BEST SUNSET

BOOKS 4-6: HOTEL SERIES

EBONY ✕❀✕ OLSON

EBANDMUSE
PUBLICATIONS

BEST SUNSET

JESS'S TRILOGY

EBONY OLSON

EBANDMUSE
PUBLICATIONS

Published 2022

Published by

EbandMuse Publications

Sydney, Australia

Paperback: 9780645157918

Cover by Smoking Hot Covers

http://ebonyolson.com/

CONTENTS

BEST MAN

Chapter 1	7
Chapter 2	10
Chapter 3	15
Chapter 4	18
Chapter 5	21
Chapter 6	25
Chapter 7	28
Chapter 8	31
Chapter 9	35
Chapter 10	38
Chapter 11	41
Chapter 12	44
Chapter 13	48
Chapter 14	51
Chapter 15	55
Chapter 16	58
Chapter 17	63
Chapter 18	66
Chapter 19	69
Chapter 20	72
Chapter 21	75
Chapter 22	78
Chapter 23	81
Chapter 24	84
Chapter 25	87
Chapter 26	94
Chapter 27	96
Chapter 28	99
Chapter 29	104
Chapter 30	108
Chapter 31	111

BEST LAYOVER

Chapter 1	137
Chapter 2	146
Chapter 3	156
Chapter 4	167
Chapter 5	175
Chapter 6	184
Chapter 7	192
Chapter 8	199
Chapter 9	207
Chapter 10	214
Chapter 11	222
Chapter 12	229
Chapter 13	237
Chapter 14	244
Chapter 15	251
Chapter 16	259
Chapter 17	268
Chapter 18	279
Chapter 19	285
Chapter 20	293
Chapter 21	301
Chapter 22	309
Chapter 23	317
Chapter 24	328

BEST KNIGHT

Chapter 1	343
Chapter 2	352
Chapter 3	361
Chapter 4	369
Chapter 5	376
Chapter 6	385
Chapter 7	393
Chapter 8	401
Chapter 9	411
Chapter 10	419
Chapter 11	429

Chapter 12	436
Chapter 13	445
Chapter 14	454
Chapter 15	465
Chapter 16	477
Chapter 17	489
Chapter 18	497
Chapter 19	508
Chapter 20	515
Chapter 21	526
Chapter 22	540
Chapter 23	551
Chapter 24	560
Chapter 25	572
Chapter 26	582
Epilogue	595
Join the Beautiful and Deadly	611
Calypso	615
Romance Suspense by Ebony Olson	631
Dark Fantasy / Paranormal Romance / Fantasy by Ebony Olson	632
About the Author	633

BEST MAN

Best Man

Hotel Series

EBONY OLSON

BEST MAN

BOOK 4: HOTEL SERIES

EBONY OLSON

EBANDMUSE
PUBLICATIONS

CHAPTER ONE

IT'S EASIER TO RUN AWAY; DISTRACT YOURSELF FROM THE helplessness inside by changing everything on the outside. I hid my wounds so deep that no one in my new life even knew they existed. Change was so much simpler than dealing with those wounds — leaving it all behind and never looking back. But family, family I couldn't let go of.

When I left the country ten years ago, my sister Sharnie had been the exact opposite of monogamous. In fact, my best friend Lizzy always described Sharnie as the whore from hell. I returned home in time for Sharnie's hens' night on Wednesday, three nights earlier.

Within an hour of arriving I determined that Sharnie hadn't really changed. She was still reckless, impulsive and entirely self-absorbed. I could only guess that Sharnie's husband-to-be worshipped her enough that she could leave her days of promiscuity and needing to be wanted by everyone else behind.

My parents standing alongside me in the front pews of a church only added to the surreal atmosphere. Sharnie getting married in a church was unexpected. Growing up, Sharnie hadn't a religious bone in her body, possibly because it required her to worship someone other than herself. The church was obviously the groom's decision.

Family members I hadn't seen in forever kept coming up and reintroducing themselves. 'Wow!' Uncle Bruce exclaimed as he gawked at my cleavage. 'Sharnie used to be the pretty one, but I reckon you'd win a wet t-shirt contest outright now.'

Bruce was the pervy uncle who all the post-pubescent girls stayed clear from at the family functions, especially once the alcohol started flowing. 'So Bruce, I remember you being taller and having more hair. What happened?' I feigned my best concerned look. Bruce chuckled, gave my breasts one last leer, licked his lips and stalked off to find a seat.

The groom's men came out of the side chapel, laughing quietly. The tallest of the three drew my attention. My heart skipped a beat as I remembered dragging my nails over his naked surfer's body only two nights ago.

One-night stands were not normal for me. In fact, I couldn't remember the last time I'd had sex before Thursday night. But the guy was gorgeous, like a young Patrick Swayze but with darker, almost black hair. He'd been out with his mates for the night and I was spending my second night back in the country catching up with my old friends.

We were catching each other's eye all night, exchanging smiles and appreciative glances. When my friends left, I used the bathroom before heading back to my hotel. As I walked back into the pub he caught my arm and kissed me. No introductions, no cheesy pick-up lines, just his mouth on mine, his body pressing me to the wall in the back corridor.

I stiffened long enough to see who I was kissing and then I went with it. The next morning, I woke totally embarrassed by my behaviour. I'd loved every minute of it, but the confusion of acting out of character saw me sneaking out of his apartment while he slept.

Now he was standing at the altar where my sister was about to get married and I feared the worst. I sidled closer to my mother and whispered in her ear, 'Who's that?'

Margaret looked over, smiled at the men and turned smiling to me. 'That's the groom of course,' she answered as if I'd asked the most absurd question in the world. I blanched and grabbed the back of the pew as my knees threatened to buckle beneath me.

CHAPTER TWO

'WHICH ONE?' I ASKED POINTEDLY. I STILL HADN'T MET SHARNIE'S fiancé. Margaret looked at me, glanced back at the men and pointed to the average looking blond guy with his back to us.

'Oh, thank fucking god!' I sat down hard, my legs giving out.

'Jessie!' Margaret chastised. Unlike Sharnie our mother was near fanatical in her piety.

I concentrated on my breathing; deep, slow breaths to bring my heart rate and quivering body back under control. The trembling legs had little to do with my sudden panic attack and everything to do with the memory of the weight of him against my hips as he plunged slow, and deep. The smell of him, vanilla and cinnamon mixed with that masculine scent all men have. The taste of his mouth, woody like oak from the scotch he'd been drinking.

I pressed my palms into the wood of the pews, pressed my thighs together as I remembered the feel of his ... 'You know one of them?' Margaret sat down next to me, breaking through my vivid memory.

'Yes,' I almost moaned as a tremor of remembered pleasure quaked through my nether regions. Margaret had stopped being motherly the first time she'd caught Sharnie having sex. Her coping mechanism was to start acting as a mature friend instead.

'The tall, black-haired gent. He was out with his mates the other night when I went to meet up with Karla and Lizzy.' I fiddled with my fingers, refusing to look up at him.

'Ah … that would have been Greg's stag night. Did Ethan go home with one of the girls?' Karla and Lizzy had been my best friends all through school. They were a bit wild — not to Sharnie's extreme, but renowned enough that Margaret had no troubles coming up with her own ideas about what happened.

I nodded, finding the marble altar suddenly very interesting. Ethan. I hadn't even bothered to get his name. Jesus, other than excusing himself long enough to say goodnight to his mates before meeting me in the car park to walk back to his place, we hadn't stopped kissing long enough to exchange more than one syllable.

'Hmm,' Margaret mused to herself, pursing her lips before rubbing them as if she had just applied lipstick. It was my mother's deep contemplation look.

'What?' I asked unable to resist the bait.

Margaret shrugged, 'Well, that just doesn't seem like the Ethan we know. He's Greg's best man and Sharnie has always complained about how "responsible" he is. To the point of being a "killjoy" — well, at least that's Sharnie's perception of him.'

I let my eyes roam to him. My sex contracted at just the sight of him. He laughed. I gripped the edge of the seat hard, my knuckles going white trying to halt my body's reaction. I took a deep breath, and considered him for a long moment.

'I don't think his friends knew. He might be very good at keeping his nocturnal habits to himself entirely.' If that was the case, I decided, I liked Ethan even more in daylight.

'Hi, Mr and Mrs Buttler,' a nice male voice greeted my parents. I looked up to find Greg shaking hands with my father and kissing my mother's cheek before his eyes met mine with a touch of surprise. 'You must be Jessie?'

I stood and was surprised when Greg hugged me. 'Um … hi … nice to meet you.' I watched the surprise cover Ethan's face as he finally spotted me being hugged by the groom.

Greg pulled back with a smile and looked to Ethan, waving him over. 'E, this is Jessie, Sharnie's twin sister, the one she reckons you'd be a perfect match for.'

'Because we supposedly have the same size sticks up our arses,' Ethan explained taking my hand firmly. 'Shit, you two look nothing alike. I would never have known you were even related. I didn't even recognise you from the photos at your parents' house. You've changed quite a bit.'

I smiled politely but didn't dare talk. Ethan's hand in mine was making my pulse race with wantonness. Ethan was right. Sharnie and I were polar opposites in appearance and personality. I had sat watching my sister at her hens' party and even I found it hard to believe we were twins.

The music started playing. 'Think that's our cue.' Greg excitedly patted Ethan on the shoulder of the arm that still held mine. 'E mate, you can hold the pretty girl's hand all you want at the reception. Let's get me married to her sister first.'

Ethan dropped my hand and blushed slightly at having held it that long. It made me laugh as he returned to the altar with Greg. Margaret stood with a certain mischievous smile on her face and my father, Lou, was trying hard not to laugh himself.

'What?' I asked cynically as Pachelbel's Canon started playing. I rolled my eyes at how cliché this wedding was turning out to be. The two wild kids meet, fall in love, and settle down with a nice white wedding. Even the music was traditional wedding stuff. The wedding procession started. I watched my beautiful older ¬¬— by twenty-two minutes — sister make her way down the aisle.

In one respect this wedding was perfect for Sharnie. Anything that made her the centre of attention and object of envy fulfilled her lifelong ambition. It's why she became a model and had aspirations to be an actress. I knew Sharnie would be good at it too. She was a brilliant actress, making people see the person she wanted them to.

I turned my attention to Greg in an attempt to keep my mind away from my deceptive sister's abyss-deep character flaws. Greg smiled warmly, tears glistening in his eyes, and I wondered for a moment what persona Sharnie had created to parade in front of him.

Deep blue eyes staring at me over the groom's head tugged mine to meet them. While the whole room was focused on my sister, Ethan watched me, and in that moment, I was powerless but to watch him back till we were forced to turn and face the front with everyone else.

———

The ceremony was short, beautiful and perfect. I stood waiting for the obligatory photos outside the church afterwards, chatting to friends and family while the bridal party posed. After a while I moved to find some shade to rescue my skin from the summer sun. Ten years ago, I was called Casper by my friends, but, while still not the bronze goddess that Sharnie was, living in Hawaii I'd built up a nice tan.

'You took off early yesterday morning,' Ethan came to stand beside me. I looked at him out of the corner of my eye, smiled and kept watching the goings-on around us.

'I had to spend some quality time with my darling sister.'

'Yeah, you two seem real close. What with you not being in the wedding party and all.'

'I've been overseas for a decade. Doesn't exactly encourage sibling bonding.'

'As I hear it, you weren't all that close before that,' Ethan continued. 'Greg tells me you two didn't even talk for a year or more after you left. Barely talk now.'

'Oh really?' I turned to face him, crossing my arms under my bust. 'What else has Greg told you about me?'

'Apparently, you're an uptight bitch who wouldn't know how to have a good time if it bit her on the arse.' Ethan smiled lightly as he reached around and pinched said anatomy playfully. 'I believe he may have been misled somewhat.'

I frowned. 'No, the other night was very much out of the norm for me.'

'Jessie,' Margaret summoned me across the church grounds, 'family photos, hon.'

I smiled and waved to indicate I was coming before stepping closer to Ethan. 'Look, I'm not as boring as my sister makes out, but I don't do one-night stands with perfect strangers either … so …'

'I'll keep our meeting two nights ago quiet. I'm not the bragger like some of my mates,' Ethan assured me.

I gave a half smile, 'Yeah, Margaret said that.'

I started to walk off when Ethan called quietly, 'Jessie?' I looked back and he smiled, 'it's nice to meet you.' I smiled and continued on as my mother called again.

CHAPTER THREE

Several hours later dinner was served, toasts and speeches were finished, and everyone started mingling and dancing. '… should be looking to settle down yourself,' Aunt Mary lectured, 'you aren't getting any younger you know.'

I rolled my eyes in exasperation before smiling. 'Well, as soon as they legalise gay marriage, my girlfriend and I will be happy to make that commitment.' I ignored the overdramatic gasp of shock my aunt emitted.

Taking my drink from the bar I started walking back to the table grumbling to myself. Aunt Mary wasn't the first person to give me the settling down lecture tonight. 'Jessie?' Greg smiled as he came to stand next to me taking my hand, 'come dance with me. I'd like to get to know my sister-in-law.'

I let Greg relieve me of my drink and drag me out to the dance floor. I looked over my shoulder to find Sharnie chatting and laughing with friends. 'I doubt Sharnie really wants us getting to know each other, or she would have introduced us before the wedding,' I mumbled, Greg unable to hear me over the music.

Once on the dance floor, Greg turned me into him and started dancing. I was shocked at how well he moved into a gentle waltz. 'Did ballroom as a teenager,' he laughed when he saw the look on my face. 'Always been handy with picking up chicks.'

'Ah!'

'So, Sharnie told me you two had a falling out some years ago and you've not been close since,' Greg started fishing immediately. 'Must have been some falling out for twins to barely have any contact?'

'We are only twins because we shared a womb thirty years ago,' I answered a little spitefully. 'Other than that, we have nothing in common.'

'Wow!' Greg looked a little shocked. 'Definitely a huge falling out. I've seen the photos at your parents' house, Jessie. You were close. Now you could be worst enemies.' I frowned. Up until we were teenagers we had been best friends. After that, the photos were all posed for our parents' happiness.

'I know Sharnie has tried to extend the olive branch several times,' Greg continued examining the obvious unhappy thoughts cycling behind my pale blue eyes. 'I also know that you are only here today because Margaret begged you to come.'

'Well, you seem to know a lot.'

'What I don't know is what made you hate my wife so much?'

'Well, as you said,' I stopped dancing and stepped back, 'I'm here because Margaret demanded I attend. She also requested I play nice, and I have no reason to dredge that shit up. If Sharnie hasn't told you by now, I daresay she doesn't want you to know. Anyway, you have it all wrong. It's Sharnie who hates me.' Greg's eyebrows lifted in curiosity. I smiled, 'Do you know how hard it is to be the centre of attention and constantly have the spotlight when you have siblings, let alone a twin, who is sportier and more academic?'

'Right,' Greg pouted, a little put out. 'So, you are the bitch Sharnie described after all.' I laughed, not surprised my sister would make me out to be the bitch.

'Let's be frank, Greg. This will probably be the last time we see each other until the next big family function. Where is the point in us getting to know each other when I have no intention of being part of your wife's life?'

I went to walk off but Greg caught my wrist. I looked over my shoulder at him, giving him a very unpleasant look at his grip on my arm. 'She did something really bad for you to hate her this much,' Greg observed, 'I have a right to know just what sort of woman I've married.'

I stepped back into Greg, leaning in till my lips touched his earlobe. He shuddered as my breath slid down his neck. Over his shoulder I saw Sharnie watching us warily, saw her eyes grow tight at my proximity to her husband, the nervous fidget of her hands on her drink as she watched our interaction.

'What happened between Sharnie and I is in the past,' I spoke quietly into his ear, 'and that is where it is going to stay. I'm not going to dredge it up and I can assure you that she isn't going to either. But I want no part of her life because I will not let her hurt me like that again. As for you … you've married her now. It's too late, so why go looking for landmines? It was nice meeting you, Greg.'

I stepped away walking straight to the bathroom to hide the tears that were threatening to escape. God, ten years had passed. I thought I'd dealt with it. But of course, if I had moved on from my sister's betrayal, if I had overcome the hurt, I would have come home from my self-imposed exile by now. Wouldn't I?

CHAPTER FOUR

'What did you tell him?' Sharnie asked as she casually walked to the mirror to touch up her lipstick.

I stood straighter giving her a disinterested look. 'Nothing! He still thinks your perfect and I'm the family bitch.'

Sharnie turned quickly, grasping my hands in hers, her face full of remorse. 'Won't you ever forgive me? Can't we forget about it, go back to being sisters?'

If I hadn't seen her pull that same contrite face on our mother as a child, used those same doe-eyes on our father whenever she wanted her own way, I may have fallen for her plea of absolution. Unfortunately, I knew my sister too well. I pulled my hands free from hers. 'When you actually mean it, I might consider forgiving you.'

I walked out of the bathroom, slipping my well-rehearsed smile back into place. 'So, you're still fucking high and mighty? Little Miss Perfect who never makes a mistake?' Sharnie yelled after me. The wedding guests in close proximity all stopped to pay attention as the slightly inebriated bride stormed out of the bathroom after me.

'I made a mistake and you're going to hold it over me for the rest of my life, aren't you?' she continued, bringing nearly everyone to a standstill. 'Perfect little Jessie, always being the good girl, never stepping out of line. You were boring then and you're just as boring now. At least I've had fun in my life!'

I'm sure she thought I'd bite and expose our family secret to everyone just so she could blame me for ruining her wedding. Ten years ago, I would have, but unlike her, I had changed. I took a deep breath, aware that everyone was now watching as I turned to face off with my twin.

'I don't hold your mistakes over your head, Sharnie, you do. I moved on with my life, created a new life, and it has been all the better without your toxic presence in it. You're the one who has to look in the mirror at yourself each day and obviously you don't like what you see.' Sharnie's smug look vanished.

'You were jealous of my happiness then, and you did what you did to take it from me. Right now, you're jealous of the fact that I'm able to be here and act civilly towards you, so you're trying to take that from me. You may have lived the wilder life, Sharnie, but who's really happier?'

Sharnie glared at me. I gave a one-shouldered shrug, then moved through the stunned crowd to my table to collect my shawl and clutch. Greg was right; I'd come back as a favour to Margaret. She'd probably hoped her girls could bury the hatchet. She'd been too optimistic as usual. My father touched my hand, giving it a gentle squeeze as the whispers started to circulate throughout the room.

'I'll see you for lunch tomorrow,' I assured him. I knew Lou was worried I'd be on the first plane out of here again. Moving to a different town hadn't been enough distance between Sharnie and I. Eventually her spitefulness had sent me running to the other side of the world. I squeezed his hand back as the music started playing again and moved to the exit.

I caught a glimpse of Sharnie bitching to her bridesmaids, of Greg standing with Ethan talking quietly as they looked between us. Ethan's intense blue eyes caught mine for a split second. I bit my lip as I pushed on the door, stepping out of the function centre into the warm summer night. Old emotions were swirling around my heart, fresh desires were surging through my body.

'Miss?' The doorman smiled.

'Taxi please,' I requested, keeping my emotions under wrap.

The doorman smiled and went to his booth. I heard the door swoosh open behind me, the music suddenly loud before the door swept close allowing only the faint beat to encroach on the stillness of the night. 'Want to share a cab?' Ethan asked as he unfastened his tie.

I appraised him for a moment as the taxi pulled up and the doorman opened the door for me. I met Ethan's hypnotic gaze unflinchingly before stepping forward. I didn't answer, just climbed into the taxi sliding over for him. Ethan smiled, tipping the doorman before closing the door and giving his address to the driver.

CHAPTER FIVE

Ethan settled back in the seat, looking down at my hand on the seat next to him, running his hand down my bare arm. I met his eyes when they flicked up to mine and couldn't suppress the sigh that escaped through my lips at his touch.

I closed my eyes as his fingers traced the lines of my hand bones to reach my fingers. A lust-filled moan slipped from my throat as his fingers found the space between mine, filling the space, rubbing back and forth a few times before sinking in and settling there.

The index finger of Ethan's other hand at my chin made me open my eyes to look at him. I met his eyes, his face so close I could feel his breath on my lips. 'Jessie …' he started tenderly.

I lifted my index finger to his lips and he quietened. 'Jess,' I barely whispered, 'only strangers call me Jessie.' I saw the understanding in his eyes. He spread his hand to cup the side of my face. I leant into it and closed my eyes. 'I shouldn't have come back.'

I turned my face into his palm, breathed in his scent, the smell of amber burning arousal through my nasal passages, down my throat where it turned the hot embers of desire into a raging inferno of need in my belly, drowning out Sharnie's existence.

Ethan opened his mouth, taking my finger between his lips, tasting it on his tongue. I hooked my finger on his bottom jaw and pulled his mouth to mine roughly, stealing his kiss before I even removed my finger. I trailed the wetness of that finger down his throat to find the top button of his tux and started getting rid of the barrier between us.

His hand left my face in favour of searching beneath my floor length silk gown for my bare thigh. The driver's subtle cough before telling us we arrived and the fee was the only thing that pulled us apart.

I opened my clutch to pay. Ethan scoffed, forcing my clutch shut as he handed the driver a twenty, not bothering to collect the change as he pulled me from the taxi into the alcove of his apartment building.

In the lift Ethan pressed me to the wall, both hands under my black dress sliding up to find my hips. His mouth at my throat as his fingers gripped the top of my scanties, sliding them down my legs, his mouth drifting south over the thin material of my dress as he squatted to help me step out of the black lace.

The elevator doors opened and we kissed our way down the corridor. Ethan's body pressed mine to his door for the second time this week as he fumbled the key into the lock. The door opened and I swung back with it.

We stood there heavy petting in his doorway for a good five minutes before Ethan lifted me to his waist, kicked the door shut and carried me into his bedroom. His hand made short work of the zip in my strapless dress while I relieved his upper body of its clothing.

He dropped me to his bed, both of us laughing while he removed the last vestiges of clothing covering his body. I slithered out of my dress, my eyes glued to his tanned athletic form the entire time and the way his cock stood rigid against his hard abdomen. It wasn't a gym-defined body. I recognised a hard-core surfer's body like those of the guys where I live.

My eyes followed the light, nearly non-existent trail of hair up the centre of his abdomen to where it disappeared at his rib cage, leaving the strong pecs and shoulders hairless. My mouth watered with the urge to kiss every part of that muscled physique, until I reached his eyes.

Those bright blue penetrating eyes that stripped me bare the first moment I met them two nights ago. They watched me now, waiting, taking in every inch of my pale flesh, while I waited half-reclined on his bed.

I suddenly felt so vulnerable and exposed under that gaze, as if his eyes did more than see the softer curves of my body, as if he could see deep to the very core of me. It was as if lying there naked before him, he was able to see all my hopes, fears, hurts and joys. I knew in that moment that I would fall in love with him, if I let myself.

'Ethan,' I sat up covering myself with my dress suddenly unsure. My self-preservation instincts were screaming for me to run for the door. In ten years since I'd left I hadn't met a man who could even tempt me to fall in love with him. Now one stood over me.

Ethan's lips twitched in a smile as he knelt onto the bed. I knew I looked worried, that the fear of getting hurt suddenly rose to the surface after being squashed down for so long. Ethan knelt over me, taking my face in his hands tenderly as he smiled with reassurance. He pulled my mouth to his, leaving only millimetres between our lips as I looked up to meet his suddenly kind eyes.

'Not tonight, Jess,' he murmured as his lips brushed mine, his nose rubbing mine in an Eskimo kiss. 'I won't hurt you.' Another brush of lips as he tugged the black satin away and set his weight forward, laying me back beneath him, 'Not tonight.'

I gasped as Ethan's thumb and finger closed over a nipple, his thigh pressing against the moist heat between mine. The arch of my body gave Ethan's mouth my neck and he took it. His lips pinched the pulse of my neck, trailing it down to my shoulder. His body pressed mine back to the bed, his hand smoothed over the flat of my tummy, cupped my heat, his mouth capturing mine in a slow, hungry kiss as his fingers pressed into me.

CHAPTER SIX

IF YOU CAN TELL A MAN'S DEMEANOUR BY HIS APPROACH TO SEX, then Ethan was patient, meticulous and an overachiever. My first orgasm was at his hands, literally. He kissed me slow and deep, matching the rhythm of his fingers as they fucked me, his thumb rubbing gently over my clit until I whimpered my climax into his mouth. Empty orgasms were always a little painful. My body seemed to overcompensate for the missing male appendage and the resulting clench set my nerve endings on fire.

Ethan lifted his fingers to my mouth, wiped them over my lips before kissing me anew, licking the tart taste of me from my lips in the process. He moaned as he tasted me, like he was eating the most delicious meal ever served up, and God I loved that sound rumbling in his throat.

When his mouth moved away in search of the delicious feast he was craving I was left gripping the sheets, back arched high on the bed crying out to the bedhead as he feasted on another two courses of my pleasure.

I expected the smile on his face to be one of arrogance when he finally kissed his way back up my body. Instead it was pure gratification, like a cat licking his lips after a bowl of cream. It was as if I gave him the treat, been the one spoiling him. That smile undid my last lock of restraint. I threw myself up to kiss that happy mouth, used the force of my rising to throw him onto his back before nibbling and biting my way over his body, satisfying my urge from earlier.

'Jesus, Jess,' Ethan inhaled sharply as I took him in my mouth and let my teeth drag up his shaft. I smirked around his thick dick as I licked and sucked at him like I was worrying away excitedly at the most delicious lollypop. His breathing picked up tempo as he throbbed in my mouth, his hands threading into my hair and pulling me up to his mouth with a gasped laugh. 'Goddamn, Jess! You suck cock like a hormonal woman eats chocolate!'

'Hey!' I smacked his chest insulted, 'what makes you think it's only when we are hormonal?' Ethan didn't answer. He hugged me tight to the front of him and kissed me, slowly and patiently. Somewhere in that kiss I felt another wall get breached as the thought I could kiss this man forever seeped into my consciousness.

'Oh God!' I gasped pulling away, burying my head in his neck which was just as bad, with that intoxicating warm amber scent of his causing butterflies to erupt in my stomach. I was never like this with guys, so why now, why this guy?

Ethan kissed my neck, my shoulder, caressing his hand down the arch of my back, over the rise of my arse to reach my thigh. Pulling my lower limb across him so he lay between my legs, he caressed back up to my waist and dragged me up his body. He hauled me over his engorged shaft trapped between us till the head of it flicked up and pressed against my nether regions.

He bit my ear lobe and in automatic response I pushed away from him, pushed away and pressed myself right onto him. I would have given him an evil look but it felt so good having the head of him surging into my molten heat that all I could do was utter expressions of pleasure and worship.

Ethan laughed at me till I pushed up on my arms and rammed him home within me forcing a groan of delight from both our throats. He growled at me then, gripped my hips lifting me the length of him, slowly, before driving me back down hard as he thrust up with his hips.

He slammed into me from below with each of my descents, a slow, hard fuck that had me crying out with every thrust. Ethan came up onto his elbows, giving me full reign. Shifting his weight to one arm he curled the other around my waist, flattening his palm in the small of my back.

Sliding up slowly as I rode him, he drew my body into a forward tilt, till my breasts were at his mouth. His tongue lashed my nipples sending rippling pulses of pleasure to my womb, causing me to struggle to keep my control as my body contracted around him.

I looked down and found his eyes intent on my face as he held me in place with his strong arms. Tongue slowly circumnavigating my areola, circling the nipple like a shark, coming closer to its prey with each orbit. I watched, hypnotised by those eyes as our bodies moved of their own accord, his ocean gaze holding my ice blue eyes in a trance. His tongue circled the base of my nipple and my body lost its rhythm.

Ethan smiled and closed his mouth over the hard nib; his eyes closed, breaking the trance. I threw my head back and came hard, my body paralysed by the intensity of the orgasm. Ethan held me in place and bucked beneath me as my cunt clutched and released him inside me.

I opened my eyes as my body relaxed, looked down to meet his smiling eyes and collapsed. My hand found his face as I fell into him, our mouths joining in a passionate kiss. He rolled me under him, taking control, and took his pleasure from me.

CHAPTER SEVEN

The morning light woke me. The smell of sex and Ethan brewed to a nice aroma on my skin. I smiled to myself, snuggling deeper into the sheets as I let the scent revive my memories of last night. I rolled over expecting to find Ethan still asleep with the intent of waking him pleasantly, but instead found the bed empty except for a piece of hotel stationery. I reached out and took the note from Ethan's pillow.

Jess,

Out for morning surf. Make yourself some coffee. I'll cook breakfast when I get back. DON'T DISAPPEAR! I know where to find you now.

E

I sighed and flopped back onto the bed. There was a little voice telling me to get out of there now, that this guy was hazardous to my heart. My body, however, was very much inclined to stick around and spend the morning working up an appetite for lunch.

I pulled myself from the bed and walked to the window where the morning sunlight was streaming through the gauze curtains. I pulled them back and was looking out at the ocean, albeit six storeys above the beach level. Surfers waited in the back break for waves, others were riding them in. I had no way of picking which was Ethan from here. Shutting the curtain, I took a deep breath, the smell of Ethan still burning on my skin made things clench tight in my belly.

I moved into the bathroom, stepped into the shower and started washing his scent from me, washing myself with slow, firm hands. When my hands rubbed over my breasts I bit my lip, put my back to the shower wall and closed my eyes. Ethan's hands were on me again, wandering my curves, pinching my nipples, fingers thrusting into me. I came so quickly with him. Normally I took ages to work up to it, but Ethan satisfied me in a way no fantasy could. For starters, he was real.

A second set of hands ran up my thighs and my eyes sprang open in surprise to find Ethan standing in the shower with me, a lascivious smile across his face. 'Couldn't wait for me huh?' he teased as he stepped under the flowing hot water to wash the salt of the ocean from him.

'Didn't know how long you'd be and I like to start the day with a smile.' I let the tease enter my eyes, my lips parting just a touch in invitation.

Ethan's smile grew into a chuckle. 'Well, I hope you saved some for me!' He pulled me under the rainmaker showerhead and ducked his head to kiss me deeply. This time when my back hit the wall, my legs were wrapped around Ethan's waist as he buried himself deep within me.

He suckled at my breasts as he moved within me, each flick of his tongue sending electrical impulses spiralling through my body till it tightened hard around him. 'Ethan?' I breathed as I came closer to climax and could feel his engorgement growing ready for his own release, 'Oh God, Ethan, I'm not on the pill.'

He growled deep in his throat before releasing my breasts and pulling my face down to his. 'I'll hold out,' he assured me, his voice thick with lust. He captured my mouth with his as he drove deeper within me. I felt him throb hard and my body went over the edge. My cunt clutching tight at his shaft, my mouth held to his so he could swallow my screams of delight. He pulled his face away, eyes tight in concentration. I dropped my legs and sunk to my knees taking him in my mouth. No sooner did my mouth closed around him he was squirting his pleasure into my throat. His flavour mixed with mine on my tongue and I had to appreciate his clean taste; he obviously wasn't a beer drinker.

Ethan threaded his fingers into my drenched hair and pulled me to stand, pressing his body to mine against the wall while he kissed me, slowly, deeply, moans vibrating through both our bodies. 'I owe you breakfast,' he smiled, pulling back to look at me. I flushed under that gaze of appreciation and he laughed. 'Come on, Jess, let's actually have a conversation.' He turned off the water and hauled me from the shower.

CHAPTER EIGHT

I SAT CROSS-LEGGED ON THE BREAKFAST BAR WHILE ETHAN COOKED breakfast. I normally would have sat on a stool or at the table, but there was a definite lack of furnishings. 'Came home one day and my wife had moved out while I was at work and taken all our furniture with her,' Ethan explained, observing my silent inventory of his apartment.

'Apparently her best friend's boyfriend had enjoyed screwing her all over my apartment so she wanted to take the memories with her.' I looked at Ethan, shocked; firstly, that anyone would cheat on him since he was possibly the best lover I'd ever had, and secondly that he said it without a hint of resentment.

He continued while he served up sausage and scrambled eggs for breakfast. 'Funny thing was I didn't know a thing about it till I came home from work to find my place empty. I'd bought all the shit too.' He shrugged, 'I figured other than the lounge to sit and read at night, and the bed — I didn't need the rest.'

'How long were you married?' I took a mouthful of egg, surprised yet again by how good it was. He was a proficient cook, a fantastic lover, seemed to be a genuinely nice guy, but his wife cheated on him and cleaned him out. He can't be perfect.

'Ha! Too long,' Ethan laughed. 'I met her just after I graduated and we married within a year.'

'Divorced?' I asked casually.

Ethan smiled at me, eyes glittering but there was wariness in them as he stabbed a piece of sausage. 'Five years now. Not bothered with a relationship since.' He popped a piece of sausage in his mouth and the look he gave me told me the rest. And I've no intention of getting into one so don't bother.

I nodded understanding and continued eating. Was there a part of me disappointed? Yes, but I was more relieved than anything. 'So, you're a hotel manager?' Ethan leaned over the breakfast bar drinking his coffee as I finished chewing on a bit of toast.

'Yep,' I answered without adding any further information.

Ethan smirked then sobered, putting his coffee down and standing straighter. 'So, who cut you up?' I raised a brow at him and took another meaningful bite of my toast. 'Not going to give me anything hey?'

'Do you think Sharnie and Greg will last?' I changed the subject.

Ethan shrugged, eyes relaxing as the topic moved away from us. 'Pilots have a high divorce rate.'

'Greg's a pilot?'

Ethan laughed at me as he moved to stand in front of me, unwrapping the towel I'd wrapped around myself. 'He's my co-pilot,' he purred ducking his head to my neck.

I inhaled sharply. 'I give it two years then, before they cheat on each other.'

Ethan kissed across my collarbone. 'Greg's wild, but moral. He loves your sister. He won't screw around on her.'

'Hmmm. Well, I wish I could say the same about Sharnie.' I gave myself brownie points for keeping the venom from seeping into my voice. Ethan paused for a moment, his breath tickling across my shoulder.

'Is that what happened between you two? She fuck some guy she shouldn't have?' I couldn't help my automatic response. My body went tense as I met his eyes, a sparkle of success shining back at me. I pushed him away and pulled the towel tight around me.

'You son of a bitch!' I roared. 'That's why you bought me back here last night. Greg wants you to find out what I wouldn't tell him and you thought you could fuck it out of me.' I pushed off the bench to go collect my stuff. Ethan's hand gripped my upper arm to stop my escape. I swung around, slapping him hard across the face. His free hand touched the bright red bloom of my hand print as he stretched his jaw quietly. His blue eyes assessed me, glassy with indignation as he released my arm.

I took a step back, shocked by my own lashing out. Tears stung my eyes as I realised just how much I was hurt by his deviousness. Ethan's eyes softened a touch as he watched my reaction. I turned and went for the room. I dressed quickly, but was unable to find my knickers from last night.

Ethan's phone rang and I heard him grumble beneath his breath as he picked it up. 'What?' he answered gruffly before his toned softened and filled with apology. 'No, sorry, of course not, I was just in the middle of something,' he chuckled quietly. 'Of course, I'll still be coming … okay see you then.'

I gave up looking for my panties as he finished the call, grabbed my clutch and walked quickly towards the front door. Ethan caught me there as I swung the door open, putting me against the wall next to it. 'Greg doesn't know about us,' he said quietly so his voice didn't carry out into the corridor. 'I had every intention of having you again the moment I saw you in the church. But yes, after the show you and your sister put on last night, I want to know what happened.'

I stared back at him blankly, determined not to be intimidated, but God he smelt so good. 'Come on, Jess! She's married my best mate,' Ethan half pleaded, 'you'd want to know if it was the other way around.' I met his eyes, giving no ground. Ethan shook his head, dropping it to look at his feet. 'Stay,' he finally murmured. Part of me wanted to, a very physical part that was highly attracted to Ethan and utterly adored what he did to my body. But I'd been shut off too long to let my physical desires rule my decisions.

'I can't. I'm meeting my parents for Sunday lunch. I need to go back to my hotel and get changed.' I ducked under his arm and stepped out the door. 'Bye, Ethan.'

CHAPTER NINE

'So how long are they away for?' I asked my mother of Sharnie and Greg.

'They're only taking the week,' Margaret said as she browsed the menu as if she might choose something other than the barramundi in lemon sauce. 'Greg has to work Thursday.'

'You'd think as a pilot he could get a bit more time away if he wanted to.'

Margaret raised a brow. 'How do you know Greg's a pilot?'

'I danced with him, remember?'

'Ah yes!' Margaret closed her menu with a look that informed me she was about to get serious. 'What else did you discuss while you danced?'

I studied my menu intently. 'His dancing ability and nothing much else,' I answered flatly. 'I definitely didn't tell him anything worthy of Sharnie's curiosity.'

Margaret nodded. 'I never thought you would be that spiteful …'

'No, that was always Sharnie's gift.'

Margaret gave me a warning look. 'You need to forgive her eventually, Jessie. She's your twin ...' I tuned out. I'd heard this lecture a million times over the past decade and it always had the same outcome. I would ignore Margaret's request to come home and she would sigh with heartache and try to guilt trip me.

I scanned the doorway to the bar attentively. Lou had gone to get our drinks. Usually he was the one who distracted Margaret from her sole purpose of trying for world peace. 'Sorry I'm late, Margaret,' Ethan's voice sang over my shoulder. My eyes went wide and my body tensed at the sound of his voice, well, except for the part that grew wet and clenched in longing at the memory of last night.

'That's fine, Ethan. We've been too busy chatting to even notice,' Margaret smiled, turning up her cheek to meet his polite kiss of greeting. 'You remember Jessie?' she asked, a light in her eye I knew all too well.

'How could I forget her?' Ethan was all charm as he turned and touched his lips to my cheek, lingering longer than necessary as he took a deep breath in appreciation of my perfume. His hand settled on the bare skin of my upper back and it stayed there even after he straightened. 'I was hoping to see you again,' he chirped for Margaret's benefit.

I smiled and nodded, terrified speaking would announce our two nights of passion to the world, or worse to my mother. Margaret was smiling with the hope that Ethan may be the bait needed to lure me home. Just the hopeless optimism I expected from her. 'Where's Lou?'

'Getting drinks.' Margaret's eyes brightened when she noticed how Ethan's hand still lingered on my back.

'I'll go give him a hand,' Ethan excused himself. From the humour in his eyes as he looked back at me, he knew just what my mother was thinking. Great!

'He likes you,' Margaret verbalised as soon as he was out of earshot.

'He knows I'll be leaving after a week. That appeals to a lot of guys.'

Margaret scowled and lifted her water glass to her lips. 'Well, even when he and Sharnie were sleeping together he never touched her like that.'

I nearly choked on my tongue. 'What?'

'Oh, that's how she met Greg,' Margaret continued as if she hadn't noticed my sudden difficulty breathing, 'she and Ethan had a fun-filled weekend together and then the following weekend when she went to see him she met Greg and that was that.'

CHAPTER TEN

HAD MY SISTER SAT ASTRIDE EVERY DICK WORTH RIDING IN THE Southern Hemisphere? *Stupid question*, I thought, *Of course she has*. Sadness sunk into the pit of my stomach. 'You didn't tell me you were expecting him to join us.'

'Ethan and Greg have been joining us for Sunday lunch since Sharnie and Greg became serious. I see no reason for him to stop coming just because they are away on their honeymoon. And anyway,' Margaret smiled towards the two men approaching from the bar area, 'your father enjoys the company. They're like the sons he never had.'

I had a knowing feeling that this set-up was years in the planning on my parents' behalf. I was overcome with the sudden need to travel back in time three nights and undo that random one-night stand. I looked up as Ethan approached the table, but all I could see now was him fucking my sister and making her scream out his name.

I wanted to scream at the unfairness of it, but as usual I sat quietly, smiled politely, and seriously considered ringing the airline and bringing forward my departure. Ethan placed my cranberry juice on the table before taking the seat next to me, his orange juice located at the tips of my fingers.

The first time Ethan reached forward to take a drink, his hand brushed over mine seductively. I flinched and took my hand off the table, setting both in my lap as I sat back. Ethan looked at me suspiciously but other than those hypnotising eyes assessing my tense posture and obvious discomfort, his face was all smiles as he joked and talked with my parents.

I let the conversation pass me by until we ordered our meals. Ethan smiled up at the waitress politely before his eyes fell on me and I knew my peace was over. 'So, Jess,' he started, sitting back casually, 'your parents tell me you haven't had a boyfriend in quite some time. Surely that can't be true?'

There was a mocking smile on his face as he lifted the glass to his lips which annoyed me. 'Yes well … Margaret tells me the last woman you fucked was Sharnie.' Ethan coughed his drink back into his glass. I smiled with satisfaction. 'So, I'm guessing their information is a little outdated.'

'Jessie!' my mother reprimanded. My father's eyes narrowed across the table before he looked from me to Ethan and back. When I met them, they were wide with surprise before he turned to my mother.

'Margaret, my dear,' he said as he took my mother's hand gently. His devotion and love for my mother had always given me hope that one day I might meet a guy who loved me like that. But that was lost too many years past now. 'Did you really think that bit of information needed to be shared considering our daughters' feelings for each other?'

Ethan's smile was gone, his eyes calculating as he watched me now. 'I thought it best she knows upfront,' Margaret returned. 'It's better than finding out years later.'

'Years?' I asked shocked. 'Margaret, I'm home for a little over a week. How does that translate to years?' I threw my napkin on the table as Margaret's eyes filled with tears and I knew the guilt trip was about to start. I really wasn't in the mood for this today. I got up from the table and walked across the bistro to the balcony door. I needed fresh air.

I pushed the door open and welcomed the heat of summer. Stagnant, humid air stole my breath and the sudden difficulty breathing through the dense heat calmed my temper almost instantly. I stepped to the railing, watching the people in the park across the road set up for their picnics. 'You shouldn't be so hard on her,' Lou said as he came to lean on the balcony next to me, 'she misses you.'

'Kids grow up and leave home all the time, Dad. Missing them is nothing new.'

'Yes,' he nodded in agreement, 'but it's not often they disappear two days before their wedding and call you a day later from the other end of the world with no warning.'

'I paid you back every cent you were out …'

'I've never cared about the deposit for the goddamn ceremony, Jessie,' Lou raised his voice just enough to be stern. 'I cared about my barely adult daughter being distraught enough to leave everything that ever mattered to her behind without a backward glance or a care of how that would affect the people who loved her.'

CHAPTER ELEVEN

I BOWED MY HEAD AND CLOSED MY EYES. IT WAS UNFAIR THAT I BORE the guilt for running away, but I did. Wrong that I accepted everyone's blame, but I had. Pathetic that I still shouldered the liability, but I always would. The silence drew out. Lou sighed audibly and softened his tone. 'It's time to come home, Jess. We miss you. Your mother worries.'

'I'm happy where I am …'

'If that were true you would have a boyfriend, you would have settled down, bought a place, and been thinking about kids. You've kept your life just as portable as when you first left.'

How could I dispute that argument? I hadn't put down roots and while my apartment was at least furnished, it wasn't mine. In truth, neither was the furniture; it came furnished. My job was the only permanent thing in my life. I'd made friends but most were transitory. God knows most of my lovers were.

'I'm not ready to come home,' I tried instead. The first year I wanted to get on a plane nearly daily. I'd missed home, missed my family and friends so badly. The first month was interspersed with crying to sleep and barely contained rage. But by the time the second year rolled around I missed it less, and by the third I had moved on and coming home just didn't seem practical after that. I had a good life where I was and for the most part I was content. Why would I want to risk giving that up?

Lou nodded but sighed. 'That answer I can accept.' He looked back over his shoulder. 'Besides it will give Ethan time to come around.' I looked at my father confused and he chuckled. 'Your mother may be naïve to that boy's nocturnal habits while abroad, but I have been privy to many a jest by Greg in regard to Ethan's activities.'

'Ah!'

Lou always was the more perceptive parent. If it wasn't for his sit-back-and-watch attitude, my parents may still not know what tore their family apart. 'You and he,' he continued, 'you're the same, Jess. One bad heartbreak and you closed yourselves off to the world. Maybe your two broken hearts can fit together to make a whole?'

I chuckled at my father's subtlety. 'Maybe one day, Dad,' I said remembering last night and the emotions Ethan stirred within me, 'but not today.'

'No,' he agreed, 'not this trip home. Maybe when you come home for your mother's sixtieth birthday next year?' I arched an eyebrow at my father's time frame. I hadn't mentioned anything about coming home again, but I knew that tone. It was the tone that as a child told us we were doing something and all negotiations were off.

'In the meantime, I've been planning a holiday with your mother,' Lou smiled as he watched kids in a water fight with super soakers across in the park. 'We've decided to visit you at Christmas this year. We will stay in a hotel, may even stay in yours … just for a week, Jess,' my father reassured me at the worried look on my face.

I took a deep breath and nodded. 'It would be good to have you guys around for Christmas actually.' For the last decade, I'd worked Christmas to avoid admitting I was alone. It worked, but it would be nice to have my parents around for once.

'Let's go back in, Jess.' Dad patted my hand. 'I'll tell Margaret to back off on the guilt trips if you forget what she told you about Ethan and Sharnie?' I looked at my father angrily. 'Don't you give me those daggers, young lady,' he pointed his finger at me. 'Your sister was just a one-night stand to that boy; you've already outmanoeuvred her there. And you know Sharnie. If you do end up in a relationship with Ethan she would find the most inappropriate time to "drop" that little bombshell …'

'Yeah, most likely at my wedding …' I stopped at the smile that flickered across my father's face and quickly back tracked. 'Not that I'm considering marrying him.'

'A-huh!' Lou chuckled as he pulled me into his side for a cuddle and kissed the top of my head. Now there was something I always missed.

CHAPTER TWELVE

GOING BACK TO THE TABLE WAS AWKWARD. NOT BECAUSE OF MY SNAP at Margaret. That was an easy 'sorry I snapped at you', kiss her on the cheek and be seated again. But I didn't exactly know how to follow up 'hey, I know you fucked my sister before me' politely, so I spent the rest of the meal rather withdrawn and avoiding eye contact with Ethan.

Lou kept the conversation light by discussing sports with Ethan while Margaret filled me in on all the gossip from her quilting group. The waitress brought out tea and cakes that my parents always finished lunch with. Margaret lifted her tea to her lips and blurted her last surprise news before taking a sip. 'Ben is married now. Just had their first child.'

My glass slipped from my hand and hit the table with a thunk, splashing cranberry juice everywhere before Ethan caught it, preventing it spilling all over the table. 'Shit sorry,' I apologised to Ethan as he studied me intently.

'Honestly, my dear, why don't you just stab her with your fork?' my father grumbled to Margaret.

I took the napkin Ethan handed me, wiping at my now wet, pale yellow summer dress. 'This will stain if I don't wet it,' I said as I excused myself from the table, my eyes brimming with tears.

'Who's Ben?' Ethan asked as I left the table.

'Jessie's ex-fiancé.'

I left any further explanation behind as I moved briskly to the lady's room. The club had one of the old-style lady's bathrooms. There was a powder room, complete with plush lounges for gossiping and mirrors for touching up make-up, before going through a separate door to the actual stalls. I shoved the door open into the powder room, catching myself on the bench and sitting down hard on one of the plush stools. I looked at my reflection in the mirror, eyes full of liquid anger.

Of course, he moved on, fell in love with someone else, and had the future we'd planned together with that other person. I expected it, but it hurt just the same. When the door opened I dropped my face so whoever was coming in wouldn't see my eyes. It wasn't until I heard the lock click that I looked up to find Ethan in the powder room with me. I stood up to face him, surprised, as he walked towards me. 'What are you doing?'

Ethan pulled me into his arms and kissed me passionately. I was stunned enough to go with it for a moment before I pulled back, hands on his chest and looked at him astonished. 'Ethan …' Ethan's fingers twined around my loose chestnut hair, gripped it in his fist, and forced my face back to his, holding our lips mere millimetres from touching.

'She meant so little to me I'd forgotten it ever happened, Jess. You I will never forget. And that ex of yours is a fool for ever letting you go. I would have jumped a plane and come straight after you.' Ethan closed the distance between our mouths, pinched my bottom lip between his, his eyes still glued to mine. My eyes shuttered. Ethan tilted his head and kissed me unreservedly. After a minute, I found my butt against the bench, my back arching so my shoulders were pressing against the mirror as Ethan's hands crept under the hem of my thigh length dress.

Ethan slid his fingers beneath the gusset of my panties and stroked me gently. He teased me till his fingers could slip in my dampness then slid two fingers into my moist heat and found the core of my lust. All the while his lips moved against mine as if my mouth was his dessert and he intended to devour me.

I moaned into him, hands gripping his shoulders and neck like I would never let him go. His thumb rubbed back and forth over my clit as he pushed a third finger into me. I lifted my leg to his waist giving him deeper access and he used it. Ethan's fingers moved in a steady controlled motion as if he used his own heartbeat to keep time. This wasn't some hurried fuck. He was making sure I knew that I was worth more than that. I bit my lip as his mouth kissed down my neck, licking over my collarbone while his free hand massaged my breast through the dress.

When his mouth started moving lower he pulled the top of my dress down for access to my erect nipple. Ethan took it between his teeth and pinched hard. My head pressed back into the mirror as that weighty feeling grew between my legs. I could hear his fingers as they moved in me now. I grabbed a handful of Ethan's hair and yanked his face up to mine, pressing his mouth in a hard kiss as I came, trying hard not to make any noise. He muted my moans, and then kissed me tenderly as he withdrew his hand, sliding his index finger around the trim of my knickers to move them back into place correctly.

I blushed brilliantly when he pulled back to smile at me. He licked a tear from my face as he straightened my dress. 'We're having dinner tonight. Be at my place at seven.' He moved to the door.

'Are we having dinner or am I dinner?' Ethan smiled, winked, unlocked the door and walked out. I nearly slid to the floor in a puddle of mixed emotions. Lust, need, confusion, and something else I couldn't put my finger on and probably didn't want to.

I steadied my legs beneath me, pushed myself to standing and unlocked the door to the bathroom. I needed to fix my dress still, but also splash some water on my face to cool down. I looked in the mirror over the sink at my flushed face. *Oh God! My parents are out there waiting. Dad is so going to know.* I cringed and took my time cleaning my dress.

CHAPTER THIRTEEN

I TRIED FOR CASUAL CALM WHEN I RETURNED TO THE TABLE AND succeeded. I daresay my parents put my behaviour down to the news Margaret had blurted out. Her face was flustered, her eyes darting to my father occasionally as we finished our luncheon. I recognised the sign of my parents having words. Lou wouldn't have liked Mum telling me about Ben. Hell, I'm sure he was pissed about her informing me about Ethan and Sharnie. It was obvious Lou liked Ethan, despite knowing his reputation.

As I watched them converse I knew Lou would like nothing better than to call him son. When Ethan stood to leave, excusing himself early so that I could have some quality time with my parents, I realised Ethan already was part of the family. The shock of just how distant I was from my parents hit me hard. I'd always been close to Lou. Thought our weekly Skypes had maintained it. But they'd never once mentioned Ethan, let alone how close he and my father were.

I was still sitting when Ethan leaned down to kiss my cheek goodbye. 'I'll see you later,' he whispered in my ear, letting his hand brush down my arm as he stood to walk away.

I blushed. I couldn't help it. The images floating through my head, of what might actually be served for dinner, made my body flood with heat in anticipation. I could hear Ethan chuckle as he moved off and I knew he'd seen my reaction, but unfortunately, he wasn't the only one. Margaret's eyes sparkled. But as she opened her mouth to say something Lou tapped her hand and shook his head slightly to indicate she should hold her tongue. She managed it for the rest of the afternoon. I loved my dad.

Arriving at Ethan's that evening I was nervous. I would be lying to pretend otherwise. I'd had the late afternoon to myself to analyse just what sort of effect Ethan was having on me. I hadn't liked my conclusions. I closed my eyes and pressed the downstairs call button. The door to the apartment complex buzzed open without a word and I made my way up in the elevator.

It took a moment for Ethan to answer the knock on his apartment door. 'Great, you're right on time!' He slipped my handbag from my shoulder placing it inside his apartment door before picking up a picnic basket and joining me in the hall. 'Let's go,' he said as he took my hand, leading me back to the elevator.

We crossed the road to the beach, then walked along the road till it diverted off onto the path that would lead us to the top of the cliff that overlooked the beach at the far end. I knew there was a beautiful park at the top and guessed that was where Ethan was taking me so didn't ask questions. I was silently thankful for my choice of flat shoes.

Ethan led us away from the main area of the park, choosing a place closer to the edge of the bluff and less open. I stood admiring the view while he laid out the blanket, slipped out of his shoes, knelt, and started setting out containers on the rug. A breeze picked up and stirred the skirt of my summer dress. I quickly held it down and turned to check if I'd flashed Ethan.

He sat with a naughty smile on his face, watching me, but simply indicated the space next to him on the blanket for me to join him as he poured out two glasses of red. 'Come eat before it gets cold.'

I looked over the spread. Salads, roast chicken, a pasta bake, cheese and fruit platter, and wine. 'Isn't this a little romantic?' I raised a brow as I folded down onto the blanket and took the proffered glass of wine. 'A picnic dinner overlooking the beach at sunset? I think we are past the seduction stage, Ethan.'

Ethan chuckled and shook his head, eyes shining as he started dishing out a plate of food. 'We're part of the same unit now, Jess. My best friend is married to your sister. I attend every family function including Sunday lunch when I'm not working. We're going to see each other whenever you come home to visit. So, I think, for both our sakes, we need to be friends.'

I took the plate Ethan handed me but watched him, unsure. 'That makes sense, but I'm pretty sure my parents are thinking arranged marriage,' I informed him honestly.

Ethan laughed and nodded as he served out his own dinner. 'Yeah, they've been talking you up to me for years. Even Sharnie kept saying how perfect we were for each other. Although she was more derogatory than complimentary.' Ethan half reclined on the blanket, picking up a fork to start eating. 'I've been married, Jess. I've no intention of making the same mistake twice.' He looked at me, a combined expression of surety and worry.

I smiled. 'Good, we're on the same page then.' I picked up my fork and pointed it at him. 'But this doesn't mean I'm going to sleep with you every time I come home either.'

Ethan smirked. 'Eat up and enjoy the view, Jess.'

CHAPTER FOURTEEN

We'd finished eating by the time the sun started sinking behind us washing the sky in pinks, purples and the darkening blue of night. The ocean reflected the sky as we lounged, picking at the fruit platter and drinking the wine. 'So why Hawaii?' Ethan took another grape and gobbled it down. His eyes were wandering the length of my legs before returning to my eyes. It made me smile that he was obviously trying to resist touching me.

'At first, I went to Canada,' I explained picking another strawberry, 'but it was too cold in winter. So, I transferred to Hawaii where the temperature is closer to home.'

'That explains the tan. You're pale, but at your parents' house your photos have you paler.' I smiled, but just gave him a sideways glance as I bit into the strawberry. Ethan smirked. 'I noticed you don't have much in the way of tan lines either. Can't see your resort allowing naked sunbathing.'

'The staff like to get away from the office on days off,' I shrugged. 'There's a lagoon that's rather remote where we can go and relax.'

'And get naked with each other?' Ethan's eyes were bright, obviously imagining a bunch of girls toasting themselves in a hideaway location, probably with the stereotypical sun-lotion body-rubbing scene as well.

I smiled. 'It's getting dark.' I indicated rising Venus now visible in the dying light of day.

Ethan knelt and started packing the basket, so I sat up and started re-lidding containers to help. Once the basket was packed Ethan placed it to the side and halted my hand as I went to replace my shoes. I met his sparkling eyes, saw the lust within them and let him take the shoe from my hand, placing it back beside the other.

He ran his hands up my legs and pushed my skirt to my waist. A smile tugged his lips as he appraised my naked hips. 'No panties?' He started kissing down my inner thigh, my legs spreading of their own accord for him.

'No, I've already lost two of my favourite pairs to you,' I berated, though with my breathing already pitching it didn't come off as the scolding as I intended. 'Though if I'd known we were going out for dinner ...' I gasped and couldn't complete the thought as Ethan's mouth made contact. He separated my labia with his tongue and dug into his third course. I was nervous about being in public. I wasn't a non-exhibitionist — but there were places that were safe to be naughty and this wasn't one of them.

The thought of getting caught just added to the heat of the moment, bringing my climax surging forward in record time. Ethan covered my mouth as I moaned my excitement to the night sky and when he pulled back he was laughing softly. 'Like outdoor sex do we, Jess?'

I felt how wet the blanket beneath me was from my orgasm. 'Jesus!' I looked at him wide eyed. 'I never make that much mess.'

Ethan just laughed as he scooted up my body to kiss me hungrily, his mouth covered in my juices. I felt him unzip, felt the head of him nudge apart my folds before he pushed forward into me. My breath caught and I clung to him as he took his time to sheath himself fully within me.

I don't think I could ever get sick of feeling Ethan press into me. 'Stop it!' I berated myself quietly.

Ethan paused and rose from where he was kissing my neck to look at me worried. 'Did I hurt you? I thought you were ready?'

'No,' I shook my head, 'not you. I don't want you to stop.' Ever! I added in my head.

Ethan smiled, kissing me as he moved within me. The stars were shining brightly now, pin pricks in the curtain of night, but the most beautiful thing I saw that night was the glint in Ethan's eyes every time he pulled back to look at me, into me, deep to the soul of me.

Our bodies started to pick up the pace as they neared their synchronised crescendo. I bit my lip as I went over first. Ethan buried his face in my neck, his moans vibrating against my skin while his body pulsed in mine. When he pulled away to remove the condom and dispose of it in his gear, I wiped the tear that escaped from my eye. I'd fallen for him, I knew it then, fallen hard and fast to someone who was as emotionally unavailable as I was to all of my lovers for the past decade.

Ethan returned with a grin and kissed me tenderly as he chuckled. I smiled, but inside I was freaking out. 'Everything okay, Jess?' Ethan asked looking down at me after a moment, 'you seem suddenly tense.'

I touched his face, smiled and nodded as I pulled his mouth back to mine. A light suddenly stung my eyes. I hid against Ethan's chest to prevent losing my night vision. 'Come on, kids. Pack it up and take it home,' an authoritative voice said from a few metres away.

Ethan laughed, covering his eyes from the light, but stood up to show he was fully dressed to the advancing policemen. 'Ethan,' a familiar voice laughed, 'should have guessed it was you seducing some beautiful thing.'

'Fair go, Bailey,' Ethan laughed back, 'we were just having a picnic.' The torch light finally shifted to the ground and Ethan stepped forward to meet the officers before they got close enough to see me. He knew them.

'Hope she's legal, Ethan,' Ben Bailey, my ex-fiancé joked with Ethan as I scrambled to put on my shoes, keeping my back to them. Ethan didn't respond. 'Miss, can I see some ID please?'

'Shit,' Ethan murmured, 'her purse is at my place, Bailey. Didn't see the point in bringing anything up here we wouldn't care to lose.' I stood up and walked over to join them. Ethan wrapped an arm around my waist and hugged me tight to him.

'Jess!' Ben looked gobsmacked. 'You're home?'

CHAPTER FIFTEEN

'Hi Ben,' I smiled, my hand around Ethan's waist gripping tightly to him. 'Just home for Sharnie's wedding.'

Ben nodded as he looked between Ethan and I, considering. 'I heard someone tamed the wild child.' He met my eyes.

'Yes, that was a surprise, but then we both know not to put anything past my sister, don't we?' I gave myself brownie points for keeping my voice neutral. 'I hear congratulations are in order for you ...'

'Thank you.' Ben's voice became quiet. 'Look what happened ...'

'Wasn't your fault,' I finished for him. Ben looked at me shocked, but he nodded. 'Sharnie told me.' She hadn't really, but her eyes told me that night; the way they'd glinted at me in the half-light with absolute delight at a game well played.

'She did?'

'She did.'

'But you didn't come back?'

'To what, Ben? What would I have been coming back to?'

Ethan's arm around my waist gripped me tightly at the acid sound of my voice, and he pulled me a step back from the policeman on duty and cut in. 'The mossies are coming out. We might head indoors.'

Ben's partner was nodding his wide eyes in agreement, obviously seeing where this was going. Ethan pulled me back another step and as I turned to go retrieve our stuff Ben stepped up and grabbed my wrist to halt me. 'To me, to us, to the life we'd planned together. That's what you had to come home to. If you knew it wasn't my fault why did you leave me days before our wedding without so much as a goodbye?'

'Because it still happened!' I yelled at him. 'You may have been innocent at the start of the night, Ben, but you knew by the end and you didn't even try to contact me till lunchtime the next day. Sharnie left voicemails on my phone within an hour and you did nothing …'

'Jess.' Ethan pulled me out of Ben's grip and put my face to his chest as the tears surged forward. 'Johnson, I think it's best ...'

'I agree,' Ben's partner said as he stepped forward grabbing Ben's shoulder. 'Come on, Bailey, we've got patrol.'

'You're with him?' Ben barked, 'He's a man-whore, Jess. He'll fuck you and dump you quick as you can spit.'

'Bailey, let it go,' Johnson growled at his partner.

'Or are you just a whore like your slut sister now, fucking everything that moves? And if it doesn't move you push it?'

I tried to pull out of Ethan's arms to hit Ben but Ethan pinned me to his chest and shook his head. 'Johnson, I think Bailey really needs to leave because he's just called my sister-in-law a slut and insinuated my fiancée is one.'

Everything stopped. The air around us was so quiet we could hear the waves breaking at the beach below. Ethan held me tight, not letting my sudden rigidness show to the police. Ben was flabbergasted. 'Come on, Bailey.' Johnson grabbed Ben's shoulders and shoved him back towards their car.

'No way! Not him? That can't be true?' Ben was saying to himself.

'You're married with a kid, Bailey. Does it matter?' his partner lectured him as they moved away.

Ethan held me tight until he heard the car pull away then he kissed my forehead and loosened his hold. 'You okay, Jess?'

I nodded my head and stepped back wiping the tears from my face. 'Thank you.'

'For what? Not punching your ex out?'

I shook my head with a smile. 'For lying.'

'About us being engaged?'

'No, about my sister and I being sluts,' I smirked, 'because we both know what he said about her was true.'

Ethan laughed and smiled at me. 'I never said it wasn't.' I thought back over his words and nodded as I realised he hadn't either. 'Come on, you floosy,' he chuckled, picking up the blanket and basket, 'let's get your panty-free arse back to my place where I can defile you without us getting charged for public indecency.'

'Now where's the fun in that?'

CHAPTER SIXTEEN

MONDAY MORNING, I WOKE TO THE SOUND OF SURF CRASHING TO shore in one ear and a steady slow heartbeat in the other. It took me a moment to realise the heartbeat belonged to the body I was half draped over. I lay listening to Ethan's deep, slow breaths and remembered the hours of fun we'd had last night before we'd finally fallen asleep in each other's arms.

My hand crept beneath the sheet to find Ethan saluting the sunrise. Moving slowly, I slipped under the sheet. I smiled at his sleepy moans and knew the exact moment he woke to realise his dream was reality. 'It's been years since I've had that sort of wake up,' Ethan purred as I kissed my way to his mouth.

'The downside to casual liaisons,' I shrugged before kissing him intently.

'Hmm ...'

'You should get going,' I breathed hard between kisses.

Ethan's fingers were entwined in my hair, making it impossible to pull away. 'Where?' he kissed down my neck.

'Surf's up,' I moaned as his mouth found my nipple, 'you'll miss the best waves of the day.'

'I'd rather stay here and make sure you don't disappear on me again.'

'I'll wait right here, I promise.' And search for my missing underwear while you're gone.

Ethan lifted his face from my neck, still halfway between sleep and waking, with a glaze of sated lust in his eyes. I moaned at just the promise of that look. 'You better be here or I'll tell your mother how you broke my heart,'

'Ha! You'd have to admit how you seduced her good little girl first.'

'Please! Your sister is Sharnie. Nothing we've done could possibly shock your mother.'

'Good point.' He laughed, kissing me breathless, and then left me longing for more in his bed while he pulled on his wetsuit and disappeared out his apartment door.

After a shower and dressing I ferreted through Ethan's laundry, which was relatively empty, under his bed, through his drawers, and couldn't find any sign of my missing underwear. I was starting to think he had a secret trophy case somewhere or was supplying a vending machine in Japan.

The sound of a key in the front door made me stop. I stepped into the lounge-room expecting to see Ethan and found a middle-aged woman. She looked at me surprised before giving me a look of distaste. She reached into the basket of clothes she'd carried and handed me my freshly laundered knickers.

'Oh, thank you. I was wondering where he'd hidden them.' The woman cocked an eyebrow at me and moved passed me to the bedroom where she started putting Ethan's clothes away before stripping and remaking the bed.

I felt a little embarrassed by her obvious awareness of just how soiled those sheets were. I decided to busy myself by making some breakfast. 'Shouldn't you be going?' the woman asked smartly.

'I …' I flushed at the insinuation of being just another one of Ethan's one-night slash weekend stands. Of course, that's all I was, but we were friends now too; had to be since he was part of my family. 'He made me promise to wait for him.' The woman raised both her brows in surprise this time. 'He blackmailed me actually. Told me he'd tell my mother we were seeing each other if I disappeared on him again.'

'Your mother wouldn't approve?'

'My mother would start making the wedding arrangements and he knows it. He's already practically part of the family.'

There was a pause of consideration. 'You're the runaway sister of the girl who married Greg.'

'Please don't hold it against me.'

The woman chuckled and came to join me in the kitchen, watching how I cooked Ethan's eggs just like he did yesterday morning. 'Not your first time for breakfast here either.'

I blushed. 'No.'

'I apologise for my rudeness earlier. I didn't realise you were a long term … friend of the boy's.'

I didn't really consider four days long term but then this was Ethan we were talking about. 'It's okay. I know Ethan's … habits. I understand the misconception.'

The door opened and Ethan stepped in, wetsuit folded down to his waist, taking in the two of us as he propped his surfboard up in its hold. He collected the towel he'd left by the door, wrapped it around his waist as he turned towards us with a smile and started working his wetsuit down his legs from under the towel. 'Morning, Sophia. I see you've met Jess.'

'Yes,' Sophia smiled back, a glint in her eye.

'Mmm. I wake to a beautiful woman in my bed who lets me go for a surf and I come back to find her cooking me breakfast.' Ethan moved to the kitchen and looked at the food I was plating up. 'And she's done the eggs just how I like them.' Ethan wrapped his arms around me as I turned to face him. 'I could get used to this.'

'Ha! I wouldn't. I fly out on Friday.'

'I go back to work Thursday,' he countered with a sly smile as he pulled my body tight to his. 'Stay with me.'

'Pfft!' I went to push out of his arms but he held me tighter.

'Just till Thursday, Jess? Three nights, three days, that's all I'm asking for. Then we both go back to our lives with nothing more than a smile and the memories of a great week together.'

'I'm home to spend time with my parents, Ethan.

'That's doable. I'm not superman. I do need recovery time you know,' he replied sarcastically. 'Stay with me.'

'No.'

'No is not an acceptable answer, Jess.' Ethan pressed my back to the breakfast bar as he seized my mouth with a teasing kiss. 'Stay with me.'

I caved. I'd already fallen for the guy. Three nights of the best sex of my life wasn't going to undo the damage already done. Come Friday I would board that plane and remember Ethan fondly, but that's all he'd be, a memory. Ethan kissed me fervently till a not-so-soft cough reminded us we weren't alone in the apartment.

'Sorry, Sophia.'

'Worse than honeymooners,' Sophia muttered as she collected her cleaning gear and disappeared into the bathroom. I took the opportunity to escape Ethan's arms and take a mouthful of breakfast as I moved to put the breakfast bar between us, because honestly, if there wasn't something between our bodies right now, we were going to become exhibitionists.

Ethan laughed at my blushing and sat down with his plate, content to let his housekeeper finish her work before he had his wicked way with me again. The glint in his eye every time we made eye contact was enough to make me squirm in my seat, which in turn encouraged Ethan's mischievous smirk to grow into a Cheshire grin.

At one stage, thinking Sophia safely hidden away in his bathroom, Ethan wrestled me to the lounge and stole the underpants I'd put on back. 'These are mine,' he smiled. 'Ow!' Ethan's hand went to the back of his head where Sophia had smacked him.

'You're embarrassing the girl,' Sophia scolded before moving into the kitchen.

I snatched my knickers back, sure I was bright red from getting sprung, and Ethan snarled, playfully catching me around the waist as I tried to escape. He carried me towards the bedroom as he put on a serious face for Sophia. 'If you're finished in here, Sophia, I need a shower.'

Sophia rolled her eyes. 'Honeymooners,' she said, shaking her head with a smile before the bedroom door closed.

CHAPTER SEVENTEEN

'COME BACK TO BED,' ETHAN GROWLED AS I PULLED MY DRESS OVER my head, freshly showered for the third time that day.

'I told you I'm spending time with my parents.' I looked at the time. I expected my mobile to start ringing any minute with my mother on the other end wondering where I was. Ethan sighed, throwing back the bed sheets, and took the few steps to me. He pulled me into his arms and kissed me intently. I melted against him and returned that hungry kiss with the same desire.

'I'll get dressed and drive you.' I went to argue but Ethan spoke sternly over me. 'Otherwise you'll be even later if you wait for a taxi.' He gave me a quick kiss and pulled away to have a quick shower.

The motorbike wasn't expected. 'I'm wearing a dress!' I said as I watched Ethan mount the bike.

'I know,' he smiled wickedly at me. 'Now hop on already.'

I threw my leg over behind Ethan and pulled the helmet into place before I wrapped my arms around him. Ethan ran a hand up my bare leg where it pressed against the side of his. I shivered. He laughed and the engine roared to life. Despite my complaint, I loved motorbikes. I enjoyed it even more snuggled against Ethan's back as he used the back streets to reach my parents' place.

He pulled up out front, the hedge along the front fence hiding us from view of the house. I handed him the helmet and went to turn towards the front path but Ethan pulled me back to him. He kissed me passionately, pinning my body to his as his hands gripped the curve of my arse and centre of my back.

The underwear I'd managed to steal back was suddenly sodden as my want for him flooded through my body. Ethan felt the change in my body and moved his mouth to my neck. I rubbed against the hardening bulge in the front of his jeans eager to free it and have him drive into me till I cried out his name. 'A-hum,' Lou coughed from the corner of the hedge.

I jumped back out of Ethan's arms and could feel the embarrassment burning my neck and face. 'Dad!'

'Jess, your mother has been waiting for you. Why don't you head in, sweetheart, while I have a word to Ethan?' I looked to Ethan who shifted uncomfortably at getting sprung by my father. I swear we both felt like a couple of naughty teenagers in that moment.

I nodded my head, gave Lou a kiss on the cheek and went up the walk to the open front door. Margaret was humming to herself in the kitchen setting out a tray of freshly cooked scones as I came in. 'Margaret?'

'Jessie!' she called, surprised, before a look of confusion crossed her face. 'But we heard Ethan's motorbike pull up out front.'

'Yeah, he and Dad were out there talking when I arrived.'

'Oh,' Margaret smiled, 'guess I should set an extra place for lunch.'

I knew that smile. She was hoping Ethan's turning up for lunch today was a sign that he liked me and another chance for her to play matchmaker. I wondered if her head would explode in a shower of streamers if I told her after I left today I would be collecting my stuff from the hotel and going to stay with Ethan till I went home. 'I have to make a call,' I said, stepping to the back door to get some privacy.

'Okay, Jessie, lunch in ten,' Margaret smiled as she set the extra place setting.

CHAPTER EIGHTEEN

'So, you're back at work on Thursday?' Ethan was the quietest I'd seen him so far, only talking when Margaret asked him a question. Lou focused on his food, intermittently smiling at Margaret but avoiding eye contact with Ethan.

'Yes. Thursday morning, I head out for my first shift again.'

'Do you ever do the Hawaii run?' Margaret asked casually. 'With Lou and I flying there at the end of the year it'd be nice to know we are in capable hands.'

For once it wasn't one of Margaret's matchmaking tactics. My father took her hand tenderly and smiled reassuring. 'We'll be fine, Margaret, whoever the pilot is.'

Ethan's face cleared of confusion. 'Have you never flown before, Margaret?' She shook her head. Ethan smiled softly. 'There isn't one pilot I've worked with at my airline who I wouldn't trust. Most of us are exRAAFies.'

'You used to be air force?' I was suddenly intrigued.

'Joined straight from high school and did ten years.' Ethan stabbed a lettuce leaf with his fork. 'Feels like forever ago now.'

Margaret scoffed, 'You are not old, Ethan. You're still plenty young enough to find a nice woman to settle down and have a family with.' Margaret's eyes flicked to me. I rolled my eyes while Ethan chuckled.

'You forget, Margaret, I tried that once remember?'

'Things are different now,' she continued taking on a stern voice, 'you're not in the forces anymore. You're not away God knows where and you're home a lot more often. No more six-month absences.'

'Still absent enough for a woman to grow lonely and look for comfort elsewhere, Margaret.'

'Not if you found the right woman …'

'What makes you so sure Jess is the right woman? You haven't seen her in ten years. She could have gone to the other side for all you know.'

Margaret sat looking agape at Ethan for a moment before that stunned mullet expression turned to me. She closed her mouth swallowed and lowered her voice. 'You're not a … a lesbian, are you, Jessie?'

Lou choked on his mouthful of scotch. 'Well, I'm finished. What's for dessert?' he queries, trying to distract from the current topic.

'Why don't you help me clear the table, Ethan?' I interrupted, standing up and taking Margaret's plate in my spare hand. Ethan smiled and took Lou's plate as he rose with his own and followed me into the kitchen.

'Thank you,' he said quietly once through the dining room door. 'I think I understand why you've not come home.'

'Don't think she doesn't give me the "I want grandchildren before I'm too old to see them" lecture over Skype. But it does help being able to hit disconnect when she does.'

Ethan laughed. 'You should give me your Skype call sign so we can keep each other company on the lonely nights.'

I sobered. 'My impression is you don't have lonely nights.'

Ethan stilled my hands from tossing the warm scones into a basket to take to the table. 'Having a strange woman in your bed doesn't stop you being lonely, Jess.'

'Maybe Margaret's right. Maybe you are in need of a good woman. You should start looking for one, after I leave.' I took my hand back and started pulling cream and jam from the fridge, handing them to Ethan.

'I'm happy how I am, Jess.'

'It didn't sound like it just then.' I spotted the freshly baked ricotta cheesecake and pulled that out also. 'Bring the scones, will you?' I called back over my shoulder as I stepped back towards the dining room.

CHAPTER NINETEEN

'I THINK YOU SHOULD TAKE A TAXI BACK TO THE HOTEL,' ETHAN said, leaning on the door frame of what used to be my bedroom. I looked up at him bewildered from where I sat at Margaret's craft table admiring her recent foray into folk art. Ethan's eyes flicked to the photo of my parents on the wall before coming back to me. It finally clicked. Lou's grumpiness wasn't that I'd been kissing Ethan, it was having realised I'd been on the back of Ethan's bike.

'Well, we'd have a hard time with my luggage on the back of the bike anyway.'

Ethan smiled, moving to the window where he could see Margaret getting clothes in off the line. 'Do you think they truly love each other that much still, or are they scared to be alone after so long?'

I looked at Ethan in surprise before I looked at the photo of my parents and thought about it. 'I believe they do, and I'm not just saying that as their daughter.' I ran my hand over the beautifully carved woodwork Margaret was currently decorating.

'Dad took up woodwork five years ago when he partially retired. It took a couple of years to get good at it, but now he's really producing some magnificent pieces. Margaret didn't take up folk art because her inner artist was dying to get out. She did it so she could share this new passion of his with him. Dad has started building stuff with the sole purpose of knowing his wife, the woman he adores, will take great pleasure in helping add a little more beauty to it. Even subconsciously they still revolve around each other.'

When I looked up to meet Ethan's eyes they sparkled, but there was sadness to it to. 'Back when my parents got married there was no way out, Ethan. You married someone for life and you took the good with the bad. All the bad shit in a relationship will usually occur in the first twenty years. Affairs, finances, kids ...'

'Kids?' Ethan queried bemused.

'Kids will test your relationship to its fullest extent. Everyone has different ideas on discipline and spoiling their kids. Kids will consciously pit one parent against another just to get their way, and Sharnie was brilliant at it. But after the kids grow up and leave home a couple has two choices. They rediscover their passion for one another, possibly in a different way to what it was before, or they realise they have nothing left in common any longer and go their separate ways.'

'And Lou and Margaret just found their passion by combining hobbies?'

I smiled and shrugged. No kid wants to think of their parents as lustful beings no matter what age they are. 'If they weren't my parents I'd be all for them going off on dirty weekends. But as my parents, I'd prefer to remain uninformed.'

Ethan laughed, walking back to the door. 'You going to stay here a while longer?' I nodded gazing around the room.

'This used to be my room. I moved out to get away from Sharnie so it was already reappropriated by the time I needed somewhere to go. Of course, Sharnie was still living here at the time, so when I needed my family the most, it was the one place I couldn't run to ...'

'She fucked him, didn't she?' I closed my eyes and nodded. 'Did she want him? Was she jealous that you had him?'

I met Ethan's cautious eyes. 'No. She didn't want him. She may have been attracted to him but she always said she could have anyone, so why settle?'

'Then why?'

I shrugged. 'She was jealous of my happiness, or maybe she just needed to prove to herself that she could, in fact, have anyone because Ben had never paid her any attention.' I dropped my hands to my lap.

Ethan shoved his hands in his pockets confused. 'If Ben wasn't interested why'd he do it?'

'Because … he thought it was me. And by the time I came home and turned the light on, he didn't care that it wasn't.'

CHAPTER TWENTY

It wasn't sleeping with Ben that had left me unable to forgive Sharnie. We both knew she wasn't innocent. Sharnie's hate for me had escalated starting right after her hospitalisation when she was fourteen. Even in the photo I held in my hand, taken a week before her betrayal, it was there in her eyes. Sharnie wanted me to hurt.

The doctor who treated her after her drug induced psychosis warned us that she would relapse. The night she had gotten high and her brain had malfunctioned; she beat her best friend into a coma with a text book. Sharnie had lost all her friends and had to move schools to get rid of the stigma. But after that Sharnie's psychotic tendencies were only ever aimed at me. I'll spend my life wondering what I did to make my twin so spiteful towards me, because she will never admit out loud that it was on purpose.

'The last photo I ever got of my girls together,' Margaret stated, observing what absorbed my attention, 'I had hoped to get one at the wedding …'

'Never going to happen, Margaret.' I put the photo of Sharnie and I on our twenty-first birthday back on the shelf. I stepped away to browse the other photos collected in my absence.

'Has Ethan left?' Margaret picked up the discarded frame and ran her thumb over her happy daughters' smiles.

'Half-hour ago.'

'I'm not ignorant, Jessie. Your father told me what happened when he found out from Ben.'

'Then you should understand,' I replied absently. I knew better than to think she would.

'No, I don't. It was an accident. Ben thought it was you and Sharnie was drunk and wandered into the wrong bedroom.'

'Wrong bed in the wrong bedroom, in the wrong house, in the wrong suburb ... yeah, I can understand the confusion.'

Margaret ignored my sarcasm. 'You hold her responsible for what happened after?'

I froze. 'Don't!' I warned through gritted teeth.

She touched my shoulder gently. 'You can't hold Sharnie responsible for that, Jessie. If it was meant to happen it was going to happen no matter what ...'

My arm swung knocking the photo from her hand causing the glass frame to smash on the floor. Margaret jumped back, surprised by my aggression. I wanted to grab her by her perfectly pressed blouse and shake her while I yelled, 'But it was her fault!' Instead I turned, slamming the front door behind me.

I made it to the curb before my father came out after me. 'Jessie?'

'She chose her side years ago, Dad. That's fine. But if she wants to keep in contact with me she needs to stop pressing for reconciliation.'

'She chose the daughter who stayed. Your mother didn't know what happened, none of us did. You just upped and left and I had to go intimidate the truth from Ben myself. What did you expect her to do? Lose both her daughters? You'd run away. You really expected her to throw Sharnie out and shun her?'

I shook my head as the tears started to fall. I hugged myself tight and looked over the front of the house that had stopped being home to me long ago. I brought my eyes back to meet my father's. 'I was happy. Why was that so offensive to her?' Lou just stood there looking at me unable to answer, or unwilling to voice the truth about his own daughter's malicious nature. For the second time in my life I walked away from my father. Left him standing there watching me leave just as he'd done at the hospital emergency room.

I was wrong. Nothing had changed. The hurt was still as bad, the betrayal, and the loneliness. Some cuts you just can't heal. They go too deep, fester and rot away your insides so that forgiveness and trusting again are unattainable dreams. They make coming home impossible.

CHAPTER TWENTY-ONE

'You know,' Karla shook her head, 'I was shocked when you came home for that bitch's wedding. Not that I haven't missed you.'

'Margaret insisted,' I mourned into my wine. One thing hadn't changed. When I needed my best friend, she was there. We met at our old local from uni days and were throwing back drinks while I caught her up on Ethan and Margaret's behaviour.

Karla chuckled, 'Margaret has been insisting for ten years now.' She sat straighter and looked me over. 'No, something else brought you home.'

'Really? Please enlighten me.'

'Well,' Karla took another mouthful, 'it could just be a kicking the dirt in the grave thing. You know, not believing the town slut was getting married until you actually see it happen — a doubting Thomas.' I shrugged at the possibility. 'But I think more likely you're dipping your toe in the water. To see if you could handle actually coming home for good.'

'Hmmm, all good theories. I'll accept them. But the water is ice cold if that's the case.'

Karla shrugged. 'Well, you know what they say … sometimes you just have to dive in and start swimming. You try to take it a step at a time you'll never get in.'

I laughed at our excessive use of euphemisms. 'Yes, but risking hypothermia and death just seems a little drastic for me too.'

'Ah, but then there is the amazing Ethan to get naked and share body heat with!'

'An option that I'm sure would quickly dry up if my visitation became permanent,' I frowned. 'He's like me, Karla. No strings attached.'

Karla quirked a brow. 'We know I've been around the block a few times, Jess, so trust me when I tell you you've both met your match in each other. It's just neither of you are willing to admit it.'

'For good reason.' I didn't bother denying it. Karla knew me well enough to spot a lie from me. Karla smiled and patted my hand. 'Speaking of meeting one's match?' I fingered the rock on her ring finger.

'Ah yes. Anthony.'

'The on-again-off-again Anthony from high school?'

'One and the same. Notably the engagement has been off three times in three years too.' Karla sighed and fidgeted with the ring. 'How can someone who is so right, be so wrong at the same time?'

'Depends where he's going wrong?'

Karla cringed. 'There is a reason I keep going elsewhere for sex. I love the guy but his idea of sex could fit into a commercial break.' Karla looked at me out of the corner of her eye, a mischievous smile creeping up the corner of her mouth, 'Think maybe Mr Sexpot Ethan would give him a few pointers?'

I laughed and joined Karla in another glass of red. 'How is it you haven't met Ethan or Greg already anyway?'

Karla shrugged. 'You know Lizzy and I only put up with Sharnie because she was your sister, right?' Sharnie didn't really make long-term female friends. 'After what happened we had nothing more to do with her. So sadly, I haven't had the pleasure of your Ethan.'

'Oh, please don't call him that!' My phone rang. It was an unknown number so I just pressed the silent button. A minute later it buzzed with a message.

'Mr Sexpot looking for his next booty call?' Karla teased.

I smiled opening the message. 'You psychic, Karla?'

'Ooh really? What seductive opener did he send you?' Karla swooned. 'Let me guess … I'm laying here naked, hand strangling the snake remembering how your tight pussy feels as it cums repeatedly?'

'Something like that,' I lied and Karla keeled over laughing.

When she righted herself, she smiled wickedly and said, 'So you going to go relieve his burning desire?'

I shrugged and put my phone down. It was Ethan but his message was one of worry. Lou called him and told him about my fight with Margaret. I didn't answer. Things with Ethan already breached the personal line. I doubt Lou would have shared details and I needed to get Ethan back to arm's length.

'Maybe later,' I winked at Karla, 'right now I want to hear everything you haven't bothered to tell me on Skype.'

CHAPTER TWENTY-TWO

I KEPT MY ARM ON THE WALL LEADING TO MY HOTEL ROOM TO STOP the world from spinning. Ethan followed the first message an hour later with a request to know if I'd reneged on staying with him. I hoped my silence answered his question loudly enough. I reached my hotel room and slipped the card in to unlock the door. I stood with the door open while I slid the card into the power key and the lights came alive. I let go of the door and walked three steps before I realised it hadn't closed behind me.

I turned around to find Ethan standing in the doorway. He stepped inside letting the door shut and leant on the wall with his arms crossed. 'Did you drink the place dry?'

I went to deny it, the world spun and I sat hard on the end of the bed. I shrugged instead. 'What are you doing here, Ethan?' I sighed kicking my shoes off.

'I was worried about you. Decided to hang out in the lobby to make sure you were okay. You walked right past me, and I followed you down the length of that hallway with you totally oblivious. You're damn lucky I'm not some psycho after you.'

'The jury is still out on that one, Mr Stalker,' I slurred at him, rolling my eyes. Ethan scoffed. 'I'm fine, Ethan. Fighting with Margaret is nothing new for me. Having a one-night stand turn up persistently is unsettling though, so goodnight.'

I pulled my dress over my head and climbed under the quilt before removing the rest of my underwear, flinging it back across the room in the direction of my suitcase. I didn't bother to wait to see Ethan leave. I was wasted and exhausted from several nights of neglecting sleep in favour of great sex. There was no chance of him getting any action from me tonight.

The sound of someone knocking on the door brought me around in the morning. I heard the door open and two muffled voices exchange pleasantries before I could incite my eyes to actually open and focus. Ethan walked from the doorway to the desk with a tray of food from room service and I couldn't stop the growl of appreciation at the sight of him half naked, just his blue denims hanging from his hips like he'd just pulled them on.

'You stayed?'

'Thought you may need someone to hold your hair back if your night caught up with you. Surprisingly though, once you passed out you stayed that way.'

'Right that's it,' I said, sitting up angrily, 'one-night stands are not recurring, they don't turn up unannounced after you fight with a family member and they sure as hell do not hang out for a full night to hold your hair from your face in case you puke your guts up.'

Ethan frowned. 'That's true. But friends do.'

I lay back down with a sigh. 'Friends do not fuck each other senseless.' Ethan just smiled and bought me over a glass of water. 'I mean it, Ethan. I can't handle this. That your close with my kin is your problem; it doesn't give you an all-access pass to my life.' Ethan's smile faltered as he sat on the bed beside me. 'You want to fuck each other's brains out till I leave? That's doable. But you stay out of my personal shit.'

Ethan cocked a brow at me. 'Out of curiosity, was the fight with your mum about what flowers she thinks we should have at our wedding, or are you suddenly so hostile because you gave up your big dark secret to me?'

'Fuck you, Ethan. You find out my sister fucked my fiancé and you think you know it all. You don't know the half of it.'

'Right.' Ethan stood and pulled his shirt on. 'Well, there's breakfast over there, mainly toast to soak up the alcohol obviously still coursing through your system. You have my number. If you get over whatever the fuck this is before you fly out again I'd love to have dinner with the Jess I met a few days ago.'

Ethan was out the door now as pissed off as I was. I dragged myself to the shower and sat on the floor enjoying the hot water pelt down on me for close to an hour. By the time I emerged to the cold toast and coffee on the desk I'd started to feel bad about my treatment of Ethan. So, I had issues. I shouldn't have taken them out on him. I considered calling to apologise, but put my phone back on the table. It was probably better just to leave it this way.

CHAPTER TWENTY-THREE

'So, your mother was quite upset about how you left yesterday,' Lou informed me casually as he filled a water bottle. I stood in my parents' kitchen happy that Margaret was at work, allowing me to avoid lunch with her.

My father, however, was partially retired so he was off to golf soon. I dropped over to apologise to my dad, knowing I had no intention of apologising to Margaret. 'It's not the worst fight we've ever had,' I shrugged. 'Did you really call Ethan to come check on me last night?'

'I figured he'd have an idea how to find you or that you would respond to his call before mine. Was I wrong?'

'Yep!'

'Oh!' Lou cringed.

'How much did you tell him?'

'Just that you fought with Margaret and left quite upset. I may have mentioned the fight was Sharnie-related.'

'So, he doesn't know about …'

'Not our story to tell, Jessie girl.' Lou touched my arm affectionately. 'That is yours, just like what happened between Sharnie and you was yours to tell.' My father pulled me into a hug. 'Will you tell him?'

I shook my head against his chest. 'None of his business. I'll be gone in two days and any future visits home may not even correspond with him being around anyway.'

'Two days?' Lou pulled back. 'I thought you were here till Friday?'

'I fly out Thursday morning now. My flight got brought forward.'

'When?' Lou asked suspiciously

'Oh, about the time I found out Sharnie would be home on Wednesday evening,' I feigned my best airy innocence. A knock at the door stalled any response my father may have had. 'I'll get it,' I smiled and walked to the front door. When I pulled it open Ethan was smiling at me in a pair of cargo pants and polo shirt.

His smile faltered. 'Jess. You're looking a bit perkier this afternoon.' Ethan stepped into the foyer and waited while I closed the door.

'Ethan, I'm really sorry about venting on you this morning and for ignoring you last night. If I'd just told you I was catching up with a friend …'

'I wouldn't have stumbled upon your bitch doppelganger?' Ethan smiled. 'Apology accepted.' I relaxed and Ethan tucked a loose strand of hair behind my ear. 'So is the nice Jess back in control again?'

I tilted my head. 'All depends on the topic of conversation really.'

Ethan leaned in close and my eyes checked to make sure my father hadn't stepped into the hallway. 'Well, how about dinner tonight? And after dinner we can discuss something relatively harmless.'

'The weather?'

'I was thinking about the various ways to fuck each other's brains out,' Ethan laughed citing my own words back at me. I couldn't help the blush that rose when my body responded to the suggestion. Ethan smiled and leant in for a kiss.

'Afternoon, Ethan!' Lou called from down the hall. 'If you could keep your attempts to corrupt my good daughter out of my house I'd appreciate it.'

'The good daughter?' Ethan raised his eyebrows humoured.

'Yes, the good twin. Until yesterday I had never even seen her do more than hold hands with a boy. Unlike her sister, Jess has always allowed me the delusion of her goodness.'

I was silently chuckling at the stern look on my father's face and the surprise on Ethan's. 'Well,' Ethan finally recovered leaning in to talk to me quietly, 'I look forward to corrupting you later tonight.'

Ethan ducked as Lou smacked the back of his head. 'I heard that. Come on or we'll still be at the ninth hole when dinner time comes. You still want me to drop you off on the way, Jess?'

I hesitated but nodded. I opened the door and walked out ahead of them. Ethan caught up to me at the footpath while Lou locked the front door. Ethan pulled me around the corner of the hedge so not only were we out of sight of my father, but also legally off his property. His fingers tangled in the hair at the base of my skull as his mouth seized mine forcefully for several minutes. The blast of a car horn pulled us apart laughing. Lou had backed up to the footpath and was waiting for us to get in the car. I opened the door and hopped in the back. Ethan went to join me.

'You're in the front, Casanova,' Lou scolded. Ethan shrugged shutting my door for me. When he hopped into the front Lou gave him an unfriendly look. 'I like you, Ethan, but I do know your reputation so I should explain something. Unless Jess is wearing a ring you paid for and a priest has blessed, you kiss her like that anywhere near me again and we'll be having a conversation over the barrel of my shotgun. Am I understood?'

CHAPTER TWENTY-FOUR

THE GRAVEYARD WAS BUSIER THAN I EXPECTED. TWO FUNERALS WERE taking place on the opposite side and a random few visitors to loved ones milling about. The grave I stood in front of was small, the inscription read *'Our beloved granddaughter Matilda Bailey, stillborn 2002'* because after twenty weeks it's not a miscarriage and the child has to be legally named and buried.

'I was wondering if you'd come to see her,' Ben said as he stepped beside me before setting a bunch of white roses down next to the yellow lilies I bought. 'It took me a long time to accept how you could just leave it to your parents to bury their grandchild. I get it now. Grief affects everyone differently.' When I stayed quiet Ben sighed heavily. 'I'm sorry about the other night, Jess. I was shocked to see you to start with, but to see you with Ethan Knight …'

I raised a brow at Ethan's surname, which I'd never bothered to find out. Ben mistook it for a reaction to his tone. 'Look, I'm married, I have a son now. I have no right to comment on who you choose to see. But don't marry the guy okay? He'll break your heart.'

'You know him that well?' I kept my eyes on the tiny pink marble headstone.

'We surf the same waves.'

'And that gives you full insight into his personality, does it?'

Ben sighed. 'Look, Jess, I don't want to fight. Just 'cause we've both moved on doesn't mean I stopped caring for you.'

I let the silence stretch out between us before I finally spoke. 'God, Ben, we were so young and when I found out I was pregnant …'

Ben frowned. 'Yeah I know. We'd not even talked about marriage before that, but I wanted to do right by you, Jess. It doesn't mean it wouldn't have worked between us. We did love each other and you were so happy about becoming a mother.' The silence stretched out again. 'Is that why you're marrying Knight, because you're pregnant again?' I looked shocked and looked down at my flat abdomen. 'I'm not saying you look pregnant, Jess, just …'

'Why would anyone want to marry me otherwise right?' I laughed at the insincerity.

'No!' Ben was quick to defend himself, 'but Ethan isn't the guy to marry …'

'Ben, stop, before you dig your own grave.' I pointed to the empty plot beside our stillborn daughters. 'I'm not pregnant. I'm not the same woman I was when you knew me. Back then all I wanted was the white picket fence, a husband who loved me and a brood of kids running around the backyard. That dream died for me the same night our child did.'

I turned walking back to the road. I made it a hundred metres down the road and was calling for a taxi when Ben pulled his Ford XR8 up next to me and wound down the window. 'I'll give you a lift back to town, Jess. Get in.' I sighed, considered the fifteen-minute wait for a taxi, briefly, and hopped into the car. 'So you still in Canada?'

'Hawaii.'

'That explains the tan.' Ben's eyes lingered on my legs.

'Tell me about your wife, Ben.'

Ben blinked and turned his eyes back to the road. 'Remember Suzanna Wilson?'

'Pretty little thing, she was always into you even at school.'

'Yeah well, after you disappeared, I finally started paying attention. We've been married three years last month and William will be one next month.' Ben's eyes were back wandering my body.

'You can drop me off at Starfish by the wharf. I'm having afternoon tea with Lizzy.'

Ben looked gobsmacked. 'Have you and my sister been in contact all this time?' I just smiled. 'That bitch! She told me she hadn't heard from you.'

'You know Lizzy's ex-boyfriend screwed Sharnie behind her back right?' I asked with little emotion. Ben nodded, unsure where I was going. 'She understood exactly how I felt.'

Ben didn't have a comeback for that one, but his brain was ticking just the same. 'If you're still living in Hawaii how did you and Ethan even hook up?'

'We met in a bar.' My phone buzzed. Ethan telling me he'd pick me up at seven.

Ben saw the message and glowered. 'Will you move home when you get married?' He pulled into the parking lot at the wharf.

'Thanks for the ride, Ben.' I got out of the car and walked towards the café. Ben had saved me cab fare but more than that, I realised I'd never really been angry at him.

CHAPTER TWENTY-FIVE

ETHAN KNOCKED ON MY HOTEL DOOR AT SEVEN ON THE DOT. HE looked good in his black slacks and button-down shirt. 'Shit,' I murmured looking down at my casual summer dress, 'when you said dinner I expected something like Sunday night.' Ethan smirked, stepping inside while I turned to pull something a bit more respectable from my suitcase. I pulled my summer dress off and slipped the maxi dress on instead, swapping my sandals for the only pair of heels I'd brought for the wedding.

When I finished Ethan raised a brow. 'Nicely done. Most girls would have taken another half-hour to change their outfit at last moment.' He looked at my suitcase and frowned. 'Have you got all your stuff together?' When I looked at him dumbfounded Ethan exhaled in annoyance. 'Remember you agreed to stay with me till you left?'

'Ethan …' I started shaking my head.

Ethan started throwing things into my suitcase. 'It's only two nights, Jess. I'll leave Thursday and you can stay at my place till you leave on Friday. Sophia will come lock up after you leave.'

'If I say no?'

Ethan hoisted my bag. 'I'll take this with me anyway.' I frowned but collected my stuff from the bathroom, ensuring I had everything I'd come with. I checked out and assured the receptionist my early departure was nothing to do with their service. In the parking lot I stopped dead in front of Lou's car.

'I only own the bike, Jess. Your dad insisted I borrow the car if I was taking you out.'

I squeezed my eyes tight. 'Please tell me Margaret doesn't know!'

Ethan laughed and said, 'She knows I'm taking you out to dinner, but that's all your father felt the need to share.' He put my bag in the boot. 'By the way she told me to tell you you're forgiven.'

'Damn it, Ethan!' I sulked into the passenger seat.

Ethan started the engine then took my hand in his. 'As far as she's concerned, it's just dinner. She was so happy about it she's over your refusal to forgive Sharnie. Is that so bad?'

'That's not what the fight was about … well, mostly. And you really don't know Margaret if you think she isn't sitting home right now picking out wedding venues and writing the guest list. You're taking the car back straight after dinner otherwise she'll be picking out baby names by breakfast.'

Ethan chuckled and put the car into drive. 'It's okay. Lou's working tomorrow so he's already told me the car has a curfew.'

Dinner was at a nice restaurant in Hamilton. It wasn't super fancy but the food and service were good. 'So how did you ever get up to no good, Jess? Your parents seem super protective of you.'

'With Sharnie, the more they tightened the leash the wilder she got. By the time we turned sixteen they'd decided just to be happy with her coming home alive each night. In comparison, I chose to give myself a curfew, had a steady boyfriend from the time I was fourteen …'

'Ben?'

'Yeah, I had the most popular boy in school tied to a leash from very early on.'

Ethan chuckled. 'And here I thought you were a good girl. Did your parents know you were having sex so young?'

I shook my head at Ethan's misunderstanding. 'I think they were more worried about Sharnie coming home knocked up. Besides, Ben and I didn't have sex till much later.'

Ethan looked disbelieving. 'You're telling me that the popular boy, who was two years your senior, stuck around all those years when you weren't putting out?'

The waiter set down a coffee for Ethan and a hot chocolate for me instead of desserts. After he walked away I smiled at Ethan who still wasn't buying it. 'Look, I swear to you I was still a virgin when I finished high school. But, as you well know, there are other things to be done to the same outcome.'

'Ah, so years of foreplay.' Ethan understood finally. 'You never felt pressured to do more?'

'Of course! He was male,' I answered dismissively. 'After our first year together, with my sister's reputation, he wanted to go further. I wanted to as well. I wasn't a saint. Thing was his mother was a stay-at-home mum so nothing ever happened at his place and Lou wasn't lying about that shotgun, Ethan. Then Ben went off to the academy. I got a year's reprieve and by the time he came back I was at uni. We moved in together and our first night under the same roof was also our first night.'

'He wasn't a virgin though?' Ethan's eyes narrowed. 'You were together from when he was sixteen. He was either an early starter or …'

'The year he went away to the academy we had a year off. I wanted to focus on my studies and, well, he was four hours' drive away. We agreed that anything that happened in those twelve months would never be discussed or held against each other.'

Ethan shook his head. 'And you honestly didn't mind he was screwing other random women?'

I looked at him exasperated. 'He came back to me, Ethan. He had a year's freedom and still decided he wanted me. And anyway, it was beneficial for me that he knew what he was doing for my first time.'

'And yet he didn't chase after you when you left?'

'I thought we agreed no personal talk?' I put my cup down and glared at Ethan.

Ethan nodded glumly. 'I tell you what. Answer just one last question about that topic and I'll let you ask five personal questions of me.'

'If I don't want to answer?'

'Then I'll still let you ask your five questions, but I have the right to refuse to answer one. Fair?' I nodded and Ethan took a deep breath. 'What is your biggest regret about everything that happened with Sharnie, Ben and you?'

I hadn't been expecting that question. I expected him to ask why I couldn't forgive her, if I thought I ever would, if I knew why Ben didn't chase me down. But that question I couldn't answer honestly. I bowed my head and shook it.

Ethan looked disappointed but took my trembling hand in his. 'Fine. Your turn.'

I took a deep breath. 'How old where you?'

'Fifteen. She was in year twelve. It was her younger brother's birthday party. She invited me into her room and …' Ethan smiled lasciviously.

'Do you even know how many women you've had sex with?'

Ethan raised his eyebrows. 'Do you know how many you've been with?'

'Of course, but this is my question time.'

Ethan smirked and said, 'I stopped counting a year after my divorce was finalised. I was married for ten years you know, so it's not as many as you think. Though admittedly the marriage itself was over many years before that, we just didn't file for divorce till she got pregnant and decided to marry the new bloke.'

'Did you want the whole picket fence scenario? Wife, kids, big backyard?'

Ethan shrugged. 'In a way yes, but I wanted to be a pilot so obviously I wasn't about staying home to raise the kids. I wanted to see the world and have fun. But yeah, I imagined coming home to my loving wife. By the time I was ready to think about kids, the wife loved somebody else.'

Ethan said it with such casual honesty and without a trace of hurt that I was instantly jealous of his ability to move on from being hurt. Except, I realised, he hadn't really. His lack of interest in having a relationship with anyone was obvious proof of that.

'Okay, easy one now.' Ethan sat forward in earnest. 'Who's better in the sack? Sharnie or her twin?'

Ethan laughed. 'I am not putting myself in for that one.'

'So, you refuse to answer?' Ethan nodded. 'Do you miss having someone permanent, someone to love?'

Ethan looked at me intently. 'Do you?' I lifted a brow. 'Right, not your question time. I'm not answering.'

'You've already used your opt out!'

Ethan glared at me. 'You asked the comparison question knowing I'd play the gentleman?' I just sat watching him. 'Fine! You're the better lay. Sharnie's a slut, and she fucks like a slut. You're all about intimacy. You get just as much out of my touch and kiss as you do out of the fucking. When I'm with you I know it's because you want to be with me. I'm not just a cock for you to get off on. Of course, I miss having someone in my life, but I'm not about to risk getting burned again either.'

Ethan stood up and pulled his wallet out ignoring the shocked looks from the couple at the next table. 'You know, I thought Sharnie was your family's shame when I first met them five years ago. Your father talks about you like you could never do any wrong. But these last few days, I've looked back on what they say and realised what they don't say. Whatever blew your family apart, it wasn't Sharnie.'

I was up and out the door leaving Ethan to deal with the bill. He caught my elbow halfway up the block. I cursed wearing heels and my inability to run in them. 'Okay, I was out of line. I'm sorry.' I just glared at him. Ethan exhaled deeply and said, 'Jess, I like you, really like you. I know a relationship isn't going to happen with you, but I have this absolute need to get to know you, to understand everything about you.'

When I just stood there looking at him Ethan led me back to the car and forcibly sat me in the passenger seat. The drive to his place was in silence. Ethan took my bag. I half think it was to stop me trying to make a run with it. Inside his apartment he put my bag in his room while I stood idle in the entry way.

'I have to take your dad's car back. I'll be about fifteen minutes. Don't go anywhere okay.' I refused to answer. Ethan dragged me over to the lounge and sat me down. He squatted in front of me. 'No more talking, I promise. Just chill out till I get back.'

Ethan left me alone in his apartment. I took off my heels, moving to the window so I could watch the waves in the moon light. When my phone rang I jumped, answering it without even looking at the screen. 'So, how'd dinner go?'

'Jesus, Margaret, has Ethan even left the premises?'

'He just rode off on his bike. So, are you going to see him again?'

'I don't know. Dinner wasn't an overwhelming success.'

'Oh!' Margaret paused. 'Well, you're having dinner with us tomorrow night anyway. Be here at six. Do you want your father to pick you up?'

'No, I'll catch a taxi.'

'Good.' Margaret hesitated. 'He's a nice man, Jessie. What went wrong at dinner?'

Ethan came through his apartment door. I indicated he should be quiet. 'Margaret, I really don't want to talk about it right now. I'll see you for dinner tomorrow night okay?'

'Okay, sweetheart. I guess I should be happy you at least went out on a date.'

I hung up. Ethan raised his eyebrows at me. 'So, what flowers did she pick out?'

'Don't you laugh. You will cop it more than I will after I leave.'

Ethan hesitated, 'Jess …'

'Ethan?' I recognised the look in his eyes. Despite promising he wouldn't intrude any further the curiosity was eating at him. I sighed and dropped back onto the couch. 'I'll sleep on the couch tonight.'

Ethan shook his head and pulled me back to standing. 'Don't be ridiculous. We don't have to have sex to share a bed.' I let him lead me to his room. I was tired. Tired of having to defend myself. Dead tired of Margaret and her insistence that I forgive and forget. Overtired of hating Sharnie. Over closing myself off out of fear of getting hurt.

I realised as Ethan kissed my cheek and turned to leave the room that Karla had been right. I'd come home to see if I could manage coming home for good. I came home looking for something more in my life and found Ethan. I reached out and tugged him back to me. I seized his face and kissed him with everything I'd been holding inside. Ethan's eyebrows rose with surprise before he wrapped me in his arms and met the ferocity of my kiss with his own.

CHAPTER TWENTY-SIX

'WHERE IS YOUR FAMILY, ETHAN? WHY SO CLOSE TO MY dysfunctional kin?' I stared up at the ceiling lying in his arms while we absently thumb wrestled.

'Well, my mother was a single mum. I never knew who my dad was and she died before I had the chance to ask. I lived with my grandparents till I was seventeen and could apply for the air force. My grandfather was a fighter pilot and made it sound like the best thing in the world.'

'It isn't?'

'The flying, yes. The war side of things, no. They died while I was still enlisted.' Ethan stopped wrestling my thumb and stroked my fingers instead.

'So, Lou is like your surrogate father?'

I felt Ethan shrug beneath my head. 'I guess. Hadn't really thought about it.' I wanted to say that made what we were doing kind of incestuous but didn't because another thought entered my head. What if what we were doing was about him truly becoming part of the family? We lay quiet for a few more minutes and I felt myself drifting off to sleep. 'Who were you visiting today?'

My forehead crinkled in confusion. 'What?'

'When we dropped you at the cemetery? Lou said you had to go say goodbye to someone. Was it a grandparent?'

I burst into tears, shocking Ethan. He pulled me tight to his chest, kissed my forehead and held me while I cried. When I quietened, Ethan didn't press to know more. In fact, my outburst seemed to silence his interrogations completely.

I woke Wednesday morning to an empty bed and knew instantly Ethan would be catching the morning surf. I didn't know what time he was starting tomorrow. It may be his last surf for a few days. I considered fixing him breakfast and decided to just go back to sleep.

CHAPTER TWENTY-SEVEN

WHEN I WOKE LATER IT WAS TO THE FEEL OF ETHAN SPREADING MY thighs as he climbed between them. 'Morning,' he murmured when I looked down at him. 'It's our last day together. Any ideas what you would like to do today?'

'You!' I answered with a giggle as he tickled my inner thigh with his tongue.

'Me first.'

I gasped gripping the pillow beneath my head while he licked and sucked me to within an inch of climax. When I started to tense up Ethan crawled over me. He kissed all around my neck before focusing on my breasts. I squirmed beneath him dying to feel him inside me. Ethan pinned my hips to the mattress and that just made me want him more. My fingers combed through his short dark hair and pulled his face to mine.

We stayed that way for a few minutes, staring into each other, breathing heavy with our want for each other. 'Jess,' Ethan finally breathed.

I gripped his hard shaft around its base and watched Ethan's eyes flutter. I guided him into me and with a final thrust he buried himself. Our desire was burning hot as we fucked each other as hard and fast as we could. But each time I came within thrusts of climax Ethan would pull away and change position, drawing me out till I thought I would scream in frustration.

'If you don't want me to cum, fuck me from behind,' I finally grumbled, 'I can't cum like that.'

'Really?' Ethan asked surprised as he pulled away from me for the sixth time. He turned me in his arms putting me on all fours and knelt behind me. When he thrust into me I cried out, but I knew my body; this would be pleasurable without the payoff. Ethan pounded me till I was breathless and he was throbbing hard. He bent over me and forced me forward to lie on my stomach. He kissed over my shoulders as he spoke to me. 'You weren't lying. You get nothing out of it.'

'I didn't say that, it's just not the way to make me cum. Sex isn't all about climax. You wanted to hold me back, it's the best way to do it, because honestly, the next time you penetrated me I was going to cum otherwise.'

'Interesting!'

'What is?' I asked breathless as his hand slid between the mattress and my tummy to find my clit.

Ethan kissed my neck. 'Ask me later.'

He started moving slowly while he rubbed my clit. I gripped the sheets and buried my face in the mattress till it was too much. 'Ethan!'

'Me too.' He lifted his upper body and thrust into me without mercy. All the hold off caught up with me in one big hit. I smothered my face in the bedding to stop from moaning loud enough to alert the neighbours. Ethan on the other hand didn't care if they heard him.

He collapsed on top of me to catch his breath. After a few seconds, he turned on his side, used my hair to turn my face to his, and kissed me deeply. 'Now,' he laughed when I moaned at his withdrawal, 'what else did you have planned for today?'

CHAPTER TWENTY-EIGHT

WE ARRIVED AT MY PARENTS JUST AFTER SIX. ETHAN DROPPED ME off a block away while he rode ahead. That way Lou didn't see me on Ethan's bike and Margaret didn't think we'd come together. When I walked up the front stairs the door was open. Lou was just inside. 'Ethan said he saw you walking up the street.'

I smiled kissing his cheek, 'Hi, Dad.'

'I'll kill him!' Lou scowled shaking his head. 'We're out on the patio. I'm cooking a BBQ tonight.'

I followed my father happily. I was so caught up in enjoying what had been a great day with Ethan that it wasn't till we stepped into the backyard that I heard the other male and female voice. I froze on the spot at the sight of Sharnie. Her olive skin darkened from the island honeymoon, blonde hair even lighter than normal, laughing as she showed Margaret pictures of their holiday. I took a step back without thinking. Lou put his arm around my waist to stop me retreating.

'I know, Jessie girl. Do it for your mother okay? It's just one night. I ha̶n't told Margaret you brought your flight forward so she still thinks she has tomorrow after Greg goes back to work to play Mrs Fix-it. That means she won't push so hard tonight in front of the men since Greg doesn't know the history.'

The fact that Lou said Greg, not the men, told me he knew Ethan was in on the part that most people knew about. Which told me they'd talked about it. 'Jess!' Ethan called out stepping away from where he'd been talking to Greg, drawing everyone's attention to me, removing any chance of a stealthy escape. I looked to my father, who just shrugged, pressing me forward as he moved to join the gathering. I watched Sharnie say something quietly to Margaret before looking at Greg with worried eyes. Greg was watching me with a tight smile.

Margaret patted Sharnie's hand then came to greet me. Obviously Sharnie hadn't known I was coming either. 'Evening, Jessie. Glad you could make it.' Margaret pulled me in for a hug then whispered in my ear, 'Please, Jessie?'

I sighed. What choice did I have now? I nodded silently, my eyes locking with Sharnie's. Her worry seemed to ease and she even gave me a friendly smile. 'Please tell me you have wine.'

'Merlot, it's up on the table. Take it easy though, Jessie. You're an emotional drunk.' Margaret moved back to the swing chair with Sharnie to keep looking at photos. I went straight for the table and poured a glass of wine. After I'd had two mouthfuls Margaret tried to reel me in. 'Want to look at your sister's honeymoon photos, Jessie?'

'Maybe later.' After a lot more wine. I forced a smile. 'Where did you go?'

'Bora Bora,' Greg smiled. 'You ever been?'

'Several times. It's beautiful.'

'So sad to go to such a romantic place by yourself.' Sharnie didn't even try to hold the cut from her voice.

I laughed. 'Who said I was alone? I may not hold a candle to your track record, Sharnie; hell, a paid whore comes up short next to you, but I'm no nun.' Sharnie went red with anger at my less-than-subtle implication. Before she could respond, a hand in the middle of my back moved me away towards the other end of the patio where the men were congregating around the BBQ.

Margaret stood, ushering Sharnie into the house to help her with the salads. I knew they'd be ready already. Our parents were just creating a buffer zone. 'Just breathe, Jess,' Ethan murmured quietly, 'you made it most of the way through the wedding.'

'There were a lot more witnesses to her brutal murder there.'

Ethan laughed as we got to my father. Lou put out his arm and I cuddled into his side happily. 'Sorry, Jessie. Sharnie was already tipsy when we picked them up from the airport.'

I laughed, which surprised the three men around me. 'Oh my God, Dad. If she's drunk there is no chance this will end well. You know her track record.'

'She promised your mother she'd behave,' Greg said, sounding unsure.

'Definitely no chance. You did hear her just now, right? She's only warming up.' Lou looked at me beseechingly. 'Fine! But if she comes at me with a knife again I'm holding you and Margaret responsible.'

'She's attacked you before?' Greg was gobsmacked. 'What happened?'

I met Greg's eyes snarling. 'Which time? Honestly do you know anything about the woman you married other than her gag reflex limit?'

'Jess!' Lou reprimanded harshly.

Ethan lifted the wine glass from my hand. 'I'm cutting you off before your doppelganger turns up.'

'The bitch is not alcohol-related, Ethan, it's Sharnie-related.'

'Still …' Ethan replaced my wine with a glass of water. 'Let's not exacerbate the situation.'

'Jesus!' Greg looked at Ethan. 'You know?'

'Not now, Greg,' Ethan urged.

'How bad?'

'Nothing that should impair your judgement of your wife.'

'Pfft!' was all I got out before Lou tugged me tight against him to cut me off.

Margaret and Sharnie came back out carrying the salads and breads as Lou moved the cooked meat into an aluminium tray. I took it to the table. Sharnie reached across grabbing my wrist, nails digging in. 'You stay away from my husband.'

I wrapped my other hand around her wrist and buried my nails into hers. 'Yes, because it would suck for me to wait till after you were already married to fuck your husband. Don't worry. I'll at least wait till you're pregnant to even the scale!'

Sharnie pulled away quickly and actually looked pale. I blinked at her sudden withdrawal. 'You're pregnant!' Everyone was watching us now.

Lou cursed and actually swore in front of Margaret for the first time I'd ever heard. 'You're fucking kidding me. You're pregnant and you're drinking like a fish?'

'I'm still in my first trimester. It won't hurt it,' Sharnie recovered. I couldn't react. I just stood there like a stunned mullet.

'Jessie?' Margaret called tentatively.

I looked at both my parents. 'You knew?'

Margaret looked away, tears in her eyes. Lou grabbed my arm. 'Jessie, let it go.'

I pulled my arm out of my father's grip and pulled out my phone. 'Karla … I need a lift. The psycho slut is pregnant and my family expect me to be happy for her.'

'Jessie!' Margaret gasped.

'Oh, get over yourself,' Sharnie slurred, 'you didn't even stick around to bury your daughter, so it obviously wasn't that great a loss.' The whole place went dead quiet.

'Shit,' Ethan whispered bringing my attention to him, 'that's why you were getting married so young. You were pregnant when it happened.' I squeezed the tears from my eyes then looked at my evil twin. Rage fuelled by decades of pain and hatred burned through my veins and without realising I'd clenched my fist I punched her full in the face. Blood spurted from her nose as she fell backwards onto the patio deck.

'That's about ten years overdue!' I roared shaking my hand out. Punching her had hurt like hell. 'Congratulations, Sharnie; you finally get your wish to be an only child. I'm done!' I stepped away not even looking at my parents as I walked out.

CHAPTER TWENTY-NINE

I WAS LEANING AGAINST ETHAN'S FRONT DOOR WHEN HE CAME HOME several hours later. He stopped and looked at me angrily. 'I just came to get my stuff, Ethan,' I admitted quietly as I stood up. 'At the very least I need my passport.'

'I've been out looking for you. Your father is worried sick.' Ethan stuck his key in the door. 'When we get inside you call him and tell him you're okay and that you still love him.'

'Better idea. When we get inside you call him and tell him I'm physically fine and I'll call him when I forgive them for tonight.'

'Any idea how long that will be?'

'Current track record is about a decade. But my father gets special dispensation. Give me a week.'

Ethan let me in, shutting the door behind us. 'Get a drink. You look like shit!' I didn't argue with him. I made my way to the wine fridge and poured a glass of red. I fished a beer out from the cold fridge for him, opening it while he dialled Lou.

'Hey, Lou, I found her … she's fine, just cut up emotionally.' Ethan watched as I opened the balcony door, stepping out to feel the cool breeze coming off the ocean. 'How's everyone there?' Ethan leant against the door frame behind me. 'I will Lou. She promised to call you within a week.' Ethan chucked the phone back in on the lounge and came to stand beside me.

'How angry is he?'

'Apparently he tried to talk your mother out of the dinner. They'd agreed to keep Sharnie's condition from you on this visit home as Lou was worried how you would react.' Ethan took a swig. 'He's only upset because now he and Margaret are fighting. Margaret wants to disown you, says she can't put up with your selfishness anymore.'

I chuckled sadly and Ethan quirked a brow in question. 'One for each, Ethan. I was daddy's little girl. Sharnie reminded Margaret of herself and so was the apple of her eye.' I waited a heartbeat. 'Tell Lou not to fight it. I don't need their money and frankly it saves me an hour of guilt tripping every week if Margaret won't talk to me. Anyway, I'm sick of Sharnie causing trouble.'

Ethan frowned. 'Lou told Margaret she could wipe you from her will and leave everything to Sharnie. He'd change his will so that on his death his estate would only go to you.'

My brows nearly hit my hairline in shock. My family's wealth was Lou's. Margaret worked, but only to give herself spending money. Lou had paid for everything else, including the house they lived in. 'God, Sharnie will have me assassinated if Lou cuts her off.' Ethan smirked but kept his thoughts to himself. We drank in quiet for a few more minutes. 'How's Greg? He's the one I truly feel sorry for in all this. I really didn't want to let this cat out of the bag on the guy. He seems decent.'

Ethan exhaled turning to put his back to the railing. 'Greg's done his fair share of bad shit. But even he drew the line at seducing your pregnant sister's fiancé three days before the wedding,' Ethan smirked. 'Sharnie is pleading it was a decade ago and she's grown up a lot since then.'

'She's carrying his kid.' I was exhausted. 'He'll let it go.'

'Yeah he will. He offered to fuck you to even the score if you like.'

'So I can sink to Sharnie's level? I don't think so.'

Ethan took my hand in his, pressing his cold bottle to my bruised knuckles. 'You have a mean hook, Jess. Sharnie's got a broken nose, busted lip, hairline fracture to the cheekbone. Sadly for her, Ben Baily was the cop who turned up at the hospital for her statement. She was going to press charges. By the time he got her blood alcohol level, found out she was pregnant and she verbally abused him, he politely pointed out that she'd basically lost her case with her history of drunken violence towards you.'

'With my medical history of her temper tantrums any court would consider her face self-defence.'

'Yeah, that's the part that worried Greg the most I think.' Ethan looked amazed. 'Did she really stab you in the shoulder just because you got your driver's licence first go and she failed?' I lifted the sleeve on the summer shrug I was wearing and showed Ethan the scar.

'Sucks for her that she did it in front of Ben too.' I let my sleeve fall and finished the wine. 'Never good to have a cop called as a witness against your character.' I stood up straight. 'I should get my stuff and get out of your hair.' I went to walk away but Ethan grabbed my arm. I swallowed hard at the look in his eyes.

'You asked me what I regret most?' Ethan nodded but didn't interrupt. 'I regret it happened, Ethan. I regret the hurt it caused our parents, that she didn't consider the fallout it would cause around her.' I closed my eyes. 'I regret Matilda.'

He put his bottle on the table along with my glass and forced me to look at him. 'The baby?'

'After I caught them together I was so upset I went into early labour. I was only twenty-one weeks; she didn't stand a chance.' The tears poured out easily. 'Afterwards I could barely bring myself to name her. There was a drunk guy singing 'Waltzing Matilda' down the corridor while I held her. It seemed apt.'

Ethan held me to him as I let it all out. 'When they said I could go home I stood there wondering where that was. I went to my place, got my passport and packed an overnight bag. I booked my flight and was gone before Ben even tried to call and apologise.'

'He didn't follow you because he felt responsible for Matilda's death?'

'I called him, after I'd called Lou. Ben was so angry at me for just leaving, for not coming to the funeral. He said some horrible things about my worth as a mother and hung up on me.' I gripped Ethan's shirt. 'After that there was no coming home.' I lifted my head to look Ethan in the eye, 'And after tonight ...'

Ethan's eyes tightened in understanding. I was never coming home again. Ethan leant down, kissing me gently. When I didn't pull away he took the kiss further. He swept my legs out from under me and carried me to his room.

This time it wasn't about passion, or sex. It was about us, the 'if only' that was us. He made love to me and he said goodbye to me without a single word being uttered.

CHAPTER THIRTY

I STOOD STARING DOWN AT ETHAN SLEEPING. IT WAS STILL DARK outside. It had taken everything in me to slip out from the warmth of his arms. I considered leaving a note for him, but I couldn't think of a thing to say. I frowned, slipping out his door much as I had that first night a week ago. Except this time instead of euphoria, I left with melancholy. I was in love with this guy, but it could never be. Not only because of distance, but because his best friend was married to the person I hated most in the world.

The taxi ride to the airport was reminiscent of the same one ten years ago. I was hurt emotionally. I was angry with my family. And I knew I would be carrying a new regret away with me. Ethan. At least this time I knew where I was going and what waited for me there — a life a damn sight better than I could ever have here. But already the happiness of the life I created was tainted with Ethan's absence.

I checked my luggage, received my boarding pass, and went for breakfast before heading to the gate. I was early, hours early, but I couldn't handle saying goodbye to Ethan. So it was down to sitting by the gate, playing online scrabble on my phone while I waited to go … home.

When the speakers announced my plane was nearly ready to board I got up to put the cup from the pint-sized raspberry slushie I'd bought for a sugar kick in the bin and ran smack bang into two pilots. 'Shit, I'm so sorry,' I apologised before looking up to see Greg and Ethan. I turned my focus to Greg and nearly burst into tears. 'Really, really sorry.'

Greg took a step forward to leave. 'Did you really unfriend your mother on Facebook last night?'

'No offence, but you're breeding with Satan. I really don't want to see the brag book of Satan's spawn that's bound to appear in a few months. Plus, you know, she disowned me. That's automatic grounds for unfriending.'

Greg chuckled. 'Guess you won't want to friend me then either?'

'Tempting as it is to send Sharnie's blood pressure through the roof with jealousy … I wouldn't wish what happened to me even on that harpie.'

Greg surprised me by hugging me. 'It's a shame you know. I think I would have really liked you as my sister.' He kissed my cheek and went to walk off. He noticed Ethan wasn't moving. 'Well, I'll be damned!' He gave Ethan a sad smile. 'I'll give you two a minute.' Greg walked away where he could watch but be out of earshot.

'You ran out on me in the middle of the night again.' Ethan took my hand in his.

'Yeah,' I blushed. 'I sort of suck at goodbyes, and since I've already set precedence for disappearing …'

'Jess, when I said I liked you …' I waited patiently. 'I lied. I more than like you.'

His smile was infectious. 'Yeah, I more than like you too, Ethan.' Ethan pulled me into a deep kiss. I moulded myself to his body; we fit perfectly. The announcement that my flight was now open for boarding brought me back to the present, but I didn't pull away.

'Hey, Ethan,' Greg called, 'Tokyo's calling, man.' Ethan smiled, stepping away. I watched him walk up to Greg and couldn't help myself.

'Ethan?' he turned back to face me. 'If you ever need to get away I know a great resort in Hawaii, and I get a discount in Bora Bora.' I held out my business card.

Ethan abandoned his carry-on with Greg and jogged back. He grabbed the card kissing me furiously this time. He was walking away before I opened my eyes. Greg gave him a playful punch on the arm. 'You are so spilling every detail on the flight over.'

I laughed, watching them till they were out of sight. At the last-minute, Ethan looked back over his shoulder, winked, and then entered the gate he'd be taking off from. I took a deep breath, grabbed my stuff and boarded my flight.

'Ms Buttler?' the attendant greeted me as I boarded. She smiled and said, 'There's been a mistake with your booking it seems. I've been informed that you've been upgraded to first class.' I followed the attendant in shock as she led me to my reassigned seat. When I sat she leant down and whispered in my ear.

'Captain Knight said we're to take extra good care of you and to tell you he'll call you soon.'

CHAPTER THIRTY-ONE

Arriving home was a combination of happiness and sadness. Neither one was better than the other. "Jess!" Mayla cheered when she answered her phone. "Are you home already?"

"Just got through customs in Honolulu. How is my hotel?"

"Your hotel? I'll tell the boss that when he calls next. Speaking of which, I think he's replaced you."

"What?" My heart pounded in my chest, eyes itching. This was too much. Not only would losing my job be devastating this week, but my boss was one of my best friends, so that would mean I lost that friendship too. "I was gone for a week!"

Mayla was laughing. "I meant romantically, Jess. He was just here the other day with a girlfriend. He was holidaying with her."

"Jesus, Mayla! You gave me a heart attack." My breathing instantly calmed. "I'm happy that he's seeing someone. He's been alone for a long time."

"So have you," Mayla sighed. "Hence, why we've all been shipping the two of you for over five years now."

It made me laugh. Some of the sly comments by my employees hadn't gone unnoticed by Sean either, but we were just friends. What none of them knew was that Sean asked me out years beforehand, when I was still working for his competitor. Arriving at the venue, I was anxious about a relationship developing between us. Notably, it was the first date I'd agreed to since Ben broke my heart. However, halfway through the meal, we realised both Sean and me carried too much baggage, and eight years ago, when the date took place, we were both too raw emotionally to want more.

The dinner we'd shared ended up a discussion about our ideas of a good hotel. The date also coincided with a phone call that one of Sean's managers had resigned, and so our meal together turned into an interview. I'd never kissed him, and definitely never got between the sheets with him. However, the date did kick-start my new dating program. Sean got me back on the horse, figuratively.

The reminder that even two weeks ago, I still wasn't interested in a relationship, made me think of Ethan. My heart sank into my stomach, and I felt my eyes water. "Well, my flight to Maui is still six hours away. I'm going to do some shopping before I fly home. Want anything?" Retail therapy would be good for me.

"Ooh, Yes! But, Trinity and I are flying to the mainland for a shopping spree next week, once you are back running things." A phone started ringing in the background. "Huh, speak of the devil. I've got to go. The boss is calling."

"Say Aloha for me."

"I'll tell him you're heartbroken he's moved on," Mayla teased. I bit my lip on admitting she was right about part of that. She just had the wrong guy. The phone disconnected. With a sigh, I turned toward the short stay area of the airport. They had a place you could leave your luggage for the island flight so you could enjoy some shopping or sightseeing on Oahu first.

My phone was ringing before I reached the desk. Looking at the caller ID, I smiled. "Sean." A smile lifted my lips. He was a good boss, and my best friend, so hearing he might have found someone made me happy for him. The irony that we both had our hearts broken the same year, both ran away to Hawaii to get over it, and now, both met someone new, hadn't escaped my attention.

"Jess, I hear you are on Oahu?" There was a panic in the question.

"Is everything okay?" My feet halted, the man behind me cursing when he had to move around me suddenly. Waiting for him to pass, I moved to the side.

"I need you to come to Turtle Bay and run the Cassidy here for me."

"What's happened? Is your dad okay?

"It's not him. I need to fly to Australia. I'm not sure how long I'll be gone, but I need you to run the Cassidy while I'm gone. Can you grab a car at the airport and head here now? I'll pay the cost."

Looking around, I spotted the closest exit and started moving. "I don't have any of my work gear with me."

"Mayla will send whatever you need over, and I'll have a uniform ready for your arrival."

Through the doors, the noise of the open air arrival area greeted me. The best thing about Hawaii, you got the smell of home right out of the gate. Well, mixed with the fumes of jet fuel, but it still let you know you were home. Taxis, busses, and the organisers of private charters were milling around. Waving to the woman who operated the Cassidy preferred charter, I moved towards her. "I'll be there as soon as I can get there."

"Thanks, Jess. I'll have everything organised by the time you arrive." Sean hung up. I'd never heard him sound frantic before.

"Are you heading to Waikiki?" The woman asked, recognising me.

"North Shore. I'm heading to Cassidy resort."

———

"Jess," Henry greeted with a hug. "You're our fill in Manager?"

"Apparently. Where is Sean?"

"His place, finalising his travel arrangements. He said you could stay there till he gets back." Henry turned to the bellhop. "Have Miss Butler's bag taken to Mr Cassidy's cottage, please, Hori."

"Yes, Henry." Hori wheeled my bag off towards the cottages.

"You got here fast," Henry inquired.

"I was already here. I was on my way back from Australia."

"Good timing. Was it a good holiday?" Henry started walking with me towards the cottages.

"My sister's wedding. I feel like I need a holiday to get over the experience."

"Weddings are like that." He stopped walking. Looking around, I realised we were out of sight, in a rather secluded part of the path. "Sean's in a frizzle. He met a woman, and they hit it off to the point that he proposed."

"He did? Oh my god! That's great!" I was so happy for Sean if he met someone he connected with that strongly. Ethan popped into my head, but I dismissed the subconscious reminder, focusing on Sean's happiness.

"It was. Then Senator Cassidy used the engagement as a political move. Holly's the youngest daughter of the Australian prime minister."

"Holly Claire? Sean got engaged to Holly Claire?"

"You know her?"

"We've met a few times at Hotel Manager conferences over the years. The two female Australians in the room tend to find each other pretty quickly."

"Okay, well, yes. Sean got engaged to Holly Claire, but when the senator announced it live on television, things blew up back home. She called off the engagement and flew home. Sean's going after her."

It broke my heart and made me happy all at once. "Good. If Holly's the one, he should chase her to the end of the earth and back."

"Well, he's chasing her to Australia at the very least. Just be warned, he's not his usual calm self."

"Consider me warned. I can find the way myself if that's the only reason you tagged along?"

Smirking, Henry's eyes flitted over me appreciatively. Having just got off a ten-hour flight and spent two hours in the back of a car; he must be hard up to think I looked appealing. "I'll see you at work." He turned and headed back to the hotel.

Following the path to the last cottage, I knocked on the door. Opening it, Hori let me in as he stepped out. "Sean?" I called. The place wasn't large, but I wasn't walking into his bedroom uninvited either.

"Bedroom." Moving to his bedroom door, I observed the suitcase he was packing, his passport sitting beside it along with printed plane tickets. "Know any good hotels in Sydney?"

"I'll give you my membership cards. I still get a discount at the Hilton from having worked there, and the place I stay when I go home has hotels all over the South Pacific. When do you fly out?"

"First thing tomorrow morning. The car will pick me up at five. Should be able to catch you up and orientate you this afternoon." Sean turned to appraise me. "How was the trip home?"

"Shit, as expected. My last night was a massive fight with the family which resulted in my effective disowning."

Sean grimaced. "What was the fight about?"

"My sister's pregnant." Sean knew the history. We'd talked about what brought us here over beer and burgers whenever he came to Maui for the quarterly report. He was my boss, but we were friends too. The fact we both ended up in Hawaii off the back of broken engagements bonded us.

"So much for karma." The look he sent my way was one of sympathy for the pain he imagined I was feeling. Frankly, I was still a little in shock by the entire event to be feeling anything but confused.

"Since the worst thing Sharnie could do is have a kid, it might be karmic. She hates anyone who takes the attention away from her. Kids instantly become the centre of your world."

"She'll end up being one of those dance mums." Sean's nose wrinkled in disgust.

"And I hear you met someone? An Aussie girl, no less."

"Something about you Aussies, I can't deny it. I think you'd like her."

"I've met Holly a couple of times. I do like her."

Sean's mouth popped open. "You know Holly?" I nodded. Sean took a step forward. "Do you know where to find her, where she lives, or where she works?"

"Ah, no. We hung out at a couple of conferences; we didn't become pen pals." Sean's face fell, and he cursed under his breath. "Wait? You don't know where she works or lives?"

"Never really came up in conversation other than she lives in Sydney."

"Sydney is huge. In area and population, it far surpasses this island. Your chances of finding her are pretty slim."

"You don't have any contacts you could reach out to for me?" Sean wondered.

"I did my training in Newcastle where I grew up. That's three hours north of Sydney. The likelihood anyone I knew, none of whom I kept in contact with when I left, that would know of, let alone where to find Holly, would be none and Buckley's."

"None and Buckley's?" Sean raised an eyebrow. He did the sexiest eyebrow raise I'd ever seen.

"It's slang for having no chance. Buckley was a convict who escaped into the bush. Back in those days, they expected him to perish."

"Great!" Sean sighed, dropping onto his bed in defeat.

"However, Buckley lived another thirty years with the indigenous Australians, so there is still a chance there."

The side of Sean's mouth turned up. "I've set up the other bedroom for you. There is a uniform on the bed; you may want to check it fits before tomorrow. Is there anything else you'll need?"

"I'll make do for a couple of weeks," I assured. "I'll go get my stuff unpacked while you finish up, and then you better take me through the roster and anything else I need to know."

"Jess, thanks for coming when I called."

"It's what friends do, Sean. Especially when your friend is your boss," I teased. "Mayla will love the extra time as the manager on her CV, so take however long you need." Sean gave me a forced smile. Unable to miss the heartbreak in his eyes, I flinched wondering if my eyes looked like that.

Making my way to the only other bedroom in the cottage, I unpacked my suitcase. Then I picked up the phone and called Mayla. She may get to stay Manager for another couple of weeks, but I needed a few things from home to see me through. The first was my work shoes.

By the time Sean had taken me through the ropes of running the Cassidy, I'd hit the wall. After our usual beer and burger dinner catch up, I went for a walk down the beach and pulled out my phone. Australia was four hours behind Hawaii time wise, but a day in front, or twenty hours ahead, whichever was easier to work out.

"Hello?"

"Dad," I sighed. Not unlike ten years ago, I wasn't sure what to say. "I just wanted to let you know I'm home safe."

"If you were home, you'd be here."

"That hasn't been home for me for a long time. I know now, it never will be again." Saying those words to my dad hurt, but it didn't stop them being true. One of the hardest things I'd learned about life, is sometimes the truest words were the hardest to say. When Lou stayed quiet, I exhaled. "Look, my boss has to travel, so I'm going to be filling in as manager at another resort for him. I don't know how long I'll be here, but I don't have my computer, so Skyping won't be possible until I get back to Maui."

"I see." The phone was static. Unsure what else there was to say, I didn't think Lou knew either. "Jessie girl, don't think I don't love you because of all this. I have never stopped loving you, neither has your mother. I will make sure my Skype is available every Sunday at the usual time. When you are ready and able to call us, we'll answer."

Swiping at the tears cascading down my face, I choked back a sob. "I miss you, dad."

"Me too, Jessie. I know you tried. That's all I ever asked of you." He exhaled loudly. "Call me when you can. I don't want to lose you over this mess. You're still my baby girl."

"I love you, dad." Hanging up, I sat there staring out at the water until my tears dried up, then I made my way back inside. Sean sat at the meals table looking over paperwork. His eyes looked me over as I came in, then they flicked to a piece of hotel stationery in his hands. "What's that?"

"A list of ideas to improve things around my various hotels. Holly left it instead of a goodbye letter."

"Can I have a look?"

"Sure." Sean handed the list to me. Each hotel they visited on their trips had a few suggestions for them. I read the one for Cassidy resort in Maui first. The critiques were spot on what I'd been thinking about for years. "Think you can look into some of those for me while I'm gone?"

My eyes lifted to Sean's ocean blues. "Of course, I wouldn't mind actioning some of these at the Maui resort either."

"Do what you can. I trust you to do a good job, Jess. You've never let me down yet."

The laugh was automatic. "That you know of, anyway." Turning to the rooms, I smiled over my shoulder. "I'll try not to fuck things up on you."

"Jess?" Sean called, his voice serious. Pausing at the bedroom door, I met his concerned eyes. "We've talked about why I'm falling apart today. Do you want to discuss what's happened to you?"

"I told you…"

"Your sister isn't what makes you look like someone died, Jess. What happened to your family is only part of that turmoil inside you. I'll listen."

Rubbing my lips together, I looked at Sean's surfboard in the corner of the room, reminding me of waking in Ethan's bed. When I switched my gaze to Sean, that damn eyebrow was hovering close to his hairline. "Maybe when you get back. I'm still confused by things. Goodnight. Travel safe."

"Thanks, Jess."

———

The moon was peaking just above the horizon. Tea lights and torches created a romantic ambience in the bar overlooking the beach. Tilting the bottle up, I groaned when I found it empty.

Grabbing another from the multitude on the table, Sean handed it to me. "Thanks." I took a mouthful then met Sean's eyes. He looked like shit. Two weeks he spent searching Sydney, going from hotel to hotel trying to find the woman who stole his heart, hounded by the media the entire time, and he'd dragged himself home looking exactly how I was sure he felt. "What's your next move?"

Polishing off his second beer, Sean placed it on the table and selected a chip from the bowl between us. "Her older sister is getting married in six months. I'll crash the wedding, see if she'll give me the time of day."

"Six months is a long time to wait," I grimaced.

"I'm open to suggestions," Sean replied disheartened. Having nothing to offer, I smartly took another drink of beer. "I tried everything, Jess. I even appealed to the media, but they didn't air it. I'm out of options. If I find her and she's moved on, then I'll know I didn't mean that much to her."

"From everything I've heard, I find that hard to believe."

"The staff are talking?"

"The staff are always talking," I reminded. "If you're back, I'll head home to Maui tomorrow."

Sean nodded. Slowly, he sat forward. "Do you like it here?"

"Are you kidding? I love Turtle Bay; you know that."

"I've got the new resort opening in Ko Olina. I was going to split my time between here and there, but I think I should focus my attention there until it's ready. How would you feel about staying on here for another three months or so?"

Tilting my head, I considered Sean. "Still running away to deal with the heartbreak?"

"We all have our coping mechanisms. The Cassidy is a higher rated resort than anything you've run before, Jess. It's a good opportunity."

"It's only an opportunity if it's a solid six months or more." I was already going to say yes. While I liked the Maui resort, being close to shopping would be good therapy for a few months.

Sean smirked. "That business head of yours is the reason we work so well together. Take on the Cassidy. When the Ko Olina is ready, the manager role is yours if you want it."

"I'll think about it," I appeased.

"Don't take too long. I'll head to the west coast in a week. I'll need you back by Friday. Should give you enough time to pack up your stuff and hand over control to Mayla."

"Do I get your cottage while I'm here?" I negotiated.

Sean laughed. He started nodding his head and took another long drink. "Sure, but you'll have to share once a month when I come back for the report."

Lifting my shoulder in a shrug, I finished my third beer. "Well, it's been a long day. If you didn't look like something the cat dragged in, I would swear you planned your escape to coincide with spring break."

Sean smirked. "Sadly, no." He waved to the bar staff and signalled another round. "Stay a while. I'm dead tired, but not ready to sleep yet."

Checking my watch for the time, I stifled a yawn and agreed. It's was Friday night, I didn't need to be up early tomorrow. Sitting forward, I looked Sean over properly. Bags under his ocean eyes, dimming their natural brightness. He looked haunted. I knew that look too well. "Are you okay?"

"Are you?" Sean sat forward too. "I need out of my melodrama for ten minutes, so let's talk about the guy you left behind this time. Was it the ex?"

Exhaling, I shook my head. "No. I saw Ben. He's married, got a little boy now."

"So, who was your Holly?"

"Why do you think it was anything like what you've been through?" I tried distracting him. Sean knew better; he used to be a lawyer for Christ's sake.

"Because I'm looking in a mirror. Spill the beans, Jess. I need the distraction."

More beers arrived. I grabbed one, tossing the crisp hops back. With a loud, lip-smacking 'ah'. I set the beer down. "He started as a one night stand."

"That's not normally your scene. You don't mess with absolute strangers," Sean's brow furrowed.

"I know, but the chemistry was undeniable," I justified. Sean lifted that damn brow at me. "We met at a bar, couldn't stop looking at each other, so we took it back to his place. I left before he woke, only to run into him at the wedding. He was the grooms best friend, work colleague, and best man."

"So, one night turned into…?" Sean prompted.

"Nearly the entire time I was home," I admitted. "To make it worse, he's tight with my dad. Almost the son my dad never had, so my parents were all about trying to set us up."

"Ooh, that's awkward," Sean cringed.

"They weren't subtle."

Sean appraised me for a moment. "Does he feel the same?" I raised a brow at him, trying to mimic his unasked question method. "Did he fall in love with you too, Jess?"

The rim of my beer bottle suddenly became very interesting. "It was great sex, then we decided, given his link with my family, we should be friends. It fucked everything up."

"Because becoming friends meant when you climbed out of his bed, he was more than a body with a head on it."

My jaw dropped open. "Is that what you think of me? I've never been that callus."

"No, but you like men who come with expiry dates. You're used to that, so this guy should have been perfect for you. Why did this one impact?"

My finger traced the rim of the bottle. "I don't know. We couldn't walk away from the moment we laid eyes on each other."

"How did you leave it?" Sean prodded carefully.

"I gave him my card and told him to call me if he wanted a holiday," I scoffed. "He wasn't a saint before we met, so I doubt I'll hear from him."

Sean considered me. "If you don't, then he wasn't the right one."

"I think he was, but it wasn't the right time," I mourned. "Maybe we needed to meet twelve years ago, while Ben was away at the academy. Maybe we needed to meet somewhere else. Who knows?" Taking another swig of beer, I gazed out at the moon. "Do you think it's ironic that we both go through the same shit at the same time in our lives? Our breakups, coming here, and now meeting someone worthwhile, but not being able to keep them."

"Maybe we walk the same path in life, Jess. Maybe, ten years is the fate designated recovery time, before she breaks our hearts again," Sean glanced at the rising moon. "I'm going to find her, Jess, and I'm going to marry her. Maybe, your best man is sitting out there thinking the same thing."

It made me smile. "The best man was pretty adamant he wasn't looking for a second wife. I'm not looking for something permanent either."

"Then what are you sad about losing, Jess? What did you want?" Sean prompted.

Considering Sean's question, I thought long and hard about the answer. He didn't interrupt me, let me puzzle through my emotions to try and find the right answer. I knew I wasn't ready for something long term, so what did I want from Ethan that left me feeling like shit that I'd never see him again. What was it I wanted, if not something short term or long term? The answer came to me as I finished the last drop of beer in the bottle. With a sigh, I met Sean's waiting eyes. "I want more. No expiry date, no commitment, just more of him in my life."

The silence fell between us. Sean lifted his beer into the air. "Well, here's to both of us, getting more." We clinked drinks, and both started laughing. "That sounded wrong didn't it?"

"Like frat brother's making a pact to get their nibs wet every weekend," I snickered.

Sean laughed harder. Finishing his beer, he stood. "Come on. Let me take you back to my place and get you into bed."

"Say it louder; I don't think the doorman heard you," I stood chuckling.

Sean put his arm around me, gripping my upper arm so he could hug me as we walked. "Maybe we were meant to be each other's recovery, Jess. Did you ever think about that?"

"We were. As friends, we still are."

"As friends, we are," Sean agreed. "We found the right people; it just wasn't the right time."

"So, we give it more time," I rationalised. "What's the worst that could happen?"

"Too true, Jess. Movie and popcorn?"

"Bed!"

A bit over a week later, I was sitting at the table in Sean's cottage Skyping with Lou when Sean walked in from work. "I'm home, and I brought dinner."

"Who's that?" Lou frowned.

"My boss," I laughed at his suspicion. "I'm house sitting for him while he's away."

"He doesn't sound away to me."

The fatherly reaction made me chuckle. I missed my dad the most. "He's leaving tomorrow. I'll be managing the hotel here until the new resort is ready, and then I'll be taking over there."

Sean stuck his head over my shoulder. "Who are you talking to."

"My dad," I chuckled when Lou's eyes widened in recognition. "Dad, this is Sean Cassidy, my boss and friend."

"He was all over the news recently, some scandal with the prime minister's youngest daughter."

Sean's smile disappeared. "Nice to meet you, Mr Butler. I'll go serve up dinner and let you finish." Watching the melancholy slip over Sean was heartbreaking.

"Okay, well, I'm going to sign off now, dad." Our conversations went so much quicker now that mum refused to acknowledge me. Well, not directly, anyway.

"Did you tell her?" Mum called from off camera. Dad lifted his eyes to the ceiling, then tilted his head as he looked back at the screen. The look an offer of pre-emptive apology. "Tell her Ben's having another baby. His wife just announced she's pregnant again. They think it's a girl this time."

Sean stopped everything at the kitchen bench. When I glanced his way, he mouthed 'are you okay?' The truth was, I was happy for Ben. Seeing him when I was home gave me at least that closure.

Lou exhaled dramatically. "I'm sure if Jess and Ben wanted to keep tabs on each other, they would have exchanged numbers when they saw each other."

There was a moment's pause. "When did they see each other? You didn't tell me they spoke."

"No, I didn't. Just like Jess didn't tell me," Lou sighed. "I only know because I ran into Ben at the golf club the other day, and while his wife was telling you about the baby, he mentioned how good it was to see Jess, and to know she was happy and had finally moved on with her life."

There was a glint in my father's eyes. The memory of the run-in with Ben on the bluff and the relationship Ethan fabricated suddenly played through my head. I covered my face and swore quietly. "Jessica Butler!" Margaret scolded. "Why would he think she moved on with her life? She's still single. My god, Lou, Jessie couldn't even behave herself on a date with Ethan. He's not exactly picky," Margaret scoffed.

"You obviously missed how Ethan was all over our daughter her last night here, Dear. For sure, if you weren't so busy trying to force oil and water to merge, you might have recognised that your insistence of forcing our girls to reconcile ruined whatever had been brewing between them."

"This again?" Margaret screeched. Lou peered over the top of his laptop, no doubt at my mother. A moment later, the sound of his office door slammed shut.

Lou let out a sigh and dropped his eyes back to the monitor. "It's a shame you live so far away; I think you and Ethan could have made it work if you stayed."

"Going now," I chimed. "Love you, dad."

"You too, Jessie girl. Thank you for not holding it against me." Blinking back tears, I disconnected the call while blowing a kiss at the camera.

"Jessie girl?"

My eyes darted to Sean smirking in the kitchen, a long sigh escaping my lungs. "Don't start."

"No, I like it. I think I'm going to call you that going forward."

"You have a death wish," I threatened, glaring as he walked toward me with two plates of food.

"I have a broken heart, and calling you a cute nickname makes me forget the woman I love ran off and left me." Sean batted his long lashes my way. He placed my plate on the table and took the seat on the other side.

"No, you're trying to distract me from the bomb my mum dropped on me, but you don't have to. I'm happy for Ben, and I'm glad he moved on."

"Oh, Jessie girl," Sean smirked when I grimaced. "You are so wrong! I'm very aware you are over your teenage love. You don't need any protection from that. Though, it looks like your mum missed the memo."

"She misses a lot." Taking the plate of Chinese food Sean pushed towards me, we started eating.

"So his name was Ethan?"

"Yes." Needing a change of subject, I turned the focus back to something that distracted us both. "What time are you heading off in the morning?"

"Way too early for you to see me off, Jessie girl."

"Drop it."

"Nope. Are you going to be okay here by yourself?" Sean assessed me.

Tilting my head, wondering why on earth he was suddenly concerned for my welfare. "Why shouldn't I be?"

"Because I have noticed how Henry has been looking at you all weekend." Sean stabbed at some noodles with his chopsticks. "You still have that rule about dating colleagues?"

"I still have that rule about dating anyone permanently located on this island."

"So, I don't need to worry?"

"About me sleeping with Henry? God, no! Nice guy, but he's so not my type, even before his being a subordinate, he's still a local. You know I like them with a visa expiry."

Sean smirked. "Good to know, Jessie girl." Picking up a fortune cookie, I threw it at his head, catching him right on the forehead. "Ow!" Sean pouted. It was so cute, if he weren't one of my best friends, I would have kissed him.

We just finished our meals when Sean's phone rang, his dad's picture flashing on the screen. "Take it. I'll clean up," I assured.

"Thanks, Jessie girl," he grinned as he walked to the door. Another fortune cookie clocked him on the back of the head as he stepped out onto the balcony. "Ouch!"

After cleaning up, I sat down at my computer to catch up on some emails to friends. My skype ringing made me jump out of my skin. My eyes went to the alert and widened. The name Ethan Knight, with a picture of a knight's armour, was on my screen, right above the green accept, and red decline buttons. My heart was in my throat as I moved my mouse to hit accept.

A video screen jumped open, Ethan, in his flight uniform, inside of a cockpit. "Jess," he almost sighed my name.

"Ethan."

"I've been trying to reach you at the number you gave me."

Damn it! "I've been filling in for my boss on Oahu. Sorry, no one told me you were calling.

"Lou told me."

"How did you get my Skype?"

"Okay, I've sorted that shit. Let's get out of Australian airspace before my wife invents another drama," Greg's voice came from somewhere in the background, followed by the sounds of another person joining him in the confined space.

Ethan looked at his side and adjusted his seating so his co-pilot couldn't see his screen. "Your dad gave it to me. He just messaged to tell me you were online now. I'm getting ready to take off. Can I call you when I get home in two days?"

A butterfly fluttered in my chest, my smile refusing my usual restraint. "I'd like that."

BEST LAYOVER

Best Layover

Hotel Series

EBONY OLSON

BEST LAYOVER

BOOK 5: HOTEL SERIES

EBONY 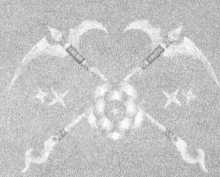 OLSON

EBANDMUSE
PUBLICATIONS

CHAPTER ONE

THUNDER POUNDED OVERHEAD, PUSHING DOWN, BUFFETING MY SIDE as I swam to the rocky outcrop on the far side of the waterfall. Gasping for breath as I broke the surface, I grabbed hold of the rocks and climbed out. Flopping onto the sun-warmed grass, I closed my eyes and swayed my knees from side to side to ease my back. Managing a hotel seemed like a cushy job, but one customer with a bout of stomach flu happy to share could ruin all your careful planning. For two weeks straight, I'd been covering the staffing shortage and doing my work while the virus worked its way through the employees.

Thankfully, most of the staff recovered and were back on deck when my immune system threw up its hands, and I spent two days befriending the porcelain throne. Unfortunately, today was Sunday, so I only scored a day of recovery before my work week started again. Closing my eyes, I let the sun lull me into an exhausted sleep.

Cool drops splashed on my face and chest. Eyes opening, I found a tall shadow standing above me, shaking out his blond hair. "Wake up, sleepyhead, or you'll burn."

Groaning, I closed my eyelids against the midday-ocean blue of my best friend's eyes. "How did you find me?"

Laughing, Sean Cassidy dropped to sit next to me. "It was here or the beach. A call to the stables let me know you'd taken my horse, so that answered my question."

Turning my head, I spotted the second horse grazing next to Sean's horse. "I'm riding the stallion back."

Lifting a brow, Sean smirked. "Thanks for the offer, but I don't sleep with my staff."

"Gross! Any chance of me riding you evaporated eight years ago." The small chuckle Sean gave me made me smile. "What are you doing here? I told you to stay away."

"Henry called and told me you all but passed out Friday trying to push through and that no one had seen you all day yesterday. You don't have anyone to take care of you, so I thought I better step up."

"You don't want to catch this, Sean. It's like having your guts wrenched out through your mouth."

"Charming, but since you were the last to get sick, I think I should be safe. How are you feeling?"

"Wrung out, but better. You?"

"I've avoided all plagues this winter. Summer is just around the corner."

"It's still a few weeks away." Making it over two months since I'd gone home for Sharnie's wedding. "I meant, how are you coping post-Holly?"

Yanking at the grass until it ripped in his fist, Sean looked out over the swimming hole. This waterfall and its lagoon were a well-kept secret by the locals and one of Sean's favorite places. "You know how it is. Have you heard anything more from the pilot?"

"We've sent messages and talked when our times have synced. It's hard with the time difference and work, especially since his job makes him incommunicado for half a day or more at a time."

"Trust you to fall for a guy who is always leaving and spending time away from home."

"He has a reputation when it comes to women, Sean. Yes, we like each other more than either of us intended, but there is a lot of ocean between us, and he knows I will not move there. Pining over him would be pointless."

"He called you, he wants more of you, Jessie girl. Trust me."

"I'm going to kill you if you keep calling me that." Ever since Sean heard my father, Lou, use that term of endearment for me, Sean had adopted it. It made me feel ten years old, and only my father was allowed to make me feel that way.

Sean's masculine laugh echoed off the rocks. Laying back on the grass, he relaxed in the sun. "Why don't you invite the pilot to come and visit for a holiday? It's getting cold in Australia, so summertime in Hawaii would be appealing. Add you, and the guy is the luckiest man on Earth."

"Considering I'm working, that makes for a pretty boring holiday for him."

"I was working, but I still managed to woo and fall for a woman. And seriously, as if I won't come run my hotel if you need a week off. I probably owe you eight years' worth of holidays anyway."

"Only six."

Snapping his head in my direction, Sean opened his eyes wide. "Are you serious?"

"A little over. I have just under twenty-six weeks of leave accrued."

Staring at the sky for a moment, Sean cursed. "You've seriously only taken six weeks of leave in all the eight years you've worked for me?"

"The week home for the wedding was my first holiday in eighteen months."

Rolling to his side, Sean propped himself up on his elbow. "Wait, that would mean it was eighteen months between guys."

"What?"

"The last time you took a holiday was when you spent two weeks boning a certain celebrity brainless in my reef resort in Bora Bora."

Frowning, I covered my eyes and glanced at Sean. "Really?"

"Mayla and the others couldn't stop waxing poetic about how smitten that poor guy was for you for months. The rumors had it that he asked you to go back to England with him and marry him."

Bursting out laughing, I groaned when all my abdominal muscles protested, reminding me I wasn't well. "Those girls are too romantic for their own good. He never proposed."

"Did he ask you to move to England?"

"Not move there. He asked if I'd want to come and visit him, maybe fly back with him, but he was only going home for a few weeks and then was heading to his next filming location, so that would have only been a few weeks."

Smirking, Sean shook his head. "You should have gone."

"God, no. Remember what the media were like when you chased after Holly?" Rising on my elbows, I looked through my brows at Sean. When his smile dropped, I nodded. "She was the unknown Prime Minister's daughter. English tabloids are so much worse. That actor started dating a woman last year, and the tabloids stalked her and interviewed her friends and everything to get any gossip on her. Hell, her ex came out and dished the juice of their relationship and sex life. There is a reason I took our fun to your private island resort."

"You were worried your ex would tell the press you rocked his world?" Sean cocked a brow.

Huffing, I rolled my eyes at him. "I have a sister who would kill to be famous and is trying desperately to break out of her modeling career into acting. If the media linked me to a celebrity and the journalists came looking for a story, she wouldn't hold back, and she wouldn't paint me in a nice picture."

"Oh, yeah, I see what you mean." Falling back, Sean stared up at the sky again. After a minute, Sean started humming.

"Don't—" He always hummed when he was about to start waxing philosophical at me.

"If you want your life to change, you need to take the risk to bring what you want into your space." Sean let the silence fall for a second. "Invite the pilot to come and see you, Jess. You've been miserable since you came back. Everyone has commented on how you never smile as you used to."

"Henry?"

"Some of the staff think you're heartbroken about me proposing to another woman."

"Did everyone think we were fucking? Mayla said something similar when I called her."

Sean shrugged. "Not a lot of people can accept a close friendship between a male and female without it involving sex."

"Yeah, but you dated other women, and I wasn't exactly secretive when I was seeing guys..."

"You were in Maui; I was here. Whenever we are on the same island, we always hang out. They just assumed..." Lifting his shoulder, Sean let the subject drop.

Sitting up, I glared at Sean. "Wait, did you know they thought that?"

Smirking, Sean jumped his brows at me.

Shoving him, I gaped. "Seriously? You were playing up to the gossip, weren't you?"

Adjusting to a seated position, Sean held up his hands. "I didn't confirm or even suggest anything, but I did notice that once you were on the scene, the amount of staff flirting with me dropped right off, so I didn't exactly put an end to the rumors when they reached me either. You didn't want anything serious, and it made the workplace less of a sexual harassment minefield for me. People knew we'd been on a date, and then you were working for me—and yeah, you ended up in Maui, but—"

"I did my two weeks of training here, under your direct supervision."

"A-huh."

"And you let me live in your place in Maui for the last eight years."

"I did."

Blinking at Sean, I opened my mouth and closed it, then licked my lips and stared at the water. "I've been your mistress for eight years. Holy shit! I thought it was them hoping we'd get together, but they thought we already were." Covering my face, I groaned.

Sean rubbed my upper back. "If it makes you feel better, you are an amazing mistress."

"We don't fuck."

"Yeah, but what we do is better than sex because we are there for each other. Plus, we were never compatible. We are—" Sean chuckled, "—too much alike."

"Too the same person," I said at the same time.

Stopping, we looked at each other and started laughing. "It's like you're my twin sister separated at birth. Except, you know, hot, and not my sister, so it's okay for you to tell me about your wild sexathons with your fun flings."

"I don't tell you about my sex life, just when there is a fling. Though the staff gossip usually tells you in advance."

"You could tell me about the wild sex, you know. I wouldn't mind."

"Pervert."

"Like you've never asked for details about my sex life."

"Only when I am going through a dry spell, and you never share anyway." Thinking about it, I laughed. "Oh, except for that model you dated who wanted to put her finger in your—"

"Oh, God, you are never going to let me forget that."

"Hey, I can't believe you passed up the broadening learning experience. You could have told me why guys wanted me to do that."

"Still haven't done it?"

"Nope. You give Holly a taste of your slap and tickle?" Going bright red, Sean looked away, making me laugh. "Did she like it?"

"I proposed, didn't I?" Sean's smile slipped, his eyes glassing over. "The pilot into any kinky stuff?"

"No, thank God. Okay, maybe outdoor sex, but it wasn't like out in the open. It was romantic," I sighed, then felt tired all of a sudden. "I don't even know how it happened. He was great sex one minute, and more a moment later."

"I fell for Holly the moment I laid eyes on her."

The mood dropped, the silence filling the lagoon. Standing up, Sean offered me his hand. "Come on, you need to go home and rest, and you need something to eat."

Taking the hand up, I shook my head. "Oh, no, I can't do food yet. Or maybe never again." Placing my hand over my stomach, I groaned.

"You have worked double shifts for two weeks, and then you were very ill. I don't need a doctor to see it; I can look at you and know it. So, I'm here for the week. You'll take three days off as time in lieu, and then Thursday and Friday, we'll do some planning for the Ko

Olina resort. We need to start looking at staffing, and we'll need to find you a place to live on this island."

"I guess we will, but what's the rush? We are still a few months from opening, aren't we?"

"Not anymore. Probably only a month until we can start getting staff in to train up."

"Oh. You know I still have most of my stuff in Maui. I should probably head back there soon for a few days and pack it all up, so you can rent your apartment out to tourists again."

"Well, that doesn't concern me as much as your pilot showing up and me having to hear you two through the wall. Plus, the morning traffic from the North Shore can be a bitch."

"Oh, that I've planned for." Smiling sweetly, I dove into the water and swam back to where the horses waited.

Climbing out, I pulled my swim dress on before Sean climbed out of the lagoon, and then threw myself up into the saddle of his horse.

"Are you sure you have the strength for that bad boy?" Sean worried.

Smiling, I patted the neck of the beautiful animal. "He likes me. We've become close while you've been away."

Peering at his horse, Sean lifted his eyebrow. "Is that true?" When the horse turned, pushing Sean away, I laughed. Sean huffed. "He's also a sucker for the beautiful Aussie girls."

Directing the stallions head for home, I started the climb back up the mountain trail. Once we reached the flat back to the resort, we picked up to a canter.

When we got back to the stable, Sean was smiling. "What?"

"I'd forgotten how good you looked in the saddle. It's been a while since we've gone for a ride together."

"When you came out to Maui for my birthday last year."

"Are you still going for long rides on your days off?"

"Most weekends. Even here, I've been doing rides into the national park." Climbing down, I walked the stallion into the stables and started removing his saddle and bridle. By the time I'd done that, the staff who maintained the horses had come to finish it off. Grabbing an apple out of my bag, I offered it to the beautiful beast.

"Oh, now I see how you won him over," Sean teased.

Giving him a smirk, I kissed the horse on his head and followed Sean back to his place. We were maybe a few meters from the door to the bungalow when I felt it. "Oh."

"Oh, what?"

Turning around with a smile, Sean met my eyes, and his smile disappeared. His eyes dropped to where my hands gripped my stomach, and I'm sure I looked as green as I felt. "Jess?"

Turning ninety degrees to the left, I started dry heaving over the garden. Not that there was anything to vomit, but I retched like a cat with the worst kind of furball.

CHAPTER TWO

"Dad."

"Jessie girl, you look like hell," Lou frowned on my screen.

Sinking further down under my covers, I sighed. "The bug that was going around finally caught up with me. How are you?"

"I've got a touch of a cold but looking better than you. Your mother made me her chicken, ginger, lime, and chili soup, so I'll be right as rain in no time. Who is taking care of you?"

"Sean has come back to cover my shifts for a few days. He's forced me into bed and just ducked out to get some dry bread rolls to see if I can keep those down. Ginger is good for nausea, isn't it?"

"I believe so; not sure how you'd keep it down, though."

Thinking about it, I grabbed my phone and sent Sean a text. "Maybe Ginger tea?"

"Possibly. Get some Hydrolyte if it lasts more than a day."

Sending Sean another text, I decided not to tell my dad this was day three. "I could handle throwing something up, but when there is nothing left and you're just retching and gagging, it's the worst."

"You've never been a good vomiter."

"There's such a thing as a good vomiter?"

Shrugging, Lou sighed, his eyes flicking to the side. In the background, I could hear Margaret chirping about something. "I can't stay long tonight, Jessie girl, we have company for dinner."

Recognizing the other female voice in the background, I rolled my eyes. "How are your adopted sons?"

Smirking, Lou relaxed. "Not here, sadly. They flew out Friday and won't be back until Thursday, I believe."

"That's a long trip."

"They often do that. They fly to somewhere in Asia for the first leg, then the next day, they do the European leg, have a few days off, and do the same coming back."

Staring at the ceiling dreamily, I sighed. "I should have done air hosting. Think of all the countries I could have seen."

"Very long and hard hours, Jessie."

"Ah, yeah, that's the case in all the hospitality industry, Dad."

"I guess so." Watching me for a few minutes, Lou tilted his head and tried for casual. "Have you heard from Ethan?"

That was the first time he'd asked me. I wasn't sure if Ethan told him when we talked or not, but I hadn't mentioned it. "We've talked a couple of times. It's not a regular thing, though. We send messages more than anything."

Frowning, Lou peered through his brows. "Are they clean?"

Smirking, I opened my phone. "No nudies, Dad. I know better than that. It's not very stimulating either, for example: 'Hey, just landed in

Beijing. Let me know if you can Skype in about an hour. Sorry, I can't, stuck working a double shift to cover sick staff.' Then last week he sent, 'Just got home. Tired as hell but needed a surf. I missed the waves and my bed. Just wish I was coming home to a cooked breakfast.'"

"And what did you write back?"

Rolling my eyes, I read from the phone. "'I've never got around to learning to surf. I should do lessons on my days off. I can use my flatmate's board. Luckily, I always get fed at the morning report with all the rest of the staff, so cooked breakfast, lunch, and dinner are a perk of the job, as long as I have time to stop for them, which hasn't been the case the past two weeks.'" Closing my phone, I threw it aside. "See, not very titillating."

"So I see. You could tell Ethan that you miss him."

"I thought you wanted it clean. If I said why I missed Ethan, I wouldn't be able to let you read it."

"Jessie!"

Huffing, I shrugged a shoulder. "Look, we had fun, and we got to like each other, but I'm never coming home, so that's all it's going to be. At least by keeping in contact with Ethan, I'm likely to be told by one person if something happens to you."

Sighing, Lou slumped in his chair. "Jessie. Who are you trying to convince?"

Heart falling into my stomach, I swallowed hard. "He's there, I'm here; that's how it is, Dad. And, as you said, it wasn't going to happen that time around anyway. Ethan and I both have baggage that doesn't allow room for someone else permanent in our lives. Two shattered hearts without even enough pieces to make one whole heart between us. There are trust issues, family issues, location issues, the hours I work, and how often he's away. It's the perfect recipe for another bad heartbreak. Neither of us needs or wants that."

Taking a moment, Lou took a deep breath. "If it wasn't for the barbecue, I don't think you would have ever moved out of his place once you went to stay with him."

"He told you I stayed there?"

"Not so much as Ethan told me you went to his place to pick up your stuff and passport. Otherwise, he doesn't think we would have found you before you fled the country again."

Well, I couldn't argue with that hypothesis because I most certainly would have headed straight for the airport and tried for an earlier flight had I been able to. "The thing is, Dad. It was always going to happen. I had a job to come back to, and even if I wanted to stay, Margaret's insufferable nagging and inability to accept that her favored daughter is a sociopathic bitch—who everyone hates—would have inevitably caused what went down at the barbecue. It was better that it happened before any attachments could form."

Averting his eyes, Lou pressed his lips together before my mother's voice scathed my ears from off the camera. "We are getting ready for dinner."

"Yes, dear."

"And you tell that selfish brat that at least Sharnie doesn't run away when things get hard, and she'll let me be a part of her children's lives."

Oh, she picked the wrong day for this. "Huh, you'll probably end up raising them when Sharnie goes down for child abuse. Or burying them like you did mine when the crazy bitch loses it and kills them, just like she caused the death of your first grandchild. Even then, you will probably think the sun shines out of her ass, and she can do no wrong. Talk about delusional. I guess we know where Sharnie gets it from now." Not waiting for a response, I pressed the disconnect button.

Slowly sliding around the door jam, Sean lifted that eyebrow at me. Scowling, I put my computer aside. "How long were you eavesdropping?"

Lifting that brow higher, Sean came in and set a mug of hot tea beside the bed. "Ginger tea, as requested."

"Thank you." Taking a seat on the bed beside me, Sean met my eyes, that eyebrow still lingering at his hairline. "Was I too harsh? I normally let what she says wash by me, but..."

"Besides the fact that you are exhausted and unwell, what you said was not out of line considering what you went through and your mother's unrealistic expectations. Plus, she just said that intending to hurt you, and it's a horrible thing to say."

Rubbing my lips together, I controlled my breathing.

Exhaling, Sean opened his arms. "Jess, you are one of the strongest women I know, but it's okay to cry when someone hurts you, and a good friend will always be there to hold you while you do."

The first sob escaped, then another as I fell into Sean's arms. Turning his body, Sean laid us both down and held me while I cried —which wasn't for too long, because I hated feeling sorry for myself.

Even when the crying finished, Sean held me, which was when I realized he was asleep. The poor guy probably hadn't been sleeping well since Holly broke his heart. Sighing, I closed my eyes and snuggled into his warmth.

My skype ringing woke me. Frowning, I rolled over to see Ethan's name flashing on my screen. Smiling, I pressed the answer button. "Hey."

Lying on white sheets, Ethan looked to be the epitome of sultry. His dark hair messed, and his eyes still glazed with sleep, a slow smile spreading across his handsome face. "Are you in bed?"

"Yeah, I'm not well and fell asleep after I got off the call with Lou."

Behind me, Sean groaned and sat up. He took a look at the screen, smirked, and stood up. "I'm guessing that's the pilot?"

"You would be guessing right. Ethan, meet Sean, my best friend and boss."

Ethan's smile had slipped at Sean's appearance, but Sean was fully dressed, so it's not like we even looked like we'd been having sex. "Hey, Ethan. I'll go refresh your tea."

"Thanks."

Waiting until Sean left the room, Ethan cleared his throat. "Did I interrupt something?"

Sighing, I got comfortable. "Margaret said something which upset me while I was on the call to Lou. Sean let me snot up his shirt."

Inhaling deeply, Ethan nodded. Margaret probably wasn't talking me up to Ethan anymore and probably did quite the opposite. "Are you okay? You look a bit worse for wear."

"I caught the stomach bug that's been going through my staff. I've spent the entire weekend worshipping porcelain. It's why Sean's home. He's covering my shifts for the next few days."

"I'm also taking care of her because she refuses to let anyone help her, but I can pull the boss card, which trumps friend," Sean added as he came back in the room with freshly brewed ginger tea. "Here, sip this. I also picked up the Hydrolyte, but I want you to keep this down before we start trying the expensive stuff."

Taking the mug, I sniffed the tea and recoiled. "Oh."

Without asking, Sean grabbed the bucket and shoved it in front of me at the same time he caught the tea. "Okay, that's a no. Seriously, Jess, it's three days; I think we need to go to the hospital."

"Aww, God." Retch. "You know how much I hate—" Retch, retch. " —hospitals. I mean, especially American hospitals." Retch, gasp, retch, retch, retch, retch, gasp, groan. "Your health care system sucks." Despite the horrible interruptions and speaking into a bucket, Sean seemed to understand me.

"Well, I hope Ethan wasn't looking for cybersex because I'm pretty sure you've killed the mood."

Waiting for the evil entity trying to wrench my guts out through my esophagus to finish, I groaned.

"She's been like this for three days?" Ethan asked.

"Yeah. Most others have only gone two, but Jess wore her immune system down trying to cover the extra shifts for two weeks straight, and now she's been hit."

"Jess, I think he's right; you need to go to the hospital and get one of those injections," Ethan worried over the line.

Glancing up, I noticed Ethan was now sitting up, and the defined pecs and shoulders that I'd bitten and gripped during ecstasy were on display. "Wait, can you just tilt the camera down a bit."

Ethan did as I asked with a frown, exposing his toned abs and surfer's body to me. Sighing, I fell into my pillow. "Better than any injection."

Sean scoffed and shook his head. "I'll call my doctor friend and ask the favor. You perv on the pilot all you want."

Putting the bucket back on the floor, Sean left the room, leaving Ethan chuckling on the other side. Lying down, Ethan just sat watching me. We both lay there like that for several minutes before Ethan sighed. "I wish you were here with me."

"So you could hold the bucket instead?"

Chuckling, Ethan shook his head. "I'm sure I could find a way to make you feel better."

"It would at least take my mind off feeling like crap. Where are you?"

"Roma," Ethan pronounced with an Italian accent. "It's exactly twelve hours' difference."

Lifting my eyes to the clock, I smiled. "So, eight in the morning there. What are you doing today?"

"Well, we didn't get in until midnight, so I expect Greg will be sleeping in, but I thought I'd call a beautiful woman first thing. By the time I'm ready to go out, he'll have come out looking for nourishment."

"I should probably let you go call that beautiful woman then since you look hungry."

The side of Ethan's mouth twitched. "Even looking like hell has worked you over and watching you hurl, I still find you beautiful, Jess."

"Ask him," Sean whispered from the door. Glancing his way, I watched Sean gesture to the computer. "Ask him."

"Ask me what?" Ethan smirked at me.

Rolling my eyes, I sighed. "Well, I didn't know when you have holidays coming up again, but we are heading into summer here, so if you wanted to catch some waves in Hawaii, you're always welcome to visit. I mean, I work Monday to Friday, but Sean has offered to cover for me if I need a few days off, especially since realizing how much leave I've accrued working for him."

Considering his screen for a long moment, Ethan said nothing. Swallowing, I looked away. "It doesn't have to be anything more than friends. I just..." Glancing towards the door, Sean was lifting that damn eyebrow at me again. "I'd like to see you again if you're ever over this way or in need of a holiday."

"I'd like to see you again, too, Jess, and I'd love to surf the waves in Hawaii. When I get back home, I'll see when I can get some time off. Will your boss have an issue with me staying there?"

"Sean's only here a few days a month right now. He'll be here this week to cover for me and to get things sorted for his new resort, but he'll still be on the west coast for most of the summer."

"I can give you some surf lessons while I'm there."

"We have a surf school at the resort. If I get some lessons before you come, I can take you to the beach where Sean likes to surf. It's got a better swell."

Smirking, Ethan rubbed his lips together. "Okay." Looking to his side, Ethan sighed. "I should get ready for breakfast. I'll call again soon."

"Okay."

"Go see that doctor and get the shot, Jess. You need to take care of yourself."

"Trust me; Sean will make sure I do. He won't want to trust his hotel to Henry."

"Henry?"

"The concierge. He's a great people person but no management skills. We're working on him, but it's a long torturous process."

"You trained Mayla; you can whip Henry into shape," Sean called from the living area.

"Unless you allow me to use an actual whip, it's going to take years, and I'm only here until the new place is up and running."

"He'd probably enjoy the whip too much."

Chuckling, I looked back to the screen to see Ethan frowning. "Something wrong?"

"Are you heading back to Maui after you finish there?"

"No, I'll be taking over the new resort. I'm still deciding if I'm going to find a place close to work or a place here in the north and commute each day. The traffic can be a bitch trying to get from the north."

There was a knock at the door, and then I could hear Sean talking to someone. "I think the doctor is here."

"You look more green now than you did vomiting."

"I hate needles."

Sympathy shrouded Ethan's features. "I'd hold your hand and distract you if I was there. Get some rest; I'll talk to you soon."

"Have a great day." Giving the screen a wave, I disconnected the call.

A moment later, Sean was leading a female his age into the room. "Jess, this is the doctor."

"Aloha, Jess. Sean tells me you haven't been able to keep anything down for three days."

"There was a stomach bug that's just gone through all our staff."

"Okay. But yours seems more severe than the rest?"

"It's gone a day or more longer, but I worked double shifts seven days a week the last couple of weeks to cover for sick staff."

"When were you last sexually active?"

"Not for a few months now."

"Could you be pregnant?"

I'm pretty sure all the color drained from my face. A second later, I was heaving into the bucket again.

CHAPTER THREE

"The look on your face."

"Can you blame me?"

Chuckling, Sean served up Chinese while I sorted papers over the coffee table. "No, but it was pure horror. I wish I had a camera for that moment."

Shaking my head, I picked up the bowl of food. Two days after the injection, I'd gotten over the bug finally, and another day later, I was famished. "The important thing is, it was just a stomach bug. Now, stop making fun of me and give me an update on my staff before we start talking Ko Olina."

Cocking his damn brow, Sean took the seat next to me. "Your staff?"

"You know they are."

"Yeah, I got told about some of the changes you've put in place. You run a tighter ship than me."

"Don't act surprised. It's how I ran the Maui resort, and look at how much better that's been since I took over. Hell, the rating went up another star level."

Sighing, Sean picked up his bowl. "True. If I let you and Holly get together, I'd be in trouble."

"Holly Claire is a damn good manager. When we've caught up at conferences, we've always discussed how we could do things better. Hell, I stole her app idea, and she took on my manager's breakfast session idea. If you manage to get her back, I'm going to have her consult on all your hotels, starting with whichever is under my management first."

Smirking, Sean lifted that brow again. "Are you paying for her to do that consultation?"

"Ah, no! You will be, and I don't want to know the details of how you go about paying her, okay!"

Laughing, Sean shook his head. "You are lucky you are the best manager I've ever had, Jessie girl."

"Argh, you are going to suffer a tragic surfing accident if you keep that up. Speaking of which, since you have no wife or kids yet, have you left me your hotels in your will? I'd hate to have to train up a new boss."

Nudging me with his shoulder, Sean snickered. "Okay. Let's talk about work."

While we ate, Sean went over the Cassidy, and what happened the past week. Then we started planning staff for the Ko Olina resort. Once we had that drafted, Sean made notes while I washed up. By the time I was sitting back down, he'd put all the paperwork away and opened his laptop.

"How many bedrooms were you thinking?"

Frowning, I peered at Sean. "It's a bit late to change how many rooms there are now; the renovations are nearly complete."

"I meant your new place."

Glancing to the screen, I noted the real estate page he'd opened. "Oh, two minimum."

"Buying or renting?"

"I should probably look at buying something, I guess. Since I know I'm never going home."

Lifting an eyebrow, Sean put in the starting parameters for the search. "Let's start close to the new resort and expand the circle."

"You want me to buy in the gated estate of Ko Olina? How much money do you think I have?"

"Well, you've lived in my place in Maui for a very reasonable rent for eight years, and I know how much I've paid you to manage my resort."

"I'm worth more."

"And your trip home a couple of months back has been your only travel expense, other than when you fly here for retail therapy, which isn't very often. You've never bought furniture, so food and utilities have been your only expenditure. Your annual is just over a hundred and fifty, with a yearly bonus between twenty to thirty thousand depending on the profit your resort brought in and reviews. So, after-tax, you are probably taking home just over a hundred. You probably spend a quarter of that on living expenses, so what do you do with the rest?"

Lifting a shoulder and dropping it, I sighed. "Saving it."

"Which would give you about six hundred?"

Tilting my head back and forth, I squinted. "A little over eight, last I checked. There's been a fair few years of interest. And I've had a few term deposits maturing all this time too, which were worth close to two hundred thousand in total. Each time they come up, I move the interest to my savings and reset them to run a few more years."

Blinking, Sean stared at me. "Where the hell did you get that money?"

"My father bought me a house when I graduated. It wasn't worth a lot when he bought it, but by the time Ben and I split and I got my shit together to ask Dad to organize the sale, it had doubled in value. I told Lou to take the money since he bought it, but he refused. He said I earned it when I graduated, and the house was in my name, so the money was mine. Since I wasn't ready to put down roots, he suggested I split it into various term deposits to earn money so that by the time I was ready to buy again, my savings would have increased with house prices."

"Wait, so you have been paying me half of what my place is worth in rent all these years when you could have been paying me full rent?"

Smirking, I shrugged. "You set the price, not me. I offered to pay its value."

Sean went back to his computer with a huff. "Ko Olina is a gated estate; I'd prefer to know you are safe."

"I'd prefer to live close to the beach."

"As I said, we'll start close to work and expand the search."

An hour later, we'd searched up the west coast and then returned to the south, finding a few places in Ewa Beach for me to view. "Nice, it's only a twenty-minute trip to the resort. Not a bad commute, and you'll be going against peak traffic, which is even better. Let me call the real estate agent and make an appointment to see these places this weekend."

"This weekend?"

"The sooner, the better." While Sean made calls to view the properties, I opened my banking app and checked where my savings was sitting, and when the term deposits would expire next. None of the places on my list were more than what I had, but there would be the need to buy furniture and all the things that people used daily to function, like plates and cutlery.

"You okay? You look stressed."

"I don't want to break my term deposits, so my max spend, including furniture, taxes, and utilities, will be eight hundred. Ideally, the house needs to be no more than low to seven hundred thousand."

"I'll help you negotiate the sale price. Don't worry. We should probably look for a car so that you can get back and forth to work."

"I was thinking of getting a bike."

"A pushbike?"

"A motorbike." Getting up, I went into my room and grabbed the pamphlet I'd been eyeing off, bringing it out for Sean to see.

"Like a Vespa, right?"

Rolling my eyes, I handed the pamphlet to Sean. "No. What a sexist suggestion."

"Well, you've never asked to go on mine."

Lifting a shoulder, I shrugged. "I got into motorbikes while back home, and so I started looking for one when I realized I'd be moving to Oahu as a way to counter the traffic."

"I've never heard of this brand."

"Zero makes electric motorbikes. The original builder was an ex-NASA engineer, and the bikes get great reviews. I like the SR/F."

Considering the details, Sean eventually sat back. "How much?"

"About twenty-five on the road."

"Jesus!"

"Yeah, not cheap, but cheaper than a car, more environmentally friendly, and you make back the money by not having to pay for petrol."

"You still have to charge it up, and electricity isn't cheap."

"I'll get solar power on my place and a battery. Since I'm rarely home during the week, this will probably use the most electricity in the house, and it will still be cheaper than air-conditioning or a whole host of other things I could waste money on."

"Surely a hybrid car would be a better investment? What about when it rains, which it does nearly daily in the west?"

"Yeah, for like an hour or two, maybe a full day's rain in winter. I'll probably work through most rains, and if it is a full day, I can get a taxi or ride-share to work. Hell, there's a bus that goes from the Kapolei shopping center to Ko Olina that I could catch if all else fails."

"That bus doesn't start until after nine and finishes its run long before you finish work."

"My point being, there are always alternative transport options."

Inhaling, Sean gave me back the pamphlet. "Let's park that for now and come back to it after you've decided on a place."

"Sounds sensible. The cost of the house and setting it up will also determine if I can afford anything to drive at all."

Sean's phone rang. Looking at the screen, he scowled. Glancing at the caller profile, I sighed. "It's been two months, and he never intended to cause an issue. You have to forgive him eventually." Patting his shoulder, I got up and headed to my bedroom, giving Sean some privacy to talk to his father.

The Holly incident strained their relationship, but they'd always been close before, so I was hoping they'd patch things up. Kind of like me and Lou. With a sigh, I open my laptop and sent an email to my dad.

Dad,
Just a quick note to let you know I'm off house

hunting this weekend. Depending on what time I
get back on Sunday will determine if I get to
catch up with you. I hope you know that I love
and miss you very much. If you ever get sick of
the carryon there and need to get away, the resort
here has a fantastic golf course.

Love Always,

Jess.

Sending the email, I sighed and fell back on my bed on my pillows.
Despite no longer being sick and finally recovering my appetite, the
virus had shattered me. Lifting the quilt, I slid my legs beneath it
and snuggled down as I turned off the lamp next to the bed.
Usually, this would be when I thought of Ethan and all those nights
getting hot and sweaty with him, and I'd relieve some tension.

Since last Friday, I'd not had the inclination. Tonight, I was horny
but too tired to put any effort into it. If Ethan were here, I'd play
little spoon to him right now, let him fuck me gently from behind
while I did as little as possible. Ethan was an overachiever, so I knew
if he were here, he would make sure I claimed at least one if not
more immunity-boosting orgasms.

Closing my eyes, I thought back to the night of the wedding and
how we fell into Ethan's apartment hot and heavy. The way Ethan
kissed me slow and deep, matching the rhythm of his fingers as they
fucked me, his thumb rubbing gently over my clit until I whimpered
my climax into his mouth.

Squirming a little, I put my hand between my legs as I recalled the
way Ethan lifted his fingers to my mouth, wiping them over my lips
before kissing me anew. He moaned as he tasted me on my lips like
he was eating the most delicious meal ever served up, and God, I'd
loved that sound rumbling in his throat.

My sex clenched, just remembering the way he pleasured me, taking his time to enjoy me before he fucked me. Shifting my hand into my pajama pants, I rubbed past my clit once, a shiver passing through my body. Exhaling roughly, I shoved my face into the pillow as I pinched my clit and held it.

My body quaked under the onslaught of my orgasm. It was short and sweet and nowhere near what Ethan could draw out of me, but my body fell limp into the mattress, my brain going into sleep mode, and my dreams bringing Ethan to Hawaii where he made up for my lazy showing just now as if he'd watched the entire thing.

The next morning, I woke up and opened my laptop before I'd barely opened my eyes, sending Ethan a private message, a cheeky grin slowly emerging as I typed.

<Jess>: I miss the way you fuck me.

Expecting to leave the message and not hear back from him in a while, I was surprised when my Skype started calling, Ethan's profile picture of a suit of knight's armor taking up my screen. Biting my lip, I pressed receive as I let my head fall back on the bed.

"Early morning?" Ethan smirked. He was in his uniform, but the background looked like a hotel restaurant.

"Where are you?"

"Getting dinner in the lounge before we board for our flight home. You're looking better."

"The injection worked. I finally could keep down a meal last night."

Pursing his lips, Ethan nodded. "I'm glad your friend talked to you around."

"There was no talking. Sean just called his doctor friend, and then they stabbed me. It was quite humiliating."

"Did you cry?"

Scoffing, I glared at him. "No. I'm not a cry baby."

"Then why was it humiliating?"

Rubbing my lips, I shrugged a shoulder. "I was vomiting, so the doctor was asking questions." When Ethan just cocked a brow, I huffed. "About the last time that I had sex. When? Protection? All those rather intrusive things, which, when answered incorrectly, can lead to further tests and lectures."

Both eyebrows up now, Ethan formed a perfect circle with his mouth. "Oh!"

"Oh, is right."

Glancing around him, Ethan lowered his voice. "So, when was the last time?"

Cocking a brow, I glared at him. "You don't remember?"

Blinking, Ethan relaxed his shoulders. "Oh, I remember the last time we..." He turned his head a little, eyeing something. "I just wasn't sure if that was the last time you—"

"As I said when we became better acquainted, I'm usually pretty selective and can go quite a long stretch without a lover. You were my first and only one-night stand, Ethan."

The sides of Ethan's mouth twitched as he dropped his gaze, then met my eyes again. "So, you miss me?"

"I believe my message was about what you do to me."

"My cock is still an extension of me, so if you miss it, you miss me."

"Who misses your dick?" Greg's voice came from the side, Ethan turned his head, and the word his lips cursed as he quickly dropped the phone down to face the table was amusing. "Was that Jess?" The table shifted, and then suddenly, I was looking at my brother-in-law as he sat down, swinging his arm away from Ethan, who was trying to grab his phone back. "Hey, Sis. So, you miss my boy's D?"

Scowling, Ethan grabbed for the phone again, looking around and trying not to make a scene. "Mind your own damn business."

Smirking, I didn't retreat from Greg's laughing eyes. "What can I say, he spoiled me while I was there, and now I'm having withdrawals."

"He can't hear you," Ethan huffed, pointing to his EarPods, "but I do like that answer."

"What did she say?" Greg asked. "I mean, I got the gist by the smile on her face and the way her cheeks turned pink, but I'd love the actual answer."

"She said, if you don't give me the phone back, I can tell Sharnie that you've been hitting on her sister using my phone."

Rolling his eyes at Ethan, Greg huffed. "Bye, Jess. You should come and visit again. Ethan's grumpy since you left."

The phone got handed over as Ethan stood and moved to the window, airplanes taxiing in the distance. "He's right. I'd love you to visit again."

"E..." With a sigh, I shook my head. "I'm never coming back. Not even to visit."

Watching me, Ethan chewed the inside of his cheek. "What about Lou?"

"He's known where to find me for ten years, E. They've never once come to see me either."

"They were planning a trip out there next year."

Going quiet, I close my eyes. "I'd love it if Lou came out here to see me, but I'm not going through all that shit again. I only stayed as long as I did for you."

"For my dick."

Inhaling, I held the tears that welled up at bay. "For you." Exhaling, I hovered my mouse over the end call button. "I have to go." Disconnecting, I closed the laptop and let one tear fall. Only one.

CHAPTER FOUR

AFTER A WEEKEND OF LOOKING AT PLACES, I'D PUT AN OFFER IN ON A lovely three-bedroom condo in Ewa Beach. Situated in the resort-like community of Lei Pauk, the townhouse had two and a half bathrooms, a private courtyard and yard, multiple covered lanais, and an enclosed two-car garage. Part of the strata included access to the Wai Kai Hale Club, plus it was just minutes away from an abundance of recreational amenities such as the beautiful surf beaches, parks, and shopping.

"If I get the place, I'll only be twenty minutes from work," I informed Mayla Monday afternoon while we ate lunch via video conference.

"I can't believe you're not coming back to Maui."

"As if I'm going to turn down being the manager of a five or six-star resort. And I'm going to be living minutes away from the second largest open-air shopping center in the northern hemisphere."

"What about horse riding?"

"I can come to Turtle Beach on the weekends and ride with Sean."

"Oh, well, that sounds lovely. Are you two okay?"

Smiling, I slurped my noodles and tucked my legs under me on the couch in the staff room. "Yeah, why?"

Lifting a brow, Mayla shook her head. "No reason." Scooping up some of her curry rice, she filled her mouth.

"We'll still be able to have shopping trips together. Just let me know when you are coming over for the weekend, and you can have my guest room."

Grinning, Mayla chuffed. "I guess that is another bonus on top of the promotion. We won't need to pay for accommodation to go shopping anymore."

Henry stuck his head in the room with a worried look. "Damn it! Mayla, my lunch break just ended."

"Problems?"

"By the constipated look on Henry's face, yes."

"Aloha, Henry!" Mayla called.

"Aloha, Mayla. Sorry, Jess."

Waving goodbye to Mayla, I shut my laptop and took my noodles to the counter, placing a lid on with the optimism I might be able to come back while they were still warm. "What's happened?"

"It looks like we've got a thief staying at the hotel. We've had multiple reports of wallets and other valuables stolen yesterday and overnight."

"How valuable?"

"One customer claims to have had a thousand dollars in his wallet, and another has had their twenty-five-thousand-dollar engagement ring stolen."

Damn it! Over the five-thousand-dollar threshold, and for insurance purposes, they would need to report it. Inhaling, I shoved my noodles in the fridge. They were going to get cold anyway. "Have the police been called?"

"Not yet."

"Okay, let's do that and then get some details from guests about when they last saw their valuables and start going through the security footage."

Much later than usual, I finally finished work for the day and made my way home. In Sean's cottage, I shrugged out of my blazer and hung it up as I picked up the phone and dialed room service. "Aloha, Jess. Hungry?" Kamryn from the kitchen answered.

"Starved and in desperate need of something nutritious, please?"

"I'll get something down to you soon."

"Thanks, Kamryn."

The thing I loved about Sean is that he always hired great chefs. I had no issue giving them a general idea of what I needed and then eating whatever they sent my way. It was usually exactly what I needed. Thinking of Sean, I groaned and dialed him next while I removed my uniform and pulled on some lounge pants and a light jumper.

"Miss me already?" Sean answered. By the sound of hammering in the background, he was still at work.

"Yes, especially because we had an incident today."

Sighing, Sean moved away from the noise until the sound of waves crashing sounded in the background. Having done a walkthrough of the site on the weekend, I could visualize he was down near the private ocean lagoon, which had a break wall to protect it from the rough seas. "What happened?"

"We had a thief staying with us. They waited until their last day, robbed a bunch of guests yesterday and last night, and checked out this morning as the victims reported the first thefts."

"So, you identified them?"

"Only just. He spent his week here, identifying all the security systems and working out the best place to target people. We got lucky, he missed the camera in the gym, and we caught him lifting a wallet there. Henry was able to identify him, and we gave the police the details. They apprehended him at the airport."

"Well, at least you caught him. Get security to do an analysis, and let's try to cover those blind spots going forward."

"Will do."

"Which means you've already ordered that, haven't you?"

"Yes."

"So, your call was just politeness."

"You're the owner. The police will call you for any follow-up. Detective Ekewaka already asked where you were."

"Before or after he asked you on a date?"

Smirking at how well Sean knew the people he dealt with, I sagged onto the lounge. "Before."

"He's a real ladies' man, that one."

"Oh, that I picked up from the way his eyes had me naked and riding him two minutes after we shook hands."

Chuckling, Sean sighed. "I know you called about work, but you seem to have a knack for picking up the phone when I need a laugh, so thank you."

"Are we still heading to Maui on Saturday to move my stuff here?"

"Yep, I've booked the yacht. I will head up Saturday morning. If we leave by ten, we should have plenty of time to pack your stuff and make it back home by Sunday lunch."

"Cool, I told Mayla, so she's going to come and help and then wants to have a farewell party for me Saturday night."

"I figured that would be the case. I'll see you Saturday."

"Will do. And Sean, you can call me anytime. I'm happy to listen to anything you need to say, or even watch a movie together and chat on the phone."

"Thanks, Jess. Have a good night."

As I hung up, there was a knock at the door. Getting up, I let room service in and tipped them. I could have ordered and brought it back myself, but I'd been eager to get out of the hotel before something else blew up, so it was only fair to tip the staff serving me.

Back on the lounge, I opened my laptop to go over reports I'd meant to read today before I'd gotten caught up with the incident. Forking a mouthful of steamed vegetables and saffron rice into my mouth, I frowned when Skype rang with Lou's profile.

"Dad? Is everything okay?" I mumbled around my food.

"Jessie. Yes, everything alright. I missed you yesterday and just saw you come online, so I thought I'd see how the house hunting went?"

"Good. I put an offer on a place twenty minutes from the new resort I'll be managing in a few months."

Lou's smile was broad. "That's good to hear. Is it far from where you are now?"

"About two hours' drive depending on traffic. It's in the south of Oahu, about thirty minutes from Waikiki."

"Oh, so you'll be near the airport?"

"I'm not even half an hour from the airport. It's a townhouse located on Ernie Els's signature Hoakalei golf course. It has views of the ponds, and you can walk straight out onto the green. So, if you wanted to come to visit once I move, you could stay in my guest room and play golf while I'm at work."

Lips twitching, Lou seemed to struggle between a smile and frown. "I'll think about it. Will your boss return to Turtle Bay after you leave?"

Frowning, I hadn't expected that question. "Ah, yeah, I guess that's the plan. I guess it all depends what happens with—" Stopping myself, I rubbed my lips together.

"With?" Lou pressed.

Exhaling, I shrugged. "Sean's had some personal stuff going on. I think he's thrown himself into the renovations to distract from it."

Huffing, Lou grumbled, "I see why you two get along."

"Yeah, we are very similar that way. We both ran away when we got cheated on, and our engagements fell apart, and we both work long hours when we need to keep our minds occupied. We also share similar interests. You'd like him, Dad. He's the male version of me."

The look on Lou's face was not impressed. "I see."

"No, really, Dad. It's like he's my twin separated at birth. Older, but so much like me. We are way closer than Sharnie and I ever were. That's why we are such good friends. And we seem to go through the same shit in our lives at the same time, too. Our engagements broke up because our partners cheated with our siblings at the same time, and now we've both met someone new, but they are in Australia, and we are here, and incidents occurred which sort of ruined any chance of things going further, and we miss them, and..." I bit my lip.

Clearing his throat, Lou blinked wide eyes at me. It was probably the most I'd ever told. "I played golf with Ethan today. He mentioned you'd invited him to come to visit?" When I didn't confirm or deny, Lou nodded his head. "Remember what I told you, Jessie girl. Ethan's done the long-distance thing before, and it broke his heart the same as yours. If you're not willing to take a chance and come home for him, it might be pointless pursuing this."

Blinking, I assessed my father. "Oh! Ethan told you if I won't come home, he's not interested."

Lou inhaled and held up a hand. "That's not what I said. Ethan's wary. You're no different. Neither of you wants to go through that situation again."

"But he did say he wouldn't do long-distance again, didn't he?"

Pursing his lips, Lou answered my question with the same look he used to give me when I complained about doing my chores as a kid.

Sighing, I deflated, throwing my hands in the air. "I've already told Ethan I won't be coming home, Dad. I've put an offer in on a place, and I already have dual citizenship, so Hawaii is my home now. I'm not asking Ethan to marry me. I'm not even sure what there is between us. I miss him, but I know Ethan's reputation too, you know. He's not a saint, but I was still willing to get to know him better. What makes you think he would stay faithful to me while he's flying around the world?"

Closing his eyes, Lou muttered beneath his breath before looking at me again. "I'm sorry. I shouldn't have said anything. I just wanted you to think about what you want before you go down a path that might lead to more pain. I don't want to see either of you hurt. I especially don't want either of you to be the cause of each other's heartbreak."

Sitting forward, I bowed my head. Ethan was like the son Lou never had but always wanted. If we got involved and fucked it up, he'd have to choose between us. But then again... "Dad, I'm here. If Ethan breaks my heart, I'm never going to know if he still plays golf with you or attends Sunday dinner. You don't mention him again, and it's never an issue. But, since Ethan doesn't want a long-distance relationship, I guess that's not going to be a problem. We can be friends. It doesn't need to be more. Tell Ethan I won't be offended if he declines my invitation to visit me on holiday, okay? There's no need to stress about it all."

My father couldn't meet my eyes while he sat with his jaw clenched tight. It made me sigh and feel how tired I was.

"It's been a long day, Dad, and my dinner is getting cold. I'll speak to you Sunday. I love you."

"Love you too, Jessie—"

Disconnecting before he could finish, I hung my head. No longer in the mood to catch up on my work, I shut the laptop, turned on the television, queued up a movie, and finished my dinner. I guess that settled the Ethan dilemma.

CHAPTER FIVE

GETTING IN THE DOOR LATE WEDNESDAY NIGHT, I YAWNED. KEEPING busy was easy because there was always work to do as a manager. Over the last two nights, I'd caught up on everything and got ahead on next week's work. Grabbing out a soup bag, I poured the contents into a bowl and put it in the microwave to heat while I went to shower and change.

Dressed in a singlet and knickers for bed, I used oven mats to take the soup bowl out and set it on the placemat on the dining room table. After grabbing a glass of water, I took my laptop to the table and opened it to check my emails while I ate.

Finishing the soup, I pushed the bowl aside and answered Karla's email, chuckling at what she shared. Anthony and Karla were finally planning their wedding, but she wanted to know if I thought booking sessions for him to see a sex therapist would be a good wedding present.

Knight's armor flashed up on my screen as a video call rang. Smooshing my lips together, I then bit my lip as I pressed receive. Ethan was in uniform, but his tie was loose and his collar undone.

"Hey," he greeted, pulling the tie over his head and throwing it aside.

"Hey. Did you only just land?"

"Several hours ago, but I just got home. I literally just walked through the door. I saw you come online while we were driving but hoped you'd stay on long enough for me to get home."

"We?" I asked.

"Greg drives us to the airport when we are flying together."

That surprised me. "Don't you always fly together?"

"If we can, but rosters don't always work out that way. For the most part, we get rostered the same, but we both pick up extra work when someone gets sick or something and end up not working together."

That made sense. I didn't know much about how the whole pilot thing worked. "So, where did you just get back from?"

Opening his fridge, Ethan pulled out a beer and knocked the top off. "Japan. We flew over yesterday and then back again today. The weather was a bitch. There was a cyclone off the coast of Queensland which caused some severe turbulence, and we had to be wary of updrafts."

Entirely ignorant of updrafts and such, I assumed they were terrible things. "Hence the beer early in the afternoon?"

Frowning at his watch, Ethan smirked. "Eighteen hundred hours is not early, Jess."

Glancing at the clock, I sighed, seeing the time, and deflated a little. It was already after ten. "Well, crap. I didn't realize how late it was."

Cocking a brow, Ethan dropped down on his couch. "Rough day?"

Lifting a shoulder, I didn't commit to an answer. The truth was, I could have finished at six and enjoyed my afternoon; but since Lou's call on Monday, I kept thinking of Ethan and how he didn't want anything more from me if I wasn't willing to move back to Australia.

"I've put a deposit on a place here today. I made an offer over the weekend, and they accepted. It's a three-bedroom townhouse on a golf course estate. When the new resort opens, I'll be twenty minutes from work and not much further from the airport."

Lifting the beer to his lips, Ethan took a long pull before sighing. "Is that so?"

"It's also near a great surfing beach. Only a five or ten-minute walk."

Ethan looked to the side with a huff. "Not that you can surf, yet."

Ethan's change in attitude when I talked about buying a place confirmed Lou's statement for me on Monday night. Chewing my lip, I looked down at my lap. "I started my surf lessons on Monday. I've been up early every day this week for them. I'm still a little weak from the stomach bug, so I haven't managed to stand yet, but I came close today."

Looking back to the camera, Ethan leaned forward on his knees, hands scrubbing through his hair. "You'll get there. Look, I'm exhausted, I only got the minimum layover between shifts, but if I go to bed now, it'll throw my sleep out, so I'm going to go out for a run. Exercise helps with the jet lag."

"Of course. I have an early morning, so I should get to bed as well."

Standing, Ethan took his beer to the counter, dumped it, and then started heading to his room. "Cool. We'll talk again soon. Night, Jess."

"Night." Finger ready to press hang-up, I sighed as Ethan dropped the phone, ready to disconnect. "Ethan, I understand where you're coming from, and I don't begrudge your attitude one bit. It's okay. I'd be the same in this situation."

Face suddenly back on screen, Ethan frowned, his brows meeting over his nose. "What situation?"

Inhaling, I licked my lips. "Lou told me what you said, about me not coming back, about us. I get it, and I'm not going to be put out if you decide to stop calling, but if you don't mind, could you make sure I know if anything ever happens to my dad? I don't trust Sharnie and Margaret to keep me in the loop if he were to get sick or something."

Still frowning at the screen, Ethan blinked a few times, then he rubbed his eyes and cursed. "Jess, I can't—"

"I know. I'll let you go. Take care, Ethan." Disconnecting, I slumped back in my seat. A tear tracked down my cheek as I shut the laptop. Swiping the tear away, I got up and started cleaning up for the night. We'd been a one-night stand that turned into a holiday romance. I was never meant to be more, and he couldn't be more for me.

Giving up on the day, I turned out the light and went to bed.

————

Sitting in front of the television Thursday night, I picked up a handful of freshly made popcorn and shoved it in my mouth. The phone ringing combined with a giant spider jumping onto Mando's ship, made me jolt and nearly spill the bowl of popcorn. "For fucks sake!" Snatching up the phone, I answered it. "Worst timing ever, Sean."

"Are you fucking some guy?"

"What? No! I'm watching The Mandalorian."

"Well then, it's not the worst timing. Are you decent?"

Frowning, I looked over my singlet and lounge pants and considered that it was a ridiculous question. "Sure. It's not like Mando cares what I'm wearing."

The door lock turned, and Sean stepped into the kitchen. "No, but I don't want to get yelled at for walking in and finding you in your birthday suit." Sean smiled as he shut the door.

Standing up, I pressed pause on the show. "What are you doing here? I thought you weren't coming until Saturday?"

"Friday night got canceled, so I thought I'd come up tonight, and we can head to Maui tomorrow. Get an extra night there, and I can catch up with Mayla and see how she's going on Friday afternoon." Walking over to the hall, Sean dropped his bag in his room and then returned to the lounge.

"I still have work tomorrow."

"I'm your boss. You can do a half-day while I'm getting a few things settled here, and then we'll take off, okay?"

"Sure. I'm not going to argue. I'm ahead on my work this week anyway, providing nothing comes up tomorrow."

"I figured, what with the late hours you've been up at the hotel."

Huffing, I dropped back onto the sofa. "You're spying on me!"

"Hey, I've been living and working here for ten years. Some of my staff are my friends too, and they talk to me as much as you."

"Argh, I'm looking forward to having Ko Olina, so we can go back to you not being able to keep tabs on me." Picking up the popcorn as Sean sat down beside me, I took a handful and offered him the bowl.

Snickering, Sean took it. "If you think I didn't have my spies in Maui, you're wrong; they just didn't have anything to report outside of how awesome a boss you are. Here, the staff is loyal to me, and they are very aware you were out of sorts taking over. After you got so sick last week, they are just worried you will make yourself sick working long hours again. This is Hawaii, Jess. People don't work extra hours for fun. If you work overtime voluntarily here, it's because you need the money or you are avoiding going home."

Rolling my eyes, I picked up the remote. "Do I need to restart?"

"Yes, please, I haven't seen this week's episode yet."

Taking it back, I pressed play and grabbed another handful of popcorn. Watching the episode in relative quiet, we shared the snacks, and I got to laugh when Sean jumped for the big-ass mother spider this time.

"Have you heard from the pilot this week?" Sean asked as the episode finished.

Grabbing up the empty bowl, I headed to the kitchen. "Yeah, last night. So, how are the renovations coming?"

Tilting his head, Sean followed me over and got himself a drink from the fridge. "Fit-out is done in the main building and about to kick off in the family suite building. I want to start interviews in a week and get our staff on board ready to be trained up, so I need to organize for you to spend a few days down there and for someone else to cover here."

"Not Henry!"

Chuckling, Sean shook his head. "No, Kilikina could jump into the manager's role for a few days."

Kilikina was the event's manager but had experience filling in for the assistant manager when she took leave. "Okay. Let me know what days you need me, and we'll get the Ko Olina staff sorted." Grabbing a drink, I walked back to the sofa. "Want to watch a movie?"

"Sure." Retaking his seat, Sean considered me. "What happened with the pilot?"

"I bought a house here."

"So?"

Flicking through the movie choices, I hit play on a new miniseries about a female chess player. "It means I'm not going back."

Exhaling, Sean looked at the screen for a moment. "You bought a house?"

"They accepted the offer you made, and I signed the contracts and paid the deposit yesterday."

Turning his face back to me, Sean laughed. "They accepted an offer nearly eighty thousand below asking?"

"Yep. The money your negotiating skills saved me will cover furniture and my new bike and car." Enjoying the way Sean's eyebrow lifted, I smiled.

"You're getting both now?"

"Well, it turns out I still need to learn to ride a motorbike, and then there is a wait in getting it shipped here. So, I thought a little hybrid car would be for work, and I can keep the bike for weekends when I come here to ride your horses because if you think I am giving up my horse riding on weekends, you are wrong."

Smirking, Sean sat back. "It's a shame you'd be like fucking my sister, Jess. We could have been perfect for one another."

Laughing, I shook my head. "Confession. I only agreed to that first date because my friend slept with you a few months earlier and told me you were hot in the sack, and I hadn't been with anyone since Ben. You were going to be my rebound. But the moment I sat down to dinner with you, I knew it wasn't going to happen."

Grinning, Sean nodded. "Me too. I mean, you are beautiful, Jess, but your heartbreak haunts your eyes. Still, your passion for your work shined through, so I didn't hesitate to make our date an interview by the time I got that call. Then, by the end of your two-week orientation to Cassidy, you had managed to get my heartache out of me and become one of my closest friends. We were meant to meet and become each other's support person."

Smiling quietly to myself, I wondered if it was fate. It couldn't be a coincidence that we had the same experience then and were going through the same thing now. "You told me once you believed in love at first sight. Was Holly your true love?"

Inhaling deep, Sean watched the screen. "Yeah. Holly's it. If I can't find her, or she doesn't want anything to do with me again, there's never going to be anyone else for me."

"I guess you'll just have to put up with me. We can move in together, get a few cats or something, be each other's family."

Smirking, Sean turned to me. "I want kids someday. I'm not exactly getting younger."

"I could find a hot guy, have a few weeks of fun and let him knock me up before he flies home, and then we can raise the kids together. What do you think?"

Lips turning up further, Sean gave a half-laugh. "Let's give it a year. If Holly won't have me back, and your pilot doesn't come to his senses, we'll do kids, but I want them to be mine, so let's look at IVF."

"Done! But you're paying for the artificial stuff."

We watched the show for a few minutes before I frowned. "Do you think it would be weird for kids growing up with parents who don't sleep together or even kiss each other?"

Cocking his head, Sean shrugged. "Nah, that's how things were back in the fifties and before. Lots of couples had separate beds or rooms and didn't kiss and touch outside of sex."

Scrunching up my face, I shook my head, and Sean laughed at me. "We'd have to have secret affairs. I mean, I can go without for long periods, but I'm going to get horny, and so are you, and we'll need to source an outlet to those needs away from home, preferably where it doesn't raise eyebrows."

Snickering, Sean grinned. "Guess you won't be able to take up with a guest for a week or two. Where are you going to sate your needs?"

Exhaling hard, I raised my hands. "I guess I'll just have to bang Henry."

Sean started laughing so hard that he curled over himself. Admittedly, I was near crying, trying to hold my laughter inside. Focusing back on the show, we fell quiet. Reaching out, Sean took my hand and gave me a wink halfway through. "I could handle this with a bit on the side, but I want Holly if I can have her."

Squeezing his hand in mine, I relaxed into the lounge. "I know, and I'm praying to all the gods that you find her and make her yours, Sean. You deserve to be happy. And hey, I can be just as happy being an aunty to your kids."

Giving me a kind smile, Sean settled in to watch the show with me. Thinking of what Sean said about Holly being it, I wondered when I'd decided Ethan was my last chance as well. That's what I'd just basically implied, right? Tired and overthinking things, I was glad when the episode finished, and I could go to bed and tell my brain to shut down.

"Jess?" Sean called as I headed to my bedroom.

Looking over my shoulder, I forced a smile. Getting up, Sean shoved his hands in his pockets, his eyes watching me for a solid minute. My smile fell away, and I stared back as I blinked back tears. "His ex-wife cheated on him while he was away in the Air Force."

Bowing his head, Sean pressed his lips together. Without a word, he picked up his glass and headed to the kitchen. Stepping into my room, I closed the door and let out a long breath. None of us wanted to repeat history. Ethan flew worldwide and encountered beautiful women who probably loved his uniform as much as I did. He'd had just as long in that lifestyle as I had in mine, and it would be insane to think he'd give it up for a woman who wasn't even living in the same country as him.

It was a holiday romance. It was time to file it as a memory and move on.

CHAPTER SIX

"JESS, I HAVE SOMEONE AT THE FRONT DESK ASKING TO SPEAK TO the manager," Henry informed me.

"Can Kilikina deal with it? I'm finishing up in a moment." Signing the order request on my screen, I sent the order approval and closed out of the screen. "That's good to go, Hanley."

"Thanks, Jess." Hanley checked her tablet and then pointed to another item to do with a wedding we were catering on the weekend.

Henry lowered his voice. "Sorry, Jess. They asked for you specifically."

Nodding at Hanley, I slipped my pen into its holder on my tablet and closed the cover with a sigh. "Okay, Henry. I'm just finishing up in the kitchen, and I'll be up."

"Thanks, Jess."

Hanging up my phone, I slipped it into my pocket. "Anything else, Hanley?"

"All good, thanks, Jess. Here are the lunches Sean ordered."

Accepting the basket of food, I picked up my tablet. "Okay, well, Kilikina will be me for the afternoon. I've given her a full debriefing, so if anything else crops up for this wedding tomorrow, she'll be right to help." Waving over my shoulder, I headed up to the main lobby.

"Jess, we ready to go?" Sean came out of a side hall.

"I've just got to deal with one more thing, and then I'll duck back to your place to change. I shouldn't be more than twenty minutes if you want to go ahead and get the yacht ready?"

Looking at his watch, Sean nodded. "That will still get us to Maui in good time. Is that our lunch?"

"Yes. What's with the basket?" Handing it to Sean, I frowned.

Lifting a shoulder, Sean peeked inside and started chuckling. "Ah, Hanley might think this is to be a romantic lunch. She's included extras to the two meals I ordered."

Leaning forward, I spotted the chocolate coated strawberries and cheese tray and rolled my eyes. "Well, while I wish they'd all get their heads out of the clouds, I'm not going to turn away treats for free." With a wink, I strode out to the lobby.

"See you at the yacht," Sean chuckled as he veered off towards the beach exit.

"Aloha, Jess." Kilikina stopped in my path to the concierge desk. "Is there anything urgent you want me to take care of?"

"Just keep an eye on this wedding. The bride keeps making last-minute changes, and it's driving Hanley mad."

"I will. I can take the pilot for you too if you like? I know he asked for you specifically, but I'm happy to say you had already left."

"Pilot?" My focus turned to Henry's desk, where a tall, broad-shouldered man in a pilot's uniform, aviators, and black hair was watching me. Despite the glasses and uniform, I'd know that face anywhere. "Um, no, it's fine. I'll handle this. Thanks, Kilikina."

Separating myself from the woman drooling over my dream-man, I strode across the lobby, trying to compose myself, but my mouth was forming into a smile the closer I got, Ethan's lips pulling up as well. "Ethan?"

"Jess." Stepping into me, Ethan wrapped an arm around my waist, then his mouth was on mine, only for a few seconds, a touch of tongue to my lips, then he hugged me to him. "Jesus, I'd forgotten how good you taste and smell," he whispered to the top of my head.

Inhaling his delicious vanilla and cinnamon scent, I murmured something like an agreement. A throat clearing pulled me back, as Henry stood waiting for me. "Thanks, Henry, I'll take it from here." Waiting for Henry to find another guest to assist, I noted Ethan's carry on by his leg. "How?"

Smirking, Ethan collected my free hand in his, massaging between the knuckles, which did things to my sex I would have never believed. "I asked my manager to tell me if any opportunities to do a layover in Hawaii came up. The pilot rostered to fly the red-eye caught the flu, and they called me up. I landed a few hours ago and thought I'd surprise you."

Blinking, I smiled. "How long are you here?"

"I fly out Monday. I could get a room and sleep for a few hours while you finish your shift, and then we could get dinner together."

My smile fell. "Shit!"

Ethan's smile disintegrated. "Jess?"

"Um, I'm about to board a boat for Maui, Ethan. I'm packing up my place there, ready to move here permanently."

"Oh."

Taking a breath, I dared a smile. "Did you want to come?"

"To Maui? Will you be back by Monday?"

"Yes, I have to work, so we'll get back here Sunday afternoon at the latest. Sean has to get back to Ko Olina, too, so we will be back in time." Picking up the phone at Henry's desk, I called the kitchen. "Hanley, can I get a third lunch made up and sent to the yacht ASAP."

"A third lunch?"

"Yes, a good friend of mine is coming for the trip."

"Okay, sure." She didn't sound sure.

"Thanks, Hanley." Hanging up, I turned to face Ethan.

"Sean?"

"My friend and boss. It's his yacht. He's meeting with the manager who replaced me there while I start packing this afternoon, and then there is a farewell party tomorrow evening."

Closing his eyes, Ethan tensed his jaw. "Jess, I flew the red-eye. I'm pretty tired. I'm not sure I'm up to sailing for a few hours."

Taking Ethan's hand, I tugged him toward the exit while I checked the time. "It's a luxury yacht. You can sleep for the trip over, and if you are still tired when we get there, you can sleep while I start packing." Ethan still didn't look convinced as I lead the way to Sean's place. "It's up to you, of course. You can stay at my place for the weekend, and we can just do dinner Sunday if you'd prefer. But, if you come to Maui, Sean will probably take you surfing both mornings we are there, and Maui has some great surf. It'll be my last time there that you can have free accommodation."

Smirking, Ethan tugged my hand, pulling me back to him as we stopped in a quiet place on the walk. "Will Sean be staying with us, or will I get you to myself tonight?"

Swallowing at the look in Ethan's eyes, I licked my lips. "Ah, I'm sure he'll opt to stay on the boat once he knows you are here."

Slipping his hand to the back of my neck, Ethan dropped his mouth to mine, his hot breath tingling my wet lips. "Good."

Pinching my lips twice, Ethan turned his head, his tongue brushing along the seal of my mouth, then as our lips locked a third time, his tongue delved into my mouth, making my toes curl under in my shoes. Melting against his muscular frame, I grabbed Ethan by his jacket and pulled him tight to me as I lifted a little out of my heels to let him know how much I'd missed him.

Moaning, Ethan pulled back as I dropped back into my shoes. Licking my lips, I smiled up at him. "Come on, Sean's waiting at the slip, and I still need to get changed." Giving Ethan's uniform a look over, I lifted a brow. "I suspect you'll want to change too."

"Ah, yeah."

Tugging his hand, I showed Ethan to Sean's cottage and then into my room. "This is Sean's place, but I've been staying here while he's away. I'll miss being able to step out the front door onto the beach each day when I leave, but luckily my new place isn't that far from a nice beach either."

Following me into my bedroom, Ethan didn't say anything, just took everything in with a critical eye. Shrugging off my blazer, I hung it up and then unzipped my tunic dress while I stepped out of my heels. Pursing his lips, Ethan put his bag on my bed and opened it, grabbing out a pair of shorts and a shirt.

Chewing my lip, I grabbed up my bikini and sundress. "I'll use the bathroom while I change. If you need the toilet, there's an ensuite in Sean's room." Stepping into my bathroom, I shut the door. Closing my eyes, I took a deep breath. Ethan was here. Was he going to try and convince me to come home and give us a chance? Not likely. If he didn't want a relationship, why was he here? Just a weekend fuckfest? It would explain asking if Sean were staying with us.

Sighing, I stripped off and slathered myself in sunscreen before dressing again. Despite the emotional hell it could cause me, I wasn't going to turn down one more chance to ride Ethan. If this were goodbye for him, then I would accept it. If he decided to make Hawaii and my bed a regular holiday location, was I really going to complain? I could go years between fuckfests—a few months between, and being friends with the guy would be a much better deal.

Back in my bedroom, Ethan was changed and sitting on my bed waiting for me. His eyes tracked my legs as I grabbed my phone and chucked it in my overnight bag before picking it up off the bed. "You good to go?"

"I hung my uniform in your closet; I hope that's okay," Ethan explained as he stood up.

"Of course."

The walk down to the jetty was slightly awkward. The shock of Ethan turning up had worn off, and now my brain was overanalyzing his sudden appearance. "So, will I get to see your new place this weekend as well?"

"I don't have the keys yet, so not this visit." Scraping my lip with my teeth, I realized Ethan would probably judge me by my place in Maui too. "Ah, look, you know how you never really bothered replacing the furniture at your place? Well, my place in Maui came fully furnished because it is a holiday rental. All I own there are my clothes and a few knick-knacks. I left all of my stuff behind when I left Australia, so don't expect it to look like anything but what it is."

Considering me, Ethan bunched his brows. "You mean, it was never home?"

"I didn't set down roots. As much as I loved it in Maui, I think a part of me always yearned to give Australia another chance. I've done that now, and I've realized it's not home there either. So, I get the chance to start from scratch. I have to buy furniture, kitchen appliances, a car, and all those sorts of things. If you come to visit again, the next place I'll be living in will be mine, and it will reflect my tastes and be the home I've made for myself."

Coming to a stop, Ethan turned to face me. "Jess, I get that you're confused by my being here after what Lou told you, and because of that, you aren't willing to consider this being more than a once-off, but could you not overanalyze this or try and label this right now? I have no idea what I'm doing here either. You asked me to visit, and it worked out that I picked up a relief shift, so I'm here. I have no expectations of this visit, so let's just feel our way through it, okay?"

Chewing on my lip, I stared into Ethan's deep blue eyes and nodded. An extended holiday romance would be no different from every other intimate interaction I'd had since coming to this beautiful island; a weekend or a few weeks of fun with a guy who would fly out and not expect anything more. I knew this and could handle it. Lifting a bold brow, I eyed Ethan as I caressed a hand across his chest. "No expectations at all?"

Lips twitching, Ethan ducked his head and pulled me hard against him as his mouth lavished mine with the naughtiest kiss ever. "Well, some expectations."

Smiling, I stepped away, making the final turn on the path to reach the jetty where Sean was standing beside the yacht's mooring, talking to one of the staff, holding a paper bag the kitchen used to provide take-away meals.

Turning his eyes up the pier, Sean crossed his arms across his chest and smiled. Suddenly, Ethan scooped my hand into his as we walked towards the yacht. My cheeks heated, and Sean's smile only grew. Giving the staff member a chin jut to dismiss him, Sean moved, ready to greet us. "Ethan, I take it?"

"You must be Sean." Sticking his hand out, the two shook hands.

"Nice to meet you in the flesh. You coming to Maui with us?"

"If you don't mind the extra?"

"Mind? God no. Anyone who can make Jess smile like that is welcome anytime. The fact you made her blush should grant you VIP status." Stepping out of the way, Sean gestured to the yacht. "Let's go. The waters only get more choppy the later in the day you wait."

Both men waited for me to go first, so I stepped across onto the swim platform and then climbed up the stairs to the main deck and moved under the shade where the lounge seats were. "Ethan just finished an overnight shift, so he needs to sleep on the way over. Can I set him up in one of the cabins?"

"Sure, use the second master." Sean moved towards the stairs for the upper deck where the controls for the yacht were. "Will you eat with us first, Ethan, or do you want me to leave your lunch in the fridge for later?" Holding up the paper bag, Sean looked at Ethan.

"I could eat."

Smiling, Sean turned for the stairs. "I'll put this on the table and then cast off while Jess shows you your cabin." Disappearing up the stairs, Sean gave me a covert wink before he disappeared.

Holding in a laugh at Sean's enthusiasm, I showed Ethan around the boat and the second master suite where he could catch some shut-eye. By the time I got upstairs, Sean was steering us out of the protected mooring and into the open sea. "He came."

"Don't read into it."

One side of his mouth lifting high to expose his dimple, Sean shook his head. "I wouldn't dare."

Before I could tell Sean to cut it out, Ethan joined us on the deck. "Hungry?"

Eyes raking me, Ethan lifted a brow. "Starving."

CHAPTER SEVEN

"You not going to tuck him in?" Sean teased after Ethan made his way downstairs to the cabin.

"He's exhausted," I dismissed. Honestly, by the time we finished eating, Ethan was dead on his feet. Given another five minutes, he'd have been asleep in his seat. The rocking motion of the boat probably didn't help.

Gazing my way, Sean merely lifted a brow and turned his eyes back to the water, which was getting rougher the further we went. Standing up, I cleaned up from our lunch, shoving another chocolate-coated strawberry in my mouth. "Do you want anything left out for you?"

"Leave me the cheese; you can take the strawberries."

Loving that answer, I stole one more piece of camembert before moving the cheese plate to where Sean could easily reach it. "Have you organized interviews?"

"Have you read through all the applications I sent you?"

"Most of them. We should interview the former staff out of politeness, so we could be setting up interviews for them while I finish the new applications." Taking the copilot seat, I bit into another strawberry.

"The previous owner had to sell for a reason, Jess. We keep on the same staff who ran it into the ground last time, and I'll have to sell it too."

"The previous owner didn't have me at the helm. You know I won't put up with shit. We interview them, give them a chance to prove they are worth keeping. One of the questions we pose is asking where it went wrong last time. If they say management, well, we know that's already changing. If it's something else, we get an idea of where we need to be careful. It's what I did at Maui."

Sean's eyebrows drew down and together. "You reinterviewed the staff when you took over Maui?"

"Of course. I dressed it up as getting to know my team, but I asked what was working, what wasn't, and all that. I got to know my staff, and the feedback gave me an idea of where I needed to focus first. Why do you think you needed a new head chef within two weeks of me taking over?"

Mouth falling open, Sean glared at me. "You told me he quit."

"He did after I told him to up his game or use the door. He was an ass with a drinking problem, and he used to throw things at the kitchen staff, which is why you had an insane turnover in junior staff members. I told him I wouldn't tolerate that shit any longer, and he threw a bowl of salad at my head. I told him not to let the door slap his ass on the way out. Then I got a fantastic chef who elevated the staff retention and the public restaurant face of the hotel. Guest from other hotels come to eat at our restaurant; we have that good a reputation now."

"He threw a salad bowl at you?"

"And the salad."

Contemplating that, Sean took a few moments. "You didn't tell me that."

Smirking, I gestured between us. "This friendship was still new, but you gave me full control with only reporting responsibilities, so I did what was needed. He was the only one I had to get rid of entirely. The rest I handled with stricter reporting, open communication channels, and clear procedures."

"And free meals as a perk," Sean grumbled. "Something I noted you introduced at Cassidy."

"Not free entirely. The managers get a relatively free breakfast at the morning report, but they deduct two dollars a day from their salary. It allows us to be comfortable and talk and get things started for the day. All the staff can have one meal a shift, and they deduct three dollars a day for it.

"Then, the leftovers from the buffet get packaged up as meals, and staff finishing their shift at those times can opt to collect a doggy bag to take home. The food would just go to waste, and it lifts staff morale, especially here in the states where the minimum wage is below what I got paid base as a fourteen-year-old in Australia. The poverty rate is ridiculous for such a rich country and could easily be addressed by introducing a guaranteed and decent minimum wage."

"I pay above award, as you know."

"And I provide a small perk to my staff, which doesn't impact your bottom line. In fact, it lifts it. When people aren't going hungry, you get increased staff morale, leading to a happier and more productive workplace. That adds to the guest experience. You've seen the results, Sean. You know what I do works."

Smirking, Sean side-eyed me. "I know, but I'm not grandfathering in the former staff at Ko Olina. They can interview, but they won't have a guaranteed position until we've interviewed all the candidates. Some of them may end up offered a different position."

"Fair enough. You know the owners used to let the staff have their families use the facilities on weekends. Is that going to continue?"

Chewing his cheek, Sean nodded. "But only in off-peak season. We do the same at Cassidy. When we are packed out or have big events on, the facilities are closed to staff benefits that weekend. When it's slow or the offseason, it's not an issue."

While in Oahu, I hadn't noticed staff having family there on weekends, but then I spent my weekends as far from work as I could get. Typically on horseback, hiking the national park, or snorkeling. Considering we'd just finished spring break and gone straight into the wedding season, it probably meant most weekends had been closed for staff recreation. We were booked out this weekend from a combination of the wedding and international surfing competition.

Finishing the last strawberry, I put the container back in the basket and pulled out another box. "How much did Hanley pack in here?" Opening the lid, I licked my lips at the fresh churros with caramel dipping sauce. "I'm going to need to jump overboard and swim the rest of the way to Maui."

Glancing over, Sean chuckled. "Those you have to share!"

An hour into our journey, Sean and I ran out of things to discuss, and neither of us wanted to talk about our personal lives right then, so I moved out to the front of the boat and took my dress off. Laying down with a book, I started reading.

When we sailed by the Kalohi Channel entrance, the waters got rough from strong winds blowing between the islands. Since Sean sailed these waters all the time to get to his place in Molokai, I wasn't worried about my safety. He could have taken us up the channel to reach the Auau Channel, surrounded by the four islands and calm. But, as it's protected and a tourist destination, it was faster to go down the south side of Lanai and come in at the Kealaikahiki Channel to reach the Cassidy Wailea resort.

The seas got better once we'd crossed the channel, but it was still a little choppy thirty minutes later. "You're awake? Do you feel better?" Sean asked up above.

"Yes, a good nap makes a difference. Where's are we?" Ethan's voice made me squirm. Glancing up, I could only see Sean, so Ethan was further back. Putting my eyes back on my book, I tried to concentrate and let the men talk.

"That's Lanai. We are about thirty minutes out of the harbor."

"Cool. Where's Jess?"

"Getting some sun and reading on the foredeck lounge. I'm guessing you two will want some alone time to catch up tonight, so please don't think me rude, but I'll drop you guys at Jess's place and then head to the resort to get some work done."

"I'd appreciate it."

"Jess tells me you are an avid surfer."

"Every morning that I'm home, or near a decent beach."

"Jess will probably want to go riding the next two mornings and say goodbye to her long-term weekend companions. I like to start my days with a surf if you want to join me? It's a drive from the resort, but I can pick you up on the way."

"The surf in the morning sounds good, thanks. Riding?"

"Horses. Jess likes to horse ride on her weekends. She's been taking my horse out since she's been in Oahu."

"Will Jess have somewhere to keep doing that when she moves to her new place?"

"There are a few places, but she'd have to pay there. Jess will probably just drive north and steal my horse."

"That's a long drive just to go riding."

"She'd be against traffic, so not that long."

At this point, I'd given up trying to read my book. Closing it, I stretched and put my head down a moment before rolling over.

"I might go join Jess."

"Grab yourself some water and take one for Jess."

A minute later, Ethan plopped himself down on the sunbed next to me. "You're not worried you'll burn?"

"I slathered myself in hundred-plus sunscreen before we left. Plus, the Hawaiian sun is nothing after growing up in Australia." Taking the bottle of water Ethan offered me, I sat up and cracked the lid. "You look more awake."

"I slept pretty well, considering." Drinking half his bottle in one hit, Ethan leaned back on his elbows. "Sean seems like a decent guy. How long has he been your boss?"

"Eight years now, and he's not just my boss." Watching Ethan's jaw clench, I put the lid back on my drink. "Sean's one of my best friends. He knows my history, about my family and Ben. He's the only one I ever told the whole story to here. My other friends know I was engaged and that he slept with my sister, but that's all they know."

"Why was he special enough to get the entire story?"

Staring out to sea, I sighed. "Because Sean went through the same thing at the same time. His ex-fiancée left him to marry his brother. That's how he found out about their affair. We were drinking together one night, and we got talking about what brought us here, and our backstories spilled out. Back then, I was still raw from it all, so having someone who knew, who understood, it helped."

Finishing his water, Ethan put the lid on and sat back up. "It's beautiful out here. I've never really gone out sailing. Up there is my haven." Ethan pointed to the sky. "But being out here, I get why this appeals to a lot of people." Turning to look at me, Ethan considered my smile. "This is your thing? Boats, being out at sea?"

Scrunching my face, I tilted my hand back and forth. "Not so much out at sea. I'll enjoy a boat trip to get out to a wreck to dive at or to sit offshore and chill with friends on deck with the occasional dip, but I much prefer being on land. As long as I'm near the water, I'm happy. How about you?"

"I love flying, but when I can't be up there, then I need to be near the beach. Riding my motorbike is my equivalent for flying when I'm earthbound."

"Sean has a motorbike. Maybe he'll let you take me for a ride on it when we get back."

Eyebrow popping up, Ethan scanned the horizon. "Do you two go riding together?"

Laughing, I shook my head. "On horses, yes, but I've never been on Sean's bike. It wasn't my thing until I got on the back of yours. When I came back, I started looking at buying myself a bike to get around. I'm still not sure if it was the bike or you that won me over there, and it probably won't feel the same without you in control, but the bug bit me."

Ethan slid his hand behind my neck as he twisted and laid me beneath him, his mouth smothering mine in the most sensual of kisses. When he pulled back, his eyes flicked to the upper deck, and then he rolled to his back.

Grinning, I found his hand next to mine and intertwined our fingers. "I'm glad you came."

"Me too."

CHAPTER EIGHT

"Right, well, I'll buzz you when I'm on my way to get you in the morning, Ethan." Sean smiled as Ethan and I climbed out of his rental car. The men had exchanged phone numbers while waiting for the hire car to pick us up from the harbor.

"Thanks, Sean. See you in the morning."

Giving Sean a wave, I led Ethan inside the place I'd been renting for the past eight years. Directly inside was the open plan living area that looked out to the southwest with great views of Lanai. Plonking my keys and bag down on the kitchen bench, I went to the stacker doors and slid them all the way open, letting in the ocean breeze and opening the house to the patio and plunge pool with an infinity edge.

Turning back, I smiled at Ethan, who was taking everything in. "Can I get you a drink?"

"Water, please. We don't drink much on duty to minimize the need to leave the cockpit."

Going to the fridge, I grabbed out the filter jug and poured two glasses of water. Handing one to Ethan, I grabbed up my backpack.

"I'm going to start packing in the bedroom. Make yourself at home. Take a swim, there should still be some food in the cupboard if you're hungry, and I have Netflix if you want to watch some television."

"Jess." Taking my hand, Ethan met my eyes. Taking the glass out of my hand, he set it on the bench next to his already empty one. Smoothing his palm over my cheek, Ethan slid it into my hair and pulled me closer. Using his hand to control my face, Ethan pressed his lips to mine, pinching until I fell into the kiss and our tongues tasted one another.

Dropping my bag to the floor, I moaned when my back hit the front of the fridge, and Ethan hoisted me up to have my legs around his waist. Kissing across my collarbone, Ethan assisted my dress strap to fall down my arm, and then his hand was pulling my swimwear down to expose my breast to him. Latching on, Ethan sucked, kissed, and nibbled my breast until I tightened my thighs around him and groaned his name.

"Where's the bedroom?" Ethan muttered as his mouth returned to my lips.

"Last door at the end of the hall." Lavishing Ethan with kisses, I nibbled his lips as he carried me down the hall. "Condoms are in the bedside table," I panted as Ethan pushed through the door into the master bedroom. Dropping my legs, I pulled my dress over my head while Ethan opened the drawer and found our protection.

Yes, we'd had unprotected sex before, but I still wasn't on the pill, and who the hell knew where his dick had been since. *'Don't think about that,'* I scolded myself. All but tearing my swimwear off, I dropped to my knees and relieved Ethan of his shorts while he yanked his shirt over his head.

Taking Ethan's big thick dick in hand, I licked the tip and loved the way he trembled and groaned. Fingers entwining in my hair, Ethan guided my mouth down his length, his brilliant blue eyes watching me bob on his cock, licking and sucking with enthusiasm for having him here and ready to fuck me.

Gripping my hair after only a few minutes, Ethan pulled me away and handed me the condom. Rolling it on, I smiled at the noises he made, then I found my feet and stood up to face him. Wrapping his arms around me, Ethan grabbed my ass as his lips assailed my neck. "I want to fuck you so hard, Jess. I've missed you so much."

Grinning, I lifted my eyes to the ceiling thanking whatever gods existed. "Please."

Falling to the bed together, I spread my thighs, and Ethan wasted no time getting between them. Ready as I was, Ethan's cock slipped right into place, and then he shoved into me as he moved us further across the bed.

Gripping his muscular shoulders, I bit my lip as my body thrilled with the way Ethan slid his body in and out of mine, adding a slight rotation of his hips as he did. Wrapping my thighs around Ethan, it took me less than a minute to be walking the tightrope of orgasm.

Feeling the change in my body, Ethan dropped his face to my breast, using his hand to pull the nipple into this mouth. The sucking made my sex clench, and a second later, I was there. "Oh, God, Ethan, I've missed you so much," I cried out as I came.

Grunting, Ethan thrust hard and fast, his cock swelling and pulsing as he gave out a yell of his own. Shivering above me, Ethan hung his head, holding his weight for several minutes while I wound my hips to draw out both our climaxes.

"Fuck!" Holding the condom in place, Ethan fell to the bed beside me, his breath just as rough as mine.

Lying there, we stared at the ceiling, enjoying the moment. Turning my head, I met Ethan's bright blue eyes and smiled lazily. Rolling towards me, Ethan kissed me slow but deep, enjoying my taste in our languid afterglow.

When Ethan fell back again, he covered his face and swore again under his breath. It made me chuckle. Sitting up, Ethan looked me over, caressed a hand over me, then he got up and went into the ensuite. Biting my lip, I propped myself up on my elbows and smiled where I could see Ethan tremble as he removed the condom and disposed of it. "So, was it worth the boat ride?"

Grinning at me, Ethan gazed at me lustfully. "Join me in the shower?" Turning, he started the shower.

Smirking, I grabbed another condom from the drawer and went to join him. Seeing the fresh packet, Ethan scoffed. "You remember I'm exhausted, right?"

"You remember I'm not on the pill, right?" I replied, stepping into his hands and the warm water.

Kissing me slowly, Ethan slipped his hands over my curves, feeling all of me as the rainmaker showerhead poured over us. "Hmm, good point."

Stepping back, Ethan grabbed the condom, ripped it open, and rolled it on to his hardened cock, then he was under the water, lifting me to his waist as he kissed me passionately.

Holding me up, Ethan took his time to fuck me slow and deep this time. Wrapping my arms around his neck, I kissed Ethan until it got too much, then I clung to him as I came again. Holding me tight, Ethan squirmed his hips, letting me finish. Lifting my face, Ethan kissed me intensely, then he lowered my legs and turned me to face the wall.

Holding me to the front of him, Ethan caressed my stomach and breasts, his mouth sucking at my neck, rubbing his hardness between the crevice of my cheeks. "Hands to the wall, Jess."

Pressing my hands to the wall, I was surprised when Ethan lifted me, his cock finding my entrance and sliding into me as he lowered me. Moaning, I bit my lip at the unbelievable feeling of Ethan's hands and mouth worshipping me as he fucked me slowly.

Dropping his hand to my pelvis, Ethan rubbed my clit, his other arm pinning me to his chest while the hand massaged and teased my nipple. Throwing my head back, I grabbed the back of Ethan's neck and held on tight as I came for him again.

"God, I love making you come." Letting go, Ethan grabbed my hips and started fucking me hard and fast. Gasping, I lifted onto my toes and pushed against the wall to hold myself against his thrusts. Fingers digging into my hips as my sex clenched around him once more, Ethan grunted hard, and as I felt him swell and start to pulse, I cried out one last time as Ethan yelled, his voice echoing off the bathroom tiles.

Panting, Ethan helped me straighten up and hugged me, his cock still inside me as he turned my face to my shoulder so he could kiss me. "Thank you for inviting me to come here with you, but I am literally drained now, Jess." Smirking at his reference, I lifted enough to release him from my body, and then I turned to face him. "The bed is comfortable. Sleep as long as you need. I'll pack up in other rooms, so I don't disturb you." Pecking a kiss to his lips, I went to step out.

Grabbing me around the waist, Ethan wheeled me back in for one more toe-curling kiss, and then he let me slip away from him. Grabbing a towel, I dried quickly and went out to the room to dress. Folding the bedding back to make it welcoming, I placed a fresh towel for Ethan in the bathroom.

Coming back out to the kitchen, I made sure I was out of sight, then sighed and leaned on the bench. My God, what that man did to my body was magical, but he touched me in a more profound way than just the physical, and that part of me ached a little for even thinking this could be a great casual set up.

Closing my eyes, I exhaled hard and turned to the fridge. Filling up Ethan's glass of water, I took it in to the bedroom for him. The shower was off, Ethan standing in front of the vanity, hands leaning on the counter and his head bowed as if he was experiencing the same sensation that I did in the kitchen. Swallowing, I left the water on the bedside table and left the room, pulling the door shut so my noise didn't disturb his sleep.

Back in the kitchen, I told Google to play me my jam, the playlist I used for house cleaning, turned the volume down, then started with the pantry. Leaving some items on the bench for snacks later and breakfast tomorrow, I sorted the rest into either transport or discard piles.

It was a matter of just collecting the few photos of my friends and family scattered around in the lounge room. Putting the small pile of photo frames on the kitchen bench to box later, I raced to my backpack when my phone started ringing.

"Hey," I panted as I answered.

"Did I interrupt?" Sean asked.

Smirking, I moved out onto the patio and sat on the bench chair for the outdoor table. "No. Ethan is sleeping, so I raced to get the phone before it woke him. How'd the run down with Mayla go?"

"Good. You trained her well. She's still a little cautious and wanted to run a list of her ideas by me."

"Did you give her the list Holly left?"

"Yes. It pulled apart Mayla's ideas, but I worked through it with her and made some compromise suggestions. I know each new manager likes to put their stamp on things, but I don't want her undoing any of your good work either. She needs to take the time and get the hang of being in charge first."

"Being the manager is a pair of new shoes you need to break in. You eventually get comfortable, and it all just works."

"Trust a woman to refer to shoes," Sean laughed. "Anyway, I have some boxes that were ready to go out to recycling. Are you okay for me to drop them up now, or want me to wait until tomorrow?"

Glancing back over my shoulder, I made sure Ethan wasn't up yet. "Whenever you are ready. I'd rather get everything boxed tonight and have tomorrow for saying goodbye."

"I gather you'll be riding tomorrow?"

"It was the plan."

"Would it be okay with you if I invite Ethan for a game of golf after surfing? I thought I'd take the boat over to the Manele golf course on Lanai."

"Seriously, are you trying to seduce him? Surfing and golf are probably Ethan's favorite things to do in his free time."

"What about you?"

Screwing up my nose, I shook my head. "Golf is so not my thing."

Chuckling, Sean took a moment. "I meant being one of his favorite things to do."

Remembering the intense fun we had on arrival, I groaned. My hormones were keen to go back into the room and see how many more times I could come before Ethan passed out from exhaustion.

"Okay, Jessie girl. I'll drop the boxes off in the next hour. Need anything else?"

"Nah, I'm about to take a walk down the shops and pick up some food for dinner and the next two mornings."

"You're cooking?" Sean sounded strangled.

"Yeah, I thought just dinner here would be nice tonight. Enjoy the views and that since we are going out tomorrow night." The truth was, I realized how much I loved this place and wanted to enjoy it a bit more before I gave it up.

"What are you cooking?"

"I don't know yet. Why?"

"Because on the rare occasion I've been blessed with your cooking, it's been awesome, Jess, and I'm jealous that I'm not getting invited. You rarely cook. I feel like I'm missing out, and this guy is getting spoiled."

Snickering, I shook my head. "Well, when I get my new place, I promise to cook you a meal."

"I'm holding you to that," Sean huffed. "Okay, I'll be there in just over an hour."

"See you then. If I'm not here, just leave the boxes on the porch for me." Hanging up, I sighed. Going back inside, I left a note for Ethan, grabbed my backpack and keys, and went to get supplies.

CHAPTER NINE

"Something smells great," Ethan praised as he wrapped his arms around me from behind.

Plating up the homemade lasagna, I smiled and tilted my head for his neck kisses. "Hungry?"

"Starving. My belly rumbling woke me, and now I know why. It could smell this."

"We're eating outside. I have wine, but if you prefer beer, there is some in the fridge. Water is already on the table." Grabbing the plates, I went out to the patio table I'd set up for dinner. I'd set our places side-by-side, so we could both enjoy the view of the sunset.

Taking the seat beside me, Ethan poured us both a water and then the wine. "How did the packing go?"

"Good. All done except the bedroom." Stabbing the salad, I cut some of the lasagna and heaped it on the fork with the greens.

Tilting his head and bunching his brow, Ethan didn't comment on it and just put a forkful of lasagna in his mouth. Pausing, he lifted his brows and moaned as he swallowed. "Holy shit, Jess. That's the best lasagna I've ever eaten. Where did you learn to cook like this?"

"Lou's mother was a private chef. She should have been one of those famous names you know and associate with cooking, but how many Michelin chefs are females? Anyway, she always took us girls on school holidays. As a teenager, I would go to Grandma Lottie's after school to avoid being home alone with Sharnie on the days I didn't have training. As a kid, I'd watch her cook. By the time I was a teen, I was fairly proficient, so she would get me to help with whatever meal she was making her clients."

"So, you are an awesome cook."

Cheeks heating at Ethan's appreciation of my culinary abilities, I set up another mouthful. "Don't get too excited. I rarely cook."

"Why?"

"The hours I work. I'm too tired to bother most days. I usually get something from the kitchen on my way home or heat a soup pouch or make a sandwich."

Peering back at the kitchen counter, Ethan eyed the food pile. "Or two-minute noodles." Smirking, I lifted and dropped my shoulder. "What about lunch on the weekends?"

"All depends on where I am. Quite often, I go hiking or snorkeling with friends in the afternoon, so we either eat out, or I grab something quick on my way home from the stables. If I'm home, then I'll probably order in unless there is someone else to cook for as well." I raised a brow as I took a sip of the wine. "You?"

"If I'm home, I prefer a home-cooked meal. It's important to keep fit and healthy. We get medicals every six months to make sure we are fit to fly, and after nine years in the Air Force, it's just a habit for me to take care of myself." Taking a sip of his wine, Ethan considered before scooping up another forkful. "When I'm working, we get the same meals as business class, and then hotel food at our layovers, so when I'm home, I prefer to eat home-cooked meals."

"I can understand that. I occasionally yearn for a good roast, or bangers and mash, or something simple but homely. It just comes down to time."

Finishing his plate, Ethan moaned. "That was truly delicious."

"There's more in the oven if you want it."

"That's all going to depend on if there is dessert?"

"There is, but it's not edible," I smirked as I sucked the fork prongs from my lips and lifted an eyebrow.

Grinning, Ethan stood up and put his mouth to my ear. "You are entirely edible." Whistling, he took his plate back to the kitchen and served himself another slice.

When Ethan came back out, I'd finished my meal and happily drank my wine watching the sunset. "I thought after I clean up, we could go for a swim in the pool?"

"Hmm." Ethan considered, chewing his food. "Or, we could clean up, fuck each other's brains out, and then swim to cool down?"

Loving his idea, I held in a laugh that he still remembered me saying those exact words to him after all these months. "God, I was such a bitch to you that night. I'm surprised you even bothered with me again."

Shaking his head, Ethan finished his wine. "You were drunk and scared about letting anyone close to you again. I wasn't much better, in all honesty, and I wasn't going to come looking for you again. When we ran into each other that afternoon, I realized that my friendship with your family meant that we had to end on good terms."

Swallowing hard at his wording, I couldn't help thinking that's what this trip was. "I wouldn't have blamed you. I have more baggage than I could take on a flight, and the excess fees would bankrupt me. Like I said to Lou, I live in another country now. If he never mentioned you to me again, I wouldn't know if you still hung out. Hell, he'd never mentioned you before Sharnie's wedding anyway."

"But he talks to you about me now?"

"Not really. I mean, the other week, you came up because Sharnie was there for dinner, and I asked how you and Greg were. Bringing you up on Monday, telling me that you'd talked about me, that's not like my dad. It told me it was important for him to volunteer that information." Shifting in my seat, I refilled my wine. "It's why I was surprised you came. I thought once you knew I was serious about staying for good, that I'd bought a house, you'd wash your hands of me. You pretty much gave that impression when I told you too."

Refilling his water, Ethan turned to face me on the bench. "I sort of figured that. The thing is, I was beyond exhausted that night we spoke, Jess. I wasn't pissed off about you buying a house here. I think it's great you are finally getting a new home, not that I wouldn't have loved this to be your home because this place is impressive."

"It's out of my price range."

"It's out of mine. Pilots do not earn as much as people think."

Frowning, I circled my finger around the top of my glass. "So, you're happy I'm not coming back?"

"Jess, I didn't want you to leave, but another part of me was glad there was always an expiration date. If that makes sense?"

Understanding what Ethan meant, I chuckled. "Yeah, it does. We aren't ready for what started between us."

Dropping his head, Ethan took a breath. "Your father asked me if things were getting serious between us and warned me you were house hunting here. Maybe he thought I could sway your mind, but I think your family seriously underestimates what a deterrent your twin is. If you think, after learning everything Sharnie put you through—the way she spoke to you at the barbecue—that I would expect you to come home for me, you're mistaken. No one is ever going to be good enough to bring you home and have to suffer that in your life."

Taking my free hand in his, Ethan met my eyes. "Does it disappoint me that it means I have to let you go? Yes, more than I can express. But I know if you gave up what you have here to come home, every time your sister hurt you, you'd blame me. Eventually, you would hate me, and it would break us both. I can't give my heart to someone only for them to break it again, and neither can you."

Taking a deep breath, I swallowed to keep the tears at bay. "So, this is goodbye?"

Ethan's forehead bunched, then he let go of my hand. "No. I know it contradicts everything I just said, but I can't say goodbye to you, Jess. Not for good. I tried. Trust me; the last few months have been hell. I've wanted to talk to you every day, to touch you and kiss you and fuck you all over my place. I can't climb in my bed and think of anyone but you. When you asked me to visit you, I didn't know how to react. My first instinct was to jump a plane straight here, but the sensible part of me keeps telling me this can't work. But when you said goodbye to me the other night, I needed to come here and have this talk face to face."

Blowing out a breath, I looked out at the lights of Lanai; the sun had set while we ate. "I get what you are saying. I really do. I'm just as confused. I want you in every way. Am I ready for a long-term commitment? No. I know that without a doubt, and I don't know how to date long-distance." Getting up, I stacked our empty plates. "We're friends now. We just happen to be friends that enjoy sex together. Let's not overcomplicate it." Picking up our empty wine glasses with my free hand, I took the dishes to the kitchen and packed the dishwasher.

As I put the leftovers away for my lunch tomorrow, Ethan brought the water jug and water glasses inside. "Can I help wash up?"

"No, it'll all go in the dishwasher," I answered as I stacked the baking pan next to the plates.

"Jess, I don't want you to feel like I'm using you for sex, and after that talk, I feel that it would come off that way if we followed our agreed agenda for tonight."

Shit, now he was backing out of fucking me brainless. No, that I wasn't having. Standing straight to face him, I met Ethan's eyes. "That's strange because I have no issue with you thinking I'm using you for sex."

Eyes widening, Ethan moved a step closer. "You don't?"

Smirking, I pressed go on the dishwasher. "Wouldn't it make this more comfortable? Your horny, I'm randy, we are mutual horny single friends who are very sexually compatible. Wouldn't it be easier to approach you being here as friends scratching each other's itches and hanging out in-between the fuck marathons? Bonus, you get free accommodation on one of the most beautiful islands in the world, and my best friend is going to take you to one of the best surf beaches, and golfing on an island."

"Golf?"

"Oh, yeah, Sean called while you were asleep to check my plans tomorrow and ask if you'd like to go out to Lanai for a game of golf. I'm going to be riding all morning, so I said yes."

"Jesus, this is turning into the best holiday I've had in a long time."

Moving a step closer still, I wrapped my arms around Ethan's neck. "See, flying out to Hawaii worked out well."

Wrapping his arms around my waist, Ethan held me tight against him, so I could feel how hard he was through his shorts. "I don't care where we are, Jess. If I'm naked with you, and fucking you, then it's heaven."

Smiling as Ethan crushed his mouth to mine, I squealed a little when he picked me up suddenly, throwing me over his shoulder.

"Condoms are in the bedroom," Ethan growled as he squeezed my ass.

Holiday fling. That was the safest way for Ethan and me to move forward. A safe, gorgeous man who could fuck me brilliantly and would leave before I could get sick of him. Sexy, secure, and sensible. I would be his perfect layover, and he was my great last weekend in Maui.

CHAPTER TEN

"So, tell me about Ethan," Mayla spoke into the comfortable quiet between us midway through our last ride together. She'd met Ethan at the farewell dinner last night and given me 'explain yourself' eyes all night, especially when Ethan put his arm around my shoulders or whispered in my ear.

"He's a pilot."

"Did you meet on the way home or the way to Australia?"

"Neither. He was the best man at my sister's wedding."

"And now he's come to help you pack up and move to Oahu?"

Shaking my head, I smiled at Mayla. "No. He flew over for work Thursday night and came to visit. It just happened he arrived as we were getting ready to head here."

"And where is he this morning?"

"Surfing with Sean again." Smiling at the way Mayla's mouth fell open, I resisted laughing at her. "Yesterday they went surfing together, and then went a round of golf on Lanai. They seem to get along well. I think in the future, Ethan will come to visit Sean instead of me."

Laughing, Mayla shook her head. "I don't get you and Sean. You're perfect for each other. You should just settle down with each other already."

"Sean and I have never been lovers."

"Right!" Mayla nodded her head, then gave me a wink.

Pulling my horse up, I patted its neck. "I'm serious, Mayla. We've never even kissed. We are just friends. I don't think we could be anything more if we tried at this point. It would just be too awkward and like banging your brother or something."

Gaping at me, Mayla stared. "Not even a kiss? Are you serious?"

"Deadly."

Blinking a couple of times, Mayla stared out at the trail ahead. "But you've kissed Ethan, right?"

"Oh, God! I've done so much more than just kiss Ethan. The guy is a sex god. He started as a one-night-stand. Then it turned out he was close friends with my dad as well, and we kept seeing each other."

Laughing, Mayla juggled her eyebrows. "Sex god? Yeah, he looks it too. And he's followed you back?"

"Well, not really. We kept in contact, and I invited him to come and visit."

Watching me, Mayla smirked. "And that was a bad thing?"

"No." Shaking my head, I glanced at Mayla and sighed. "It's just hard to think about him leaving again so soon."

Eyebrows in her hair, Mayla struggled to close her mouth. "I don't think you have ever said that about one of your lovers before."

"Well, none of them were sex gods." I winked, then squeezed my thighs to get up some speed for the open plain ahead.

After a tearful farewell at the dock, we set sail back to Oahu. Unlike the first trip, Ethan was wide awake and deep in conversation with Sean about surfing and golfing worldwide. Since this wasn't a conversation for me, I retreated to the front deck lounge, stripped down to my bikini, and laid down with my book again.

After thirty minutes, Ethan joined me, lying beside me and closing his eyes. "You okay?"

"Sure. Why?"

"I got the sense it was hard for you to leave that place for good."

Smiling on the memories, I kissed the tip of his shoulder. "I had a lot of years there. Each time you leave a place, you leave friends, memories, and places you love behind. The longer you're there, the harder it is."

Turning his face to me, Ethan shaded his eyes from the sun. "I can't say I've ever really moved overseas. Even in the RAAF, I made good friends, and they became like my family."

"Did you stay in contact with them when you left?"

"Most. Half of us all work for the same company still."

Nodding, I went back to my book. "As you said. I found good friends, and they became like family. And that house was an amazing place to live. My new place is nowhere near as nice."

"So, you're mourning the very nice accommodations?"

Smirking, I turned the page. "Totally."

"I've heard great sex is a fantastic remedy for grief."

"Well, you may have to come and visit again to help me mourn my loss when I'm in my new place. You might need a few more days, though, so that I can grieve all over my new place, multiple times."

Lips twitching, Ethan put his arms behind his head, stretching out that very fit surfer's bod. Licking my lips, I glanced up to Sean and then focused back on my book.

After we docked in Oahu, Ethan and Sean took my boxes to Sean's car to head south with him. Sean was going to keep them at the hotel until my house was ready.

"Should we get dinner before I leave?" Sean asked quietly. "Or would you prefer it just be the two of you?"

"You sailed me over to save me money and helped move my stuff. I think dinner can be shared," I assured him. "What do you think, Ethan?"

Smiling, Ethan came up beside me and took my hand. "Of course. You can tell me where to surf in the morning."

After dinner, Sean hugged me and told me he'd see me in a few days to start the interviews, and then he farewelled Ethan as if they were old friends. "I think he liked you," I murmured to Ethan as we headed back to Sean's cottage.

"He seems like a nice guy. Did you two used to date?"

"Sean was the first guy I gave time to after Ben. I thought he'd be a good way to get back on the proverbial horse. Five minutes into our first and only date, we quickly realized a romantic situation didn't suit us. Our dinner turned into a job interview when his Maui manager quit during our meal. I had to do my two weeks training here at the Cassidy, and Sean and I became friends. Over the years, he became my best friend. Sean's like that with all of us. His managers are like his family here."

Getting to the beach bungalows path, Ethan looked toward the beach. "Want to take a stroll before we go back?"

"Sounds lovely." The moon was full overhead as we strolled along the beach in front of the bungalows, hand in hand.

"So, I was thinking," Ethan led. "What if I tried to get Hawaii on my roster once a month?"

My heartbeat hard in my chest. Yes, it would be wonderful to have Ethan there regularly, but would once a month be too little or too much? "Doesn't that start to complicate things?"

"As you said, two horny friends enjoying each other's company between fuck frenzies. Once a month isn't a commitment, but it would allow us to explore where this could go from a safe distance."

"Like a testing stage. What if we find monthly leaves us wanting?"

"Then we talk about the cure." Coming to a stop, Ethan turned to face me, his fingers caressing my cheek. "You are the first woman who I've desired for more than a weekend in a long time, Jess. If I leave tomorrow and just leave things open, we'll go back to online video chats randomly when we are both available, and we'll both be frustrated with that. Eventually, it will peter out, and we will both regret not chasing this thing between us."

Swallowing hard, I stared up into Ethan's eyes. "So, you'll fly in, fly out once a month for how long before we reevaluate if it's working for us?"

"No time limit. We'll know if it's going well or not and naturally shift with whatever direction it's taking us."

"You'll stop coming if it's not."

"We'll make excuses if either of us wants out," Ethan smirked. "I've been the relationship avoider for a long time, Jess. I know how people like you and I work."

Blowing out a breath, I stepped out to start walking again. If we were just friends getting off, then I couldn't expect him to give up his weekends of fun.

"Jess? Tell me what you are thinking."

Licking my lips, I eyed Ethan. He was gorgeous in the moonlight. "You say there is no commitment, but organizing to see each other even once a month requires some commitment."

"It will once I put my hand up to do this run. You should know that sometimes the roster might have me flying here more often, or not for the full weekend. I'm senior enough to ask for a run, but not enough to get set flights. A senior officer will retire later this year. At that point, I'll go up a level in seniority and be able to start asking for set flights then. That gives us time to try this before I demand the run regularly."

"What about Greg?"

"He's a senior first officer, so he can ask to be appointed to the majority of my flights, and he'll get it. That's what he's done for years now. It will just be a different direction."

"It will mean weekends away from his family."

"Which he'll make up for when he is home. That's nothing new to how it is now." Walking a few steps quietly, Ethan brought us to a stop again. "Look, you don't have to decide tonight. I've got another week before they look at the roster for next month, so just think about it and tell me if you want to give this a try sometime this week."

"It's not that I don't want to see you, Ethan. I do, and my first instinct was to say yes. But a few days ago I thought we were over, that you didn't want to know about me anymore. Then I thought this weekend was a goodbye. The goalposts keep changing, and it's happening quickly, and I'm getting a little scared of it."

Smiling down at me, Ethan lowered his face and pinched my lips. "That is no different to how I felt seeing you at Greg's wedding. At first, I kept thinking that I just need her one more time. Then it was for the length of your holiday, but as our last day came around, I knew it wasn't enough. I need more of you, Jess. I can't say how much yet because you're not the only one scared here, but I can't say goodbye, get on a plane tomorrow, and wonder when, or if, I will get to see you again. I need to know there will be more for now."

God, he was saying my thoughts back to me again. "Okay."

"Okay?"

My smile lifted into my cheeks. "Let's give this trial a chance. I'll give you my new address, and when you come to visit next, I'll have a key waiting for you. That way, if you arrive while I'm at work, you can let yourself in and get some sleep rather than having to come and find me."

Lifting a brow, Ethan grinned. "You're trusting me with a key, already?"

"Shouldn't I?"

Shaking his head, Ethan kissed me heatedly. "Let's get back to the bungalow. I know outdoor sex gets you wet, but I've done the beach thing, and sand is no one's friend."

Smirking, I stepped back and pulled my top over my head. "What about the ocean?" Dropping my skirt, I loved the look on Ethan's face when I turned and ran for the water. Pulling his shirt over his head, Ethan chased after me.

As soon as he was waist-deep, he paused and then threw his shorts back to shore before diving in after me. The waves were gentle here in the protected bay, just enough of a current to keep the water clean. Stopping when the water was chest-deep, I turned and waited for Ethan to catch me.

Reaching me, Ethan pulled me into his arms. Kissing me heatedly, he found the back clip of my swimming top and released it. Moaning as his hand cupped my naked breast, I wrapped my legs around his waist. "What if we get caught?" Ethan asked, eyeing the resort. "You work here."

"We're far enough down the beach that no one will see us," I breathed as his lips kissed over my pulse. "Just pull out, okay?"

"Shit, Jess, we're in the water. Pulling out is not going to protect you. Give me a second." Setting me aside, Ethan floated to his back as he tore a condom open, then rolled it over his thick cock. Righting himself, Ethan pulled me close again, tucking the wrapper in the back of my bottoms as he lifted me to his waist again. Our mouths found each other, working up the heat as our bodies rubbed against each other. Moving my swimwear aside, I guided Ethan's cock to my opening, then pushing down through my butt, I sank my hips.

As Ethan guided me gently over him, I dropped my head back and cursed. He felt so much more extensive here in the water. We didn't rush. We bobbed there in the water, kissing, our bodies moving steadily in time with the gentle sway of the waves. Feeding the heat into a small inferno, lovingly tended and nurtured until my body tightened and I slammed my mouth against Ethan's to cry out when my pleasure took me.

As the waves of ecstasy stole me away, Ethan lost his gentleness and fucked me harder until he was throbbing inside me, his teeth gripping the flesh of my shoulder as he came.

As our breathing evened out, Ethan held me tight to him. "This week, you need to go get on the pill, okay? I want to fuck you spontaneously when I'm here and not have to worry about killing a turtle if I lose the condom."

"That's your only worry?"

"It's the primary one right this second."

Sighing, I rubbed my nose against his. We hadn't discussed the going bare thing, but we'd need to, especially with his philandering. "Can we discuss this later?"

"Sure. Now, stay put until we surface. I'm serious about feeling guilty if I lose this." Laughing while he carried me until the water was only knee-deep, Ethan helped me dismount, then he disposed of our protection responsibly.

CHAPTER ELEVEN

"I'M GOING TO BE LATE FOR WORK," I GIGGLED AS ETHAN PULLED ME back to bed and rolled over me for a second time this morning.

"It's going to be weeks; I need you at least one more time," Ethan susurrated to my breast before he sucked the nipple between his lips.

"Shower," I moaned.

"Soon." Grabbing a condom, Ethan kissed me heatedly as he rolled it on, then he was nudging between my lower lips to find my heat.

Cringing a little on the soreness after another night of intermittent fucking, I groaned as Ethan slid as deep as he could. Then he lifted my legs to his waist and went a little deeper.

"So tight, Jess," Ethan growled as he circled his hips.

Our mouths pinched and licked each other slowly, enjoying the last session for several more weeks. But as much as I wished we could stay there all day, my body was still sensitive from the previous orgasm, so it didn't take long for me to be walking that tightrope again.

Kissing me one more time, Ethan lifted and smiled down at me with the most wicked glint in his eyes. Hooking my knees over his elbows, Ethan forced my legs wide, and then he was pounding me hard.

As big as he was and as deep, I felt it deep in my core. "Fuck, Ethan!" My nails scratched down his arms as my back bowed, and then I was coming harder than I had all weekend.

Falling over me, Ethan chuckled breathlessly, kissing all around my neck and massaging my breasts some more. "God, Jess. I can't get enough of you."

Smiling as he kissed me, I couldn't disagree with the sentiment. "Ditto. But I really do need to get to work."

Falling to the side, Ethan moaned as he withdrew, causing me to suck in a breath on the sensation. Rolling out of bed with a groan, I made my way on unsteady legs to the bathroom to shower. By the time I'd finished washing my hair, Ethan had joined me. Kissing gently, I finished up and gave him the water.

"I need to be at the airport by ten. What time would I need to leave here?" Ethan asked as he came out with the towel around his waist.

Zipping up my tunic dress, I turned to consider him or just admire that gorgeous body. "With the morning traffic heading to Waikiki, it can take two to three hours."

Looking at his watch, Ethan huffed. "I guess I'm leaving now then."

Moving to him, I ran my hands up his chest. "Bonus of my new place. It's not even twenty minutes from the airport. Maybe forty in peak hour traffic."

As Ethan cupped my butt in his hands, I pecked his lips then stepped back before he could wrestle me back to bed. "I'll make you breakfast and organize a car for you. At least you'll be able to sleep for the drive."

Whipping up some eggs out in the kitchen, I soaked the thick-cut bread in it before frying it. "French toast? Why don't I believe this your normal breakfast?"

Glancing at Ethan, my breath caught for a second. He was so hot in his uniform. I seriously needed to peel that off him or have him fuck me still in it. "I quite often have to eat lunch as a snack, so I try and have a big breakfast." Filling two bowls with overnight oats, I then plated up the french toast dusted with cinnamon instead of syrup, a glass of juice, and coffee each.

Sitting down to eat, Ethan eyed me as he loaded his fork. "Can we talk about you going on the pill now?"

"How offended will you be if I say I don't want to have unprotected sex? As in, if on the rare occasion that we have something spontaneous take us, I'm still going to need you to withdraw."

"You're worried about diseases? I told you we have regular medicals."

Licking my lip, I bit it as I took a sip of juice. "You're still going to be fucking other women at times. Things slip through the cracks."

Lifting a brow, Ethan didn't refute the claim. "Okay, but wouldn't the pill help alleviate concern about an unplanned pregnancy?"

Inhaling to get my courage up, I focused on my meal. "I was on the pill when I fell pregnant with Matilda." Unable to look at him, I cringed slightly even bringing it up. "I'm thirty-one. If I go on the pill now, and then we decide we want a family in a year or two, it could be difficult to conceive. I'm already scared I'll never fall pregnant again, more so than I am of an accidental pregnancy. I'd rather use condoms and the withdrawal method on the odd unplanned sexcapade."

Ethan was watching me intently. Taking a long drink of his coffee, he put it down to keep eating. "I haven't changed my mind about marrying again, Jess. If you hope this affair will lead to marriage and kids, you should tell me to leave and never come back. I gave that dream up years ago."

Ouch! "I've never considered marriage and a family with anyone since Ben. But as a female who has engaged in the occasional holiday fuck frenzy, I have made my peace with the fact that a condom may break, that I may conceive accidentally, and if that happened, I would more than likely end up raising a child on my own.

"This is something every female should make themselves comfortable with before letting a man inside them because while modern society is more accepting of a single mother, men's tendency to dump and run has not changed. I'm not hindering my chances of becoming a mother later so that you can fuck me and have it feel better for you. I'm also not going to demand you put a ring on it and stand by me. You've made your positioning quite clear twice now.

"Having said that, I'm not going to be actively trying to get knocked up without your permission either. I have a demanding career that doesn't lend well to raising a family by yourself. I'm just not sabotaging my chances either. If that's an issue for you, well, I guess you've got a week to decide if you still want to see me again." Getting out of my chair, I took my empty dishes to the kitchen.

Slamming the dishwasher shut, I leaned on the bench and exhaled long and controlled. Inhaling again, I turned back to see Ethan frowning as he finished his coffee. "I'm sorry."

Turning his gaze my way, Ethan popped a brow. "Are you?"

Smirking, I bowed my head. "No, not really. I've had eight years to think about these things. While I made my peace with it a long time ago, it's not something I've had to discuss with anyone before. Before this, my 'affairs' have lasted two to three weeks at best. It's not something that comes up in conversation since you're not exactly rushing out to get tested for STDs just for the benefit of riding bareback for a few weeks."

Rubbing his lips together, Ethan finished his coffee and stood up. "I guess not." Carrying over his dishes, Ethan set them down on the bench and took my upper arms in his hands before dropping a kiss on my lips. "I respect your stance. Give me a few days to process what you just laid down, and I'll let you know how I feel about it. I don't want to react impulsively to this. Not with you."

"You prefer unprotected sex?" Definitely going to need that health report if he wanted to keep sleeping together then.

"Actually, I've never seen a woman long enough since my wife left me for it to come up. I've always used condoms, Jess, so you can erase that panicked look from your face. You were the first woman I've been inside of bare in over seven years. Hell, you are the only one I've had in a shower, or pool, or ocean, ever. My ex hated water, so she wasn't into water sports.

"You obviously missed just how well prepared I usually am. The picnic on the clifftop, the ocean last night? I typically have protection on me. That morning in my shower, I arrived home and found you touching yourself, and my brain went haywire, it was so fucking hot. I couldn't believe I did that. I'd forgotten how good it felt.

"Which is why I know I can't go bare with you if you won't let me come inside you, Jess, because it was hard to pull out that day in the shower, and I know it's only going to get harder now that you are more than a weekend of fun."

Wow! Okay, that was more than I expected to hear. "Okay."

"Okay?"

"Take the time you need to process it. I'm not going anywhere." Glancing at the clock, I swore under my breath. "Except to work. I really need to go."

Smirking, Ethan kissed me heatedly, pulling me into his arms, so my body molded to him, my nipples hardening at the feel of his body pressing against mine. Weaving my fingers into Ethan's hair, I kissed him with everything I was, in the hope it would be enough to make him come and see me again.

Closing out the kiss, Ethan continued to hold me for a long fraction of a minute, licking the taste of me from his lips as we gathered our breath. "I'll go get my bag." Slowly releasing me, Ethan stepped back and adjusted his pants around the rather obvious erection. "Damn, Jess. What you do to me." With a chuckle, Ethan headed to the bedroom.

We walked hand in hand up to the resort, silence and small smiles passing between us. Ethan handed off his bag to the waiting driver at the entrance, then pulled me into a tight hug. "I'll call you in a few days."

"Okay." Holding on tight, I breathed in the scent of him. Shifting to meet Ethan's gaze, I stared into his deep blue eyes. "I kind of hate this part when it comes to you."

Caressing my face, Ethan pecked my lips and stepped back. "Ditto." Moving away, he handed the driver a fifty. "I need to sleep on the way. Play something soothing and keep it quiet for me."

"Yes, sir."

Watching Ethan dropping into the back seat, I felt my stomach drop with him. I'd never struggled to say goodbye to a guy before. Why was it always so hard with Ethan? Waving once more as he pulled away, I smiled at the kiss he blew me, then he was disappearing down the drive. Closing my eyes, I heaved a sigh. Now, the waiting game began.

Nearly three hours later, I got a text from Ethan.

<E>: Sitting in the airport lounge having a second breakfast. I got a good sleep on the way here; it helped me think clearer. So, I have a compromise. Let's just fuck bare, and if we have a kid, so be it. Hell, if Greg and Sharnie can breed, why can't we? We can't do any worse a job.

Smirking, I shook my head.

<Jess>: I think you need more sleep. Fly safe

<E>: I'm in the jumpseat, just getting a lift back, so the passengers are in safe hands. You're probably right. We should get a plant first. If we don't kill it, then we can throw caution to the wind, and I can fuck your brains out everywhere and anywhere you want.

<Jess>: I'm sensing a theme to where your thinking is, and I believe it's all happening below your belt.

<E>: *Wink* Talk soon.

Closing the phone, I caught myself smiling. Damn, what that man did to my hormones. Taking a clearing breath, I got back to the reports on my desk, visions of Ethan and I screwing all over my new house already in my head. God, I hoped he didn't change his mind.

CHAPTER TWELVE

"Well, that's all the questions we have for you. Do you have any for us?" I asked the former manager of housekeeping at the Ko Olina resort. She was already gray in her early fifties, but she wore it with a class and sophistication I barely managed with my natural hair color at thirty-one.

"When will you be making your decision?"

"We hope to make offers by the end of the week, with a view for all staff to start training in three."

Licking her lips, the manager eyed Sean, then set her eyes back on me. "I'm aware the current head of housekeeping for Cassidy Turtle Beach has applied for the role here in Ko Olina. She lives down here and is hoping to reduce her travel. It happens that I live at Waialua, so Turtle Beach would be closer to home for me. So, if Jean is successful at getting this role, I'd like to be considered to replace her at Turtle Beach."

"Of course," Sean assured her, writing a note on his interview sheet.

"Thank you." Getting up, Talin offered her hand to me. "It was lovely to meet you both.

"Thank you. We'll be in touch soon," I smiled as I shook Talin's hand, and once Sean had done the same, she left.

Sighing back into my seat, I looked over my notes. "She's good."

"Yes, she is. Right down to being aware that Jean stood a good chance of stealing her job here and trying to jump ahead to interview for that role as well." Checking his watch, Sean gathered his interview sheets into a folder. "We've run overtime, but that was the last for the day. Let's have dinner and discuss our final preferences. I can't think when I'm this hungry."

Packing up, I followed Sean out. Fifteen minutes later, we were seated at a table in Roy's in the Ko Olina golf course. After ordering, Sean pulled out the folder and set aside his preferred candidates sheet. "Okay, let's talk managers. Who did you like for your assistant manager?"

"Can we start with all the other roles and come back to that one? I have issues with all the applicants, but they all had different positives, so I'd like to hash that one out with you. The others weren't as difficult for me to have a preference."

"Okay, Let's start with your head of housekeeping?"

"Jean."

Shaking his head, Sean wrote her name on the sheet. "I knew you were going to choose her."

"I've already worked with her, and she's good. But I think you should give Talin Turtle Beach and bring her in to start next week so that Jean can train her up. That way, she'll have two weeks with Jean before she moves here."

"I liked Bronwyn as the second option." He wrote Talin and Bronwyn's names in the second position.

"Not enough experience."

"I could have said that about you when I hired you."

"It's not just years. Bronwyn's been a manager for three months at a three-star inn. She's not in the same league as Jean and Talin, who both have extensive service at four stars or above resorts. If Bronwyn wants to step into this circle, she needs to start at a lower level as a floor team leader."

Lifting an eyebrow, Sean made a note. "Okay, we'll come back to Bronwyn after we interview teams tomorrow. How does that sound?"

Nodding my head in agreement, I picked up my glass of water and took a drink. We'd interviewed for the management roles today. Tomorrow was the housekeeping and kitchen staff, and Friday would be front of house. Taking a mouthful of his water, Sean lifted his eyes to me again. "Manager of Cuisine?" And so it continued, even while we ate our meals. By the time we'd finished eating, we had our preference list completed.

"So, how did you leave things with the pilot?" Sean sat back smiling. "Will we be seeing him again soon?"

Exhaling hard, I picked up the glass of wine Sean had ordered me. "He talked about changing his roster to include the occasional flight to Hawaii."

Brows drawing together, Sean tilted his head. "Occasional?"

"He doesn't want a relationship. It's sex between friends, that's it. So, yes, occasional."

Sitting forward, Sean assessed me. "And you're okay with that?"

"It makes sense. I don't know what I want yet. I just know I don't want to end things either." Licking my lips, I smirked. "And hey, occasional hot weekends with a guy I know leaves me very happy is better than the random one to two weeks every couple of years I've made do with until now."

Forehead heavy, Sean shook his head. "If you say so."

"What? You're the one who insisted I invite him to visit," I reminded him. "What were you expecting to happen?"

"More than an occasional booty call. Seriously, Jess, that's all you want from this guy?"

Inhaling deeply, I stared at my wine glass. "That's all that's available."

"Bullshit! I saw the way you two looked at each other, how just seeing you smile affected him; there is more than sex between you."

Yeah, but that's the most either of us was willing to push it as well. More than sex, less than whatever it was Sean found with Holly. "You're right. There is also half the Pacific Ocean, cheating exes, and some fucked up family history. Ethan's made it very clear he's not interested in a long-term commitment, but he also can't bring himself to say goodbye to me any more than I can. So, this works for us. It will either evolve into more or dissolve into nothing, but it's our starting point."

Reaching across the table, I put my hand on Sean's. "You had over three weeks straight with Holly to work out that she was the one you wanted for the rest of your life. Ethan and I haven't even managed a week together."

Closing his eyes on the reminder of his loss, Sean covered my hand and squeezed it. "You're right. I'm sorry. I just don't want to see you get your heart broken again."

Knowing it came from a place of caring and empathy, I wasn't angry with Sean. "I know."

"Have you at least heard from him since he left?"

"A few messages." That they happened before he got on the plane and that Ethan had been radio silent since then didn't bear mentioning. With the time difference and our busy jobs, our communication was sporadic since I returned to Hawaii. No need to go looking for something more there as well.

Heaving a big sigh, Sean averted his eyes. "Well, whatever the arrangement, as long as you are happy, then I'm happy for you."

God, I hated how depressed he sounded. "Should we get out of here? We have another full day of interviews tomorrow."

"Sure."

When I climbed into bed, I checked my messages. Still nothing from Ethan, but it had only been three days. Maybe he'd decided it wasn't worth his while. Blowing out a breath, I decided to break the silence.

\<Jess\>: Missing your cock. I wish it were here inside me now.

He would be in bed asleep by now if he were home. Turning out the light, I lay down and stared at the ceiling. I really did wish Ethan was here. Double-blinking when my phone screen lit up, I picked it up.

\<E\>: I wish I was inside you right now too.

Smirking, I started typing.

\<Jess\>: Where are you that you're awake?

\<E\>: London. We flew the direct flight from Perth here.

\<Jess\>: That's a long flight.

\<E\>: It's a seventeen-hour flight. Add on prep and post-arrival work, and it's over twenty hours. We can only fly ten hours straight, requiring two cockpit crews. We got flown over

---

for the second shift. Maximum layover means we get to do some sightseeing.

\<Jess\>: Wow.

A few minutes ticked on by before he replied.

\<E\>: BTW. I didn't tell Lou I was there last weekend.

Chewing my lip, I considered I'd missed my Sunday talk with dad and would need to explain that.

\<Jess\>: Is that your way of asking me not to mention you?

\<E\>: I'd appreciate it.

Inhaling deep, I closed my eyes and took a moment to steady myself.

\<Jess\>: Sure. Not a problem. Just be aware that he tends to keep tabs on where you guys fly. I think he likes to imagine going to those places himself. If you start not telling him, he might get suss.

I'd never lied to my dad. I didn't want to start now.

\<Jess\>: If it's about seeing me, just tell him I wasn't in town. I'll have to explain that I missed our call on Sunday because I was in Maui anyway. So, it'll cover you.

A few more minutes.

\<E\>: Thanks. *smiley-face*

\<Jess\>: It was nice seeing you again.

Fifteen minutes went by without a reply. Blowing out a breath, I typed one last message.

\<Jess\>: Anyway, I've spent all day in interviews and have another two days of them to prep for early in the morning. I should get some sleep. Take care. Enjoy the sightseeing.

Setting the phone back on my nightstand, I turned it screen-down so it didn't wake me and snuggled down in bed. The air was muggy tonight, summer well and truly in effect. Not that it ever got really hot here, but the humidity could be a bit much sometimes.

Tossing and turning for a while, I eventually gave up sleeping. Grabbing a large glass of water, I took the folder with the CVs for tomorrow's interviews out on the balcony and read through them again, making fresh notes. The new hotel was beautiful and staying there the next few nights was a test run. Sean was in the penthouse apartment next door, probably sound asleep.

Finished going over the applications, I set them aside and relaxed back to look out at the view. Fourteen stories up, it was all dark ocean. There was some light below, around the pathways on the grounds, but it was reasonably dim this far up.

Banging on the door woke me up to see the sun was up. Frowning, I sat up on the sunbed and groaned. Damn it; I was going to spend the rest of the day regretting sleeping out here. Taking my glass and folder back inside, I answered the door.

"You're not dressed yet?" Sean frowned.

"Tell me you have coffee or prepare to meet your maker."

Lifting a brow, Sean passed me a large takeaway cup. Taking it, I sipped it as I went back inside. "Didn't sleep well?"

"I don't think the air conditioning is working in here. I had to go out on the balcony and ended up falling asleep on the sunbed."

"I'll get someone in to look at it. I'm guessing the doorbell also wasn't working?"

"I didn't hear one. Your banging woke me up." Glancing at the time, I cursed. We planned to do our meeting prep over breakfast in ten minutes. "Give me ten minutes to shower and dress."

"Of course. I'll call the service company."

A quick shower and cleaning of teeth, followed by hair and clothes, and I was ready to start my day. Grabbing my phone from beside the bed, I noted the message icon. Opening it up, I bit my lip.

<E>: I've spoken to Greg and applied for the occasional Hawaii run. Greg's onboard with it. I'll let you know when you can expect me. And thank you for understanding about Lou and everything else. I'll call you when I get home. Xx

---

Closing my eyes, I smiled up at the ceiling for a minute. Then, getting my head about me, I got back on with my life. Ethan wasn't part of it. He was just going to be the fun on the side.

CHAPTER THIRTEEN

"THAT'S EVERYTHING." SEAN CAME BACK DOWNSTAIRS, BRUSHING OFF his hands. His eyes grazed over the new sofa and small meals table before coming to me at the kitchen bench. My new furniture got delivered this morning, and Sean brought over all my stuff he'd stored after lunch. "How are you going?"

"I think I've found places for most of it." I smiled, shutting my now full cutlery drawer. "Most importantly, I've got the coffee machine working. Want to try my brew?"

Smiling, Sean leaned on the kitchen counter. "Yes."

Finally, I had the keys to my new place, and after spending the weekend shopping after the interviews a few weeks ago, I now had my furniture and appliances. Making Sean and me a coffee, I looked over the living space. "You finally get your place back to yourself."

"As much as I appreciate that, I'm not ready to go home yet."

Gazing at Sean, I understood. "Come sit out on the patio." Heading out onto the patio, which overlooked the green, I took one of the seats of my new outdoor setting. Sean sat down beside me, and we both spent a few minutes watching the handful of golfers whack their balls.

"When I come down for the monthly reports, I'll have to bring my clubs."

Snickering, I shook my head. "The only way you are getting me out on that green is if I'm driving the buggy while we talk work."

"Maybe Ethan will play a round with me. Have you heard from him?"

"Yes."

Cocking that damn brow of his, Sean side-eyed me. "Defensive much?" Keeping my eyes on the green, I sipped my coffee. "I gather things are not going well there?"

"Things are as they have been since I came home. We talk when we can, which always seems strained, and that's about it." God, I'd never found chatting to someone so awkward, but while our video calls seemed to be short and sweet, our chat messages were stilted and never went very far.

Turning to face me, Sean leaned on the table. "You haven't heard if he will be visiting again?"

"Next weekend, he'll be flying in for two days again. It's why I wanted to get everything moved in this weekend because with the training kicking off on Monday, I won't have time during the week."

Both eyebrows in his hair, Sean tilted his head. "Why aren't you happier about seeing him again?"

Shrugging my shoulders, I drank my coffee. "I mean, I am excited to see Ethan again. It's just the last visit was hard. I thought we were done. Then he showed up unannounced. I was sure it was a goodbye visit, only for it to be a 'let's fuck and see' sort of thing. It wasn't like this when we first got together, but now we seem to both be too guarded for it to get comfortable. Honestly, if it's going to be like this, I think we'd be better off not bothering."

Considering me, Sean sighed. "You two have something. You both feel it but are also too scared to act on it. I think this thing between you is out of character for both of you. You've had ten years avoiding romance and relationships, Jessie girl. Ethan started as a holiday fling with no intention of anything developing. This is huge for you, and from what you've said, it's a big step for Ethan too. You are both anxious about this. There is nothing wrong with it. Just take deep breaths and let this thing move slowly. I think after one or two more visits, you two will find your groove, and it will stop feeling so awkward for you."

Relaxing back in my chair, I met Sean's eyes. "That makes sense. Still, the last three weeks feel like we've been forcing this thing."

"Why don't you text him a picture of your new furniture and tell him you've moved in and are looking forward to seeing him next weekend. If you can't bring yourself to treat him as a lover, just talk to him like a friend. Save the sex stuff until he's here with you. It will ease the burden for both of you."

Turning my body to face him, I studied Sean. "Are you nervous about seeing Holly again?"

Blowing out a breath, Sean fidgeted with his cup. "Yes. She may not want to see me. May just have me thrown out on my ear."

"You are crashing her sister's wedding."

"It's the only chance I have of finding her. It's not like I'm going into the actual ceremony. I'm going to wait outside and ask for five minutes to talk to her after the ceremony. Hopefully, she gives me that much."

"She will. If she loved you at all, she would give you that, even if it's just to say goodbye."

Looking heartbroken already, Sean bowed his head. Reaching across the table, I took his hand in mine. "Just be honest with her, Sean. I can't promise she'll forgive you, but if you are honest, if you tell her how much losing her hurt you and how much you still love her, then you stand a chance of getting her back again."

Taking my hand back, I watched him for a long moment. "If you need me, I'm here."

Side of his mouth twitching, Sean pulled himself together. "I know. Thank you." With a sigh, he stood up. "I should go. I need to drop my car back at the hotel and pack my stuff up and take it all home. Are you sure you will be right to handle the training this week?"

"I have a program planned. I'll be fine." Rising out of my chair, I followed him back to the kitchen and rinsed our cups before putting them in the dishwasher. Seeing Sean to the door, I hugged him tight. "Good luck. Call me, no matter which way it goes."

"I will. Try and relax and enjoy Ethan."

Holding in a laugh, I couldn't resist the grin. "I plan to."

Chuckling, Sean gave me one last squeeze, and then he left me to settle into my new place. The first thing to hit me was the lack of a beach. Over the last three months, I'd grown accustomed to the sound of the water right outside the bungalow. Even in Maui, I could hear the surf crashing at night. The beach was only a few blocks away, but you wouldn't know it during the day. Here's hoping I could hear the beach at night, or I would probably have to get an app with beach sounds on it to sleep.

First things first, I took out my phone, lined up a shot of the kitchen view through the lounge and out to the green, and sent it off to my dad. Then, I sent the same picture to Ethan with a quick message.

<Jess>: Finally in my new place. I can't wait to give you the tour this weekend.

<E>: It's a naked tour, right?

<Jess>: It will most likely end up that way.

<E>: I want guarantees. My cock has been begging to be inside you for three weeks. I don't think I've masturbated this much since I was a teenager.

<Jess>: Okay, naked tour guaranteed. It starts from the front door, so be ready to go.

<E>: Deal!

<Jess>: What time will you get here?

<E>: The flight should land around ten on Thursday night, your time. All going well, I should be with you an hour after landing.

<Jess>: I expect we will both be pretty exhausted, so let's split the tour. Front door and bedroom Thursday night. Rest of the house on Friday evening.

<E>: I believe the kitchen should be Friday morning. *Wink-emoji coffee-emoji wink-emoji wink-emoji*

<Jess>: If you're up on time. *Cheeky-emoji*

<E>: When have I ever not been up on time for you?

Smiling to myself and liking the ease in which we just managed to communicate, I thanked Sean for his advice as I typed out one last text.

<Jess>: See you Thursday night. Fly safe.

Putting my phone aside, I got back to unpacking. The beds still needed to be made, and then I needed to go shopping for food to fill my bare fridge and pantry. Smiling to myself, I turned on the music and got to it.

"The new place looks nice. Have you settled in?" Lou asked on Sunday night.

"Mostly. I'm not used to having neighbors so close, and I got used to having the beach right outside, but I can hear the waves crashing at night, so it has that at least."

"And the new resort opens tomorrow?"

"Next week. We are training staff all this week, and then the soft opening is next week. It will be a hectic few weeks until the official opening. Hopefully, we'll have ironed out any kinks by then, and things will get up to speed quickly."

"Are you excited?"

"More anxious right now. I miss my old team at Maui and even the Turtle beach staff. Taking on an entirely new team in a brand-new hotel is hard work. Before this, I've always taken on established teams in existing hotels, so all it required was a few changes to how people did things. This is all new for everyone."

"Sounds stressful." Checking over his screen, Lou lowered his voice. "I hear Greg and Ethan are flying to your island this weekend?"

"Ethan mentioned."

"I know you missed out on catching up the last time he was there but are you seeing each other this time?"

"We're hoping to get dinner on Friday night. Ethan said he wouldn't get in until late Thursday, and with my work schedule, the earliest I'll be free is late Friday if there are no issues at work. It'll be good to catch up with him if we can." All true. Mostly.

"Good. I'm glad you two have kept in contact."

"Well, I need someone close with you, so I get told if anything happens. I certainly doubt Margaret or Sharnie will bother calling me." Snarky? A little.

Pursing his lips, Lou considered me. "So, there is no romantic interest with Ethan?"

"Dad, you were the one to tell me Ethan won't do long distance. It's better just to be friends." With the best friggin' benefits.

"Jessie girl…" Lou sighed. "Just keep an open mind, okay? You two seemed to really connect when you were here, and I think if you could sort the long-distance thing out, maybe you could again."

Yeah, I got where he was coming from, but I didn't want to get his hopes up any more than mine. "It is what it is, Dad. Friends are better than nothing."

Dropping his head for a moment, Lou blew out a long breath. Lifting his eyes back to the camera, Lou nodded once. "I understand. I'm a little disappointed, but I also don't need to see you hurt again."

"Well, it's something I'd prefer not to go through again either."

Sitting back, Lou looked over the monitor. "Well, dinner is being served. Will we talk next Sunday?"

"Of course. I don't have any other plans so far. Night, Dad. I love you."

"I love you too, Jessie girl. Good luck this week."

Waving through the screen, I disconnected. Slouching on the lounge, I looked up at the ceiling. Ethan was flying out Sunday morning, which worked well in the timing. It gave me time to get myself organized for Monday and no risk of being sexnapped and running late for work in the morning.

Smiling as I thought about Ethan and the kitchen, I packed up and went to make dinner. If nothing else, the visit would relieve my sexual frustrations. All of which were Ethan's fault.

CHAPTER FOURTEEN

Sitting on my kitchen bench by the window, which looked over the entry courtyard, I sipped my glass of wine. The lights were off inside except for the stairs, but the courtyard lights were a beacon. Was I nervous about Ethan's arrival? Yes. Was I hornier than a hetero teenage boy at a Victoria's Secret photoshoot? Hell, yes!

Lights flashed on the path between the garages. Slipping off the bench, I finished off the wine and rinsed the glass. Ethan appeared. God help me, but that uniform kicked my sex drive into overdrive. Moving around to the door, I turned the handle as he knocked.

"Hey," I smiled up at him, offering him a bottle of water as I stepped back to let him inside. "I thought you might be thirsty."

Cheeky smile in place, Ethan removed his pilot's uniform cap and accepted the bottle as his eyes drank me in. "Thanks, I'm parched." Setting his carry on aside, Ethan opened the bottle and skulled it while I shut and locked the door. "God, I needed that, thank you," Ethan sighed, screwing the lid back on the empty bottle.

Smiling at Ethan, I fidgeted with the black satin tie of my short summer robe. "How was the flight?"

Smirking, Ethan reached past me to put the bottle on one of the inbuilt decorative shelving niches in the wall. "Too fucking long when all I could think about was you." Grabbing my waist, Ethan pressed me to the wall, his mouth closing over mine, devouring me in his need.

Hands caressed over the black satin of my robe, then slid up to find my bare hips. Moaning, Ethan dropped his mouth to my throat as his fingers gripped my ass, kneading the muscles as his lips drifted south, kissing and licking over the exposed skin between my breasts and then over the thin material.

Dropping to his knees, Ethan swept his hands up to my waist, lifting my robe to expose my nakedness to his hungry eyes. "Fuck, Jess. You're the best thing I've seen in weeks. Never get dressed when I'm here. I need you like this every single time."

Diving forward, he licked straight over my clit. Crying out, I gripped at the wall and his head, back arched, face to the ceiling as he feasted on me. Lifting my thigh to his shoulder, Ethan delved deeper, sucking and licking me senseless. Lost in sensation, I moaned and writhed as my body was winding tighter and tighter, barely noticing I was trembling until my supporting leg let go, and I nearly fell.

Using his hands at my waist to hold me up, Ethan stood. "Fuck, I've missed you, Jess," he murmured as his lips brushed mine, his nose rubbing mine. "I haven't called because I knew if I heard your voice, I wouldn't be able to wait for work to fly me here." Another brush of lips as he tugged the black satin belt away, the robe falling open, exposing me.

Setting his weight forward, Ethan trapped me between him and the wall. "You fill me with such want. It's more than getting off. It's like you're this deliciously sweet drug that I got addicted to after just one night. Just your voice turns me on."

Gasping as Ethan's thumb and finger closed over a nipple, I moaned loud when his thigh pressed against the heat between mine. The arch of my body gave Ethan my neck. His lips pinched my pulse, trailing it down to my shoulder. His body pinning mine against the wall, Ethan smoothed his hand over my tummy and cupped my heat. Capturing my mouth in a slow hungry kiss, he pulled back just enough to watch me as two of his fingers pressed into me.

Eyes rolling back in my head, I bit my lip as my body clenched tight around him. "God, you're beautiful, Jess. The way your body reacts to me haunts me." Kissing me slow and deep, Ethan matched the rhythm of his fingers, his thumb rubbing gently over my clit until it all became too much, and out of nowhere, I whimpered my climax into his mouth.

Lifting his fingers to my mouth, Ethan wiped them over my lips before kissing me anew, licking the tart taste of me from my lips. He moaned as he tasted me, just like he did the night after the wedding —God, what the rumbling in his throat did to me.

Throwing him back against the opposite wall of the entry hall, I kissed him eagerly as I unbuckled this belt and opened his slacks. "I've been fantasizing about you fucking me in this uniform for weeks," I whispered against his lips as I took him in my hand.

The week's exhaustion was gone with Ethan here. Nibbling and biting his neck while I stroked him. "Jesus, Jess. Did I mention how fucking horny I am?"

Dropping to my knees, I took him in my mouth. No hesitation, not licking my way up to it. He was in my mouth, and I was sucking him with renewed energy. When I felt him thicken, I dragged my teeth up his shaft.

Ethan inhaled sharply, his hands threading into my hair and pulling me up to his mouth with a gasped laugh. "You know I love that."

"I do!" I smirked wickedly, licking my lips, the taste of his pre-cum salting my tongue. Shaking his head with his cheeky smile lighting up his eyes, Ethan hugged me tight to the front of him and kissed me, slowly, his tongue tangling and caressing me until I melted into him. I could kiss this man forever.

"Let me wrap up, then I'm fucking you here," Ethan murmured in my ear as his hands at my waist stepped me back. Floating until my back hit the wall, I chewed my smiling lips while Ethan opened the wrapper and rolled the condom over his long thick shaft.

I haunted him, and Ethan preoccupied my dreams, but the fantasies never sent butterflies swarming through my insides like this moment right here. When he got ready to have me, that heated look in his eyes, burning me up with his want. That intoxicating warm amber scent of his made my head spin and my pulse go nuts. The way his hands reached out and took control of me, setting his weight against me as his lips possessed me.

Gasping for breath, I pulled up from suffocating on my desire. Kissing my neck and shoulder, Ethan caressed his hand down the arch of my back, over the rise of my ass to grip where it met my thighs. Lifting me calmly, Ethan dragged me up, hauling me over his engorged shaft until the head of it slid between my folds and notched in my opening.

Leaning my shoulders hard into the wall, Ethan bit gently on my ear. "Let me in." Ethan eased me down, slowly.

It felt sensational having the head of him pressing into my molten heat, but it wasn't enough. Groaning, Ethan propped one hand on the wall beside me and widened his stance. Then, with one hard thrust, he rammed all the way home within me, forcing a cry of delight from my throat. Growling, Ethan gripped my hips, his fingers pulling my butt cheeks apart, then he started driving into me slow and hard.

The force of his body slamming me into the wall had me crying out with every thrust. Shifting his weight, Ethan dropped his face and lifted my breast to his mouth. His tongue lashed and nipped at my nipples, sending rippling pulses of pleasure to my womb, causing me to struggle to keep my control as my body contracted around him.

Lifting his gaze, Ethan kissed me heatedly, his thumb teasing and tweaking my nipple, making my cunt clench tighter around him.

"Ethan!" I gasped, my body just on the pinnacle, winding so fast I thought I'd die any minute. "Oh, God, Ethan!"

Pulling back, Ethan watched me intently. Biting his lip, he closed his eyes for a second and cursed. His cock swelled and pulsed. "Jess! God, fuck, Jess!" Clenching his jaw, Ethan picked up speed, grunting as he fucked my tight body hard. "Jess!" The strong jerk of his cock was more than I could take. As Ethan groaned his climax, I threw my head back and came hard.

As I relaxed, Ethan fell against me, both of us breathing hard. Holding me in place, Ethan held his hands on the wall, both of us gasping when my pussy clutched and released its stranglehold on him.

Opening my eyes, I met Ethan's smiling face. Caressing his jaw, I pulled him to me, our mouths joining in a passionate kiss for several minutes. Pulling back, I tried to catch my breath. "So, this is the entry hall."

"I love it. Great design. Very functional for greeting your guests in the best way possible," Ethan murmured, dropping kisses on my neck.

"The bedroom is upstairs. Let me grab you another bottle of water, and I'll take you to bed."

Smirking, Ethan kissed my lips tenderly. "Sounds great." Lifting me, we both reacted when he withdrew, my body clenching in a complaint about suddenly being empty.

My cunt was obsessed with Ethan and his cock and what they did to us. She was in love already. Fuck whatever my heart and brain thought. Ethan's cock was her soul mate, and how dare I deprive her of him.

Getting my legs to hold me up took some work, but by the time I tied my robe closed again, I could make it to the kitchen and grab

Ethan another cool bottle from the fridge. Following me in with his pants closed, Ethan carried the knotted condom. "The bin is the pull-out drawer just to the right of the sink."

Opening the drawer, Ethan disposed of the waste and then put the empty water flask on the sink. "Do you just refill it?"

"I always wash them at the end of the day. Especially if someone else used it." Grabbing the flask and my wine glass, I put them in the dishwasher and set it to run. Collecting my water bottle, I took Ethan's hand. "Let's go to bed. I have to be at work early tomorrow."

Picking up his carry-on, Ethan followed me upstairs. Taking him into the master bedroom, I let go of his hand and opened the balcony sliding door before shutting the plantation shutters and angling them down so the southerly breeze could blow in, but no one lurking outside could see us.

"How far are you from the beach?" Ethan asked, coming to the window and wrapping his arms around me. We could hear the waves crashing in the distance.

"About a five-minute walk. My surfboard is in the laundry. I'll leave you a map on how to get there with your keys in the morning."

Kissing my ear and neck, Ethan held me tighter. "What time do we need to get up?"

"I have to get up at six. You don't have to get up until you want to."

"You're so sweet, but I want to wake up with you. Remember, you promised my official tour of the kitchen naked with breakfast. Plus, if waking up with you gets me another one of your cooked breakfasts, it's worth getting up for."

Turning in his arms, I started helping Ethan out of his clothes. "Let's see how you feel in the morning. You may be exhausted breaking in my new bed." Rising on my tiptoes, I sucked his bottom lip between mine.

Moaning, Ethan gripped my waist. He let me undress him, kissing me tantalizingly the entire time. Once he was naked, I pulled the tie on my robe and dropped it to the floor. Picking me up, Ethan carried me to bed and christened it in the best way.

In the morning, Ethan slept through my showering and getting dressed. Taking extra time to cover the love bite Ethan gave me, I was running a little late. Before heading downstairs, I kissed him softly. He barely even stirred. Possibly something to do with the four o'clock fucking he gave me after he woke up dreaming of me.

While making myself breakfast, I left him a note, the map to the beach and shops, and keys to my place. The smile I'd gone to sleep with stayed on my face all day, even when one of the kitchen hands dropped an entire tray of brand-new glassware. Honestly, Ethan was the best method of stress relief.

CHAPTER FIFTEEN

It was on television. Drinking my morning coffee on Sunday, I watched my best friend get escorted by security guards from the wedding he crashed. "Shit!" Grabbing up my phone, I dialed Sean's number then put it on speaker. "Hey, are you okay?"

"You saw then?" Sean grumbled.

"Yeah, it's all over the news."

"Interesting because it's not getting a minute of airtime here. It's like the media in this country is radio silent for anything but painting me as a stalker."

Sitting back in my seat, I didn't tell him that was unusual. While Australian media aren't to the level of British tabloids and the stalker paparazzi in America, they seemed to be more focused on sensationalism than actual reporting facts over the last few decades. "Are you heading home then?"

"Actually, no. I met someone on the flight over who has a resort on a private island they need to sell as part of their divorce settlement. I'm going to fly up and take a look."

"A resort in Australia?"

"Yeah. The Hideaway. Have you heard of it?"

Double blinking, I sat forward again. "Of course. Very exclusive, adults-only, absolute luxury. There is a second family-friendly resort at the other end of the island."

"Huh, he didn't mention another resort."

"Well, yeah, the wife owned the family-friendly Retreat Resort. Margarethe Zimmer. Real bitch in person, but an amazing interior designer. She did all the internal work on The Hideaway as well. It was beautiful last I saw it ten years ago. If you are going to buy only one, you want the Hideaway."

"Why?"

"They share everything, but on paper, it's all the husband's. It will cost more, but you don't want to get stuck with a resort that no one can get to, no spa, and minimal land. If both are selling, take them both or leave them alone."

"Should I ask how you know all this?"

"Bradley Zimmer was my boss before I left Australia. He showed me all the plans and designs, and he flew his management teams from all his hotels up there for a team bonding workshop before it officially opened. Including those in the trainee program."

Quiet for a moment, Sean finally asked. "He showed all his management team the plans, or just you?"

"Oh, I was doing an assignment for college that required designing and decorating a new resort from scratch. Either as a new build or a renovation after a buy-out. I knew they were doing exactly that, so I asked for an hour of Mr. Zimmer's time to talk me through the process. He was generous about sharing his knowledge and giving you tips and tricks to do better than others. As far as I knew, he never messed around with his staff. Mrs. Zimmer, however, had a real thing for the bellhops."

"You know all that, but not where Holly works?" Sean huffed.

Feeling bad, I finished my coffee. "Did you see that there is an international hoteliers conference in Sydney in October?"

"No? How do you know about that?"

"You received an invite. It came through your inbox a few weeks ago."

"You read my emails?"

"I had access to deal with Cassidy stuff since you are still officially the manager there as well as the owner."

"Oh, right."

"My point being, it would be a good place to throw around Holly's name and see who perks up. I know she worked for one of the big Australian hoteliers who had international reach, so they would be bound to be there."

"Except she quit her job at that place and got a GM role elsewhere."

"Sean, you don't have a staff member like Holly and not know where she ended up. Every other hotelier whoever dealt with her boss would know her too."

"Except you."

"Hey, I know her; I just don't know where she works."

"Grr, useless woman," Sean sighed.

"I'm saying you should go. Last chance run at finding her. Honestly, if you don't find her then, that's fate slamming the god damn door in your face."

"I feel like I've already got the black eye and fat lip from that one."

"And if nothing else, the place it's being held looks amazing. It's Holmes City Resort. Roger Holmes Junior opened it. He took an old run-down hotel and made it feel like you stayed in the Daintree

Forest in the middle of the city. I'm hearing great reviews about the place."

"Again, you hear all of this stuff but can't find the love of my life for me."

"That's because I already work for you."

"Haha."

"Deny it all you want; I know I'm the best you've ever had. Managers of my caliber don't grow on trees, you know." The laundry door slammed shut. Jumping up, I found Ethan standing there, eyes glaring at me. Hair damp but mostly dry after the walk back from the beach. He'd already changed into board shorts and a t-shirt. Grabbing my chest, I forced myself to breathe. "Shit, you scared the hell out of me. How was the surf?"

Blinking, Ethan tilted his head, then his face softened. "Good. A great swell was coming in this morning. Who's on the phone?"

"Sean. He was on the news, so I rang to make sure he was okay."

"Hey, Ethan," Sean sighed. "Do you like the new place?"

"It's faster to get here, and the beach is good."

"I took him snorkeling yesterday and up to the Dole plantation for Dole Whip." Pineapple soft serve had become my sex replacement since moving to Oahu. I didn't need it yesterday but wanted to share the miracle of it with Ethan. He wasn't easily convinced to try it but relented to his great pleasure.

"Do you like Jess's new bed?"

"Don't!" I reached for the phone.

"Because shopping with her for it was humiliating," Sean continued. "She seriously asked the sales assistant for the sex rating on each mattress and then continued to make herself comfortable in several sex positions to make sure it offered maximum sex-friendly comfort."

Snatching up the phone, I huffed at the snickering coming from Ethan's direction. "Don't you have a flight to catch?"

"I don't have to leave for an hour."

"Oh, look, they are showing you getting thrown out of the wedding on the news again. At least you got dressed in a tux. Looking seriously smooth as the Australian secret service throws you out the gate." Frowning, Ethan looked at the screen, which was up to the weather segment.

"Going now," Sean huffed. "I'll say hello to Bradley Zimmer for you."

"If he even knows who I am, I'll be impressed."

"Me too. Enjoy your day together." The line went dead. Throwing the phone on the sofa, I chewed my lip, worrying about Sean. He'd sounded so depressed. The fact he was awake that early in the morning was telling. It would have been four in the morning there.

"Sean was on the news?" Ethan checked as he went to the kitchen to get some coffee.

"Yeah. He got escorted out of the prime minister's eldest daughter's wedding."

"Why?"

"Oh, he crashed it hoping to see Holly?"

Raising a brow, Ethan took a sip of his coffee, then set it down. "Who's Holly?" He started grabbing eggs and bacon out of the fridge.

"Seriously? How did you miss all of that? It was all over the news three months ago, especially in Australia."

"Besides the fact I spend half my life airborne with no access to the daily news?" Ethan asked sarcastically.

Huffing, I finished my coffee and went to help him with breakfast. "Holly Claire is the prime minister's youngest daughter. Three months ago, she was out here on holiday, and she and Sean had an affair. Sean proposed, then she found out his dad was a senator the same time her family found out about them, and she ended the engagement and took off. He's been trying to find her since. He's so in love with her after only three weeks together. He's been miserable since."

Face scrunching, Ethan eyed me, then his face smoothed. "Wait, you're serious. Sean's in Australia chasing after some holiday tail?"

Lifting a brow, I lifted myself to the kitchen counter. "Where are you right now?"

Furrowing his forehead, Ethan shook his head. "Not even the same, Jess. We became friends, and I'm not about to propose marriage after a few weeks of fucking." Turning his back, Ethan went back to making breakfast.

Wetting my lips, I took a breath to gather my thoughts. "I wasn't dropping hints. You asked; I'm telling you what happened. But you can't judge Sean when you are cooking breakfast for the one-night stand you had three months ago either."

Pausing in his movements, Ethan gritted his jaw, his shoulders tensing while he took a deep breath, and then his entire body relaxed again. Running my tongue over my teeth while I assessed his body language, I chose to let it go. If things kept getting awkward between us, then it wasn't working.

"Sean's the sort of guy who believes in love at first sight. He steered clear of commitment for ten years, but the moment he saw Holly, he knew there was something more about her. Eventually, Sean will find her, and I'm hoping for his happiness that it works out between them. He deserves it. We all do."

Looking over his shoulder, Ethan assessed me. "If he loves her that much, I hope he finds her and that she loves him just as much, if not more."

Smirking, I slid off the bench and wrapped my arms around Ethan. "What we have suits me. I wouldn't settle for less than I thought I deserved, Ethan." Kissing his shoulder, I got two plates out.

"You don't believe in love at first sight, I gather?"

Setting the plates on the bench, I blew out a breath. "I did. The way Lou loves my mother filled my head with lots of bullshit romantic notions growing up. Don't worry; Ben cured me of it." Handing the first plate to Ethan, I waited for him to dish up breakfast, then swapped plates with him. "Should we eat out on the patio?"

"Sure."

Gathering the cutlery, I grabbed two glasses and filled them with water, taking it all out to the outdoor table. Ethan carried the plates. I didn't ask if Ethan believed in first sight because it was apparent he didn't. Someone who thought they'd had it once didn't ridicule another for still considering it. My experience might have broken my romantic notions, but I remembered what it was like to be in love. Worse yet, I remembered losing it. "What time is your flight?"

"Eleven."

"So—" Cocking a brow, I gave Ethan a cheeky smile. "—back to bed after breakfast?"

"No." Ethan shook his head, lips lifting in a sinful smirk. "I missed out on my naked kitchen tour on Friday morning. I expect you to remedy that."

Laughing, I eyed Ethan up. "Well, eat up already. There is still the laundry to christen too, and lucky for you, I have a load of washing that needs doing."

Chuckling, Ethan shook his head. But after I made good on the naked kitchen tour, he helped me put on a load of washing.

Walking him out to the car a few hours later, I eyed the driver. "I would have driven you to the airport."

Taking me in his arms, Ethan met my eyes. "Please don't take this the wrong way, but you seeing me to the airport is a level of affection that we're not at."

Cocking a brow, I held in a laugh. "Okay. It's not like I was going to get out and walk you to the door."

Pinching my chin, Ethan smothered me in a very intimate kiss. "Still, let's not do the airport drop-off pick-up thing. Work pays for the driver to transport me back and forth; I may as well take advantage of it."

"So, you'll let me know when you are coming back again."

"I will."

As Ethan opened the car door, I remembered something important. "Oh, Lou asked if I was going to see you this trip, so I told him we were having dinner Friday night." Technically, this wasn't a lie. We'd gone out to a restaurant for dinner.

Lips mushing together, Ethan gave a stiff nod. "I'll call you." Dropping into the car, Ethan waved as the driver pulled away.

"Famous last words."

CHAPTER SIXTEEN

Two days after Ethan left.

\<E\>: Two weeks. Arrive Thursday close to midnight. There until Monday evening. I can go to the hotel on Thursday so that I don't wake you up. And then I can come over after you finish work on Friday if you prefer.

\<Jess\>: I gave you keys for a reason.

\<E\>: *smiley face*

Two days before Ethan was due again.

\<Jess\>: I've got to go out to the Cassidy in Bora Bora. Want to come? I can delay a day so you can go with me.

\<E\>: Why are you going out there?

\<Jess\>: Work. I will get us a room, and we can stay the weekend—flyback on Sunday. I'll be busy on and off all weekend, but only for an hour or two each day.

\<E\>: Sounds good. Do I need to pay for the flight?

\<Jess\>: No, I scored us a free ride. I'll meet you at the airport Thursday night. I need to be there first thing Friday.

\<E\>: Okay, sounds fun.

_____

_____

"This is not fun!" The beautiful blonde complained once again. "What are we waiting for?"

Giving me an apologetic look, the reason I was making this trip took her hand. "Bae, we discussed this. The pilot for the return flight has to fly out with us."

Lifting an eyebrow at the lie, I tilted my head at the rock god sitting across from me. As his model girlfriend draped herself over him like he was a couch, he mouthed sorry to me, and then his mouth became occupied with the blonde.

"God, they'll be done by the end of this trip," Dylan's assistant whispered to me. "I'm sorry you have to endure this, but Dylan insisted if he stayed at the Cassidy, you had to see to everything."

"Since I'm getting a free flight in a private jet and a weekend away with my boyfriend, I'm not going to complain. I've endured worse than a hangry tantrum before."

Snickering, Dylan's assistant and sister pulled a chocolate bar out of her pocket. She could probably model herself, but she wasn't interested in fame. She worked for her brother because they were orphans, and Teille was the only person Dylan trusted with his life and money.

"Watch the look I get with this." Unwrapping the chocolate, Teille lifted her volume. "Jess, want some chocolate?"

"That'd be great. Thanks."

The blonde's head whipped around, and her mouth hung open as I snapped off a cube of chocolate and put it between my lips. Her eyes narrowed on the chocolate as Teille also put a piece in her mouth. "Dylan, Bianca?" Teille offered the block towards them.

Screeching, Bianca stood abruptly. "How dare you. That's just so rude!" She stormed off towards the bathroom.

"That gives us five minutes of peace." Teille shrugged.

"Teille!" Dylan sighed. "Don't tease her." Eyes coming to me, Dylan appraised me the way a man who's seen you naked and wouldn't object to doing so again does.

"Don't," I warned.

Licking his lips, Dylan shook his head and smiled his pantie-dropping grin. "What's it been? Two years? You're still hot, Jess."

"Put your tongue back in your head and forget we are anything but a client and service provider. I don't need to hear any more songs about the way I ride cowgirl."

Beside me, Teille covered her mouth to stop her from laughing chocolate everywhere. Dylan threw back his head and chortled. "You inspired more than just that song, Jess, but that was the best one."

Over Dylan's shoulder, I saw two pilots approaching. They discussed something heatedly by their gestures and attention on each other. Their steps slowed when Dylan's two big bodyguards stood up to greet them.

"He's here," I sang, my smile spreading wide across my face seeing Ethan in uniform. Standing up, I was striding towards him, keen to kiss the ever-loving hell out of him.

"Guys, they're with us," Teille called as she stood up and grabbed her stuff.

The guards stepped away and went to confer with their boss. That's when I realized the other pilot was Greg. "Hey," I greeted both of them, but before I could ask more, Ethan swept me into his arms and kissed me breathless.

"Holy hell, is that Dylan Neptune from the Burning Beds?" Greg gasped beside us.

Pulling back, I tasted Ethan on my lips, smiling up at Ethan before I regained my composure and looked at Greg. "Yeah, he's my job this weekend and also our ride. Shouldn't you be heading to the hotel?"

"Ah, yeah, I just wanted to say hi, but Dylan Neptune?"

"Jess," the rockstar in question swaggered forward. "So, this is the boyfriend?" He appraised Ethan. Both of them were tall, dark hair and striking blue eyes. While Ethan's eyes were the deep blue ocean, Dylan's were more the sky blue of summer. Ethan's hair was short, Dylan's hung clean and silky around his heavily tattooed shoulders. God, they were even the same age. "The girl has a type. Dylan Neptune, nice to meet you."

Rolling my eyes, I sighed. Ethan's grip on my waist tightened a touch as he put out his hand. "Captain Ethan Knight. Thanks for letting us get a ride with you."

Dylan brushed it off. "I need Jess. When she told me that came with letting her boyfriend tag along, it wasn't even a hesitation. When you find people who are damn good at their jobs, you make allowances for them." Turning to Greg, Dylan shook his hand. "Are you coming too?"

Eyebrows jumping, Greg gripped Dylan's hand, and his grin bloomed. "I wouldn't say no. Greg. I'm Jess's brother-in-law."

Frowning, Dylan cocked his head to the side and met my eyes. "I thought you only had the one sister? The evil twin?"

"Ah, yeah, I do. Sharnie married Greg a few months ago, and she's pregnant too."

Eyebrows jumping, Dylan shook Greg's hand anew and gave him an upper arm a pat. "You must be one hell of a man or in great need of booze."

"I'd like to say the first, but I'm not going to turn down the second," Greg answered. "Didn't realize you and Jess knew each other beyond her work?" Great, Greg had caught the scent of gossip and was hunting it out.

Smiling politely, Dylan stepped back. "Jess and I go way back. I grew up in Newcastle too."

"Dylan, babe, can we get on the plane now?" Bianca was back.

"Of course, bae." Dylan smiled and waved.

"Is that Bianca Turnop?" Greg's jaw slackened. Ethan reached over and helped it close up.

Snickering, Dylan ran his hand through his hair. "Yeah. Be careful; her teeth are sharp. Oh, and I told her you guys were our return flight. I hope you don't mind?" Before they could respond, Dylan went over to the blonde and smooched her hard. "Let's go!"

Everyone started heading for the exit out to the tarmac, but Ethan held back. "Do I want to ask?"

"I actually can't tell you—any of it, but especially how we met. I signed a non-disclosure a long time ago. It's why, when Dylan wants to get up to mischief off the radar, he comes to wherever I'm working. His assistant Teille is a friend, and we have kept in contact. It took me a while to realize he encouraged that so he could always find me when he needed me."

Taking Ethan's hand, we started following the rest. "Sorry about the boyfriend thing, but it was the easiest way to explain you this weekend."

"I get it," Ethan huffed. Yep, that sounded convincing.

"Also, you'll have to sign an NDA yourself. Sorry, but it's become Dylan's standard practice. Too many people want their fifteen minutes of fame or easy money for selling him out."

"Fuck, I'm tired, Jess. Does it have to happen now?" Pursing my lips, I took my hand back, but Ethan grabbed it back again and quickly turned to kiss my mouth. "Sorry. That came out harsher than I meant. I appreciate that you have to work this weekend and swindled it for me to come along; I do. Really."

Grabbing my bag off the chair, I pulled out a bottle of water and handed it to Ethan. "It's a six-hour flight. You can sleep on the way. I need to make a call and see if I can get Greg a room, then speak to Teille and make sure they'll cover it since Dylan invited him."

"Crap, Greg probably didn't even consider needing to pay for things." Ethan rubbed his forehead.

"It's okay. Dylan is fairly generous. If he invites you somewhere, he usually intends to pay. Go ahead, get settled on board. I'll sort things out."

Kissing me once more, Ethan headed out through the doors where Greg was waiting and across the tarmac. Teille waited at the gates for me. As I walked to her, I pulled out my phone and called the Cassidy in Bora Bora to get Greg a room. Teille fell in beside me while I made the call. "Just the most basic room you've got."

"Jess, this isn't the sort of resort where you get a hotel room. Our basic room is the equivalent of your junior suite."

"Yeah, Linal, I know. I've got an extra coming in with the Neptune party who needs a bed."

Exhaling exasperated, Linal groaned. "I'll have it sorted by the time you arrive."

Hanging up, I looked at Teille. "I woke him up."

Teille shrugged. "It's not like we are coming in and renting two rooms. Who's the extra, by the way?"

"Ethan's best friend, co-pilot, and my brother-in-law."

"Wait, Sharnie got married?" Teille looked awed. "Wow. Well, don't worry, we'll cover him. Dylan invited him, so it's only fair."

"Thanks, I got the feeling he was only here because he and Ethan were arguing about something."

"Yeah, I saw that when they were walking up. Hopefully, it was nothing too serious." Reaching the top of the plane stairs, Teille gave me a shoulder bump. "Your boyfriend is very nice, Jess. Very nice."

Smiling, I let her go before me and took a deep breath. "Yeah, he is."

Going to the two seats at the back Ethan had chosen, I put my bag away and grabbed out a pillow and blanket. When I met Ethan's eyes, my body heated at the way he was watching me as he took off his jacket, turned it inside out, and folded it up.

Smirking, Ethan put his jacket and tie in his carry-on, then zipped it closed and stored it.

"Here." I offered him the bundle.

"Thanks." Taking it, he settled down into the seat by the window and started getting comfortable.

Grabbing a pillow and blanket for me, I dropped into the seat next to him and buckled myself in. Teille came back and put her mouth to my ear. "Have you told him about the NDA?"

"Can it wait until morning? The guys have been flying for half a day. They're tired and dehydrated. A good lawyer could argue they are not of sound mind."

"Yeah, of course. I'll tell Dylan to mind himself until morning."

"Thanks, Teille." With a squeeze to my shoulder, Teille went back to the front and murmured something to Dylan. He gave the nod, and they put their heads together to talk for a while.

"Did you work today?" Ethan asked as he opened the lid on his second bottle of water.

"Yeah. I ended up working late as well. I got changed at the hotel and went straight to the airport to meet them. They landed at nine, we got a late dinner together in the lounge, and then waited for you."

"So, you're just as tired as me?"

"I don't fly a plane with three hundred souls on board. My job is significantly less stressful."

Taking my hand, Ethan caressed along my hand bones. "I do what I love. I've never worked a day in my life."

"You looked like you worked a double tonight." Cuddling into the ultra-comfy seat to face him, I rubbed my thumb across the dark circles beneath his eyes. "What were you and Greg arguing about?"

Gritting his teeth, Ethan turned his lips into my palm and kissed it. "Nothing. So why does this guy need you specifically beside the NDA?"

"We've known each other a long time. Nothing Dylan does shocks me anymore, and there's the NDA. So, when he needs to get away, I get the blessing of playing intermediary between him and my staff. I wanted him to stay at the Maui resort. They're my staff, and it's no issue for me to step back into that situation. Bora Bora is more complicated. The manager there resents Dylan having a preference, but I've agreed to act more like a concierge while here."

"Sean knows about this?" Ethan eyed the rockstar at the front of the plane as we taxied for take-off.

"Yeah, I cleared it with him."

Plumping his pillow, Ethan made himself comfy. As soon as we were airborne, he laid his seat back until it was flat. "Lay back, Jess. Let me hold you."

Smiling quietly at the half-asleep sound of his voice, I put my seat back and snuggled as much as the seatbelt allowed. Greg was already snoring lightly across the plane, everyone else settling down to sleep, except for Dylan, who was scribbling in his songbook. Oh, the sleeplessness of the creative mind.

CHAPTER SEVENTEEN

"How was Bora Bora?" Sean asked as we ate breakfast together four weeks later.

"Good."

"No issues keeping Dylan Neptune happy?"

"Who? I have no idea who you are talking about. We've never had anyone by that name stay with us."

Chortling, Sean shook his head. "Of course. But no issues?"

"The girlfriend was very demanding, but the staff managed to keep her happy. Other than that, it was all standard behavior for King Neptune."

"How did Ethan cope watching you deal with all that?"

"He didn't. Greg came along, and the two of them entertained themselves while I worked. Then when I was free, Greg made himself scarce, for the most part."

"Probably a good thing. The first time he stayed at my resort, one of your staff called worried about you. If you hadn't reassured me, or he'd have tried that shit with another staff member, I'd have had him charged."

"Yeah, well, with Ethan and his girlfriend there, he treated me a little more professionally." Okay, not really, but I was a lot more firm about the boundaries on this visit. "I got to know my brother-in-law a little better. He's a decent guy. No idea what he sees in Sharnie, but there is no accounting for taste."

Nodding, Sean chewed another mouthful. "You took the last two Fridays off work. Is everything okay?"

"Besides the fact I have eight years of leave accrued?" When Sean cocked that brow at me, I rolled my eyes. "I'm taking the Fridays off when Ethan is in town if he arrives on a Thursday. That way, I get a full day to spend with him. The last two visits have been short. He arrived Thursday night and flew out again Saturday lunch time. I'm trying to make the most of it." Trying being the operative word.

"So, the occasional trip is already weekly. How many times has he flown here since it started nine weeks ago?"

Had it been over two months since Ethan turned up unannounced and came to Maui? "This last trip made five. Two visits in the first month after he got Hawaii added to his roster, and then weekly all this last month, but for shorter stays. He's here again this Friday. If you are still around, you should have lunch with us."

"I just might." Sean sipped his coffee. "How are you handling it?"

"Aren't we meant to be discussing the resort?"

"Friends first," Sean argued.

"Okay. How are you?"

"Keeping busy. Now, back to you."

It had been six weeks since the wedding fiasco. Sean had been home only once since then. Done a whirlwind tour of the resorts to make sure they were all operating as they should be, and then disappeared again. "I'm enjoying having a regular sex-friend."

Inhaling, Sean cocked that god-damn brow. I was going to shave it off one day. "He's just a sex-friend?"

"Yes."

"Okay, Jessie girl. Whatever you need to tell yourself."

"Can we talk work now?"

Opening his notepad, Sean pulled out my monthly report. "Shoot."

———

Cuddled up in the nook of Ethan's shoulder, I caressed my hand over the ridges of his abdomen. The welcome back sex was ridiculous. Every single visit where I was here when he walked in the door, we fucked there and then. After that initial welcome, we'd retire to the bedroom for sleep, if it was evening, or Ethan would go to bed, and I'd make myself busy. This morning, I'd gotten to wake in Ethan's arms for the twenty-first time since he came to Maui ten weeks ago. Not that I was counting.

"Do you have your roster for September yet?"

Turning his face, Ethan kissed the top of my head. When Ethan woke me up just before sunrise, it was intense and slow passion—the sort that melts your heart and leaves you a wrecked mess by the time the orgasm subsides. Now, as the sun came up, I knew he'd want to go out to surf soon. "Yeah. Are you okay with seeing me once a week still?"

"Of course. I'd be happier if you were here a little longer than a day."

"I've got two three-day layovers, a two-day layover, and then a five-day one. For that one, I arrive on a Sunday. Will you be okay with me being here when you are working?"

"If it's towards the end of the month, I can try for a few days off. Maybe we can get away together again?"

Squeezing me tighter, Ethan caressed his nose against my temple. "Hmm, five days of Jess. That could be good."

"Put the dates on the calendar in the kitchen, and I'll get the time off," I decided, already planning to take Ethan to Kauai. Last month, Ethan started adding his roster to my calendar on the fridge so I'd know when to expect him. We rarely talked when he wasn't here at first, but over the last few weeks, I noticed he was sending me messages about random stuff all the time, and the communication was a lot easier between us now.

"We should go surf." Ethan turned his head to the rising sun outside the window. Ethan bought a second board last month so we could surf together when he was here. He'd been helping me improve my technique too.

"In a minute," I sighed, enjoying lying like this with him.

Kissing my temple, Ethan slipped out from beneath me and went into the bathroom. Well, that ended the moment. Getting out of bed, I grabbed my swimsuit and went into the main bathroom to rinse off and change. I'd have a proper shower when we got back later.

Moving downstairs, I twisted my hair up into a top knot and secured it with a band, and then I turned on the coffee machine. Ethan preferred to get straight out in the waves, so the coffee would percolate while we were away. Opening the fridge door, I poured myself a glass of milk, then shut the door to find Ethan standing on the other side. "Thought you weren't ready to get up yet?" His eyes cast over my two-piece swimsuit.

"But you did and removed my comfy pillow in the process." Leaning against the counter, I drank the milk.

Ethan's brows furrowed, and then his mouth formed an O. "I thought you meant your legs weren't up to walking, or you hadn't recovered yet. I didn't realize you wanted cuddle time."

And now I was the needy female who liked to cuddle after sex. Great! Argh, I am not that woman. "You know, the best conversations we've ever had, the real stuff, it's happened in a bedroom."

Moving a step closer, Ethan filled his water bottle from the fridge water filter. "That's important right now, why exactly?"

"Because I just realized since we started this, you avoid being in the bedroom beyond sex and sleep. Once you're awake and got your load off, you're out the door, and unlike your place where you would come back from your surf and take me back to bed for half the day, we now go out and do things. And I own that is mostly my fault because I have very active weekends to make up for my long workdays. But I've taken the last three Fridays off to be with you, made no plans other than to be with you, and it's been you avoiding having alone time with me."

Smirking, Ethan raised a brow. "I haven't been avoiding alone time with you. Greg and I usually spend time together on our layovers. Now that he's married and expecting a child, it's the only time we get to see each other. You have a great golf course on your doorstep. Of course, I was going to invite him for a game occasionally."

Movement in the entry courtyard caught my attention. Huffing, I rinsed my glass, set it in the dishwasher, and walked to the door as the doorbell rang. Pulling it open, I smiled at Greg. "Hey, kind of early, aren't you?"

"Ethan said we were surfing this morning." Greg grinned, his eyes roaming over my body.

"Oh? Did you bring a board?" I raised my brow.

Frowning, Greg scratched his head. "Shit, I didn't actually—"

"It's fine. You can use mine. I wasn't in the mood for surfing this morning anyway." Throwing the door open for Greg to catch, I turned to see Ethan frowning from the business end of the hallway. "You were saying?"

Grabbing my arm as I went to walk past, Ethan tugged me close until our bodies were touching. "He was meant to bring his own board. I wasn't pushing you out."

"I think that's exactly what you've been doing since Bora Bora. I just can't work out what I did to cause it. You're coming more frequently but spending even less time with me." Tugging my arm free, I headed for the stairs. "I'm going to head up the mountain for a horse ride since I have the morning to myself. Enjoy the surf."

"Jess, I wasn't pushing you out." Ethan groaned when I kept walking. "Good one, Doofus!"

"Sorry, when you said come for a surf, I didn't realize there wouldn't be a board I could borrow. Jess looked really shitty about me being here. I thought you checked it was okay with her. You told me last week she was okay with us hanging out. I mean, you told her about Sharnie, right?"

Stopping at the top of the stairs, I hid around the corner, intrigued by this change of events. "I haven't told her."

"E, it's her sister."

"Exactly! Her twin sister, who stole her fiancé and caused her to lose her baby, and who inflicted untold misery on her for years. This time with Jess is about us enjoying ourselves. Bringing up Sharnie is about as pleasant as a root canal."

"Sharnie says Jess blows things out of proportion."

"And you believe that with everything she's putting you through." Ethan huffed. "Jess has told me fuck all about the things Sharnie did to her. She doesn't talk about it. Most of the shit I've shared with you, I got from Ben."

"You spoke to her ex about her? E, that's a fucking death trap."

"I saw him out one night, and he asked me how the wedding plans were coming. I told him Jess left after what went down with Sharnie at her parent's house. Ben bought me a drink and spilled the beans.

More than he planned, I think. It wasn't the first time he cheated on Jess with Sharnie. I damn near nearly knocked his teeth down his throat."

At the top of the stairs, my breath rushed out of me. I had to cover my mouth to hold in the sound of getting winded.

"E, you two have something going on here. You can deny it to Lou and me all you want and pretend it's just a booty call on a layover, but I know you. You've never changed your roster for a regular piece of ass ever. This is Jess. Lou's daughter. His precious princess."

"I told you not to go there with this. Lou doesn't need to know. Jess barely tells him anything as is. She didn't even tell him we went to Bora Bora with her."

"Look, I get that, but if you aren't going to tell her why I'm hanging around, then I'm better off going back to the hotel and being a misery-guts by myself. Whatever this is between you, I don't want to be the cause behind it falling apart. You are more than capable of fucking this up on your own."

"Dude!"

"I've never lied to you, man. Don't expect me to start now. You suck at relationships. You sucked at them even before Natalie screwed you over. Now, if this morning is anything to go by, you're even worse."

"For the last time, Jess and I are just friends. That's all it is."

"Wake up, dude! I saw you two at the airport when she was leaving. I've seen you two the last few weeks too. There is something more than just sex-friends between you."

The laundry door slammed open. "Let's hit the waves already."

Listening to them leave, I hung my head. Horse riding wasn't going to cut it today. I needed something in the water, something that drowned out the world. Grabbing my diving bag, I pulled on my dive-skin pants and got in the car.

There was an excellent place for both snorkeling and scuba diving on the west coast. It was right near a power plant, so the warm waters attracted lots of marine life, but because of the currents, it was for advanced divers only as you had to be a strong swimmer. Something physically demanding and slightly dangerous and therefore requiring lots of focus was what I needed today.

When I got back to my car hours later, I had messages from Sean and Ethan.

<Sean>: What time is lunch?

Hello?

Are we still doing lunch?

I'll try Ethan's phone in case you switched yours off to avoid getting work calls.

<E>: Sean called and said you'd asked him to join us for lunch. I invited him down early for a round of golf. I'll get rid of the guys afterward, and we can go out to dinner—just the two of us.

<Sean>: So, I'm playing golf with your BF and his BFF, and I've got the sense shit went down this morning. Are you okay?

We are now doing dinner instead of lunch. Are you okay with that?

Scratch that. I got it wrong. I'm to disappear, and dinner is for you two.

Jess, come on. You never ignore me like this. Where are you?

Sighing, I chucked my bag in the back seat and stripped out of my skins, throwing them in the bag before pulling a sundress over my cossie. Laying out my towel on the driver's seat, I stood looking across Kahe Point Beach Park and leaned on my car while I texted Sean back.

\<Jessie Girl\>: I'm at Kahe Point. I'll drop by work, make sure everything is good since I'm just next door, then I'll do some shopping on the way home. I should be back by the time you guys finish thrashing your balls around the paddock.

\<Sean\>: Guys said you went horse riding, not diving. That explains the radio silence. Ethan wants to know why I call you Jessie Girl now.

\<Jessie Girl\>: Tell me you do not have me called that on your phone?

\<Sean\>: Okay, I won't.

\<Jessie Girl\>: Seriously! I'm writing my resignation letter when I get home. I can't work for you under these circumstances. It's harassment to use an employee's father's pet name against them like this. Wait until you hear from my lawyers.

Smirking, I shook my head. Bloody best friends get away with murder. Thinking about that, I wondered what was going on with Greg that had Ethan babysitting him. The following message went to Ethan.

\<Jess\>: Sorry about this morning. I overreacted. Greg's welcome to come and use my board anytime. In fact, why doesn't he stay in the guest room when you are in town, so he doesn't have to get up so early?

\<E\>: I can't tell if you are being sarcastic or not.

\<Jess\>: Not.

<E>: Oh, well then, Hell. No! You couldn't be quiet to save your life, and I don't want you trying to be. Plus, that would severely handicap the welcome I get, and I am doing nothing to jeopardize that!

Shaking my head, I couldn't help the smile that spread across my face. Okay, well, if Ethan wasn't the problem, why was I so pissed off about things today?

<Jess>: Sean and Greg should stay for dinner, then we should go out to a club Sean told me about once. I could use a night out, and by the sounds of it this morning, Greg could too.

<E>: How much did you hear this morning?

Knowing what E was worried about, I chose not to hide anything. Greg didn't lie to him, and Sean and I never lied to each other. If we were going to make it, even just as friends, we couldn't lie to each other either.

<Jess>: All of it.

Nothing for several minutes. Then the phone rang. "Jess. I'm sorry. You weren't meant to know."

"Why?"

"They'd hurt you enough. You didn't need to know more."

Staring at the ground, I kicked at the gravel. "What's going on with Greg and Sharnie?"

Blowing out a breath, Ethan took a moment. "They're fighting. She accused him of taking the Hawaii run to have an affair with you. Sharnie thinks you two are fucking. I won't let him tell her about us, so in her mind, it's about you and him."

Huh, typical. Sharnie always expected of others what she would do. "Jeez, Sharnie is going to lose it. Maybe you should just tell her that it's you fucking me and solve this for him?" Ethan was quiet. "Except you don't want that. You don't want anyone knowing about us, do you?"

When Ethan stayed quiet, I nodded to myself and stood straight, turning around, ready to get in my car. "Sharnie uses transference. If she's accusing Greg of cheating on her, he should be checking out what she's been doing while he's not in town. I've got to go. I'll see you this afternoon."

Dropping into my car, I sent one last message to Sean.

<Jessie Girl>: All four of us are going out to dinner tonight, and you are all staying over. Don't ask. Just be my friend.

<Sean>: Whatever you need.

CHAPTER EIGHTEEN

"So, you got to meet Jess's rock god?"

"Sean!" I scolded as he refilled everyone's glasses, finishing the third bottle.

"That was awesome. An all-expenses-paid weekend in Bora Bora and meeting one of my favorite guitarists in the world," Greg answered with way too much enthusiasm. "What sucks is that we can't talk about it. I can't even tell my wife!"

"You can't talk about it to outsiders, but you can with us, just don't mention his name while talking about him," Sean coached.

"Dude, you're right!" Greg started prattling on about Dylan and meeting him for a good twenty minutes. "Of course, once we got to the island, I barely saw them. My room was at the other end of the resort, but Jess and Ethan were in the bungalow next door."

"He likes to keep Jess close at hand when he stays." Sean nodded.

"Yeah, we noticed they're close," Greg agreed, eyes flicking to Ethan. "Do you know the story there?"

Shaking his head, Sean eyed me a moment. "No. Jess couldn't talk about it even if she wanted to. All I know is the guy is in love with her, and she just shrugs him off."

"Sean, you're drunk," I scoffed.

"She denies it, of course. But every time he visits, another album gets released not long after, and there are lyrics suspiciously close to things I've witnessed and been told by the staff not restrained by a piece of paper." Sean's eyes glittered at me across the table. "I bet you a grand that the next album has a song about the girl he loves and her new boyfriend."

"Now you're just making shit up!"

"Really?" Sean cocked that brow. "Care to explain the song Goddess of Heartbreak? The one about the late-night call begging for help. Take her anywhere in the world, as long as it wasn't home. Never to go home. She'll never Waltzing Matilda again. Because if I were a betting man, I'd put good money on that one being about you."

My eyes stung as those words made the scars of my heart itch. Bloody musicians using your life for their creative processes.

Sitting back with wide eyes, Greg stared at me like I was a unicorn. "Holy shit! You're Obsession, Rejected!"

Brows drawing together, Ethan looked from the others to me. "You're his muse?"

"Wait! Are you Ride Me, Cowgirl?" Greg jumped his brows at me.

"For fucks sake!" Rolling my eyes, I glared at Sean. "See the shit you've started now. They're going to associate me with any song that he writes from now on. I suppose you'll all think his song Angel of Snow and Razorblades was about me too?"

"The one about the psycho chick? Is it?" Greg asked, his smile going wide.

Standing up, I snatched the empty bottle and my glass away. "No! It's about your wife and how she got herself fucked up on drugs then tried to beat Dylan's sister to death with a fucking textbook." Going to the kitchen sink, I dropped the bottle in the recycling bin and put the glass on the bench.

The years between Sharnie's psychotic episode and my running away from home had brought Dylan and me together time and time again. As tragedy impacted his and Teille's lives repeatedly, I'd always ended up there somehow, as if fate ensured I'd be there for the siblings. As luck would have it, Dylan was there for me when it was my life falling apart.

Sean was right; Dylan got me out of Australia, and a few of the incidents that brought us together inspired his songs, but there were a lot of embellishments too.

"I'm going to bed."

After dinner out, we'd come back home and drank and played cards and talked. It was friendly and nice, but talking about Dylan and me was crossing a line. Forget the legal one. Bringing up our past was opening my personal well of hurt, which I was never keen to do.

Coming out from the shower, Ethan was sitting on my bed. "I want to ask about you and him, but I read that NDA pretty thoroughly, so I get that you can't talk about him, even with me. I'd still like to ask you to be honest and tell me whether I'm his replacement?"

Not sure I heard him right, I frowned. "Replacement?"

"We look a lot alike."

"If you mean in height and coloring, sure. But if you held a lineup of most of the guys I've been with, including Ben, you'd all meet those physical criteria. As Dylan said, I have a type. That doesn't mean you are anything alike."

"We're both orphans with commitment issues."

"That's reaching."

"Is it?"

Gritting my teeth, I grabbed my phone and googled Dylan Neptune and his parents' funeral. Tapping on a picture, I held it out to Ethan. "Recognize the girl he's holding hands with?"

Frowning at the picture, Ethan couldn't see the face. One of the things I'd always excelled at was never letting my face end up in any photo with Dylan. Zooming in on the picture, Ethan studied it as he stood up. "That's the scar on your arm. It's you."

"I knew Dylan long before he was an orphan. Google Dylan Neptune and the word tragedy. I'll wait."

Frowning, Ethan googled it. Image after image appeared of Dylan. "You're in the background or beside him in a lot of these pictures? His parent's funeral, sitting outside a hospital after the attack on Teille when she was fourteen, his sister's attempted suicide when she was sixteen—are you covered in blood?"

"I don't have to tell you how we know each other or what we are to each other because it's there for you to find—every horrendous life-changing moment in all three of our lives.

"I'm not his muse. I'm his shoulder to cry on when it all gets too much. I'm his confidante. I have cried with him more times than I can count. If you're asking if I've slept with him, I think the answer is obvious. Does he love me? I don't think so.

"It would be hard for either of us to separate the knotted-up mess of emotions we've endured together to define what we are. The best I can give you is that we are friends who have been there for each other through some of the worst things life has thrown at us."

Stepping closer to Ethan, I gazed up into his hypnotizing eyes. "You may have similar appearances, but you are very different people. That's all you'll get from me on this topic." Moving by Ethan, I climbed into bed. "I'm exhausted. Goodnight."

"Jess..." When I kept my back to Ethan, he let it go. After he stepped into the bathroom and shut the door, I wiped the tear from my eye.

After cleaning his teeth, Ethan turned out the light, climbed into bed, and put his arm around me. Pulling me tight to the front of him, Ethan nuzzled my neck.

"I don't think this is working," I admitted. "I feel like you are always judging me, waiting for a reason to end this. Fighting with you feels like shit, and so does the way you are only too keen to point out you're just here for the sex."

"That's not true."

"You keep implying it. You don't want anyone to know about us, to the point you are willing to destroy your best friend's marriage. You may be selfish like that, Ethan, but I'm not. No matter how much I dislike Sharnie, I won't stoop to her level."

Pulling back a touch, Ethan took a moment. "Are you saying you want me to go?"

Rolling to face him, I caressed the side of his face in the dark. "God, Ethan, I never want you to leave, but I'm not going to be complicit in hurting Greg because of your selfishness, and I want to be more than just sex."

"You are! You know you are."

"That's not what I've heard several times today. That's not how I feel when you've been here the last few visits. Maybe you are trying to shut your internal shit down, but you hurt me when you do it because you're the one person I'm okay with feeling something towards."

Caressing my face, Ethan hesitated when he brushed against my tears. "God, Jess. Don't cry." Wiping my tears away, Ethan pressed his lips to my forehead. "Don't cry, Jess. Please. I'm not worth this." His pleas only made the tears come faster.

"I'm sorry you think I'm a selfish ass, but I don't want Sharnie to know about us. I don't want Margaret to know I've changed my roster to see you. I don't want Lou knowing we are sleeping together because I know he's hoping I'm going to win your heart and convince you to come home and marry me and give birth to my children. We both know that's not going to happen, and I don't want to break his heart when it doesn't."

Trying to turn my face away, I couldn't meet Ethan's eyes. Sweeping my hair back from my face, Ethan forced me to look at him again. "Jess, come on. I never lied about my intentions here. We are more than sex, more than friends, but I won't offer you anything more."

"If I'm more than sex, talk to me about things. Don't hide things like Sharnie and Greg, don't lie to me, and avoid being alone with me to avoid talking about the real things. Treat me like a friend. Talk to me. If you can't do that, then don't pretend it's anything more than getting your rocks off." Rolling over again, I put some distance between our bodies and hugged my pillow tight.

In the morning, I was out of bed before Ethan woke up. After getting dressed, I went downstairs and turned on the coffee maker. While I was making myself breakfast, Sean came out. He tilted his head and assessed me. "Oh, Jessie girl. What's happened?"

"What time's your flight?"

"Lunchtime."

"You're probably on Ethan's plane then. Feel free to borrow my board for a surf before you go. I'll see you when you come back next month." Grabbing my keys, I went to leave, but Sean grabbed my elbow.

"Jess?"

Closing my eyes, I looked away for a moment. "Tell Ethan that I won't be back before you all leave and to fly safely." Kissing Sean's cheek, I left. There was a horse on the north shore missing his owner, who I had an apple for and all day to ride.

CHAPTER NINETEEN

<E>: I missed you this morning. I was hoping to talk to you before I left.

Looks like Sean is on our flight.

I don't like how we left things. Can we talk when I get home?

LOOKING AT ETHAN'S MESSAGES AGAIN, I BIT MY LIP AND CLOSED THE screen. Unlocking my door Sunday afternoon, I stepped inside and considered the empty living room. After spending most of the day out riding, I'd decided to stay the night at Sean's place so that I could ride again in the morning. That resulted in me missing Ethan's two attempts to call while I was out of service.

Going to the kitchen, I cooked up something light for dinner, then sat down at the table and opened my computer. Lou would be on soon, and I wanted to make sure I was here on time for him. Just as I finished eating, knight's armor came up on my screen, and the ring tone sounded.

Biting my lip, I answered the call. Ethan was sitting outside holding up his phone to talk. "Jess, hey. I saw you come online. I hope you don't mind, Lou is just in the shower, and I thought I'd steal the time until he was ready."

Surprised by how upbeat Ethan was, almost like he used to be before he started coming to visit, I tried to meet the same level. "Hey. You look like you could use a shower yourself."

"Yeah, it was hot here today. We were roasting on the golf course. What did you get up to?"

"I went for a surf when I woke up and then a ride."

"At home?"

"No. I stayed at Turtle Beach last night. I dropped by the Dole plantation on the way home to get my Dole whip fix."

"Pineapple soft serve would have gone down nicely here today." Someone called Ethan's name off-screen. Lifting his eyes, Ethan waved, then returned his attention to the screen. "So, I'll land late on Thursday. Are you okay for me to let myself in when I get there?"

Biting my lip, I looked down at my keyboard. "Maybe you should stay at the hotel on Thursday night."

Ethan's smile dropped. "Oh."

"If you tell me which hotel you're staying at, I'll meet you there for dinner after work on Friday."

Taking a moment, Ethan considered the screen. "You're not taking the Friday off?"

"No. That's been rather pointless of late." Meeting his eyes, I didn't bother shying away from answering that one truthfully.

"Okay. Should I expect to stay at the hotel on Friday night as well?"

"Couldn't hurt."

Ethan looked away for a moment, then nodded. "I'll get a room for the length of my stay and give you your space."

Wetting my lips, I nodded. "I appreciate that. I'll see you Friday then."

Frowning, Ethan opened his mouth, then shut it. Blowing out a breath, he dropped his head, then inhaled and looked back at the screen. "Have a good week."

"You too. Fly safe." Disconnecting, I exhaled hard. Getting up, I went to the kitchen and poured a glass of wine, drinking half of it before I came back to answer Lou's call.

"Jessie girl, did you have a good week?" Lou smiled.

Forcing a smile, I lied. "Yes, Dad. How about you?"

"Yes, good." Dad carried on telling me all about his week for five minutes before asking me about mine. I told him about some of the things that happened at work, about the place I went diving on Friday, and how I went back to Turtle Beach to ride. I just left the timeline out, so it sounded like I did all that on the weekend.

"Was your boss home?" Lou questioned.

"He flew out on Saturday. I think he was on Ethan's flight."

"Oh, did you see Ethan this visit?"

Forcing a smile to stay in place, I nodded. "Yeah. Sean and I had dinner with them on Friday night. They played golf at the course I live on, on Friday. My strata fees include free membership—not that I'll ever use them, so I've offered for them to use it when they are here."

"With them?" Lou frowned.

"Yes, Ethan, Sean, and Greg. I overheard that Greg and Sharnie have been fighting. Is everything okay there?"

Forehead furrowing, Lou shook his head. "You know your sister. I'm sure it'll settle down again. Greg's a good man. He takes a lot of your sister's antics in his stride."

"Love makes people put up with a lot of crap. When I was younger, I used to think you and mum were perfect for each other, and I used to dream of finding that sort of relationship for myself. I've realized that love just makes people complacent to being treated like shit by one person in particular."

"Jessie girl, that's not what love is. It's about accepting someone's flaws because you love them."

"That's just the romantic way of saying you put up with someone's shit because you love them. It doesn't mean you should. You used to tell me that you can't help who you fall in love with, only what you do about it. I think that was the best advice you've ever given me. I also think it was your way of telling me Ben wasn't the one for me without saying it."

"You had to choose your own path. We all do."

Bowing my head, I nodded to myself. "I get it now. I want you to know that I finally understand and value what you were teaching me. I don't think I tell you enough, but I love you, Dad. Thank you for being you."

Eyes flicking over his screen, Lou blinked and returned his focus to me. Leaning forward, Lou frowned. "Jessie, is everything okay?"

Smiling, I chuckled and quickly wiped away the tear that escaped. "Yeah, Dad. Just a little emotional this week."

Sitting back, Lou blinked. "Oh, do you have plenty of ice cream? That was always your preference, if I remember correctly. Your mother liked cheesecake, Sharnie chocolate, and you preferred some overly chocolatey ice cream."

"Connoisseur Chocolate Obsession. Triple chocolate with a cherry brandy sauce," I chuckled. "Sadly, they don't make it anymore."

"Have you found an alternative?"

"I have. There's a tub in the freezer. I'm going to sit down with it and a movie once I log off."

The doorbell rang. "That'll be Greg and Sharnie. I'll let you eat your ice cream. Love you, Jessie girl."

"Love you too, Dad." Disconnecting, I closed the laptop and took my glass out to the patio. Taking a seat at the outdoor setting, I closed my eyes and listened to the beach in the distance while I finished my wine.

Taking out my phone, I opened my phone book and pressed Mayla's number. Holding it to my ear, I waited for the call to connect. "Jess, hey?"

"Hey. What are your plans next weekend?"

"Just the usual. Why?" Mayla shut a door and the noise of music and laughter cut off in the background.

"Did you want to come and visit? I could use a wingman." Trying not to laugh and sigh simultaneously was difficult.

"A wingman?" Mayla mulled on it for a moment. "Does this visit include a full day of shopping?"

"God, yes!" I huffed. "I need a bit of girl time."

"And am I playing wingman for any particular reason?"

"Ethan and my brother-in-law will be having dinner with us on Friday night. Potentially Saturday night too, but that could just be me, and you can entertain yourself if you like?"

"The brother-in-law? Sharnie's husband?"

"The only one I've got, so far."

"Ooh, I get to meet the crazy guy." Mayla's excitement made me smile.

"He seems quite sane."

"Then what is he doing with your insane-ass sister?"

"That has everyone stumped. So, Friday night. Can you be here by seven?"

"I'll look at flights now and get back to you tomorrow."

Leaning back in my chair, I stared up at the starry night. "Thanks, Mayla."

"Hey, I get a shopping trip with free accommodation. That means more money to spend. I can't pass that up. Plus, I'm looking forward to seeing your new place. I'm not sleeping on the couch, am I?"

Chuckling, I shook my head despite the fact Mayla couldn't see me. "No. I have two guest rooms for you to choose from."

"Excellent. Then it's a win-win situation, isn't it?" You could hear Mayla's smile on the other side of the line. "I'll message you tomorrow to let you know what time I'll get in."

"Great. Mayla, there's one more thing." Waiting for a heartbeat, I wet my lips and scraped my teeth over my bottom lip. "I need a couple of photos that may suggest you're my girlfriend."

Silence on the other end of the line.

"Nothing pornographic, just subtle like friendly, but easily misconstrued by a paranoid mind."

"What am I missing?" Mayla asked accusatorially.

"Sharnie thinks I'm fucking her husband."

Mayla started laughing hysterically. Pursing my lips, I tried waiting her out, but after nearly a minute, my smile broke through, and my laughter, half-born of stress, broke through. Eventually, after several attempts to respond, we both calmed enough to finish the conversation. "Hell, Jess, I needed that laugh. That was awesome."

"Me too."

"I'd love to say I can't believe your sister would think that, but from what I've heard about her, it seems right in the circle of her brand of crazy. I just know that you would never be that kind of woman; that's why I laughed so hard."

"Thank you. At least someone recognizes that I have morals."

"Okay, okay, this weekend is sounding like a ball of fun. I'll message you my flight time later. I might try and get the afternoon off, so I have time for a little beautification before we head out."

"Perfect. Why don't you fly over at lunch and come to the spa here? I'll give you the staff discount."

"You know how to sell a girls' weekend, Jess. I'm emailing Sean now for the time off. I'll see you Friday."

Relieved, I smiled. "See you on Friday."

Hanging up, I finished my wine. A little girl time is what I needed, and if it allowed me to put Ethan in the fuck-friends space only, double bonus. If he wanted us just to be friends who had sex, I'd show him exactly how that was going to work.

As if he heard me, my phone pinged with a message from Ethan with the hotel's details and asking which restaurant I'd prefer. Calling the hotel, I enquired about the atmosphere and food at each of their restaurants, then booked a table for four at the one she didn't describe as romantic.

Putting my phone down from letting Ethan know, I went to the fridge for my pint of Dole Whip, then turned on the television.

<E>: Four?

<Jess>: My friend Mayla will be in town and is joining us for dinner. You met her in Maui. She threw my farewell party. I thought it would save Greg from feeling like a third wheel.

There was a long pause, so I put my phone aside and went back to watching my movie. When I'd finished cleaning up for the night, I grabbed my phone and headed upstairs for the night to sit down and do some prep work for the week ahead. Just as I was climbing into bed, I rechecked my phone.

<E>: Is Mayla staying with you? Is that why you asked me to stay at the hotel?

It'll be just us on Saturday night, right?

I take it that Mayla is there all weekend. I fly out Monday morning. Can we find time for just us, please? I really want to talk to you about last weekend.

Chewing my lip, I sent a reply.

<Jess>: Sunday night. I'll cook.

Setting my phone aside, I turned out the light and put my head on the pillow. It took me much longer than I would have liked to fall asleep. My mind was busy analyzing my feelings for Ethan and whether pushing him away to arm's length was what I wanted. In the end, I'd fallen asleep determined that it was for the best.

CHAPTER TWENTY

Trying to catch my breath, I fell to the side, head hitting the pillow, tempting me to close my eyes.

"You look exhausted," Ethan murmured as he rolled to face me.

"Shopping with Mayla can be the equivalent of running a marathon." I smiled. After dinner Friday night, we'd gone disco bowling. While Mayla and Greg were busy playing their fourth game of pool, Ethan and I had taken the heavy petting up to his room for an energetic romp. Afterward, I'd gotten up and left—something Ethan hadn't expected.

Saturday, Mayla and I spent the day shopping at the outlet stores. Then we met up with the guys for dinner and dancing. Ethan coerced me back to his hotel again after a few hours bumping and grinding on the dance floor, only for me to get up, find Mayla, and go home again.

Tonight, we were in my bed after dinner by ourselves. Mayla and I spent the day shopping again, and then I'd dropped her off at the airport for her flight and picked Ethan up from his hotel. We'd spent the meal talking about what we got up to separately during the day but hadn't talked about us.

Kissing over my shoulder, Ethan caressed my stomach. "I'm going to go clean up. Then, can we talk?"

"Sure, I'll go put the kettle on. Do you want some tea?" Sitting up, I reached for my robe and pulled it around me.

"I was hoping we'd stay here." Ethan frowned.

Smiling as I tied the sash on my dressing gown, I met his eyes. "I'm thirsty. I'll call a car to take you back to the hotel."

"Jess—"

Heading downstairs before Ethan could argue, I grabbed up my phone and ordered a lift for Ethan while I set about making us both peppermint tea. Something calming was best. Ethan's arms wrapped around me from behind as I stood looking out my kitchen window at the entry.

"I'm sorry I hurt you, Jess. It was never my intention."

Glancing down to where his hands held me, I closed my eyes and shifted, so he had to let me go while I fixed the tea. Before we decided where we were, I wanted to know what took us off track. "What happened at Bora Bora?"

"What do you mean?"

Sighing, I put a mug on the bench for Ethan, then took mine back to the window and pulled myself up into the seat I liked to wait and watch for him. "I mean, we were good before that, right? That's how it felt. We were getting along, the sex was fantastic—"

"It still is."

"We were making this work. Then we went to Bora Bora. From the moment you arrived at the airport, you were cranky with me, and you barely talked to me the entire weekend. The sex was still hot, but everything else…" Wetting my lips, I met Ethan's eyes. "Then you gave me your roster, and you were here every week for two nights for a month. Thursday to Saturday. I took the Fridays off to be with you, but you arranged Friday with Greg. I was just the girl you bounced on your dick each night you were here, and that was it."

Ethan's jaw clenched. "I never thought of you like that. I promise. It wasn't like that."

"Yes, it was, Ethan. It was like that to me! I've had the occasional holiday hookup, and never have I ever felt as used as you made me feel for the last month."

"Is that what this weekend was about? Trying to repay the favor by treating me like a cock you were just there to ride?"

Lifting a brow, I assessed Ethan. "Is that how you felt?"

Frowning, Ethan shook his head and exhaled. "No. Dinner and dancing were still fun and friendly. We laughed and flirted, and that was all good, and the sex was hot, but once it was over, the way you'd say goodnight and leave... It was a slap in the face. Even the first time we ever had sex, you stayed the night and snuck out before I woke up in the morning."

"This weekend wasn't about revenge, Ethan. Not to me. You were very clear last week that we are friends who happen to enjoy sex together. That's all that you are offering. That's all I can have. Right?"

Licking his lips, Ethan nodded.

"This weekend was me putting those boundaries in place. When you stay here, fuck me all night, then push me aside to go golfing with Greg, surfing with him, I feel used not for sex, Ethan, but my house, for my location, for my fucking golf club membership." My voice cracked a little, and Ethan suddenly stiffened as I wiped away a tear and took a deep breath to steady myself.

"I can handle us being fuck-friends, Ethan. If that's all you want, then it's going to be like it was this weekend. We'll hang out, have sex, but at the end of the night, I'm going to come home alone, or you will go back to your hotel. You can use the club membership to play golf with Greg. I don't care, but you won't feature in my life, and you won't sleep in my bed."

My phone buzzed with the notification that the driver was nearby. Sliding down from the bench, I met Ethan's eyes. "If this is more. If we are building towards something more, a commitment of some kind, something permanent, then we can go back to you staying over and work towards that. But if all you want is a regular fuck-friend on your layover, don't pretend it's anything more."

Lights flashed out in the driveway, and my phone pinged again. "Your lift is here."

Taking his empty mug to the sink, Ethan rinsed it and set it aside. With a sigh, he turned to look at me. His jaw moved as if he wanted to say something but couldn't bring himself to say it or wasn't sure the words were correct. He didn't look angry or upset. If anything, he looked humbled, or maybe guilty was the better word.

Cuffing my cheek, Ethan kissed me. It was quick and sweet. "Thank you for a fun weekend. Let me know what's on the cards for next week. I'll stay at the same place again."

Nodding my head, I took the hit with barely a flinch and walked Ethan to the door. "Fly safe," I farewelled, opening the door.

"Always." Staring into my eyes for a moment by the door, Ethan caressed my cheek again, his eyes glassy as his thumb wiped the damn tear that escaped. "I'll call you Wednesday."

"Okay," I agreed, forcing a smile while Ethan looked me over one more time, and then he headed down the courtyard and out to the waiting car. Shutting the door, the deluge of tears that poured forth did so quietly. It was okay, really. Ethan and I would be great fuck-friends. I just had to let go of that hope that had developed somehow that we'd be more.

It was my fault. Ethan told me from the start he wasn't ever going to marry me and want a family. I hadn't expected having Ethan in my bed every weekend would make my feelings so strong for him. Then again, it's not like we went into this with the expectation he would be here so often. It was meant to be once a month, maybe twice if I was lucky. If I'd known it would be so often, I'd have set the boundaries in place sooner.

Washing my face, I fixed myself a snack, then opened my computer. When Lou logged on and asked me how I was, I lied through my teeth. Then I sent him the photos of Mayla and me that Greg took for me. To the innocent eye, we were friends hanging out and having fun. To Sharnie, it would be her sister playing for the other team and having something with which to stir up my mum. If it got her to let the idea of Greg and I hooking up go, then I didn't care. Let her think whatever and move on to her next drama.

———

<E>: Flight ran late. We are driving home now. Are you still okay for me to call you?

<Jess>: Not if you are tired.

<E>: All good. It was only a trans-Tasman flight—eight hours round trip to New Zealand and back. I'm an hour out if you'll still be awake?

Looking at the time, I sighed.

<Jess>: Still got thirty minutes on my movie, and then I'll get ready for bed. Should be just getting under the covers when you call.

<E>: Perfect. Just the sort of mental imagery I need too.

Rolling my eyes, I put my phone aside and focused on the movie. I was in bed reading a chapter of a book when the phone rang. Picking it up, I pressed to answer, then put it on speaker. "Hey. Home safe?"

"Just walked in the door," Ethan answered. "How has your week been so far?"

"Busy, but good. You?"

"Tolerable." The phone went quiet for a long moment. "Um, so I'll land at ten-thirty Friday morning. By the time I do my flight report and get to the hotel, it will be lunchtime. I'm going to get some sleep and was hoping to meet you for dinner again."

"Sounds good. Will Greg be joining us?"

"Not this weekend. Since he missed out on seeing Maui, Greg's decided that he's going to spend the weekend there. He's catching a flight straight after we land."

Was I suss that Greg was going to Maui after two nights of hanging out with Mayla last weekend? Yeah, a little. I'd be calling Mayla to ask her what the go was after this. "Oh, okay. I was going to suggest the Cheesecake Factory if he was coming, but we can leave that until next time and try somewhere else."

"Your choice, just let me know when and where to meet you."

"Okay, I'll see where I can get us in."

"Maybe we can go out dancing or something afterward again?" Ethan suggested.

"After working all day? And you'll have only had a few hours of sleep. Maybe something a little less strenuous?"

"You choose. I'll keep up with you."

Smiling at Ethan's ease, I took a breath. "You know, I think 'Eat the Street' is on this weekend. It's a festival held once a month where we celebrate all things edible in Hawaii."

"Sounds intriguing," Ethan answered skeptically.

Yep, this was perfect. "You'll love it. I'll meet you at your hotel around six. Wear something comfy as we'll walk there and back."

"Okay, I'll see you in the lobby at six. Enjoy the rest of your week."

"You too. I'll see you Friday." Hanging up, I sighed and stared at the wall opposite my bed for a few moments. Then I remembered the Greg drama.

\<Jess\>: What is happening with you and Greg? I hear he's heading your way for the weekend????

\<Mayla\>: We talked a lot last weekend and agreed that E was using him as a buffer as much as you were using me. So, I suggested he get away and see the other islands and areas here, so E had no excuses. Don't worry, I know he's married. Considering I know his wife is an absolute psycho, I can promise you there will be nothing naughty happening.

\<Jess\>: I think we've decided to keep things simple. Dinner, hang out a bit, sex, and that's it. Anything else seems too much for us.

\<Mayla\>: Yeah, I could see that. Still, a bit of alone time won't hurt. Let's do another girls' weekend again next month.

\<Jess\>: You're on. And thank you.

Putting my phone aside, I slid down beneath the sheets and planned out the weekend as I closed my eyes.

Friday night, I met Ethan at his hotel, and we walked to Kaka'ako Waterfront Park for 'Eat the Street.' There was a wide variety of different food truck companies offering a vast array of styles and eats. Not only was it a culinary delight, but also a way to mingle with locals and foodies alike.

Once we'd eaten way too much, we walked back past Kawalo Basin Harbour and through Ala Moana Regional Park onto Waikiki beach, ready for the weekly fireworks. With our bellies full and walking hand in hand through the moonlight, it was a beautiful, dreamlike journey.

Once the fireworks were over, we meandered down Kalakaua Avenue. There was live music, and when one of the street artists played one of Ethan's favorite songs, he took me in his arms and danced with me under the street torch lights. The whole scene had an otherworldly glow to it.

By the time we made it back to Ethan's hotel room and took our time enjoying each other, it was late, and my eyes drifted closed when he held me in his arms and kissed me slowly. When I woke a few hours later, I slipped out of bed and dressed without waking him. Leaving Ethan a note, I headed downstairs, got in my car, and went home.

My bed was cold and lonely, but it wasn't confusing. That was an important distinction. No warm body was worth doubting your head and heart or breaking it recklessly.

CHAPTER TWENTY-ONE

WAKING WITH THE SUNRISE, I WENT INTO THE BATHROOM AND washed my face. This was the third weekend since I'd set the no sleepover boundary in place, and while things were better than ever between Ethan and me, leaving after we had sex was getting harder.

Next week, Ethan would be here from Sunday to Friday. I'd put in for the week off to take him to Kauai before it all went south, and while I was still keen to go, I was wondering if I needed to book separate rooms. "Fuck!" I leaned on the sink and stared at my tired reflection. "You're overthinking it. Just treat next week as a holiday fling. It can be just like it was when I went back home."

Pulling my hair up back in a low ponytail, I pulled on my leggings, boots, and a loose shirt, ready to go horse riding. Skipping down the stairs, I slowed and frowned at the smell of coffee already brewed. Turning my head, I found Ethan standing in my kitchen. When we made eye contact, he pushed a mug across the bench towards me.

"Morning. I knocked, but you were in the shower. I had the key, so I hope you don't mind."

"Hey," I approached, unsure why he was here. We hadn't spent the daytime together since our dynamic shifted.

Rubbing his lips, Ethan took a breath. "I know you probably had plans today, but I was wondering if you could change them and spend the day with me?"

"E, I—"

"I hate this," Ethan cut in. "I miss you." Staring into his coffee, Ethan looked tormented. Eventually, he took a breath and met my eyes. "There is something I love to do. It's my escape. I want to share it with you. Please."

Chewing my lip, I looked down at my horse riding outfit, then back up to Ethan. "What should I wear?"

"It's casual attire. But bring some swimmers." Picking his phone up, he sent a text message. "We'll leave as soon as you are ready."

Unsure how to take this development, I headed back upstairs. Texting the stables to let them know I wouldn't be coming today, I changed into a flowing mid-thigh summer skirt and singlet top. Packing swimmers, a hat, and sunscreen into a bag, I went downstairs and finished my coffee while Ethan stood out on the patio talking on his phone.

The door opened, and Ethan locked it behind him as he came back inside. "Okay, I've got it all locked in. Are you ready?"

Giving Ethan a nod, I followed him out the door and gave him the keys to my car when he asked for them. Driving us to Kalaeloa Airport, Ethan went to the general aviation section and asked me to wait in the car while he stepped out to talk to someone. When he came back, he had the broadest smile on his face. Ethan drove my car to a park, then led me to a hanger with several small aircraft.

"You rented a plane?"

Grinning, Ethan lifted a brow. "I want you to fly with me."

Licking my lips, I eyed the airplane. "I've never been in a small plane."

Walking around the plane, Ethan started assessing it. For what, I had no idea, but he seemed to know at what he was looking. "I've been flying for twenty years, Jess. I started in a Cessna 172 when I was sixteen. Then I joined the Air Force and flew fighter jets for nine years. I've been flying commercial for eleven years, but when I'm on holidays, I still like to take single engines up and get away from everything."

Coming back, seemingly satisfied from his external assessment, Ethan took my hand. "Trust me. Please."

"Why?"

Wetting his lips, Ethan looked at his toes. "Because it's my first love."

Inhaling, I eyed the plane then nodded. Leading me onto the plane, Ethan set me in the co-pilot's seat, then checked some more things before taking the pilot seat and starting the aircraft. We sat there for another twenty minutes while Ethan checked gauges and instruments, and I watched on, fascinated by everything that a pilot had to do before a plane even got out on the runway.

"Okay. We're good to go." Checking my harness, Ethan put a set of headphones on my head, then applied his own, and the door closed. Talking into the headphones, Ethan navigated us out of the hanger and to a waiting area by the runway. I didn't understand a word that the man talking to Ethan said, other than that he was talking to Ethan.

When they gave us the green light, Ethan taxied out to the runway, his smile growing. "Ready?" he asked me.

What was I going to say? 'No, let me off!' Giving him a false smile, I clung to the seat as the craft suddenly accelerated, and then we were lifting into the air, and I was praying to any god that would have me that I'd live through the day.

Chuckling, Ethan flicked a few switches as the plane leveled out. "You can open your eyes now, Jess."

Peeking first, I saw blue sky. Then, braving it, I looked out the window and saw the ocean below us. "Um, where are we going?"

"Nowhere. We're just flying." Ethan was still watching the instrument panel. "I've lodged a flight plan to do a lap of all the Hawaiian Islands. So, currently, we are heading up the west coast to Kauai, then we'll fly down the east coast to Big Island and back. I'm limited about how high or low I can fly because of all the helicopter tours, and also the flight paths of the commercial flights, but—" the plane tilted a little, and Ethan smiled, looking out my side of the cockpit, "—you'll have all the views on your side for the trip."

Looking out the window, I could see the west coast of Oahu, the reefs, the beaches, though, from this distance, it almost looked like a watercolor painting. Getting comfortable, I watched the view, spotting a pod of whales crossing the channel. "It's beautiful up here. A different world."

"Yeah, it is."

When I turned to look at Ethan, he was smiling at me. Chewing my lower lip, I turned my eyes back to the scenery. We flew around the top of Kauai and then headed south. "Are you still keen to get away together next week?"

"Very much so," Ethan assured. Reaching out, he took my hand. "I've missed you, Jess. I've missed adventuring together or just being with you while we read our books."

Swallowing hard, I kept staring out the window. It was on the tip of my tongue to say I missed Ethan too, but I couldn't open up to him again. If I did, he'd break me the next time he pulled away. When I didn't respond, Ethan let it go.

"That's Molokai," I pointed out after a while. "Sean's private residence is there. It's where he took Holly to propose." Turning my eyes to Ethan, I worried about my friend. "He's trying to find her again this weekend. There is a conference in Sydney for international hoteliers. I told him it was his best bet for finding where she works and finding her."

Frowning, Ethan eyed me. "Do you think he will find her?"

"Yeah, he will. Holly works for the hotel holding the conference. She's organized it all. I found out last week when Holly emailed me directly to ask how I am and was surprised to find out I work for Cassidy. I wasn't here when she was, so I missed her. I'd flown home for the wedding a few days before they came to Maui."

"You look stressed. Does it bother you?"

"She hurt him, E, but he never really let it hit him because he was so intent on finding her. I'm worried if he gets there and she's moved on, or she rejects him, that it will break him. He's my best friend. I worry. It's no different to you trying to get Greg out of his funk when he was down."

"Worrying about my friend and the impact my decisions were having on his marriage damaged what I had with you."

Swallowing hard, I took a breath. "I would say it refined what we have. It needed to happen, E. You can't deny things have been way better since we did."

"Except that I miss you. I wake up in the morning, and you're not there. I'm surfing by myself—and at home, I do that all the time—but here, it seems wrong to hit the waves without you. Then I'm left longing to see you all day."

Closing my eyes, I watched Maui cruise by the window. "I've missed you too. It's hard to come back to an empty bed, to leave your arms after having a few months getting used to sleeping in them, but when I agreed to this setup, you were going to be here once a month. Having you in my bed weekly confused things, and I think it was a problem for you too."

"I'm not good at relationships, Jess. Greg was right about that. Even before Natalie left me, I sucked as a husband."

"That doesn't excuse her cheating on you or her cleaning out your place."

"I know. Ben said you were the perfect girlfriend, and he still cheated on you. He said the hardest part was he would come back from fucking Sharnie and lie to your face, and you would smile and believe him, and you never doubted him, and it ate away at him. Each time, it just got worse."

Flinching at my past being dug up, I looked out the window. "Ben hated Sharnie. I never suspected for a minute. I truly thought the time I caught them was the first, and I blamed her entirely."

Ethan was quiet for a moment. "Ben told me the first time was before you two met. He met Sharnie at a party when he was sixteen, and they got high together and then had sex. It was both their first time. Ben met you a few months later and was besotted. You were a virgin, so he lied and said he was too because he didn't want to scare you away. When he realized who your sister was, he worried she'd tell you, and he asked her to keep it quiet. Sharnie had her psychotic break a few months later, and she used that secret to manipulate him from then on."

Nodding my head, I turned to meet Ethan's eyes. "What else did Ben tell you?"

"He told me there was another guy. That he was just a friend to you, but he saw how the guy looked at you and knew he wanted you. Ben said he expected to come home from the academy and find you'd taken up with him. He was surprised you waited. I'm guessing the other guy was Dylan?"

Gnawing on my lip, I turned my focus back out the window. We were circling the Big Island, the volcanos easy to see out the window, and despite the height, the lava lake visible. "I've never been to the Big Island. Volcanoes scare me. Ever since I saw Dante's Peak, but they are pretty amazing and fascinating. I just don't want to get caught anywhere near one if it erupts."

"That would be scary," Ethan agreed. "I had a friend on White Island when it erupted."

"I'm sorry."

Shaking his head, Ethan kept his focus on his instruments. "He's still alive."

"He's lucky to have survived." God, I couldn't imagine the trauma of such an event.

"I don't think survived is the right term, and I don't think he considers himself lucky."

Thinking about what it would be like to be highly scarred from the burns to his body and lungs from breathing in the toxic gas, I could understand that frame of mind. We fell into silence, my mind now thinking about how long-lasting a traumatic event's impact could be. Not just the big ones that leave physical scars, but even losing a baby, getting your heart broken, or being betrayed could scar your soul for life. Just one of many trauma victims walking around this planet trying to get through their day without anyone noticing.

"I did this last weekend," Ethan started out of nowhere. Blinking, I realized we were passing Molokai again. "Normally, if I'm feeling lost or out of sorts, I get up here, and I can get my thoughts sorted, my focus back. But last weekend, the entire time I was up here, I was wondering where you were and what you were doing down there."

Is that a good thing or a bad thing? Shouldn't he be thinking about keeping the plane in the air or calculating the landing?

"That's why I had to bring you with me today, Jess. I've never taken anyone up with me who wasn't part of my crew, not even Natalie. But I knew this was something I wanted to share with you."

Staring at Ethan, I realized my mouth was hanging open and forced it closed and turned away. "Um, thank you. It's been amazing."

"Maybe tomorrow, you'll take me horse riding with you," Ethan suggested as we swung out over the ocean. When I looked his way, Ethan smiled at me. "I know riding is for you what flying is for me. I want to try doing that with you, Jess."

Blinking a few times, I nodded before I found my voice. "Sure. We can go riding tomorrow."

Smile getting bigger, Ethan started flicking switches on the panel and asked for permission to land.

CHAPTER TWENTY-TWO

"It's beautiful up here," Ethan murmured.

Cuddled into the nook of his shoulder, I stared up at the sky. After the plane trip, Ethan picked up a hamper from his hotel, and we drove to the north-west to a lookout. After a picnic lunch, we'd relaxed back on the blanket together just to enjoy the peace and the view.

Playing with a strand of my hair, Ethan kissed the top of my head. "I want to tell you something, and I don't want you to judge me because of it."

Frowning, I brought my mind back to being here with Ethan. "Okay."

"You know about my family. How I never knew my dad and my mum died when I was young." When I nodded, Ethan dropped another kiss on my hair. "My grandfather died when I was a young teen, and my grandmother went the same year I joined the Air Force. That was it. At age seventeen, all of my family were dead. They'd all gone.

"Natalie and I met in high school. We'd only been together for six months when Nan died. It wasn't a great relationship. I was young and always away with the Air Force. She was already eighteen and always out drinking with her friends and pissed at me for being away. But when Nan died, she was all I had. So, I asked her to marry me."

"You wanted to know someone would be there," I realized.

"Yeah, I guess. At the time, I thought it was because I was in love with her. When she said yes and planned the wedding to happen a year later, I was happy. She wanted to stay with me. I'd always have her to come home to. The thing was, when I was home, it wasn't any better. I'm a homebody. I like to sit and read, or I want to do adventurous things if I'm going out. Natalie was a social butterfly, but she wasn't very active. Even going out to the club, she preferred to sit and drink instead of getting out on the floor and dancing.

"I hated going out drinking with her and her friends because they'd just sit around and gossip and talk about hooking up or having babies. So, she'd go out without me. I could have just walked in the door after three months away, and she'd kiss me hello and go out all night. The number of times she'd wake me up drunk, coming to bed at sunrise and crawl up on my dick then pass out before I even finished was too numerous to count."

Sitting up suddenly, I turned and gawped at Ethan. "Wait, she passed out while having sex with you?" When Ethan nodded, I closed my mouth and blinked at him. "Were you on top? Were you not as experienced back then or something?"

Chuckling, Ethan caressed my cheek. "She was always on top. Natalie was very dominant in bed, and she was the only girl I'd ever been with, so I guess I was inexperienced. But before I joined the service, she'd trained me up to give her what she liked. As I said, she was older, and I later found out, was a lot more experienced than me."

"I cannot even imagine being so drunk I'd pass out on top of you. I mean, you make a girl feel you, so how—"

Putting a finger to my lips, Ethan shushed me. "The ability to pass out on me is not the point of this story."

Inhaling, I nodded. "But we are going to come back to that. I mean, that's appalling!"

Chuckling, Ethan encouraged me back into his nook. "As I said, I was sure I was in love with her. I gave Natalie everything she asked for. I was lucky to have gotten a good inheritance, but it was all in trust. My apartment, my trust bought it, which meant Natalie couldn't touch it when we divorced. She didn't know that at the time. Still, I'd leave myself short money for food or fuel just to spoil her.

"It wasn't too bad since I wasn't as social as her. Other than flying, surfing was my only other passion back there, and that was free. Since I got to fly fighter jets, I was okay to go without my joy flights when I was home. As long as she was there, it didn't matter about all the other shit. I let her live her life and just tried to fit in with it when I was home. I thought she was happy with that."

Rolling to face Ethan, I rested my hand and chin on his chest. "You weren't happy, were you?"

Combing my hair off my face, Ethan caressed my cheek. "No. But I thought loving someone meant accepting their shit. After that last weekend here, I knew I'd pushed you too far, and when you told me to stay at the hotel from now on, I realized I was on the verge of losing you. Then, I heard you talking to Lou that afternoon. It made me realize I was treating you like Natalie used to treat me. It wasn't intentional. I was pissed that everyone was trying to interfere in what was happening with us."

Sitting up, I frowned. "What do you mean?"

Sighing, Ethan sat up as well. "Lou told you I wouldn't want you if you wouldn't come home. That was the first thing to set this in motion, Jess. You called me to tell me pointedly about your new place, and I was too tired to realize you were gauging my reaction to determine if his words were true. By the time I realized I'd somehow ended things, you'd hung up. So, I picked up the next shift I could to get over here and talk to you personally. The thing was, once I saw you again, I couldn't walk away."

Stroking my face, Ethan looked miserable. "I thought I could pick up the Hawaii shift once a month, and that would be enough. Then I got rostered more regularly, and I didn't mind that because, Jess, I've never been able to get enough of you. I hoped I would. That we'd grow bored of each other, or you'd get sick of my coming and going and tell me to piss off. I didn't want you to, but part of me hoped that would be the outcome.

"But you didn't, and things just got hotter, and it got harder to leave you without knowing when I would see you again. Then Sharnie accused Greg of screwing you. That flight over, Greg was nagging me about how serious we were; if I was going to marry you and move here; if I had told Lou yet? The entire flight, Jess. He wouldn't let up. It triggered me.

"Then I arrived, and Dylan was looking at you the way he did, and I knew instantly he'd had you, and he still wanted you. Every time that guy looked at you, it was with the same longing I know I have whenever I'm not with you. But you, you totally ignored the way he looked at you, and suddenly, I knew when this was over, I'd be just like Dylan. Longing for you still while you moved on with the next guy."

Frowning, I got ready to object, but Ethan held up a hand. "I know now, you two have so much history that there is more there than I realized, but at the time, all I could think was if I didn't put space between us now, you were going to break my heart because Jess, I never felt for Natalie like I do you. I never longed for her the way I long for you."

Bowing his head, Ethan shook it. "So, I tried to convince Greg and you, and myself, this was just two friends having sex. And fuck, Jess,

I did such a good job of convincing you that's all this was, that you made it exactly that. I think Greg was the only one I couldn't fool, and he was quick to tell me how badly I'd fucked it up when you brought Mayla to dinner with us and left with her instead of staying with me."

Listening to Ethan, I was sure he was trying to tell me something, but I didn't want to misunderstand. "Ethan, are you telling me you think you're falling for me?"

Scooting forward, Ethan took my face in his hands, his long legs creating a prison around me. "No, Jess. Falling suggests it's still happening. But it is very much a past tense situation. I fell for you back in Australia, Jess. I've been in denial all this time, but I can't deny how much I hate you getting up and leaving once the sex is over. Or how much it kills me to go to sleep with you in my arms and wake up to find you gone. I miss you every minute I'm not with you to the point even my first love, flying, feels less without you."

When I sat with my mouth gaping, Ethan met my gaze. "I'm in love with you, Jess. I don't want to be your fuck-friend. I want to be your boyfriend. I want you in whatever way you will let me have you. Just please, let me back in, because while being your friend is good, I hate how guarded you've become when you look at me. It's like you tell yourself over and over I'm not yours. That you can't look at me with anything but lust because I'm not yours to keep, and I hate it."

My eyes widened because I'm pretty sure those were the exact words I told myself for the past three weeks. "Ethan—" Feeling his chest, I dropped my watering gaze. "—be sure. I can't... I know how I've felt about you for months already. If you say this, if we do this and you change your mind again, you'll break me, and I won't come back from that. So, if you only think you love me but you might change your mind, please, don't go any further with this."

Ethan smashed his mouth to mine in the fiercest, most possessive kiss I'd ever experienced in my life. Every nerve ending came alive as he turned me to put me beneath him on the blanket, and he kissed me senseless. Pulling back, Ethan sucked a tear from my cheek and used his thumb to wipe away the rest. "I'm in love with you, Jess. I want you. I want us. I want to make this work between us. Tell me we can try this again."

The smile broke through, and fireworks seemed to be exploding in my chest. "We can. We will."

Kissing me passionately, Ethan found the gusset of my scanties and rubbed me while we stole the air from each other's lungs. "Fuck, Jess. I've never wanted anyone like I want you. I love you. I need you in my life."

"I love you too," I breathed.

Kissing me insane, Ethan relieved me of my underpants, then he was back between my legs and feeding his naked cock between my lips. "Fuck, Jess, I never thought I'd have this, that I would feel like this. I love you so much."

"Ethan!" I gulped as he went to push in. We stared into each other's eyes for a moment.

Caressing my cheek, Ethan watched me. "I want to make love to you. From now on, Jess. I'm in this for the long haul. Let's see where it takes us."

Blinking away more tears, I searched his eyes and knew he meant it. That if I took this risk to love him, he would see it through.

Knowing this is what I wanted, that Ethan was what I wanted, I gave him a slight nod. Crushing his mouth to me, Ethan pushed into me. Clinging to him, I prayed for the second time today that this was it. We'd found each other, and we would love each other.

We were high on a mountain, but I was flying so high I was in the stratosphere as Ethan and I made love. Not sex, not fucking, but love. And it was different. The way he touched me and kissed me was more intense than ever before. Even my orgasm was better. And when Ethan lost his rhythm and cried out his climax into my shoulder, I felt it, deep down in my soul. We were in love. We would make this work, and we'd never regret this.

Afterward, Ethan held me. Even after we cleaned up and redressed, he cuddled me to him while we looked out over the valley and ocean beyond.

"I love you, Jess," Ethan murmured. "Let's go home and make love again."

Smiling as Ethan took my hand and helped me up, I loved seeing the joy in his eyes. The way he looked at me with those ocean eyes as if I was his everything. When we got home, we made love again. Then, we ordered dinner and spent all Saturday night exploring this new way of being together.

Sunday morning, Ethan made love to me again. Then after our surf, we headed to Turtle Bay, and I took Ethan horse riding. He wasn't a great rider, so I kept it an easy trail for him, but he got the hang of it, and Ethan laughed joyously after his first gallop.

Sunday night, I cuddled into Ethan's shoulder and smiled at how happy the last twenty-four hours had been.

"I'm going to miss you," Ethan sighed. Both of us were tired.

"I've missed you since I left Australia. I can handle a week as long as I know you will come back again. And then we get five days together."

"I expect you to greet me naked when I come home again. I'm pretty sure that welcome home you give me was the icing on our love cake. Like, I had no chance of resisting you after that."

Smirking, I bit his shoulder playfully. "Totally naked? I thought a see-through slip with easy access might work too."

Grunting, Ethan pulled me on top of him again. "I'm exhausted, but I know you are going to sneak out in the morning, and having to wait seven days seems unbearable, so I'm going to need you to put up with me having you one more time tonight."

Giggling, I appeased Ethan, both of us done for by the time we finished again. Lying on top of me, Ethan collapsed and snuggled in to sleep while still inside me.

"Do you have your new roster?" I whispered, already drifting.

"I'll add it to the calendar before I go," Ethan breathed. "I love you, Jess."

"I love you too. I'll miss you."

CHAPTER TWENTY-THREE

Setting the timer, I checked the time and smiled. Ethan's flight should be landing any minute. Over the last three months I'd worked out on average, it took him an hour after landing to get here. Of course, it was late Sunday afternoon, so the traffic might be a mess—but if he got a good driver, it shouldn't be that much longer.

Running upstairs, I turned on the shower and stripped off. I'd promised we'd get back into routine and fuck as soon as Ethan got in the door. A quickie to take the edge off, then, since he would be here for the week, dinner, and he'd try to stay awake at least until nine to get him on Hawaiian time. Of course, tonight, we were flying out to stay at the Cassidy in Kauai for the week. A surprise holiday I'd organized. It was only a forty-five-minute flight, so I'd still have him in bed by nine.

Surprisingly, the doorbell rang when I was doing my hair. Looking at the time, I raised a brow. "Must have landed early." Grabbing my midseason robe—purple satin with a fleece lining—I wrapped it closed tight and rushed downstairs. "You're earlier than I expected." I smiled as I opened the door.

"You were expecting me?" Sean looked like shit as he stepped inside. His eyes perused my ensemble, and his feet faltered. "Ethan?"

"Just landed."

Swallowing, looking like he was holding back tears, Sean turned around again. "Sorry. I'll get out of here."

Yeah, like I would throw him out when he looked like a garbage truck hit him. Grabbing his arm to hold him back, I shut the door. "Don't be silly. Get in here. Ethan will be a while yet anyway." Was it wrong that I was now hoping for traffic? "Go pour us both a glass of wine while I get some clothes on. I just got out of the shower." Sean didn't need to know this is how I dressed to welcome Ethan home.

Home. That was not the case. Not yet. Not that Ethan had admitted anyway. Yes, he was here most weekends now, or longer if he came through the week. He may as well be living here, but he'd only called this home once. But Ethan had told me he loved me last week; stared into my eyes and said those words to my face. And I'd said them back. So maybe it would be his home soon too.

Fully dressed in lounge pants and a backless sweater, I skipped back down the stairs to find Sean standing in the kitchen, finishing off his first glass of wine. As I approached, he poured a second. Taking mine, I moved to the bench near the window. The place I liked to wait for Ethan but sat so I could face Sean.

"I take it the date didn't go well?" Holly had agreed to a date and to talk.

"It went really well. Too well."

Shit! So, that means she rejected him for him to be here on the brink of breaking down. Sean was flying up to his new acquisition in Queensland after the date. "I thought you were heading north after the date?"

"I meant to, but after I left, I just found myself on a plane home. I didn't even realize where I was going until I got off the plane and asked the driver to bring me here. You're my best friend, Jess. You've suffered the same as me. You're the only one who's going to understand this."

Damn, I was so not the person to give this advice. "Tell me what happened. What did she say?"

Skulling the rest of his wine, Sean told me his story. Thankfully, he spared me the intimate details but told me enough to let me know there had been an emotional goodbye. "I left her the ring. I can't see me ever loving anyone like that again, and I don't believe in recycling those sorts of things." Setting his glass aside, Sean lifted his watery eyes to meet mine. "I let her go. It's what she wanted, but it's killing me." The tears poured out in a deluge of emotion.

Fuck! Sliding off the bench, I met him halfway and wrapped my arms around him. Burying his face in my neck, Sean held me tight as he cried. Sometimes, you didn't need words or advice; you just needed someone to give you physical comfort.

When you're heartbroken, things like 'it's for the best,' or 'it's meant to be,' are absolute shit. There was nothing fair or reasonable about having your world ripped out from under you and torn asunder. The same went for matters of the heart.

I'd held my baby and cried for over an hour when my world fell apart ten years ago. Then, when they took her away, Lou held me. He taught me the value of silent comfort. I'd probably never have been able to walk out of that hospital if he hadn't hugged me and kept his thoughts to himself.

For forty minutes, I stood there in Sean's arms, his tears and most likely his snot covering my neck. Yeah, I would have to wash my hair, but that's what being a best friend meant some days. Even after the crying stopped, Sean held me. Were my feet and back sore from standing like this for that long? Yes. Did it matter? Not one god damned bit.

Inhaling deeply, Sean trembled. "I'm sorry."

"Don't be." The timer for the oven started buzzing. "Hey, Google. Turn off the timer and turn off the oven." God, I was loving having smart devices when I heard the oven click off.

Squeezing me once more, Sean stepped back. "I'll use the bathroom." Turning away before I could see his face, Sean went into the downstairs bathroom. Needing to clean up myself, I ducked upstairs, grabbing my phone off the bed on my way into the bathroom and shooting off a message.

<Jess>: Hey, where are you? Is traffic that bad? Dinner's ready.

Putting the phone down, I grabbed a washer and wiped down my face and then my neck and surrounding areas. Yeah, I'd cried a bit too. How could I not when my best friend's heart just smashed all over my feet. The phone started ringing, and Ethan's profile showed up.

The sun came out in my heart, and I felt a little guilty that my love life was in absolute contrast to Sean's for once. "Hey, did you get delayed?"

"Are you fucking kidding me?"

My heart stuttered at the rage in Ethan's voice. "Wait, what did I miss?"

"I was there, Jess. I saw you and your '*friend*.' His mouth and hands all over you. I guess I was earlier than you expected. Since it looked pretty intense, I turned around and left. God, I knew you were going to do this. Just like her. Long-distance never works. Nothing has changed, and nothing will. You're all cheating bitches."

"Whoa! That's not what was happening here. Sean just got dumped."

"And he came running to his precious *Jessie girl* to comfort him!"

While I couldn't deny that's what happened, the venom in Ethan's voice-over Sean's pet name for me, chilled my spine. Had he always reacted to Sean's presence this way? He'd laughed when Sean explained why he called me that, but I'd been relieved that Ethan hadn't started using it because that would have been an instant turn-off.

"We're done!" Ethan hissed.

The phone disconnected. Sliding it down, I clutched it to my chest. Seconds. That's how quickly a heart could shatter. As devastated as I'd been catching Ben fucking Sharnie, it was nothing to Ethan accusing me of cheating on him. Of his anger. The tears fell silently for several minutes while I died inside.

The sound of Sean downstairs snapped me out of it. Closing my eyes, I acknowledged I'd set myself up for this last week, believing we could make this work. Yeah, he'd told me he loved me, but I'd learned years ago those words meant very little to some people.

Sucking in a reviving breath, I went back into the bathroom, washed my face, and pulled myself together. Once I could fake a smile, I grabbed my already packed carry-on and went back downstairs. Sean was back in the kitchen with another glass of wine. He was typing into his phone as I approached. "You okay?"

Looking up, Sean sighed. "Yeah, trying to get a flight back to Australia and a connection through to Queensland."

"So, you're heading back?"

"Yeah, I was meant to be there today. The contractors were expecting me to approve the planned works. I have to go. Frankly, it suits me to be somewhere else and keeping myself busy."

Yeah, I knew that feeling. "Do you want dinner?" Walking into the kitchen, I pulled the homemade lasagna out and set it on the stovetop.

"Isn't Ethan meant to be here any minute?"

I grabbed out two plates and some leftover containers and started serving up, keeping my back to Sean. "He's not going to make it."

"Flight delayed?"

"A-huh." Setting the empty dish in the sink, I filled it with hot water to soak, then picked up the plates. "Come eat. I don't want to waste it, and it's your favorite anyway."

Lips twitching, Sean took Ethan's spot at the table. Eyeing my suitcase, Sean tilted his head. "Weren't you going to Kauai?"

"Yeah, I'm going to head over to the airport and meet Ethan before the flight."

"Well, I'm glad one of us is happy." Digging into his food, Sean missed how I cringed, but it's for the best. I wasn't going to dump this on him while he was so heartbroken he flew to the wrong continent. God, he'd feel guilty as hell for Ethan misreading what he saw and insist on trying to fix it. Then he'd probably get punched in the face again.

"What are you going to do with the Hideaway once it's up and running?"

"What do you mean?"

"Who are you going to get to run it?"

Frowning, Sean considered me. "Are you putting your hand up?"

"No. Maybe. I mean, that's a pretty big thing on a resume. A six-star exclusive resort."

"It's a boutique resort. The only way it is beneficial is to go to another boutique resort. You'd lose all the experience you have now of managing a big five-star resort in a popular tourist destination.

This isn't a stepping stone for someone like you." Sean shook his head. "Though, I might bring you over for a few weeks for training. Do you think Adrien could manage that long with you gone?"

"We won't know until we try."

Sean's phone beeped. "They've got me on the first flight out in the morning. I guess I need to find a place to stay near the airport."

"Stay here," I smiled, getting up and taking my plate back to the kitchen. Taking out my phone, I messaged Greg.

\<Jess\>: Where can I find Ethan?

"Are you sure?" Sean asked, following me over.

"It's not like I will be here, and you already have a set of keys, so you can lock up when you leave in the morning. Just use the spare room and book a driver to get you."

\<Greg\>: Isn't he with you?

\<Jess\>: We fought. Please, I need to speak to him and clear this up.

"Everything okay?" Sean asked as he rinsed his plate.

"Yeah, just organizing to meet up with Ethan." Forcing a smile, I loaded the dishwasher.

<Greg>: He's at the same hotel as usual. Room 5083.

<Jess>: Thank you.

"I've got to go. Are you sure you're okay?"

Huffing, Sean pulled me in for another hug. "I'd already lost her. This was just closing the book for good. Go live your life. One of us deserves a happy ending." Damn it. When Sean pulled back, I quickly swiped the tear that escaped. "Hey, don't feel sorry for me, okay. I caused this when I wasn't honest with the woman I love. Had I told her my dad was a senator to start with, she would have never left me. I dug this hole. Don't go getting in it with me."

Forcing a smile, I nodded, then hugged him quickly before heading for the door. "You know where I am if you need me. I'll be at the Cassidy by nine."

"I won't. Go be happy."

Shutting the door behind me, I bit my lip and held it in. I would find Ethan and clear this up, though I already knew it wouldn't change anything.

Going against traffic, it only took me twenty minutes to get to the hotel. Telling the concierge the room number, I told him my boyfriend had already checked in, and I didn't have a key. He let me up without even calling the room first. That shit would never fly in my hotel. I'd remember to reassert that with my staff when I got back.

Finding the room, I took a deep breath and knocked. I shouldn't have. The air was knocked out of me when another woman opened the door wearing just a hotel robe. "Hi," she greeted with an awkward smile looking over my casual clothes, ready for the flight.

"Is Ethan here?"

Cocking an eyebrow, she turned back to the room. "E, it's for you."

Swallowing at her use of his nickname, I forced myself to stay there, but when Ethan came into view shirtless and just doing up his pants, his hair still wet from a shower, it was hard not to step back to avoid stepping on the pieces of my heart on the floor.

"Jess?" Ethan frowned, seeing me. "What—"

"You could have just told me you wanted out. You didn't have to make up some contrived bullshit that painted me as the villain."

Clenching his jaw, Ethan stepped close so he could all but close the door behind him. "I know what I saw!" he growled low.

"Really? Because I was in that room. Sean was crying his heart out. Yes, I was hugging him, but we were both fully dressed. For forty minutes, he cried his heart out because the woman he loved refused to give him a second chance. Has it ever taken us forty minutes to get naked and fuck once we start getting heavy? No, it hasn't. So, I call bullshit on your accusation. You fucked up last week when you told me you loved me, and so you came there looking for any excuse to end this. Sean being there just gave you your out. But you could have just said you didn't mean it, that you don't want me, that you don't want this anymore. You could have been honest."

"This isn't about last week. It's about you and him and the fact I can't trust you!" Ethan snarled.

A tear tracked down my cheek. "See, that is the truth of all this." Double blinking, Ethan straightened, giving me space and getting him out of my face. "You told me when this started that if it wasn't working for you, you'd find reasons to end it. Well, you did, but don't for a second blame me or anything I've done for it. I've been there, Ethan. I know too well what it's like to have my heart broken that way. I would never do that to another person." The tears were cascading now. No amount of wiping at them could ease the flow. "My only mistake was falling in love with you."

Drawing his eyebrows together, Ethan watched me, the side of his eyes creasing. "I told you—"

"I know. No marriage, no kids. I fucked up believing the way you loved me last week was more than what you said months ago. I set myself up for this heartache, but I refuse to let you blame me for how it's ending. That's all on you and your trust issues."

Watching me, Ethan gritted his jaw. His eyes were staking me to the ground. No longer about Sean, but for making him wear this. Clearing my throat, I met his eyes one more time. "I need the keys to my house, please."

Frowning harder, Ethan shoved the door of the hotel room open, nearly clobbering his female friend, who was eavesdropping on the other side. Disappearing from view for a moment, the woman eyed me, her eyes glassy as if she felt my heartache. When Ethan came back, he dropped my keys into my outstretched palm. "Thank you."

Turning, I started to leave. I'd taken two steps when Ethan grabbed my wrist. "Jess…"

Looking back, my heart hurt anew at the confusion Ethan was showcasing. His lack of trust was so powerful that he'd imagined me cheating on him when he needed a reason to tuck tail and run, scared of what we'd become. "You told me when this started that if I wanted more than you were offering, I should tell you to leave and never come back."

Shaking his head slowly, Ethan's grip on my wrist tightened.

Wiping at the increased flow of tears, I made sure my voice didn't waver. "Leave. Don't come back."

"Jess," Ethan whispered, his voice suggesting he was in as much pain as I was. I didn't care. He did this. As I walked away, I closed my eyes, squeezing all those tears out. Trying to calm down before I had to cross the hotel lobby.

Out of the elevator, Greg appeared. He eyed me, then looked down the hall, his face falling, mouth opening in surprise. "Jessie?"

"Let me know if something happens to my dad, okay? That's all I need."

"Sure."

Stepping onto the lift, I pressed the ground floor, refusing to turn around, to see Ethan standing there, watching me leave, fresh from his shower after fucking someone else. Or maybe, I didn't turn around in case he'd already gone back in to her, taking his frustration and hurt out on her.

Sobbing once, I hugged myself tightly. Closing my eyes, I leaned on the lift wall and willed myself not to fall apart yet. It could wait until I was in the Cassidy honeymoon suite in Kauai, with that big super king bed to remind me exactly what I'd just lost.

CHAPTER TWENTY-FOUR

"Are you sure about this?" Mayla asked, leaving her suitcase against the wall. "It's a backward step."

Signing the shipment slip for the boxes I was sending, I handed it to the delivery guy and shut the door. "I'm sure. It's not like it's permanent. Three to six months will give you a good block of experience running a five-star resort. Plus, I've trained all the staff here, ready for you. You can hit the ground running, and some of those ideas you wanted to instigate in Maui will fit much better here."

Moving around my place, Mayla looked it over. "This is a nice place. You've barely even lived here."

Avoiding looking around because Ethan was everywhere, I grabbed my bag, ready to go. "Make yourself at home. The beach is five minutes down the road, and it takes twenty minutes to get to work in the morning. Adrien is good, but he needs a firm hand, so don't let him sweet talk you."

"I won't." Eyeing me, Mayla blew out a breath. "Are you going to be okay?"

"I just need not to be here. Thanks for agreeing to this."

"Please, like I didn't jump at the chance to get back to Oahu. Close to shopping and stuff. If Sean's okay with it, of course, I am." Wincing, I bit my lip. "Wait, you've told Sean, haven't you?"

Exhaling roughly, I bowed my neck. "Sean was going through his own shit, and I didn't want to burden him. He's due back next week for a check-in with all of us. I'll explain then."

Eyes filling with sympathy, Mayla pulled me into a hug. "I'm here if you need a friend."

"Thank you. And you have been. Who else would pack and move island with only two days' notice?"

Smirking, Mayla plopped onto the sofa. "The bitch who wants your job running a five-star resort and living in this sweet house. Plus, did I mention the shopping?"

Grinning, I headed for the door, wheeling my suitcase behind me. "Call me if you have any questions." Heading out, I handed my bag to the driver who was waiting and dropped into the back seat. My car was staying here along with most things. Only a few boxes of items I always took with me were coming.

―――――

"Where are you?" Lou asked, frowning at the background.

"Oh, I've moved again." He didn't need to know more than that. Did I make sure the background wasn't familiar on purpose so that he couldn't even guess where I was? Yes. "It turned out the new resort wasn't where I wanted to be."

"Are you back living with your boss?"

"No. Sean's not even living there right now. He's been living overseas for the last three months and just goes back for monthly reports."

"Oh, you didn't tell me." Shifting uncomfortably, Lou looked away.

"How have you been?"

"Good, good." The doorbell rang in the background.

"Sharnie and Greg?" I asked, suspecting the usual Sunday dinner.

"Yes. Ethan too." Lou couldn't look at the camera. I guessed that meant he knew.

Licking my lips, I took a deep breath. "I didn't cheat on him, Dad. I wouldn't do that."

Eyes coming back to the screen, Lou frowned. "Is that what Ethan thinks happened?"

"He didn't tell you?"

"No, Greg told me you two fought and that you've ended whatever was happening between you. No one told me why. Truthfully, I didn't want to know. I thought the less I knew, the better."

Nodding in understanding, I blinked back tears. "Then let's leave it there. It just wasn't to be."

Watching me a minute longer, Lou finally exhaled. "Okay, sweetheart." Tapping on Lou's side of the screen drew his eyes over the monitor. "I'll be out in a minute."

"Could I talk to Jess for a second?" Ethan asked off-screen.

When Lou's eyes came to me, I shook my head and wiped a stray tear that escaped. "Not this time, Ethan," my dad dismissed him.

"Can you… Jess, I'm sorry for how I reacted. You're right about what happened, why it happened. I just… I'm still flying the Hawaii run. Could we maybe get dinner next Friday—"

Hanging up, I hung my head, breathing through the hurt. "No. We can't." If I knew anything about trust issues, they didn't just vanish in the sudden realization of losing someone. We could get back together, but his mistrust and his paranoia about Sean and I was there now, and it wasn't going to disappear.

The week I'd spent in Kauai gave me plenty of time to process all those moments where Ethan reacted to my friendship with Sean. Even that first weekend in Maui, before we ever got on the boat. It was always there, and I'd not seen it. I'd been distracted by the voice reminding me he'd never promised not to have others, and then it was replaced with that stupid romantic one, thinking all the signs pointed to Ethan being in love with me too. What an idiot I'd been to think that would be enough.

Closing my laptop, I walked out to the pool and dived in. Turning on the swim jets, I worked it out of my system. By the time I dragged myself to the kitchen an hour later, there was a message on my phone from Lou.

<Dad>: I love you.

<Jessie Girl>: I love you too. I'm sorry.

<Dad>: You tried. For a short time, I got to see my two favorite people in the world happy again. Hopefully, the heartache won't last as long. I'm here if you need me, Jessie girl. I'll always be your father, and you will always be welcome home if you need it.

God, it stopped being my home so long ago. I'd felt like a stranger there when I'd visited. No, it wasn't home, but I had been happy with Ethan while it lasted.

———

A week later, I got home from my horse ride on Saturday morning and let myself in the door. Standing at my kitchen counter, Sean was pouring two cups of coffee. "So, I arrived back early this morning and went to my best friend's place to catch up and maybe see if her boyfriend was around and wanted a game of golf. But Mayla answered the door, rather unhappy about the early hour, and had to tell me you swapped back to your old role and moved back to Maui. What the fuck happened?"

Moving to the kitchen counter, I dropped my bag and picked up one of the coffees. "My boyfriend dumped me. I needed to get away, and since I'd always been happy here alone, I set it up so I could come back. Currently, it's only a temporary arrangement. But I need this. I need the routine I had here."

"I meant, what happened with Ethan? As I hear it, he never went with you to Kauai. That was three weeks ago, Jess. Why didn't you call me?"

Sipping my coffee, I sighed, then set the cup between my palms. "Ethan came to the house that night. He saw you holding me, your face against my neck, and instead of seeing a man heartbroken, he saw a lover's twist. He dumped me over the phone while you were composing yourself."

Mouth falling open, Sean shook his head. "What? Did you explain?"

"I did. When I got to the hotel, he'd just finished fucking some other woman who knew him well enough to call him by his nickname. I explained what he saw, but it was over. You were just the excuse Ethan was looking for to end it."

"Jess, I'm sorry."

Taking another mouthful of coffee, I shook my head. "Always the same. Same things, same times. It's like we are living the same life almost."

"I was hoping one of us would be happy coming out of this," Sean said mournfully.

"I guess that's not my fate."

Eyes glassy, Sean watched me. "Did you love him?"

"Yeah, I did. My mistake was telling Ethan that the last time he visited. He said it first, and I thought it meant we were ready to progress our relationship. While I was dreaming of more, he was looking for reasons to end it. I guess we took it to two very different places."

Moving around the bench, Sean wrapped me in his arms as the first sob escaped. "My turn to hold you," he murmured as I fell apart.

Later, we sat watching movies, discussing everything but the pain in our hearts. "So, I was thinking of spending Christmas at the Hideaway this year. Dad's going to fly out for it. Why don't you come over for the training and stay for Christmas and new year?"

"Sounds like a plan."

We sat silent for several more minutes. "Did you want the Hideaway?" Sean finally asked. "I know it's a lot smaller than you're used to, but I know you'd do a great job of it."

Chewing my lip, I considered Sean, then the view out the window. "No. If I decide not to go back to Ko Olina, I'm going to stay here. I might even buy the house off you."

Sean scoffed. "You don't earn that much."

"I own my place outright. Mayla is paying me rent. I could afford the mortgage."

"Just rent it for now. We'll work the rest out once you sort yourself out."

The silence was drifting between us comfortably again. "Are you ever going back to Turtle Beach to live?"

"I don't know."

Watching the television, I didn't really process the show. My mind couldn't focus anywhere. "I never thought I'd fall in love again.

Ethan came as a surprise, but I don't regret him. I just need the time to get over him."

Reaching out, Sean took my hand. "I understand." Giving it a gentle squeeze, he removed himself to a safe distance. Yawning, Sean slumped down in his chair.

The show was boring. Getting up, I got myself another drink and went to the bathroom. Getting changed into my swimmers, I went out and did laps again. At least my fitness was picking up again.

When I came back in, Sean was asleep. Smiling, I put a blanket over him and switched off the television. Going to bed, I checked my phone. There was a new message.

<Mayla>: So, first Sean came here looking for you. I told him where you are. Then this evening, Ethan turned up. He seemed pretty shocked to find me here. I told him you'd gone away for at least six months. I hope I did the right thing. He looked pretty upset.

<Jess>: You did. Thanks.

Closing my eyes, I fell back on the bed. I wasn't Ethan's layover anymore. I'd taken the risk and loved him, but it hadn't paid off. That was life. That was my lot when it came to love.

BEST KNIGHT

Best Knight

Hotel Series

EBONY OLSON

BEST KNIGHT

BOOK 6: HOTEL SERIES

EBONY  OLSON

EBANDMUSE
PUBLICATIONS

CHAPTER ONE

He looks at her, like I look at her,
But her eyes are all for him.
He's the only guy on earth
When it comes to her,
And I'm standing here unseen.

I'm jealous of him,
I'm jealous of them,
Seeing them together, I realize,
They have the kind of love
That a man like me can't reach.

The way she smiles at him,
The way she looks at him,
The way she touches him,
The way she kisses him,

He's the luckiest guy on earth,
And I'm jealous as all hell.

"WHAT DO YOU THINK OF THE NEW SONG?" TEILLE ASKED OVER THE phone once the music finished playing out.

Sobbing, I tried to hold it in but couldn't. "I hate it. Please don't release it."

"Jess?" Teille softened her voice. "What's wrong? You didn't even say that about 'Ride me, Cowgirl!'" Teille waited, my sobs filling the line between us as I tried to reign my emotions in but failed to do anything but avoid crying outright. "Jess, did you break up with Ethan?"

"I shouldn't have done it, Teille. I should never have let him become more than a holiday fling. I knew he'd break my heart. I did. I just hoped…"

Teille sniffled on the other side of the line, then coughed to clear her throat. "I'll speak to Dylan. See if he can maybe delay the release on this one. Bring one of the other songs forward as the new release instead."

"Thank you." Trying to rein my out-of-control emotions in, I swabbed my face with a tissue. "None of them are about Ethan, are they?"

"There is a song about a threesome that I'm telling myself was a fantasy. One about a siren on a faraway island—pretty sure that's you too, but no mention of love or anything in that one; and the other one they've finished recording so far is about the friends you keep close, no matter the distance between them. I really like the last one. It's got this sweet melody to it and is one of those songs the music just sort of steals your soul."

Smiling as the tears finally came to an end, I exhaled.

Sighing, Teille fidgeted on the other side of the line. "They are still in the studio recording a few more songs. The manager just really liked 'Jealous as Hell' and wanted it to be the early release. I'll ask if we can sit on it until they finish recording, though, and try to persuade them to pick something else."

"Could you maybe ask your brother not to write about me at all? It would go a long way to my sanity. My staff and boss think everything he writes is about me now."

"Please, over a decade ago, there were songs about the grief of surviving when someone you love tried to commit suicide or having your world implode or losing those you love. At least his songs about you are upbeat and not reminiscent of the lowest point in your life."

"Goddess of Heartbreak," was my only answer.

"Oh, yeah, okay. Fair call." Teille and I sat for a few moments in silence.

"He needs some new friends who can inspire him instead," I finally huffed.

Snickering, Teille moved around on the other side of the line. "I suggested that a long time ago. He said only those he cares about deeply ever inspire his heart."

"Sounds poetic. Maybe he should write a song about that. Or even his own issues, maybe."

"I know what you mean," Teille chuckled. "Okay, I better go. It's getting late here. I'll give you the heads up with what they decide to go with for the release."

"Maybe don't. That way, when I hear the song on the radio, I might have the chance to like it before I realize who wrote it."

"Honestly, I always give you the heads up because I think if I were driving along and heard a guy I've been close to for years start singing about how awesome my butt looked bouncing on him, I'd probably crash my car while staring in horror at the radio."

"He was rather complimentary about my ass in that song, so I wasn't too upset. Plus, a few of his lady friends were more than happy to claim it was about them, so you know it was all sorts of positive for my self-esteem."

Laughing, Teille hummed in agreement. "I guess you're right. We'll talk soon."

"Take care, Teille. Oh, I'm back in Maui now too."

"Really? Why? You said you loved living on Oahu. Didn't you buy a house there?"

Closing my eyes, I dabbed the tissue at my eyes again. "I ran away again. It's my coping mechanism."

"I'm sorry, Jess. I really thought Ethan was your happy ever after."

"Yeah. Me too." Especially after our last weekend together. "Talk soon."

"Will do."

Hanging up, I swallowed my nightly multi-vitamin and went to sit by the pool. I was staring out at the island's lights, the stretch of darkness across the channel, and the faint lights at the Lanai harbor. Ethan and I once sat here eating dinner and looking out at this view together. It ached to think he'd ruined this for me.

Sighing, I stood up, pulled my dress over my head, and started swimming laps again. This was my answer now. Think of Ethan, make sure I was either too busy or exhausted to keep doing so. I'd never been fitter in my life.

As I pulled myself from the pool, my phone was ringing. Tired, I grabbed my phone and put it to my ear before grabbing my towel.

"Hey. Everything okay?"

"Yes, I just got back to Turtle Beach from Kauai and wanted to call and finalize plans for the next few weeks. Did you get your flight confirmation?"

Like me, Sean was also about distracting his thoughts with work and such.

"Yes. Business-class. Finally, a boss that appreciates me."

"It's tax-deductible. What time will you land in Oahu?"

Going to the itinerary I had printed out, I looked at all my flights. "I'm flying over Thursday night and staying with Mayla."

"Great, I'll pick you up from there on the way to the airport. I'll be there at nine. Now, we have a layover in Sydney, any thoughts on how we can fill time?"

Smiling, I took the itinerary to the dining table. "Lou will come to the city so we can have dinner Sunday night. I'd like you to meet him. I think you'd get along."

"I'd like that. Maybe then your father won't glare at me through the computer screen anymore."

"Maybe he thought we were fucking like everyone else did."

A heavy sigh came through the phone. "Is our friendship that unusual?"

"I don't know. I mean, Dylan hasn't written a song about it yet, so it can't be that unique."

"Oh, did his new song come out?" Sean sounded like he was shifting around on the other end of the line.

"Not to the public, but Teille called tonight to give me the heads up. I've asked them not to release it as a single. Or at all."

"That bad?"

"I bawled my eyes out from the end of the first verse till the damn thing stopped playing and then some. It's all about how in love I was with Ethan. Like I need that shit out there, playing over every radio haunting me for the worst mistake of the decade."

"Damn. What do you think your chances are that he will sit on it?"

"None. Their manager loves it. Even if Dylan wanted to kill it—which he won't, because it is a great song if it's not about you—the label knows it will get the downloads, so they'll release it." Sighing, I fidgeted with the itinerary. "I just hope Teille can delay them until I've had time to pull my shit together better."

For a moment, my mind cringed on the idea of Ethan hearing that song. Would it hurt him or anger him? Did I really care? Groaning, I slumped back in my seat and lifted my face to the ceiling.

"How are the renovations coming?"

Exhaling hard, Sean hummed. "Yeah, good. We did all the guest rooms before the peak season kicked into gear. I've got them doing the staff accommodations right now. The staff lives here for five or more days a week, so they deserve the creature comforts. I've left my place till last. They've been working on it for the last week that I've been back here. They'll have finished by the time I get back, and then we'll start organizing when to work on the upgrade of the other side of the island."

"Peak season probably isn't the time to do that."

"No, it isn't, nor is it the time to renovate the grounds and stuff, but everything here needs an upgrade. So, I'll probably look at upgrading facilities first. But, I want to get your opinion on a few things first."

"Like?"

"The spa. It's right in the center of the main hub here, which can get very noisy. So I'm thinking of building a separate building further away, keep it surrounded by nature, maybe overlooking the cliffs out the east side so that the treatment rooms have views of the ocean."

"That sounds like a great idea. If you put the yoga space up there too, maybe with a covered deck, it will provide a nice oasis to relax."

"Ooh, a yoga deck. I love that idea. We'll go over plans during the flight to Australia. I've got the resort layout with me." Shuffling papers sounded through the phone. "Have you got your training plan written? I want to look it over on the flight too."

"I do plan to get some sleep on this ten-hour flight."

"Is that a yes?"

I rolled my eyes and looked at the folder with my plan all written up. "It's in draft form. I've taken the pointers you gave me and developed it with those as the foundations."

We spent the next twenty minutes discussing how Sean wanted to utilize my skills across both resorts while I was there, if possible. Then, when he'd finally run out of things to talk about for the work trip, he turned his mind to Christmas.

"Are we doing presents for Christmas?"

"Don't we always?"

"I have no idea what to get you this year. You own shit now."

"Huh, you're right." I'd already packed Sean's present in my bag.

He was easy to buy for this year. He was getting this mini projector which he could plug into his phone or any other device and watch movies on any blank wall he could find. With all the traveling he did now, I thought it would be great no matter which resort he visited.

"Remember how I was going to go home for a week on the way back after New Year? Well, you booked my flights accounting for the extra week, so I'm still going to take that leave and catch up with my friends and spend a few days with Lou."

"Sounds fair. You're not worried about seeing your sister or someone else?"

"No. Lou won't tell them I'm there if I ask. And I know Ethan. I can avoid him easily. Karla offered for me to stay with her, so I don't have to worry about trying to find a room somewhere either."

"Okay. So, I'll still meet up with you in Sydney to fly back to Hawaii on the sixth of January."

"Will do." Looking at the time, I moved to the kitchen and made myself warm milk and honey. "I should get ready for bed. I have a lot to get done before flying out to Oahu tomorrow. I'll see you Friday morning."

"Are you sleeping?"

Huffing, I pressed start on my latte maker. "You'll know the answer when you see me, so there would be no point lying. How about you?"

"I sleep. I don't sleep well, but I sleep. But then I've had longer to get accustomed to the pain in my chest."

"You know what sucks the most?" I stared at the milk vortexing as I sighed. "When I get horny, my heart aches too. I can't think of sex without thinking of Ethan. I have no chance of ever getting myself off again or with anyone else because he's ruined that for me, too."

Sean blew out a long breath. "Yeah, I know what you mean. That last night with Holly was the only time I've gotten off since she left me. I've been distracting myself from sex with exercise now."

It made me laugh. "Me too. It's the fittest I've been since high school when I played representative sports. Which is even worse because guys are hitting on me all the time now, but I can't even give them an ounce of attention."

"You were the same last time as well. You got there after a few years."

Hanging my head, I turned off the frother and poured the hot milk into a mug. "No. The last time my hesitation was that I'd only ever been with guys with whom I had emotional connections. This time is completely different. I think Ethan ruined me for all other men."

"Even Dylan?"

I huffed out a breath. "I don't know. I can't even contemplate that right now. Let's just say it's a solid no to even wanting any other man."

"I'll make sure to drag you surfing with me every morning and sign you up to all the fitness classes while you are at The Hideaway."

"Perfect. I need access to the pool after hours too."

"Done."

Loving my best friend and the fact I could talk this stuff over with him, even if it killed me that he was going through it with me. Not that we weren't alone in our hurt, but at least we knew there was someone who understood, who we could talk to without having to apply filters to what we said. Everyone needs a no-filter friend who just gets them without judgment.

"Night, Sean."

"Night, Jessie Girl."

For once, I didn't threaten his demise, because I felt vulnerable enough emotionally for my father's term of endearment to be comforting. Hanging up, I took my hot milk to the bedroom and finished packing.

CHAPTER TWO

Knocking on the hotel room door, I waited. When it finally opened, Sean had his phone pressed to his ear and an apologetic look on his face. Sean pushed the speakerphone as he took the phone away from his ear so a man's voice with a real ocker Australian accent filled the entryway, nodded, then followed it up by hitting mute.

"Dealing with an issue with the foreman for the construction work on the Island. Get a coffee with your dad downstairs, and I'll catch up to you," Sean apologized.

Smiling at him, I walked down the hall to the elevator and pressed the button. I'd heard the words sand and pylons and decided not to even ask. Anyone near the ocean knew building solid foundations meant drilling holes deep into the ground to overcome the shifting sands. Unfortunately, that usually meant extra cost. Now take it out to an island where everything you needed had to be transported across by helicopter or barge, and the potential of not getting heavy equipment on-site became a multiplication factor that could drain the bank.

In the foyer, I smiled when I spotted Lou. Despite being in his sixties, he was still tall with broad shoulders and a healthy and fit appearance. My best friend Karla once told Lou he was a DILF when we were teens. I was traumatized. Lou was flattered and horrified that a teenage girl was giving him bedroom eyes. As always, Lou's brown hair was cut short, and his pale English skin tanned from spending a lot of time at the golf course in his semi-retirement.

Lou's blue eyes were scanning around the hotel lobby, and when they spied me, they crinkled at the edges, giving away his advanced years. Damn, the moment my eyes found my dad they got itchy, because the last time we saw each other was the night of the barbecue where I punched Sharnie in the face and disowned myself. The night Ethan found out about Matilda.

Ethan.

That heartache was still too fresh—only two months since I went all in, only for him to destroy it a week later. By the time tears were streaming down my face, I was in my dad's arms, him holding me tight.

"Jessie Girl," he murmured, his faded British accent comforting as he hugged me tightly.

It took a moment to pull myself together. Thirty-one, and I still felt like a child who had a bad nightmare when he held me. Lou's hugs had that power. To banish bad dreams and make me feel safe and loved.

"Sorry," I whispered as I pulled away, wiping away the evidence of my loss of control for a moment. It was late March when I'd last been home, and now it was December. Nine months had brought me full circle. "A little emotional of late," I excused.

"I understand." Lou rubbed my upper arm comfortingly, then looked around us. "I thought your friend was joining us?"

"Yes, he's just stuck on a work call."

"He?"

Ignoring the rise of my father's brow, I indicated the cafe. "How about we get a coffee? I didn't get much sleep on the flight over and am a little jet-lagged."

"You look like you haven't had much sleep, ever," Lou grumbled as we made our way to the coffee shop and found a table.

"Work's been busy, and I've been preparing for this trip, updating my training manual to suit two different resort types in very different locations."

"You've lost weight since I last saw you, too."

Rubbing my lips together, I considered the menu. "Exercising keeps me sane."

When Lou gave me a worrying gaze, I held up my hands to appease him.

"Don't worry. I'm eating. I'm just more active than I used to be. It's good for creating endorphins to put you in a good headspace and to get your mind off things."

Pursing his lips, Lou considered me, then browsed the menu before calling the waitress over. His eyes gave away his understanding of what—or more, *who*—I didn't want to think about, but he respectfully didn't bring it up. "Do you know what your friend will have?"

"Large cap for my friend, and I'll get a mocha, please," I told the waitress who stopped by our table.

Giving his order, Lou waited until she walked away to reengage his smile. "So, where are you off too, and for how long?"

"Sean's newest resort off the coast of North Queensland. I'm running the training and development sessions for the staff there. Then I'm hoping to come to Newcastle for a week and catch up with Karla and Lizzy and spend some time with you before I head home again."

"That would be lovely," Lou smiled, obviously surprised.

Giving him a half-smile as the waitress placed our drinks on the table, I chewed my lip. "I'm going to ask that you don't tell anyone that I'll be around. I want to enjoy this visit without the family drama."

"You expect me to keep your presence from your mother?" Lou lifted an accusing brow at me. "I have never kept a secret from Margaret in my life."

Cringing, I felt terrible. "I know. But I meant what I said, Dad. I'm done with that mess. I just want to get on and live my life. This last attempt at a relationship pulverized my heart, and I wasn't lying about being overly emotional. I cried watching a horror movie when the villain had a sad back story."

Reaching across the table, Lou put his hand on mine. "Are you pregnant?"

Blowing out a breath, I understood the question. Both Sean and Mayla had already encouraged me to check that shit out due to my hyper empathic state.

"No."

Lou stared into my eyes like when I was younger, and he was trying to determine if I was lying.

"I've done a couple of pregnancy tests and then went to the doctor for a blood test to make sure, Dad. It's not that." Cracking a smile, I chuckled. "My doctor's formal diagnosis is that I'm heartbroken. I questioned if they taught that in medical school. He said it's a life experience most encounter, and that too many doctors are quick to dismiss the impact that grief and love have on our physical bodies."

"Sounds like you have a good doctor."

"Either way. Sorry, no grandbaby. You'll just have to endure parenting Sharnie's little psycho."

Sitting back with a sigh, Lou picked up his mug. "Greg is a good man. He'll raise the kid right."

Lifting a brow, I gave my father a look that betrayed my mirth at his statement. "Greg is a pilot who spends days out of the country at a time. That child has little chance of growing up well-adjusted. Maybe start saving for the therapy bills now."

"Have you thought about therapy?" Lou asked casually.

Thankfully, Sean chose that moment to join us.

"Mister Butler," Sean greeted, offering his hand to my father across the table. "Nice to finally meet you in person."

Eyeing Sean, Lou shook his hand, his forehead furrowing. "Sorry, Jessie said she was traveling with a friend, not her boss."

"Well, Jess and I are friends as well as colleagues, and she is also my employee, so I guess that could be confusing," Sean answered with a smile as he took his seat. "But we always consider ourselves friends before all else. Is this mine?" He pointed to the coffee I put in front of him and takes a long draw when I nod. "God, I needed that," he moaned, his trademark smile filling his face. "Sorry, I'm late. The contractors at the resort are trying to claim I've exceeded the brief of the initial project."

"Really? How?"

"They have to drop piers to stabilize a building and claim that it was never costed. They didn't know that I used to be in contract law before making that call. They may have realized their mistake now."

"Did you move locations or something?" Lou was now fully engaged. He was an engineer, so this was his passion. Other than golf, which I knew Sean could talk all day about as well… but I was hoping that wouldn't happen.

But for the next thirty minutes, Sean and Lou discussed the works he was having done at his new resort and the issues the land presented, alongside ensuring marine conservation and maintaining minimal environmental impact.

"Perhaps we should head to the restaurant?" I suggested when I could see that this conversation wasn't fading.

Both men nodded and got up to follow as we headed out into the early evening. The restaurant was walking distance from the hotel and gave them plenty of time to delve into Sean's plans to bring the resorts online with the United Nations' sustainability goals.

"I want to offer luxury without an environmental cost, and Australia is the perfect location for that. The best sunlight in the world should make your country the leader in renewable energies, but it seems to be lagging."

"A sad fact," Lou agreed. "Our government is in the pockets of the oil conglomerates. Just recently, instead of encouraging the shift to hybrid technology, one of the states imposed a tariff on anyone buying electric cars of over five thousand dollars. It's insane."

"I agree. So, I'm trying to set an example with my resorts here. It's costly, but luckily the buildings are just over a decade old at the most. We've just upgraded all the rooms at one resort and the staff housing with better insulation and taking better advantage of the elements of nature around it.

"The pools at the Hideaway have been converted to ultraviolet and natural filtration systems so that the water will be completely free of chemical processes. Also, within twelve months, both resorts will be fully reliant on a combination of solar and wind power, and I'll have replaced all the generators with power cells."

This conversation continued the entire walk to the restaurant and the table. By the time the two of them had taken that topic to its end, I'd picked my meal and was sipping the glass of water poured on our arrival.

"I have to ask, Sean," Lou began. "Are you involved with my daughter?"

Smirking, Sean tilted his head. "One of the great things about Jess is how perceptive she is. She tells me it's a trait she gets from you, so I think you already know the answer to that question. So, you are either asking just to play the protective father or to understand why Ethan used me as the excuse to break your daughter's heart."

I nearly choked on my water. Sean shot me a sympathetic glance while Lou pursed his lips.

"Sorry," Sean apologized.

Waving it away, I gestured he should continue.

"I'll answer anyway. Jess is my best friend. I care deeply for her. She's the sister I never had. We tease each other, and we have been there for each other. We are alike in so many ways that it's spooky at times. It's like we were twins born years apart and to different parents."

"A sister?" Lou questioned.

"No, not a sister. A soul on the same journey, maybe." Sean considered, then nodded. "A twin soul, but I do consider her to be family."

Sitting forward, Lou furrowed his brow, his eyes focused and alert, a clear sign his curiosity was piqued as Sean continued.

"Do you know, at the same time Jess ran away from home with a broken heart, I found out my fiancée was cheating on me with my brother? Or that we both arrived in Hawaii months apart fresh from that heartache?"

Lou shook his head slightly.

"I bought my first resort, and Jess went to work for the Hilton. We became friends when fate brought us together under false pretenses, and Jess then became my employee. Soon enough, she was not only my colleague but the friend I felt comfortable pouring my heart out to."

"I see."

"Then this year, I met Holly the same time Jess met Ethan." I winced, but Sean just squeezed my hand as he continued. "Once again, we find ourselves heartbroken together."

"Maybe there is more than friendship between you," Lou suggested.

Sean turned his gaze to me. Our eyes locked while we each considered that statement, and then we both started laughing. Politely, of course.

Shaking his head, Sean gave my father a huge smile. "I appreciate the sentiment, Mister Butler. That two lonely souls who are so alike might find something more together, but honestly, if those feelings existed for either of us, we would have acted on them years ago, not waited to have our hearts crushed again. We love each other as we are, but there is no sexual attraction between us."

Frowning, Lou glanced at me, his eyes telling me how hard it was for him to hear that. When his phone rang, Dad pulled it from his pocket and sighed. "It's your mother. I'll step out. Order me the scampi?"

"Of course."

Kissing me on the top of my head, Lou left.

"I think your father is like many of our colleagues and doesn't believe a female and male can be friends without one of us wanting to fuck each other."

"Again, if it were that unusual a thing, Dylan would have a song about it by now. He's never been bothered by our friendship."

"Jessie Girl. The man is a whore with intimacy issues. I may not know what fucked that guy up, but becoming a world-class musician and rockstar didn't cure him. If it did, he would have proposed to you years ago."

"Okay, you need to stop with that shit," I warned.

"Jess," Sean demanded my attention. "The guy is in love with you, but knows he would break you. You know it too. I even think you were in love with him once, but when you understood his damage would destroy you, you untethered your feelings for him and treated him like every other holiday fuckboy."

Bowing my head, I stared at the water and wondered when the friggin alcohol we ordered would arrive. "I didn't untether anything. He burned them before they could attach. He was messed up. I had a long-time boyfriend who was kind." Lifting my watering eyes, I met Sean's sympathetic ones. "I wanted to give Ben up for him, but Dylan told me not to be a fucking idiot. That he'd take my innocence and leave me just as fucked up as he was, and he didn't need that on his conscience."

The waitress set down a tray of drinks on the table. As soon as the wine glass was in front of me, I picked it up. "I'm going to need a second," I directed, then promptly downed half of it, my tears adding to the flavor of my specific brokenness.

"Shit," Sean muttered. "I'm sorry for picking that scab, Jess."

Waving away his concern, I kept swallowing until the glass was empty.

Thank God I wasn't pregnant, because having this discussion and not drinking would have sucked.

CHAPTER THREE

"T<small>HANK YOU FOR ALLOWING ME TO CRASH YOUR DINNER</small>, M<small>ISTER</small> Butler, but I'm jet-lagged, and we have an early flight. So I might say goodnight," Sean excused himself as soon as we finished the main meal.

Rising out of his chair, Lou shook Sean's hand. "It was nice to finally meet you, Sean. And thank you for taking care of Jessie."

"Honestly, she takes better care of me," Sean admitted. "I'll see you in the morning, Jess."

Giving a small wave, I sat back in my seat and finished another glass of water. After three glasses of wine, I'd calmed down. If Lou noticed when he finally returned from his call with Margaret, he didn't say anything. Then again, he probably attributed my emotions to Ethan.

In all honesty, they probably were. Dylan would have broken me. Ethan did. At least Dylan knew he was toxic and convinced me to keep him at arm's length, even if it did lead me to a loss so much worse.

"I like him," Lou states after Sean leaves. "But I can see why he raised Ethan's insecurities. You two consistently finish each other's sentences. If I didn't see the lack of attraction between you, I would assume there was something too."

Sitting forward, I put my empty water glass back on the table. "Why are you in the city?"

"So I can see my daughter who disappears for years at a time. Twice in a year, sharing a meal almost feels surreal after ten years of Skype calls."

"Nothing stopped you from buying a plane ticket, Dad." Before Lou could sweat it, I brought it back around. "But, I also know that you wouldn't have made this trip just to see me if there wasn't a way to explain it to Margaret without causing her to flip her lid about what an ungrateful bitch I am. So, let me rephrase. Why does Margaret think you are here?"

Giving me his fatherly glare for questioning him, Lou pinched his shoulders, and when he spoke next, his pompous English accent was in full effect. A dead giveaway I'd caught him out. As a child, it was reserved for when I'd question why he and mum had the bedroom door locked, and why was mum praying, and–

Oh god! Why am I even going there?

"What makes you think Margaret is unaware you are here?"

"You left the table to take the call."

"That's just good manners, Jessie. I taught you manners."

"And Sharnie taught me how to tell when someone is being evasive in the way they answer questions, and you are, Mister Butler. Spill."

Blowing out a big breath, Lou sagged a little. "I have a specialist appointment, just to check my heart and stuff."

Before I could freak out, Lou held up his hand.

"There is nothing wrong, Jessie. I am a sixty-year-old man with a family history of heart disease. I am fit and healthy, and my doctor just wants to make sure I stay that way. So you have nothing to worry about."

"You promise me?"

Squeezing my hand under his, Lou met my eyes. "I promise. I will be pinging your zoom every Sunday for another twenty years or more, bearing any factors out of my control, of course."

"Thank God."

"Dessert, coffee, tea?" the waiter asked with a smile.

"Definitely tea," Lou answered.

"Definitely dessert," I countered, gaining a warm smile from my dad.

"You haven't asked about Ethan," Lou finally prompted on the walk back to the hotel.

"Does he ask you about me?"

"He did. When I couldn't tell him where to find you, he stopped."

"My number didn't change, Dad."

"He didn't feel it was a conversation for the phone or online. He thought he had more chance of you hearing him face-to-face. He probably didn't count on you packing up and disappearing again. I know he tried seeking you out at both the Ko Olina and Turtle Bay resorts."

Maybe it didn't occur to him to try where I took him on that first visit.

"He's still doing the Hawaii run. I think he's hoping to encounter you or maybe your boss."

"I left the island." Pinching my lips, I struggled to keep my voice calm. "Ethan probably shouldn't be so keen to run into Sean. He did use my comforting Sean in his moment of heartbreak to insinuate I was a cheating whore like his ex. There was nothing sexual in anything we were doing."

"Men blinded in jealousy will see guilt in something innocent."

"Dad… Ethan was always going to end things that weekend. Sean crying on my shoulder just gave him a reason. Now, you are his friend, and we promised that it wouldn't impact your relationship with either of us if things didn't work out. Ethan made his choice. If he regretted it in the light of day, that is for him to deal with, just like how he hurt me is what I have to work through. I know you hoped for us, but it turned out our two broken hearts didn't fit together after all."

"I'm sorry, Jessie Girl. I just thought if you still loved him, maybe…"

I was grateful Lou chose not to finish that thought. "You know, when Ethan came to visit, Sean took him to play golf on Lanai. It's one of the smaller islands, and it's nearly all a golf course. So I'm sure Sean would take you there if you ever decided to visit Hawaii, and he was there."

Putting his arm around my shoulders, Lou kissed my forehead and gave me a side hug as we approached the doors for the hotel. "I love you, Jessie. I just want you to be happy."

Well, I think that boat sailed, but there was no need to voice that. Walking to the elevators, we pushed the call button. As we stepped in and pressed the button for our different floors, I turned to my dad.

"I have to leave early for our flight north, but I'll see you when I pass through in a few weeks. Maybe we can have brunch?"

"Just let me know when you will be there, and I'll move things around to see you, Jessie. God knows how long it will be before you come home again."

Giving Lou a big hug, I groaned a little when the elevator pinged open at my floor. "Love you, Dad."

"Love you too, Jessie Girl. Travel safe." Dropping a kiss on my head, Lou let me go. Stepping off the lift, I gave my dad one last smile as the doors slid shut.

Blowing out a breath, I made my way to my room and let myself in. Sitting on the bed, I stared out the window at the view out over the city for a moment as a few tears escaped. Then, picking up my phone when it buzzed on the bed beside me, I read the message and smiled.

\<Sean\>: You okay?

\<Jessie Girl\>: Stop eavesdropping through the walls and go to sleep.

Putting my phone down, I went to have a shower and followed my own advice.

———

Twelve hours later, I was alighting a domestic flight and catching a shuttle to the helipad with Sean.

"Once you get settled into your room, take the time to familiarize yourself with the Hideaway. I've allowed for you to spend the rest of this week observing and making small adjustments. For the next two weeks, I've booked formal training for four hours a day from Monday to Thursday. Friday to Sunday are our busiest times currently, but it'll get busy after Christmas, so I want the staff whipped into shape by then."

"You know they will be, but what are you going to do if I want to fire someone?"

"I'll remind you Australia has some pretty stringent laws around reasons to fire someone. So don't get me sued."

Smirking, I nudged him with my shoulder, and then we were boarding the helicopter and flying out over the ocean. It was only a twenty-minute flight to reach the island, but flying low over the water with no land in sight was not reassuring. In Hawaii, it was rare not to see one island from another.

After ten years there, it was easy to forget just how small the islands that make up Hawaii were when compared to Australia and its surrounding islands. Australia is the largest island on this planet. But, since the definition of an island is an independent landmass entirely surrounded by water but smaller than a continent, and Australia itself is the smallest continent on earth, it can't technically be called an island. But it is informally called the island continent because it is both.

When the island finally came into view, I smiled. It was over ten years since I'd flown out here to attend the managers' retreat under the employment of the original manager. They hadn't built the second 'family friendly' resort at that time, nor half of the facilities now on offer. It was impressive back then, but I was even more amazed since I could see all the amenities added over the years.

"Welcome back, Mister Cassidy," the staff greeted as we cleared the helipad.

"Thank you. This is Jess Butler, one of my senior managers. She's in the staff cabin adjoining mine. Have her luggage sent there. We're going to walk around a bit."

"Of course."

Leading the way, Sean started talking business.

"Hey. I thought I got to settle in first?"

Smirking, Sean headed towards the Hideaway. "I changed my mind. I want to show you where I'm thinking of moving the spa to, and we can discuss other planned changes on the way."

Not missing a beat, Sean started pointing out things and explaining his ideas of how to improve or completely overhaul them. I didn't argue; Sean was like me. Work distracted from the pain. I just wish he'd told me so I could have grabbed my tablet to take notes and photos as we went.

When we finally reached the cliff that Sean was considering building the spa on, my brain was racing with everything he'd already thrown at me. But once I was standing on the rocky ledge, waves crashing against the stone below, my mind emptied, and it was just me and the roaring ocean.

"It's perfect," I murmured after several moments.

"It just wipes the brain clear, right?" Sean sighed as we stood there staring out to sea.

"Exactly. Build me a house here, and I'll never leave."

Snickering, Sean stepped back and looked around. The moment broke, and we started discussing design plans. When we sat down to dinner that night in the resort restaurant, I flicked open my tablet and began making sketches of the spa, what the rooms should look like, or how we should position them to take in that view, including a float pool room. Imagine just floating in healing Epsom salts while the waves crashing against the cliff face was all you could hear. It'd be nirvana.

"I think I've changed my mind."

"About?" Sean asked, looking over my sketches while he ate his meal.

"Being your manager here."

Smirking, Sean took my pen and added a note to one of the designs. "Let's get through the next three weeks first. I don't want you to make a heartbreak call on this place and change your mind less than six months later."

"What do you mean?"

"Canada?"

"To be fair, that's where Dylan was flying for his tour, so that's where I went. The first snowfall, I knew I wasn't going to survive there."

Lips lifting on one side, Sean didn't comment, just went back to discussing the spa, but he was right. I shouldn't make career decisions while in my current emotional state.

Groaning, I stood up. "I need to swim."

Meeting my eyes, Sean considered me quietly, the skin around his eyes tightening with his concern. "Go for it. Do you want the rest of your meal sent to your room for later?"

"That'd be great. Thank you. And Sean," I waited until he was looking at me again. "Thanks for understanding."

With a nod, Sean went back to his meal, but as I left the restaurant and glanced around, Sean was watching me leave with his elbows on the table and hands clasped, a furrow in his brow. Dropping my head, I focused on getting to the pool. The last thing I wanted was Sean worrying about me. I was okay. Or I would be, eventually.

CHAPTER FOUR

"This place is aptly named," I considered, staring out the window at the darkness from Sean's room.

My room was next door and had the same view: ocean on one side, bush on the other. It was secluded and serene. Well, it was until this storm hit. The wind was howling outside as rain lashed the windows and the door on either side. Occasionally, the lightning lit up the ocean outside, and I could see the waves and dark clouds stirring around. Both beautiful and ominous.

The staff quarters were located around the middle of the island's east side, down from the helipad, in a gully just before the cliff's edge. The managers of both resorts straddled the ridge alongside the owner's suite, which was effectively two joint bungalows—one for the owner and the other for his guest.

Beside me, Sean snored. How the hell he could sleep in this was beyond me. The movie we'd been watching when Sean fell asleep still played on the wall opposite his bed from the projector I got him for Christmas. He had a lounge room, but it adjoined the manager's place. We moved in here after the first movie so the noise didn't keep him awake. My bathroom was on the other side of this wall, so no harm done.

Snorting, Sean rolled over in his sleep and threw his arm over me. Chuckling to myself, I poked him until he rolled away again with a murmur of Holly's name. My heart broke for him. Which made me think of Ethan, and then my heart ached again. Maybe I should have let Sean hold me and tried to sleep. Perhaps that's what I missed and why sleep had become so elusive.

Dismissing the idea as soon as it came, I reached up on the bed head and turned off the projector, then grabbed the empty popcorn bowl and my glass and took it out to the kitchen to wash up. Once done, I stepped out onto the wrap-around balcony and shut the door.

The storm was raging, lightning flashing to show the trees thrashing, and leaves and twigs from the branches littered the ground. Cursing came from my left, and I turned my head to see Daniel Spicks, the assistant manager of The Retreat, step out of his door quickly, pulling on a raincoat. His eyes widened, seeing me standing out there watching the storm.

"Everything okay, Daniel?" I asked, having heard the cursing.

"No. A beach chair got hurled into one of the beachside bungalows. The place is trashed."

"Shit. Was there anyone in the room?"

"Yes, a young woman was staying there. She's fine, but shaken. We've never had anything like this happen before. On top of everything, I don't have another room for the woman."

"I know we've got two suites still available at The Hideaway. We can offer her one of those. You see your guest, make sure she is okay, and ask her what she wants to do. We won't be able to get her off the island tonight, but if she would prefer to leave tomorrow, we can put her on the first flight out, or she can see out her holiday at The

Hideaway. Just let me know how long she's staying, and I'll move things around if need be."

"Thanks, Jess. I can wake Cara to deal with this."

Waving it away, I started for my place. "I'm awake. Get down to your guest then we'll get her transferred. Just call me, and I'll deal with it at this end. Once the storm calms down, I'll do a damage assessment with you. Then we'll need to take good photos and organize an insurance adjuster to come and inspect as well. Oh, and check if anyone else is booked into it soon. The bungalow will be out of commission, so we may need to move some bookings around."

With a nod, Daniel pulled up his hood and jumped into his electric cart, which was more a city car—you know, like a two-seater golf cart if it had a curved roof and doors—and headed towards the south end of the island.

It was like a gift of the gods. The weather meant I couldn't swim, but an emergency at work was just the thing for a restless soul. Grabbing my laptop, I logged into The Hideaway reservation system. Sean had given me access for the training, but it also meant I could help out while here. I was here for work, and Cara, like Daniel, was only the temporary manager until Sean appointed someone. Then they would both revert to their assistant manager roles.

That was the other part of my role here—helping Sean decide who would be best to take the Manager role. Previously there was a manager for each resort, but Sean decided one manager could oversee both. The money he saved from having two full-time managers onsite would allow for more staff in other areas.

My phone rang twenty minutes later. "Hello?"

"Hi, it's Daniel. Our guest has accepted your hospitality; I'll have her brought over now."

"That's great. Can I get her details, and I'll have her booked into a room so she can go straight there?"

"Yes, of course, her name is Miss Holly Claire."

I froze. "As in the Prime Minister's daughter?"

"Ah, yes, as in that Holly Claire."

"The Holly Claire who was engaged to your boss seven months ago. That Holly Claire?"

After two weeks here, I'd heard the staff whisper about what went down. One had even been brazen enough to ask me about it, right before they asked me if I was sleeping with Sean. The look I'd given them followed by a lecture on professionalism probably didn't dissuade the rumors, but it shut them up around me.

"I just remembered about all that mess. If it's an issue?"

"That all depends. Is Holly with someone?" God, if Holly were here with a new boyfriend, Sean would be devastated.

"Ah, no, she's by herself."

I was up and heading back to Sean instantly. Outside, the storm had calmed down. The rain had stopped, and it was just the wind sweeping across the property now. "She's not hurt?"

"No injuries, just a bit shook up by the ordeal, and all her belongings are inaccessible currently."

"Okay. I'll send someone right away to collect her. Then we'll head over to the bungalow and do an initial risk assessment."

"Okay, Thank you."

Hanging up, I charged into Sean's place. "Sean! Sean!"

"Jess? What's wrong?" Sean was sitting up as I got to his bedroom door. Tired but concerned as he stood up to appraise me.

"It's Holly."

"What?"

"Holly is here."

"Again, what?"

A smile broke over my face. "Holly was staying at The Retreat. The storm damaged her bungalow. Let's go."

Sean was still blinking at me as I grabbed the keys to his electric buggy and led the way out the door. By the time we'd loaded into the cart, Sean was wide awake and peppering me with questions about what happened. By the time I explained about the sunbed crashing through Holly's ceiling and landing on her bed—which thankfully Holly wasn't in at the time—Sean was in a state.

As soon as we reached The Retreat, Sean was out of the cart and charging towards the manager's office. Daniel was just walking down the corridor when he saw us.

"Where is she?" Sean asked, sounding like a wounded lion.

My fingers crossed behind my back as Daniel backtracked and pushed the door open to his office. "She's just in here, boss."

As Sean strode into the office, I heard a gasped breath followed by, "Sean?"

"Jesus, Holly." Sean pulled Holly into his arms and planted his lips on her. The way she melted against him and clung to his shoulders desperately was a burning reminder of what I'd lost when Ethan got cold feet.

"I'll meet you at the bungalow," I told Daniel and made my way back towards the door while Daniel cleared his throat. Probably to stop Sean banging Holly on his desk.

Outside, my heart cheered for joy for Sean and grieved for Ethan. Finding a dark area of the path, I hugged myself tight and allowed the emotion taking me to escape. Just for a minute. Just enough to take the edge off. I knew Daniel wouldn't be too far behind me, and

I didn't want him to see me crying. He'd think it was over Sean, and then all the staff would feel sorry for me.

Getting my shit together, I wiped my face dry and focused on my job. The job was my escape. It wasn't hard to find the damaged bungalow. There was staff down there already trying to get a tarp over the hole in the roof and tie it down so that it didn't blow away. Seeing the damage, I felt my eyes widen. Holly was damn lucky she wasn't in that bed. Sean would have a heart attack when he saw how close she was to being badly hurt.

"Should I try and get her things?" Daniel asked when he joined me.

Glancing to Holly's luggage, I took in all the timber and structural damage in the way. "Not tonight. You can't see what is what. If you move that post and it's the only thing stopping the rest of the roof caving in, then they'll be calling the medivac for us. Let's wait until morning when we can see where everything is leaning."

"You've seen this sort of damage before?" Daniel took a step back.

"My dad's a structural engineer," I answered, as if that explained my understanding of support systems.

After taking numerous photographs, especially of the amount of water and debris in the room, I headed back to the staff lodgings. Daniel offered to drive me, but I needed the walk. By the time I was back in my room, showered, and climbing into bed, it was nearly three in the morning. Tired didn't cover it.

"Sean!"

Sitting up in bed, I blinked, still half asleep, wondering if I'd dreamed the woman's desperate sound. The clock told me it was nearly seven, but the sun was bright outside and the air incredibly humid after all the rain last night. My body was slick with sweat, and the sheets tangled around me.

Rubbing my face, I groaned. I'd told Daniel I'd meet him in thirty minutes to try and get Holly's stuff out of the bungalow and to survey the damage in daylight. Going into the bathroom, I started my shower and stepped under the cold water. When I turned off the taps, I frowned at the banging against my bathroom wall. Then the moans, both masculine and feminine, started getting louder.

Smirking, I decided to finish getting ready in my bedroom. And when the fuck noises made it into that part of the room, it was time for me to stick my hair in a bun and escape before I would never be able to look Sean in the face again.

By the time he arrived at the bungalow, the contractor in tow, I was focused on work.

"How bad is it?" Sean asked.

"The bungalow will be out of commission for a few weeks. Daniel is checking the reservations now to see the damage from that perspective. But I think, all in all, it was worth it."

"Worth it?" Sean furrowed his brow at me.

I smiled up at him, biting my lip to try and stop laughing. Sean's trademark cheeky grin appeared as he comprehended my meaning. Then we were both laughing, and my joy for Sean pushed away my heartache for the first time since Ethan answered his phone and told me we were over.

There were three things good for forgetting pain temporarily:

Work.

Exercise.

Your best friend's happiness.

CHAPTER FIVE

"So, the engagement is back on?" I smirked over my coffee.

"Not formally." Holly fidgeted with the ring on her finger. "I told him he has to ask me again and not cock it up this time."

Loving that answer, I checked the time. My train to Newcastle would leave in thirty minutes. Sean was still at Holly's asleep when we left. Her flatmate Tessa was away for Christmas, so Holly offered for me to crash there after we flew back to Sydney last night. This morning, Holly was meeting with her boss to discuss the future of her career. She offered for us to get a coffee at their pseudo-office before I had to catch the train.

"Have you decided where you two are going to live?"

Holly sighed, sweeping a few loose strands of her brown hair back from her face. "Not here, and not the Hideaway. I think I'd be happy to make Sean's home, my home."

"You know he's barely been there since you left?" When Holly blinked up at me, I shrugged. "We're like that. We don't like to stay with the painful memories. We are heartbreak runaways, Sean and me. He spent three months after you left living in Ko Olina until that resort opened. That coincided with your sister's wedding. On the way, he met Bradley Zimmer and then bought The Hideaway. He's spent most of the last four months either there or island hopping between his hotels to check on things. He's never at Turtle Beach longer than a week anymore."

Holly's face fell. "He loved his bungalow, and I drove him out of his home?"

"To be fair, the media drove you out of yours if I heard the reports correctly."

Sighing, Holly shook her head. "It was hell for a few weeks, but I like where we live now. I'm going to keep paying rent there and use it as my base of operations here for now. Tessa would kill me for leaving her high and dry for a flatmate, and I still have commitments."

"Sounds sensible," I smiled. "I'm just happy that you two are making this work. You both look so much happier now."

"Sean told me you go through the same shit at the same time in your lives. That he wasn't the only one heartbroken on that island."

Rubbing my lips together, I considered my coffee, the hurt of Ethan's actions still a seeping wound in my heart. Holly reached over and took my hand without a word, squeezing it.

"If that's the case, he should find his way back to you, begging for forgiveness soon."

There was no way I could ever see Ethan begging. Not even playfully.

"Did Sean beg you? From what I saw on YouTube, it was more a profession of his undying love."

This made Holly chuckle. "He said he was sorry. He told me he loved me. Isn't that enough?"

"It wasn't enough for you when he did that. That's how he ended up flying back to Oahu instead of Queensland, and I was holding him as he cried on my shoulder about losing you for good when Ethan turned up and accused me of cheating on him with Sean."

Yeah, that wound was still gushing precious heart blood.

After blinking a few times, Holly's smile dropped away. "Oh."

We both took drinks of our coffee, letting that sink between us. Closing my eyes, I took a deep breath.

"I'm sorry. Ethan's shitty trust issues are not on you. Sean being there just gave him an easy cop-out. And I hope you aren't concerned with any of that being remotely true. Sean and I are best friends. We have no romantic entanglement at all."

Tilting her head, Holly smiled. She was younger than me by a couple of years, but I think her childhood as a politician's daughter made her mature faster. People in those circles tended to put more pressure on their kids to be perfect.

"I know we barely know each other personally, but Jess, I remember that guy you were with at the Hotel Manager's conference a few years ago, and I'm a huge fan of Burning Beds. I've seen you in those photos online with Dylan Neptune."

My head snapped up at that. No one has ever openly linked me to Dylan. Holly blushed a little.

"The reason I approached you ten years ago at the conference in Sydney when I was just a concierge was that I recognized you as the girl who was always holding Dylan's hand in those pictures. I wasn't sure if you were a sister or anything, but I was curious about you. We got to know each other professionally, and I liked you, and you never once mentioned him, so I didn't ask."

Holly's smile was infectious.

"Anyway, my point being, Sean showed me a photo of you and Ethan on his phone. Dark hair, bedroom-blue eyes. You have a type, Jess, and my fiancé is not it."

My mind flashed back to Dylan meeting Ethan and his comment that I have a type. "I guess you could put my former lovers in a line-up, and you'd never pick the culprit," I admitted with a sigh.

"So, Dylan Neptune is a former lover?" Holly's eyes sparkled, her smirk growing into an infectious grin. Swallowing my smile and shaking my head, I let out another sigh.

"All I can say is what is a matter of public record. We grew up in the same town, and I went to school with his sister."

"Hmm," Holly smirked, then took a sip of her coffee. "So you knew him before he became famous. Interesting. Has Sean met him?"

Lifting a shoulder in a shrug, I didn't answer. I couldn't. But Holly's eyes only lit up brighter, her smile growing even more.

"So, he's still on the scene, but if you're heartbroken over this Ethan guy, then you're not in love with the rockstar."

God, I was once. A very long time ago.

"Have you ever met Benjamin Henderson?" Holly suddenly asked, making me frown.

"As in Henderson Hotels, Benjamin Henderson? No, I don't think I have."

Holly kept smirking. "He's totally your type. I wouldn't recommend him for a relationship. But if this thing with you and Ethan doesn't mend and you need a rebound that can make you forget about him, I can introduce you."

Nearly snorting my coffee out of my nose, I swallowed and choked on a laugh before eyeing the woman across from me. We met each other's eyes, and then both started laughing.

"I'll keep that in mind." Then, noticing the time, I finished my coffee and stood up. "I should go catch my train. I'll see you in a week when we fly out again."

Rising out of her chair, Holly hugged me. "I know that you convinced Sean to come to the conference knowing I worked at Holmes. Thank you."

"I didn't know you worked there until you emailed me back about the conference. But yes, once I saw your email signature, I knew I had to get Sean to go. He'd been angry at me for months for not knowing where you worked."

Pulling back, Holly gave me a weird smile. "Huh, yeah. I never knew you worked for Cassidy. How had we never talked about where we worked before?"

Shrugging a shoulder, I smiled at her. "Because the 'where' was never important. I'll see you next Thursday."

Grabbing my suitcase, I headed off to the train station to catch the CountryLink, which would deliver me to Newcastle with minimum stops.

As soon as I was on the train, I pulled out my phone and brought up Dylan's mobile number to send him a message.

\<Jess Muse\>: Been thinking about that night. You could've saved me a lot of heartaches.

Karla was waiting with a big smile and a tight hug at the other end.

"Twice in one year after a decade of staying away. Punching Sharnie out must have healed something in your broken heart."

It made me smile as we started towards the car park.

"Just opportunity. I was in Queensland for work over Christmas and New Year and took a week off to visit on the way home."

"Does the family know you are here?"

"Only Lou. I've asked him not to tell anybody."

"Including Mister Sexpot Ethan?" Karla snickered.

Swallowing hard, I focused on the way forward. "Especially him."

Grabbing my arm, Karla pulled me to a stop.

"Whoa, hold up. What happened there? Last I heard, he was banging your brains out on his layovers in Hawaii. I thought you were just staying with me because he was away for work or something."

Meeting Karla's eyes, I managed to hold back the tears, but only just.

"Can we wait to have this conversation until there is alcohol on hand?"

Staring into my eyes for a moment, Karla went to say something, stopped herself, and groaned. "Well, fuck the devil with his pitchfork. Okay, yeah. We're having dinner with Lizzy tonight. We'll eat then drink her under the table and compare broken hearts."

"Compare?"

"Anthony and I broke up again, and Lizzy and Hale have separated."

That made me pause. Not about Karla and Anthony. They were constantly breaking up, but Lizzy and Hale had been together since university. "Really? Why?"

"Argh, Anthony's best friend is in love with me, and decided to tell Anthony how we've been fucking on and off for years behind his back whenever we weren't together. That makes me the slut in Anthony's eyes, but he's still friends with his mate. I've resisted telling him that Darren lied, and it wasn't only when we were taking breaks from our relationship. But I'm taking the high ground when he calls me all those names and not telling him how Darren pounded me into the mattress only two nights before he got drunk and confessed his love for me to my fiancé."

"I meant Lizzy and Hale. I knew why you and Anthony broke up. That hasn't changed since high school. Great guy. Bad at sex. You fuck someone else, get guilty, and end it. Rinse. Repeat."

Sighing, Karla lifted her face to the sky as we reached her car. "Yeah. Is it bad I didn't feel guilty these last few times? I mean, I've been asking for him to put more effort into things between the sheets, and his answer was to ask for anal."

"Because that's going to improve his performance?"

"Right? Anyway, as you said, I've been holding on because he is the nicest guy, and I've loved him since I was fourteen, but I keep stepping out on him. There's a serious flaw in our relationship that he's unwilling to fix. I've even tried a sex therapist."

"No good?"

"I ended up fucking our therapist," Karla mourned. "Anthony has a big dick. He should be perfect. But it takes longer for me to undress than it does for him to finish, and that includes the foreplay. I haven't even had an orgasm with him involved for—fuck, I can't remember." She throws her arms up. "And he doesn't care!"

"Oh, babe." Pulling my best friend into a hug, I hold her tight as she cries on my shoulder.

"Every other time, I've ended it, so he's never known about the other guys. He's always thought I just had commitment issues. Darren told him that it was when we'd broken up, but Anthony hates me now. He said he could handle me sleeping with other guys while we weren't together, but not his best friend. I can handle the breakup, but not how he looks and talks to me now. That's what's breaking my heart."

Holding her tight, I rubbed Karla's back to soothe her while she cried it out there in the car park for the train station. Of course, we got looks from people walking past, but it didn't matter. My friend was hurting. I'd hold her together while she fell apart and then try and help her glue herself together again.

It's not anything I allowed anyone to do for me. Not with Dylan. Not with Ben. And not with Ethan. Sean came the closest. He was my sounding wall and confessional, but not the friend with the heart glue.

Later that night, after drinking a significant amount of alcohol with my heartbroken besties, I was still lying awake when my phone lit up with a message from Dylan.

<Rockstar>: Don't kid yourself, Jess. It wasn't Ben that broke your heart. It was Matilda.

<Jess Muse>: As I said. You could've saved me.

<Rockstar>: No, I wouldn't have. I would have destroyed you. You know why.

He was right. Dylan didn't want kids. So as soon as he made his first million at age eighteen, he got himself sterilized to make sure of it. Yes, males can get it reversed, but Dylan never would. He broke my heart on purpose to give me the future he thought I deserved.

Dylan and I wanted different things from life, and the only thing we could agree that we wanted was each other, and that wasn't enough to compete with all our other dreams. Not back then. Not when I was dreaming of a home and a family.

On our last trip to Bora Bora, Dylan tried to kiss me one morning while his girlfriend was at the spa. When I wouldn't let him, he asked me if Ethan was a family man, if we were going to have babies together. The look Dylan gave me when I admitted Ethan didn't want marriage and kids stuck in my mind.

<Jess Muse>: Yeah, well, Ethan did it instead.

When you said I had a type, you didn't mean the looks, did you?

<Rockstar>: I'm sorry about Ethan.

That was it. That was all I got. The phone stayed dark, and my eyes filled with tears, but I wouldn't let my hurt disturb the sounds of the night. My grief was my own. I couldn't keep inflicting it on the world. At least, not out loud.

<Jess Muse>: I hate you.

CHAPTER SIX

"I can't believe it. Lizzy and Hale?"

Nodding confirmation, I sipped my tea as Lou gaped at me. Because Lou was only partially retired and played golf most weekends, it had taken until Wednesday the following week to catch up with him. Not that he was upset. Two visits from his daughter in a month were better than one in ten years.

"But they were so in love. What happened?"

"They have been trying for a baby for years now. When they realized there was a problem, they went and got tested. Hale is shooting blanks. He can't have kids. Lizzy told him it was okay, that they could foster or adopt or use a sperm donor, but Hale just refused, then he packed a bag and moved home to his parents."

My dad blinked, then lowered his gaze to his dining room table where we were sitting. "How devastating for both of them."

"Especially Lizzy. She loved Hale enough that she would have gone without kids altogether for him," I mourned, my mind trying to stray to thoughts of Ethan. I'd been willing to sacrifice a family to have him, and he'd been willing to risk one to have me—for a

385

moment at least. Then his lust cleared, and he'd changed his mind again.

"Did he explain why he left?" Lou asked. When I nodded, he sighed. "Was it to do with his family's religious beliefs?"

"Yeah. Some shit about marriage and sex only being for the propagation of the species, and if they can't breed, then there was no point in him taking part in either of those things." I shook my head. "I knew his family was scarily religious, but I never picked Hale as being like that. I didn't even know until Lizzy told me the other night that Hale insisted they wait until they marry for sex and that their wedding night was the first time for both of them."

I'd known Lizzy waited and was gun-shy after her high school boyfriend cheated on her with Sharnie. It's not that she wanted to wait for marriage, but just to make sure her first time was with someone who truly valued and respected her.

"Hmm, some people have some strange beliefs. It could also be that he's ashamed he can't give her the family they planned together and needs time to deal with those emotions. Women like to talk things out. Men prefer to retreat, process, and then move on," Lou counseled. "Given time, he may come back."

The way Lou was looking at me made me feel like he wasn't just talking about Lizzy and Hale anymore.

"So, you're playing golf this afternoon?" I asked to change the subject.

"Yes, did you want a lift?" Lou's eyes traveled to the yellow lilies I'd bought to take to Matilda's grave.

"If it's just you, I'd appreciate that." The last time I'd been home and gotten a lift to the graveyard, Ethan was with Lou. While I'd been clear that I didn't want Ethan to know I was in town, it also wasn't fair to put Lou in the position to have to lie. So it would be better for him just never to have it come up.

"It's just me. The guys should be flying to New Zealand today."

"Then yes, I'd love a lift, thanks."

Taking a sip of his tea, Lou considered me. "How did the work trip to Queensland go?"

"Good. Really good, actually. I brought the staff up to par with their training, Sean rescued the love of his life from a horrendous storm, and they flew back to Sydney with me to organize for her to move home with him."

"The love of his life? As in the prime minister's daughter?"

Grinning, I met my dad's wide-eyed gaze. "The same. The engagement is back on, but let's not spread that around. They'd like to avoid the media this time around."

"I bet." Still taking that in, we both jolted when the front door opened.

"I thought Margaret was at work?" I hissed.

Pushing away from the table, Lou started for the front door. "She is." A few moments later, that turned out to be a lie. "What are you doing home early?"

"Oh, you're still here. I thought you would have left for the golf club by now. We had a blackout at work. A crane driving up the road took out a power line, and it's going to take hours to repair, so they sent everyone home," Margaret explained as her voice came closer. "You look anxious. Do you have a woman here?" Margaret joked.

"Actually, yes," Lou answered as they entered the kitchen, and I got to watch my mother's face fall.

"What?"

The last time I heard my mother's voice break and sound so small and weak was when the police explained what Sharnie had done to Teille when we were fourteen.

Lou looked over Margaret's head to meet my eyes. "We have a visitor."

Margaret swung her head to the dining room, and her jaw dropped for a moment as she took me in, sitting at her table. Her mouth worked for a second as she pulled herself together, and then she forced a smile onto her face.

"Jessie. What a surprise. What are you doing in Australia?"

"I'm just passing through for work. But, since I was this close, I thought I'd catch up with Karla, Lizzy, and see Dad while I was in town," I offered in explanation. She didn't need to know how long I was here or that Lou knew I was coming in advance.

Catching sight of the yellow lilies, Margaret swallowed, her spine stiffening. "You're going to the grave?"

Deciding it was time to leave, I got up from the chair and carried my empty cup and saucer to the kitchen. "I am."

I wasn't sure how to deal with Margaret anymore. But because this wasn't awkward enough, fate decided to make things just a little tenser by having someone knock at the door.

"I'll get it," Lou decided and strode down the hall, abandoning me with Margaret, who was looking me over with a critical eye.

"You look terrible, Jessie. Are you jet-lagged?"

"Ethan?" Lou's voice echoed down the hall. "I thought you were working?"

My heart pounded in my chest as my stomach crumpled to nothing.

"The flight got canceled, so I thought I'd try to catch you for a round of golf," Ethan's deep voice followed Lou's as the front door closed, filling my heart with agony and anxiety. "I hope that's okay?"

"Yes, of course. I just need a minute to finish something here."

"Do you mind if I use your bathroom?" Ethan asked. It was a request Lou couldn't reject without things being weird. But I couldn't see him. I couldn't cope with my broken heart while Margaret and Lou watched on.

Freaking out, I yanked the pantry door open. "I'm not here."

"What?" Margaret scowled.

Stepping into the pantry, I closed the door, then put my back to the wall and tried hard to keep my shit together. Tears slid down my face as I focused on controlling my breathing.

"Where's Jessie?" Lou murmured outside the pantry door.

"Being weird and hiding in the pantry. What is going on?"

Groaning, Lou pulled the door open and stepped in. One look at my face and his own filled with sorrow. "I'm sorry, Jessie Girl."

Shaking my head, I stepped into the hug he offered me. "Not your fault, Dad. I'll get a taxi. Don't stress."

"I'll take you," Margaret offered, giving me a bizarre look as I wiped the tears from my face. Her head turned towards the hallway, and she forced a smile and stepped away. "Ethan."

It surprised me to realize Margaret had moved away to block Ethan from coming into the kitchen and seeing me. Grabbing a trail mix from the shelf, Lou dropped a kiss on my forehead.

"Stay safe. Call me when you get home," he whispered, then stepped out. "Okay. Let's go."

Taking deep breaths to calm down, I stayed in the pantry until I heard the front door close, then I eased out into the kitchen. Margaret was waiting, her nails tapping on the countertop as she stared at me as if I was alien to her.

"The boys started flying to Hawaii because you and Ethan were seeing each other, didn't they?"

Swallowing, I moved to pick up the lilies. "We lied when I was here. Ethan and I met before the wedding. I just didn't know he was involved in my family until then. We were sleeping together the entire time I was here, and yes, after I returned home, he changed his roster to keep seeing me. But it didn't work out, and I'm still feeling the burn of another failed relationship."

"What happened?" Margaret's fingers were still on the counter, her eyes still watching me like I was a mystery.

"I don't want to discuss it if you don't mind. I didn't come here for Ethan. I truly was just passing through for a work trip." Putting my handbag on my shoulder and the bouquet in the crook of my elbow, I turned to face the woman who gave birth to me. "I'm sorry I'm a bitter disappointment to you, but I can't be anyone but me. I should go. Take care, Margaret."

Putting a hand to my shoulder, Margaret waited for me to pause, then she moved that same palm to my cheek and swiped away my tears with her thumb. Then, after a moment of staring into my eyes, her own glassy, Margaret took her hand back and pursed her lips as she collected the keys from the bench.

"I said that I'd take you." Grabbing her handbag, she turned for the front door without another word.

Thirty minutes later, I stood before the small pink marble headstone of my stillborn daughter, Matilda Bailey. Margaret stood beside me, using a manicured finger to dab at her inner eye.

"My heart broke the day your father came home and told me what happened to our first grandchild. Then you disappeared. I wanted to hold my baby girl and comfort you. I wanted to be there for you, but you weren't there. I was terrified you'd killed yourself or something equally as bad in your grief, but then you called, and all that fear and grief turned into rage. How could you just leave me to bury your daughter? How could you refuse me the right to be your mother and comfort you?"

Closing my eyes, I turned my head away. A decade of pent-up hate and rejection was coming my way, and as much as I wanted to deny I deserved it, the truth was, I did. I couldn't cope, so I ran away and left my parents to sweep up the shards of my life I left behind.

"I didn't plan it. I just walked out of the hospital and then ended up on a plane heading to the other side of the planet," I answered. "I didn't mean to subject you or dad to that. I was just drowning and couldn't catch a breath long enough to consider the repercussions. By the time I did, Ben was saying ugly things to me, you were screaming at me, and as much as I knew I'd made a mistake, I also realized it was too late to fix it."

"So you stayed away?"

"No, I didn't come home because I couldn't. It was peaceful away from here. After years of Sharnie's tormenting, I didn't want to give up that peace. So, I built myself a new life, and I was happy. I was, Mum. I was happy."

"Until you fell in love again?"

"It wasn't the falling in love that was the problem." Taking a moment, I waited for Margaret to be her usual self, but she stayed quiet. Turning around to face her directly, I wrapped my arms around her, squeezing a little tighter when she stiffened. Margaret never liked anyone touching her except my dad. "I'm sorry I hurt you when I ran away. I'm sorry I left you to deal with that mess. I hope you can forgive me one day."

Turning away, I started to walk between the graves.

"Jessie," Margaret called. I turned back to see her still standing at the grave. Meeting my eyes, she hesitated. Then, after swallowing, she stood straight and pulled her shoulders back. "Do you need a lift back?"

"No, I can walk. Thank you."

I made it a few more graves away before she called again.

"Jessie." This time, there were tears in her eyes when I looked back, betraying the stiff upper-lip she was trying to hold. "No matter our differences. I love you. I always have. You're my baby girl."

"I love you too, Mum."

When the side of her mouth lifted slightly and she blew out a sigh of relief, I faced forward and walked back to town. I'd hurt her with my actions, and I knew that was her turning point—the moment when I became the devil child in her eyes. Everyone was entitled to their perspective.

If there was something that I learned over the years, it's that the ideology of forgiving and forgetting was flawed. Yes, forgiveness was good—more for you than anyone else. You should forgive. It's a weight off the soul. But you should never forget when someone harms you on purpose, physically or emotionally, and you certainly should never allow them the opportunity to do it again. Sharnie taught me that.

She was my sister, and for the first fourteen years of my life, Sharnie was my best friend. Of course, I loved and missed her. But who she became, how she treated me in the years since, I would never forget or allow it to happen again.

\

CHAPTER SEVEN

<Sean>: Are you here yet?

<Jessie Girl>: Yes. Just got through security. Where are you?

<Sean>: Past duty-free. In the lounge.

WE WERE ALLOWED TO USE THE AIRLINE'S LOUNGE WITH US FLYING business class rather than finding a seat in the food court or the uncomfortable chairs by the gate.

<Jessie Girl>: Okay. I'll get my pie and shake and then come and find you.

<Sean>: Pie and shake?

<Jessie Girl>: It's a thing. Does Holly need a sausage roll or pie before leaving Oz?

<Sean>: Weirdly, she was very enthusiastic about the sausage roll. You better grab me one, so I can understand this strange behavior.

Chuckling, I slipped my phone back into my pocket and navigated towards the shop I needed. Once I was the owner of two meat pies, three sausage rolls, and caramel milkshakes, I wheeled my cabin bag to the escalator that took me up to the airline's lounge.

International flight check-in in Australia required you to arrive at least three hours before your scheduled take-off. As long as there was no issue getting through security, you had plenty of time to browse duty-free and get something to eat before the flight.

Not that the food was cheap at the airport. Sydney was one of the most expensive cities in the world to live in, and its airport was probably the most expensive food in Sydney outside of a five-star Michelin restaurant. I swear they just doubled the prices of what you would pay anywhere else.

Locating Sean and Holly in the lounge wasn't hard either; just look for the most loved-up couple there. I swear, if I weren't so happy for them, I'd have gagged. Popping the tray of shakes and grub on the table, I announced my presence and smiled when they unlatched their lips from each other to be polite.

"Okay, unattainable Aussie grub for our last meal in Oz," I announced as I portioned out the milkshakes, then put a sausage roll in front of Holly and a bag containing a beef pie and sausage roll in front of Sean. Then, pulling out my sausage roll, I took a bite and enjoyed the hell out of it.

"Thanks, Jess. I totally forgot it might be a while before I can get my hands on these again," Holly smiled, taking a bite of the pastry-wrapped sausage mince and smiling.

Sean tentatively took a bite while watching Holly and me eat the sausage rolls with narrowed eyes. Both his brows went up as he chewed, and then he wolfed it down in no time.

"So, why is it a thing to eat this before you leave?"

"Can't get them like this anywhere else," I explained. "Sausage rolls and meat pies are a staple of any Aussie kid's upbringing. The biggest sellers are at the school canteen, and football matches. They are the backbone of every birthday party along with Cheezels and Fairy Bread."

"It's not a party without Cheezels and Fairy Bread," Holly assures him with a grin.

"Right?! We have shops dedicated just to making our meat pies and sausage rolls. I mean, Pie Face is good, but growing up, it had to be Darby's in Newcastle. They were the best."

"Ooh, Harry de Wheels," Holly added enthusiastically. "Mitch and I still go there to get our pie fix after clubbing."

Nodding, I chewed and swallowed. "Yes! We always went there when we were out clubbing as well. A meat pie with mash and gravy poured over the top."

Sean screwed his nose up at the sound of that, but it shit all over the American biscuits and gravy when it came to taste and satisfaction.

"Anyway, when I left Oz, I discovered that you can't get our version of pies and sausage rolls overseas unless it's a place with a lot of Aussie expats. And you can kiss caramel milkshakes goodbye once you leave our shores. Like, how is Australia the only country in the world that discovered caramel in milk is awesome?"

"It's insane," Holly agreed. "I'm glad I'll be coming back home regularly, so I won't miss it as bad. I don't know how you've done without them for ten years."

Shaking my head, I finished my sausage roll and pulled out the pie. "I haven't. I make my own sausage rolls. I'll make a batch and then freeze them and have them for lunch every other weekend, and I make pies out of leftovers."

"Really?" Holly sat up, appearing intrigued. "What leftovers?"

"Anything with mince, really. Spag Bol, tacos, shepherd's pie. I'll use the pie maker to spoon the leftovers into the pastry, cook them up, then freeze them to eat later."

"Yum! I might have to raid your stash," Holly joked.

"Jess is in Maui. That's a long way to go for a pie. But Jess is a great cook, so it's worth occasionally visiting for lasagne."

The next hour we chatted about food, work, and travel, and then it was time to head to the gate to prepare to board for our flight. Holly announced she needed to stop for her take-off candy as we walked through the terminal. I offered to share my Minties, but her chewing preference was Fantales. Minties were too soft and didn't last long enough to keep her ears from blocking.

Going ahead of them, I was at the gate getting my boarding pass ready for checking when a shadow fell over me. The pilot's uniform confused me as I looked up until I reached the broad shoulders and then masculine handsomeness of Ethan's face.

His cap covered his black hair, and his deep-blue eyes focused on me as the air rushed out of my lungs, tears itching my eyeballs, but I wasn't going to cry for him again. It had been two months. I needed a little self-control at this stage.

"Jess, you were home?" Ethan asked, looking hurt and maybe a little angry.

Clearing my throat, I glanced to the side and spotted Greg keeping this distance. "Just passing through. I was in Queensland for work. Hey, Greg," I waved, hopeful he'd come over and alleviate the awkwardness of this encounter, but he just waved and waited. Great!

"Are you heading back to Hawaii?"

"Ethan—"

"We need to talk, Jess. I've got to get to my plane right now, but please, have dinner with me tonight when I land?"

Swallowing hard, I licked my lips. "I won't be there. I have a connecting flight to catch." Totally true. It was just an island-hopping flight and not a flight to the mainland. Looking to the gate, I noticed the business class was boarding. "I have to go."

Putting his arm out to block me, Ethan stepped in my way. "Please, Jess, we need to talk. We need—" Someone stepped up beside me, and Ethan's eyes flicked over before turning hard, his jaw grinding.

"Ethan," Sean greeted.

"Sean." Ethan backed up a step, his eyes flicking back to me. "You're traveling together?"

Sean huffed. "I see you still haven't got over your paranoid jealousy. Maybe you should seek out a therapist to help you with that."

As Ethan's eyes narrowed on Sean before coming back to me, Greg finally joined us. "Sean, how have you been?"

"Good, Greg. Great, actually." Putting out his arm, Sean pulled Holly in next to him, and both Greg and Ethan's eyes widened a little. "I'd like you to meet Holly, my fiancée. Holly, this is Greg, Jess's brother-in-law, and his best friend—"

"Ethan," Holly acknowledged. "Yes, I recognize him from the pictures you showed me. It's nice to meet you both." Holly shook hands with them, her eyes flicking to me as she pulled back. "Our flight is boarding."

Nodding, Sean looked between Ethan and me, then kissed Holly's cheek. "Right behind you." Sean waited for Holly to head to the priority boarding before turning to me. "You okay?" When I nodded, Sean gave Ethan a look that could have been sympathy or disgust. "You hurt my best friend dearly. I encouraged her to give you a chance, and you fucked it up, for what? So you could go and fuck some other woman and not feel guilty for it?"

"Wait, what? What other woman?" Greg chimed in.

"The one in his room when Jess went to try and set the record straight," Sean answered. "She found them naked together."

"Cindy?!" Greg looked stunned.

"I didn't sleep with her!" Ethan argued simultaneously, looking just as surprised by the allegation.

"So, my friend cries on my shoulder, and I'm a cheating whore, but I find you literally naked with another woman, and it's totally innocent?" I scowl. "Fucking hell, Ethan. I didn't realize you were a hypocrite as well. We've got to go."

"Jess—" Ethan stepped in my way again when I tried to step away, moving us back from Sean and Greg. "I'm sorry I hurt you, but I didn't fuck Cindy. Please, give me another chance."

Holding back my tears became impossible with my heart aching in my chest as I shook my head. "I told you that night at the lookout. I warned you what it would do to me if you changed your mind again. There's no going back, E. You broke me, and there is no glue strong enough to repair the damage you've done."

Shouldering by Ethan, I made my way to priority boarding.

"I'm still doing the Hawaii run," Ethan called as I walked away. "I'm not going to stop. And I'm not going to stop begging you to forgive me."

The lady at the gate watched Ethan as she took my boarding pass and scanned it. "Is everything okay?" she asked.

"My ex," I explained, wiping away a tear. Boy, was I grateful we ended up flying Hawaiian Air for this trip! Sean occasionally flew with Ethan's company if he couldn't get flights for the dates and times he wanted.

Biting her lip, the woman checked Ethan out as she handed me back my pass. "Have a nice flight."

"Thanks," I scoffed and stepped through the gate.

Sean was right behind me now and caught up, putting his arm around me as we walked and giving me a side hug. "You okay?"

"No."

Sighing, Sean squeezed me tighter.

Boarding the plane, the attendant at the door gave me a gentle smile as she checked my pass and pulled back the curtain for business class.

"Is everything okay?"

"Just allergies," I forced a smile and stepped by her.

"To her ex, who she just ran into," Sean muttered behind me, then went to the other side of the plane where our initial seats were. Holly and I had traded places so she could sit with Sean.

As I got comfortable and unpacked what I needed for the flight, my phone buzzed. Setting it aside, I put my cabin bag up, then sorted out my headphones, book, and phone for the flight.

"Can I interest you in a drink, Miss?" the flight attendant asked.

"A vodka-lime twist would be great right now, please."

The attendant then took the order of the man who was about to climb into the seat beside me. He was tall, blond, and middle-aged, and gave me a great smile as his eyes casually checked me out.

"Hi," he said, taking the seat.

He then proceeded to chat to me while the plane boarded about his law firm and that he was flying to Hawaii for a big client's divorce settlement. He had to travel all that way to be on site for negotiations and the final signing. It was a distraction from the ache in my sternum, so I listened and asked questions and was just polite.

It wasn't until the cabin crew started preparing for take-off and I went to turn my phone to airplane mode that I remembered the message I'd received.

<E>: Cindy is a friend. I didn't book a room with work that weekend because I thought I'd be staying with you. She checked out an hour later for her flight, and I grabbed the room for the remainder of my stay. I swear, I didn't fuck her, Jess. Please, let me see you and explain?

Taking a breath as my eyes filled with tears again, I closed my eyes and wished it mattered. It didn't. Whether Ethan banged Cindy that night was the least of our problems.

<Jess>: Too little, too late. You don't trust me. You made that clear. And now I can't trust you not to break my heart again. Goodbye, Ethan.

An hour later we were airborne, and I was tucked away on the opposite side of business class from Sean and Holly already reclined, the blanket pulled up as I sobbed into my pillow.

CHAPTER EIGHT

"I'M SENDING YOU THE LINK TO THE NEW SONG. IT GOES LIVE AT midnight tonight, but Dylan wanted you to see it first," Teille explained as I was walking home.

"Do I want to hear it?" I asked, talking handsfree as I crossed the road from the resort and started up the street, which would wind up the hill to my place.

"It's the video clip too. When I told Dylan to hold off on 'Jealous as Hell' and why, he immediately penned this new song and recorded it within the week. The label loved it and made it the release. As soon as the album was recorded and going through post, they had the guys on set filming the video," Teille explained.

"Am I going to like it?" I asked. Code for, 'is it going to be about me again?'

"The topic? Unlikely? But it's a great song, Jess. Like it could be the best they've written since Goddess of Heartbreak."

"Teille!" I stopped, bowing my head. Tears were already in my eyes. "He's written my heartbreak again, hasn't he?"

"Not just yours, this time. Jess, you're the only one who's going to know this, but he's basically just showed the world how you became his muse."

I swear my heart stopped in my chest.

"Of course, they'll pass it off as just the creative vision of the director, but I thought you should know that any die-hard fan is going to connect some of the scenes in the video with photos of you two over the years."

The silence stretched through the line.

"Okay. I'm sending you the link now. Please don't share it, not that I think you want this out there."

"How much of our past is there, Teille?"

She hesitated too long. "If I said blood on the sheets, would that tip you off?"

"Fuck!"

"I'm guessing no one knew?"

"Did you?"

Teille hesitates again. "No. Not until I saw the storyboard for the video and asked Dylan about it." There was another long pause. "Was Matilda my niece, Jess?"

Tears escaped my eyes without warning. "No," I whispered.

"It's just that Dylan had his surgery after you found out you were pregnant and looking back, I thought maybe—"

"I never cheated on Ben. Once he came back from the academy, he was my only until nearly two years after I left, and Dylan came to Maui and sought me out."

"Does Ben know that you and Dylan…?"

"Were close? Yes. I never hid that."

"No, I meant that you and Dylan had sex while he was away?"

My mouth ran dry, but my eyes were anything but waterless. "It's not what you think. We…" God, how did I explain this? "Dylan and I were close ever since Sharnie attacked you. When Ben and I separated the year that he was at the academy, Dylan and I only got closer, and it shifted to a physical thing. I thought we were more. The night of your parent's funeral, things got hot and heavy, and we nearly…" Tears poured down my face as I started walking again.

Teile was quiet on the other side of the call, listening intently to the details of what happened that night. She already knew the fallout, the what came after. But I'd never told her the details of how her brother broke my heart.

"When I say nearly, I mean we did, but the moment Dylan was inside me, he froze, cursed, and was gone again. My body was still aching from the first penetration while he was pulling his jeans on, telling me he'd never be good for me, and I was better off with Ben. Then he told me to go home and stormed out, and you know the rest from there."

"What a dick!" Teille sighed.

"I never considered it my first time because we didn't actually have sex. Considering it so would be the equivalent of putting a tampon in and claiming it was masturbation because your finger was in your vagina."

"I can't believe he did that to you."

"Really? I mean, this is Dylan Neptune we are talking about here. The guy who comes to my hotels to go on benders, trashes my hotel rooms, leaves his sheets covered in blood from his kink, torments my staff as if he's Satan unleashed, fucks me wherever he finds me whether I'm working or not, and has twice required me to bail him out after getting arrested for assaulting other assholes he gets into fights with while drunk," I ranted.

"Yeah, but this is you, and what guy gets his dick wet with the woman he's always wanted and then freaks out before he's even finished the first slide? It's not like my brother was a blushing virgin by that time either."

With Dylan over four years older than me, no, he certainly wasn't. Hell, his band had been doing the club circuit for six years by then and had just signed to their label and released their first album. I'd been in shock when Dylan first pushed inside me, only to have him jump off me like my vagina bit him.

"I can't believe you stayed friends with him. That you still slept with him years later."

"Argh," I groaned as I tilted my head up to the sky before bringing it back down. "Do you know the thing I've learned over the years, Teille? Lust will fade or burn out, but love doesn't die. Instead, it changes to hate, morphs into friendship, or starves like a lit ember without oxygen, only needing the right settings to reignite. I thought I loved Ben until I had what I felt for Dylan to compare it to."

"And Ethan?"

The tears grew fatter and ran faster as my heart cramped in my chest.

"I'm sorry. It's still too fresh," Teille apologized when I failed to answer.

I'd had thirteen years to get over Dylan, to work through his issues, and make what we have work for the two of us in some weird and casual way. Ethan was still a gushing wound. Our run-in at the airport only a month ago showcased I wasn't anywhere near over Ethan yet. Hell, it took me two years to speak to Dylan again, and he'd only been inside me once for all of five seconds before breaking my heart. Ethan had made me his; he'd engraved his ownership of my body into my marrow.

"Well, I'm halfway home. You better send me this link so I can divert to the bottle shop if I need to after watching it."

404

"Okay, we'll talk soon," Teille chuckled, but it didn't have the energy of her usual humor. "Don't kill my brother, okay, Jess? He's all I have left."

Snickering, I said goodbye, then pulled out my phone and clicked on the link for the new Burning Beds song 'I Pity the Fool'.

The video opened with a younger version of Dylan racing into a hospital yelling, "Where is she?" at the emergency reception as if the nurse should know who he or his sister is. I guess if it happened today, or even four years after the initial attack, the nurse might have known.

A guitar starts playing a catchy riff, cutting out the hospital sounds as Dylan turns and spies a girl who resembles a younger me across the waiting room, still wearing the bloody clothes of the night and battered and bruised.

Striding over, he pulls her into his arms as the rest of the band kicks in. But that's certainly not how it went down in real life.

When Dylan found me in emergency that night, he stood over me, yelling at me to tell him what happened to Teille. What did we do? He certainly did not pay any attention to the injuries I sustained protecting his sister long enough for the paramedics to arrive or comfort me in any way, shape, or form.

Hell, Dylan hated my guts for months until Teille woke up and told him her version of events. Even then, it wasn't until the day that I found Teille with her wrists slashed and took steps to save her again until help arrived that he genuinely forgave me for Sharnie's actions.

The scene changed to Dylan and the girl hanging out, talking, reading, playing guitar together, and cuddling while writing lyrics. And then the music died down as Dylan's voice slid in over the top like a lover's caress.

"Summer chestnuts, silk, and cream
A beam of naughty, a slice of pain

Rushing blood, a darkened stain
Mountains and passes, my end of days."

A funeral. It was a replica of the photo the media snapped of us at his parent's grave. It shifts to his bedroom, where the girl holds him while he sobs, tears in her eyes, and then he starts kissing her, undressing her, and making love to her while they both cry. After they finish, he gets up, dresses, and leaves, yelling at her until she's huddled naked in his sheets and he's storming out the door.

"Whispered nothings, hidden secrets
Non-disclosure, a blight of regrets
Vacant beds, blood-stained linen
Old torments, new beginnings."

The camera pans across the room. My breath caught as I recognized that everything about that room is precisely Dylan's bedroom thirteen years ago. When it gets back to the bed, the girl is gone. Dylan comes back and sees the small bloodstain she left on his sheet. He grips it in his hand and breaks down, and cries.

"But who's the bigger fool?
The one who loves from a distance,
Or the lover who lets her go?"

The same girl walks down the street with another guy, her abdomen swollen with child. She notices Dylan, the smile falls from her face, her hand rubs over her baby bump, and then the guy holding her hand captures her attention; she smiles at him, and away they go.

"That's why Teille asked if Matilda was his," I muttered to myself. Usually, I'd be home by now, but stopping to fret with Teille delayed me, and now I was walking so slow, it wasn't funny.

The scene shifts to the new guy in bed with a blonde, my character walks in on them, and she runs away. It's not until she slows down and sits on the bench crying that the pain hits, and the girl grabs her belly and doubles over.

Ambulance lights, a hospital, and then the girl is crying to herself all alone.

> *"I pity the fool who gives you up,*
> *I pity the fool who makes you cry,*
> *I pity the fool who has it all,*
> *Then breaks your heart with a selfish mind."*

She's with a new guy, and they seem so in love, but whenever she's talking to other guys, the new guy glares at them. I had to admit, the actors are good. Even though the words aren't clear, the actors tell an entire story about a jealous boyfriend without any words needing to be said.

> *"Green eyed-monsters, friends for life*
> *Imagined looks, laughs, and fucks,*
> *Hugs and kisses, tears and lies,*
> *A broken heart that bleeds all night.*

> *But who's the bigger fool?*

The one who loves from a distance,
Or the lover who lets her go?

I pity the fool who gives you up,
I pity the fool who makes you cry,
I pity the fool who has it all,
Then breaks your heart with a jealous eye."

The inevitable breakup and the girl is left crying her heart out again. Now the scenes are a combination of flashbacks to her and Dylan before he broke her, to her—and, let's face it, Ethan—when they were happy.

By the time I got home, all the crying would have left me dehydrated, but the tears were the same reason I hadn't diverted to the bottle shop for some good vodka.

Hell, part of me wanted to mimic the vision on the screen of Dylan opening a bottle in the shop, sinking onto the floor and drinking it straight off the shelf as the music shifts into the coda.

"He had everything I wanted.
He was everything you needed.
He could have loved you for life,
But he gave you up,
He broke you apart,
He made you cry,
He made you bleed,
For an imagined sin,
An imagined touch,
A soft heart,
An imagined fuck!

Who's the bigger fool?"

The music cuts off for a breath. Modulates, and then it's Dylan and me again, so there is no doubt that the first chorus wasn't even about Ben, but Dylan breaking her heart.

"I pity the fool who gives you up,
I pity the fool who makes you cry,
I pity the fool who has it all,
Then breaks your heart with a selfish mind."

The girl and Ethan replay on the screen.

"I pity the fool who gave you up,
I pity the fool who made you cry,
I pity the fool who had it all,
Then broke your heart for a jealous lie."

The music drops and changes again as a guitar solo plays. It's a cabin in the woods. The girl is all alone. She looks sad but resolute as she moves through the trees like she'd been on a Sunday walk to clear her mind.

As she gets back to the cabin, Dylan is there with a bunch of flowers. He professes his love, his regret, and snatches her up into a passionate kiss as the music swells again. And then, as the final chorus plays out, they are happy together, in bed together, cooking, playing guitar, and cuddling while he writes music just like they used to together.

> *"I thank the fool who gave you up,*
> *I thank the fool who made you cry,*
> *I thank the fool who lost your love,*
> *Because he left you alone, and now you're mine."*

I stopped. Sitting in the gutter, I hung my head and cried for probably an hour.

CHAPTER NINE

I GOT TO THE STAIRS FOR MY PLACE, MY FEET, AND MY HEART stopped.

"Hey," Dylan closed the notebook he was writing in and met my eyes as he set it aside. He assessed my eyes and rubbed the back of his neck as he stood up, brandishing a bunch of lilies in his hand. "How much trouble am I in?"

Crossing my arms, I glared at his gorgeous and annoying head. "You breached your own NDA."

"Nah, it's all just acting," Dylan said as he came down the steps to stand in front of me. "That's the official response anyway."

"And no one who knows the truth can say it without declaring bankruptcy," I scoff. "Double standards, Dylan. Some people know us. People who know I'm the girl in those photos you used as inspiration. Ben, Sean, Ethan are all going to think I lied and that I was sleeping with you before leaving Australia. Hell, Teille asked me if Matilda was yours."

"All of them irrelevant to our truth, Jess." Holding out the flowers, Dylan waited for me to take them. I did with a sigh.

"What are you doing here, Dylan?"

"I came to see you."

"Why?" I pressed. I'd seen the video, but I doubted Dylan was here to profess his love to me and promise me matrimonial bliss.

Rubbing the back of his neck again, Dylan looked up at me through his long black lashes, his black hair falling across his face, almost hiding his cobalt blue eyes.

"Could we go inside, Jess? I could use a drink." When my back stiffened, Dylan sighed. "Of water, Jess. I'm not looking to get drunk and fucked up."

Gritting my teeth, I charged past him and shoved the key to the door in the lock, pushing it open and storming across to the kitchen. Putting my bag on the counter, I found a vase, filled it with water, added a splash of lemonade, then snipped the stems and set the bouquet in it.

Dylan observed my place, following me inside, a slight crease appearing between his eyebrows as he frowned. "This is not what I imagined your place would look like."

"It's not my place. I just live here."

"Yeah, but it looks like a holiday rental. You've added nothing of you to the place."

Sighing, I grabbed a glass down and went to the fridge.

"This isn't our arrangement, Dylan. You don't just show up. You don't come to my home. When I agree to shelter you for your self-destructive time, you book in advance; you stay at one of my hotels. We keep it discrete and away from our personal lives."

"This isn't that."

Shaking my head, I handed Dylan the glass of water he requested. "Then why are you here?"

"Thank you." Taking a big drink, Dylan eyed the outdoor deck. "Can we sit and talk?"

Exhaling, I bowed my head. "I need to shower and change." Grabbing my phone, I opened my foodie app and my past orders list. "Here, pick one of the places, order me my usual and then order something for you as well. I didn't get a lunch break today, and I'm starving."

Not giving Dylan time to reply, I grabbed my bag from the kitchen bench and stalked back to my bedroom, throwing it on the bed and shutting the door. This was the last thing I needed today. It'd been a shit day at work. One of the cold rooms for food storage broke down overnight, leaving some of the food to spoil before the day staff realized this morning, and a staff member failed to turn up to work with no notice, leaving the front desk short.

Now, this. Dylan Neptune was on my doorstep the same day he revealed my love life to the world. Great. Just what I needed.

Going into the bathroom, I groaned at my reflection. I wasn't one for wearing heavy makeup, but the little I had worn to work today was mostly washed away by my hour-long sob fest in the gutter, from which I only recovered fifteen minutes ago.

Freshly showered and dressed in lounge pants and a light sweater twenty minutes later, I pulled on my UGG boots and went out to find out why my first heartbreak was here. Dylan stood with his hands in his jeans pockets, staring at the view from the deck by the plunge pool. Turning on the kettle, I made two mugs of peppermint tea, then went out to join him.

The thing I loved about Hawaii was that the weather fluctuations were minimal. Even in the depth of winter, a light coat or sweater was enough.

"Here," I called Dylan's attention as I slid open the door and handed him the tea before turning to close it.

Taking a seat at the outdoor dining table, I waited for Dylan to join me, then lifted a brow to indicate the floor was his. Dylan smirked and took the seat opposite me, putting his tea on the table.

"I've been in love with you since you saved my life. You're my angel, Jess."

It took everything in me not to gawp at Dylan. He'd never told me those words before. The L word was forbidden on his lips unless it was song lyrics. I don't think he'd ever whispered it to a single person, including himself.

"I knew I loved you, but then your psycho twin tried to kill my sister, and by the time I got over that, you were with Ben. I considered that a good thing for you. You know my past, and you know my trauma. You know I'm fucked up. I didn't want to be the person who fucked you up, so I tried to keep it platonic between us. I knew you would never cheat on Ben and that as long as you were together, I couldn't hurt you. But God knows I wanted you, Jess. More than I wanted the record deal, I wanted you. Then Ben left for the academy, and you told me you'd decided to separate and see where that year led. I knew that Ben wanted to sow his wild oats, but it didn't matter. I was determined not to change our friendship. You see, I was too selfish to give you up, yet, I had to protect you from me. As my dad always said, it was trouble waiting to happen."

Gripping his mug, Dylan closed his eyes, then lifted the tea to his lips and took a mouthful. When he put the cup down, his eyes fell on me, glassy with the most emotion I'd not seen from him since I was seventeen.

"I couldn't keep away from you. Every free moment, I craved to be near you. I knew you were focusing on your studies, so I found myself offering to help you. I didn't even realize how much I'd drawn you into me until Mathew called you my girlfriend one night after we finished performing. I denied it, but then all of the band called me out on even trying to claim we were only friends. Evan said if that were the case, I wouldn't mind him making a move on you, and I realized I did fucking mind. As much as I should have let him, I couldn't, and after that night, there was no telling myself you were just a friend. We all knew you were so much more, and I either had to push you away or face the fact I was going to be the reason I'd look into your eyes one day and see a world of hatred aimed my way."

Picking up his mug, Dylan stared at the hot tea. "I got both anyway."

"And you chose your parent's funeral to be the day to fuck me over?"

Swallowing his mouthful, Dylan shook his head. "I didn't choose it. I knew I would end our friendship, and I planned to do it before things got that far, but then they died, and after everything, I felt like I buried my last shred of morality that day. I was off my face when you came to get me for the funeral. You knew it, and you let me rage until it became unsafe, and then you stepped in and took my hand. That's all you did, just took my hand, and all that rage just vanished, leaving a fucking ocean of pain. And still, you held my hand and kept me afloat. For a moment of insanity, I didn't care that I was going to destroy you. I wanted you, and I needed your love to keep me alive. But fuck, Jess. A darker part of me lusted for the innocence that you possessed. I wanted to take it from you as they took it from me. When you let me kiss you, and touch you, and undress you that night, my demons chortled with victory."

Tears streaked down my cheeks, the humiliation and pain of that night an old wound that I could still feel the scar of across my heart. Tensing my hands around my mug, I refused to wipe my face. I'd been overemotional since Ethan stomped on my heart. No, not just my heart. Me. He broke me entirely. Now Dylan was here shattering the shards.

"Why didn't you just fuck me then? Why did you stop?"

We'd never had this out. We never discussed what happened that night. He'd gotten dressed and told me to get out, never to come back. And yet, he's who I called when I needed to escape. Years later, when Dylan turned up at my hotel and asked to see me, he'd been a silver-tongued devil full of dirty promises of how hard he could make me come for him. When Dylan kissed me, I could feel his anger, and I'd unleashed my pain on him.

That's all our fucking had been since. Mutual torture. Brutal fucking that finished with mind-blowing orgasms and silence. We never really talked. Not about our feelings. The damage to the room, yes. The hard limits of our fucking, occasionally. How fucked up his kink was that he came to me to fulfill? Absolutely. But never what we felt for each other before or since.

Huffing, Dylan set his empty mug aside. "You're kidding, right?"

"No. It would have been worse. You didn't even use a condom. You could have fucked me and kicked me out of your bed with your cum not even dry between my thighs and treated me like every other groupie who spread their legs. It would have been more humiliating. Hurt me more."

Dylan licked his lips and avoided my angry gaze.

"Your eyes, Jess. Always, you're fucking eyes. I was hurting you. I wasn't fucking gentle about getting inside you, and you opened your eyes, still in pain, a tear falling free, and your eyes were full of your fucking love for me. My resolve nearly fucking broke in that moment. I wanted to kiss you, whisper the sweet nothings to ease the pain, but I knew if I did, I'd make love to you, and there would be no going back for me, Jess. That year we were together, I was at constant war with myself. I loved you, but I knew my demons would devour you. That moment. Those seconds where I buried inside you, and you accepted my violence with love, I realized that was the crossroads, the moment I chose to be selfish or to protect the one good thing left in my life by giving you up."

Hanging his head, Dylan clenched his fist with his other hand.

"I couldn't be selfish with you, Jess. Not then. Not when you were innocent."

Releasing the cup, Dylan eased back, slicking his hands in his pockets where he sat.

"That first time I came to your hotel and asked to speak with you, I only got drunk to build up the courage to face you. I wanted to tell you the truth finally; every secret I kept from you poised in a rehearsed speech ready to make my amends, to have you understand, to beg for our friendship back.

"Then you arrived, and the way you looked at me. The hurt you showed me in those pale orbs of yours, fuck, my good intentions went out the window. My inner demons came out, and the next thing I knew, we were fucking up a storm. Sex filled with hate and anger, and when you scratched your nails down my back and made me bleed, I'd found my new drug of choice."

"You had to get drunk to fuck me?"

"Never," Dylan denied. "Shit, I wasn't even drunk half those times, Jess. I would have one or two and then let you think I was fucked up for the rest of the night."

Blinking, surprised by that admission, I glared at Dylan. "What? You faked being drunk to fuck me?"

Blowing out a long breath, Dylan looked away. "It was better that way. If you thought I was off my face, you wouldn't let your feelings for me grow or heal or release them from whatever dark, damp place you'd hidden them. Time changed nothing, Jess. Only your innocence. I have known since we first met that you would be so good for me, Jess. You were my angel. But I've always known I'm bad for you. So I couldn't let you fall in love with me again."

The doorbell rang. Standing up, I wasn't even sure where to start dissecting Dylan's confession. There was so much to be hurt over, and I just didn't have the energy to let it cut as it should have.

"That will be dinner."

Going to the door, I took the bag and paid the delivery guy, then grabbed some cutlery and the bottle of vodka on the way back outside.

"I told you I didn't need that sort of drink," Dylan objected when I came back out. I knew he was primarily a non-drinker, but he'd binge drink when his darkness dragged him down.

"The alcohol is for me, numb-nuts. You came here and laid all this shit on me, knowing that I'm still bleeding from the last asshole who tore me apart. What the fuck did you expect?"

Unscrewing the bottle, I poured some into my empty mug and shot it down. Then, cringing on the burn, I screwed my face up and held it until I couldn't, then stuck my tongue out with an 'argh.' I followed it up with a second and then a third.

"When you messaged me, I realized that I'm partly to blame for all your hurt. That I needed to come here and tell you the truth like I planned to eight years ago. I needed to give you—"

"Stop." Another shot.

"Jess—"

"Shut the fuck up, Dylan!" I snapped, then shot another.

I couldn't take anymore tonight. There was already a lot to unpack, potentially feel, and I didn't want to feel any of it. My heart couldn't take it. Dylan claimed he was protecting me, but wouldn't the truth have been better from the start? Stopping for a moment, I remembered something Dylan said to me when I was sixteen.

"When I told you I was thinking about sleeping with Ben in year eleven and you lectured me on waiting to make sure he's the right guy, and on using condoms even if he 'claimed' it was his first time, did you know he was fucking Sharnie behind my back?"

Dylan winced. All the answer I needed.

"You're an ass."

Forgetting the mug, I picked up the vodka bottle and started swallowing.

CHAPTER TEN

S ILENCING THE ALARM, I WAITED FOR THE PIERCING ECHO TO STOP piercing my brain. I would have groaned, but that probably would have caused brain damage as well. Slowly opening my eyes, I was grateful the blinds were drawn so that the early morning light didn't stab my retinas. Not that I remembered drawing the blinds. I usually slept with them open, so the light helped me wake up.

Sitting up, I was in lounge pants and a sweater instead of pajamas. There was a glass of water, paracetamol, antioxidant tablets, and a tube of Berocca tablets on the bedside table. Frowning, I took the pills and then dropped the effervescent in the remaining water.

"Argh, Dylan," I groaned as I pieced the hangover repair kit together.

Not having the energy for my morning surf, I showered and dressed for work. Dylan wasn't beside me when I woke up, so I must have kicked him out at some stage, or he'd taken the spare room. Dylan wasn't an early riser. In all the years we'd bumped uglies, he'd always still been asleep when I had to get up and go to work the next day.

Ready for work, I headed up the hall, the smell of bacon reaching me, making my steps slow as I realized someone was cooking in my kitchen.

"… can keep trying—" a very American male voice was saying, making my feet slow.

"No. Throwing money at them for us to trespass there is not acceptable. It would help if you respected the Hawaiian people and their lands," Dylan answered. "I would never ask to film a music video standing on Uluru, so I won't have you asking to film on Niihau."

"What's Uluru?" the male replied.

"What about Bora Bora?" Teille offered, probably sensing her brother's frustration with the other man as much as I could down the hall.

"Keep it as a backup. I might be basing myself here in Hawaii between commitments for now, so if we could film the music videos here, I'd prefer it." Plates clanged on the kitchen counter, and the coffee machine churned.

"Why the fuck are you moving to Hawaii?" the guy asked. "Wait, is this about your girl? She lives there, doesn't she?"

"So, you'll have the location scouts try and find another location, Gary?" Teille cut in.

"Yeah, yeah, I'll keep them looking."

"Good. I think that's everything for today. Teille, stay on the line for me," Dylan asked as Gary said goodbye.

"How did it go?" Teille asked.

"Not great. As you suspected, Jess already wasn't in a good place. Me coming here and giving her my perspective was ill-timed, but I know it had to happen now. Pity the Fool was the opening I needed to face what I put her through and be honest after all this time."

Closing my eyes, I leaned against the wall, holding back tears as Dylan's words bashed through my brain again.

"But you're considering staying in Hawaii?"

"Honestly, she's been there for us, Teille. Through every fucked-up thing that should have killed us. She saved my life, saved yours twice, was there when we lost mum and dad. Jess is struggling. I'm not leaving her again."

"Jess may not want you there, D. You know how independent she is and how much you hurt her."

"I'm going to be here for her for once."

"As a friend, or are you finally going to admit she's the woman you always wanted and pursue her again?"

Dylan exhaled hard, then the coffee machine clicked off, and he just kept throwing instructions. "Look at renting a place here in Maui. Try and get one big enough to fit all of us. We'll need a rehearsal space to prepare for the tour as well."

"Okay, I'll start shortlisting places and then organize flights over. I'll email you the listings to look at once I have them."

"Thanks, Teille. Love you."

"Love you too, big brother."

Pulling myself together and in desperate need of the coffee I could smell, I finished the walk down the hall and emerged into the kitchen, where Dylan was plating up breakfast.

"Morning." He smiled. "How's the head?"

Wincing, I closed my eyes and put my finger to my lips. "Shh."

Smirking, Dylan watched me slide onto a stool at the bench, and he slid a plate with french toast, bacon, and a grilled banana in front of me, then followed that up with a mug of coffee and a glass of water.

"If I remember correctly, your breakfast is always poor knight's bread, bacon, and fruit. I know you usually have oats first, but I can't cook those for shit, so you get the fry up," he explained in a gentle tone.

Picking up the coffee, I nodded my head and tried to ignore how my brain seemed to slide around with the movement.

"You stayed?"

"Hope you don't mind. I crashed in your spare room."

"You were up early."

"Meeting with the label's visual media director about our music video for Siren's Call. It's the next single we'll be releasing. They're on L.A. time."

This wasn't a side of Dylan I saw often. The businessman. But I knew it existed. Teille told me Dylan was very serious about the business side of things with the band. It was their brand, and in this day and age, you couldn't just write and play music to succeed in the music industry. Dylan had a degree in music management and his MBA, which he finished online while touring with the band.

"So, which is it? Are you here as a friend or hoping last night would give us a reboot?"

Lips twitching upwards, Dylan piled bacon and a piece of french toast on his fork. "This morning, I'm here as a friend."

Accepting that, I started eating.

"But I'd like to take you out to dinner tonight."

Glancing up, I peered at Dylan. "As a date?" He shrugged but didn't confirm. "Is that wise?"

"No one knows I'm here, and even if someone recognizes me, so what? It's not like there aren't a hundred photos of us circulating the internet already, Jess. So what's a meal between friends?"

"Just friends?"

Sighing, Dylan put his cutlery down and stretched across the kitchen island to place his hands on my wrists and meet my gaze. "I dumped a lot on you last night, and I get that after all this time, my being here and not taking every opportunity to molest you is foreign to you, but we were never just sex, Jess. Go to dinner with me?"

Biting my lip, I considered Dylan, then nodded. Dylan finished his breakfast and cleaned everything up before stacking the dishwasher, giving me a soft smile. By the time he'd finished, I was sipping the glass of water, trying to figure out his angle.

"Okay, I'm going to head back to the hotel. I've got to practice these new songs. I'll pick you up at seven."

"I'll message if I get caught up at work."

Kissing me on the cheek, Dylan smirked then left while my brain was still trying to catch up with this turnaround. He was almost the Dylan I knew from back home. The pre-fame Dylan.

It wasn't until I got to work and noted the bunches of red roses that I remembered today was Valentine's Day. That's when Dylan's cheeky smile about dinner tonight clicked into place.

"Friends, my ass."

———

"Hey, how are you tonight?" Sean's voice came over the line.

"I'm fine. Shouldn't you be out with Holly?"

"We're about to go out to dinner. I just wanted to check in with you. Did you see the new Burning Bed's video yet?"

Ah, that's what the call was about. "Yes. Teille sent it to me before its release yesterday."

"Interesting subject. Some of it quite close to home for you, it seems."

"The creative director decided to use photos from Dylan's past to create a story for the music."

"Right!" Sean didn't sound convinced.

A door opened behind me, the restaurant's music getting louder, along with all the voices of the loved-up couples on their romantic dates.

"Are you still at work?"

"No. I'm out to dinner, just like you should be, so I'm going to say goodnight and get back to my date."

"Did Ethan track you down?"

"Dylan."

"Oh!" Sean sounded surprised. "Wait! He wasn't waiting at home for you with flowers like in the music video, was he?" Sean started laughing until I didn't. "Oh! He used the music video to send you a message. That's romantic."

This shit was precisely the sort of attitude I worried would happen. Rubbing my temple, I tried to stave off the headache, which was a combination of last night's drinking, the stressful day at work, and the tense dinner conversation with Dylan. We were currently waiting for dessert, but other than talking about the food and music, we hadn't ventured to discuss us again yet.

"Trust me. It wasn't romantic. Not that I can talk to you about anything, but please believe me when I say that there were a lot of creative elements in that music video. Currently, the ending is one of those."

"Okay, Jess. I better let you get back to your date then so you can work on that."

"Thank you. I'll see you on Monday for our monthly report catch-up."

"Sure thing, but you'll be catching me up on more than just work by the sounds of it."

"Dessert's on the table. See you later," I sighed, and hung up.

Taking a moment, I headed back into the restaurant and took my seat.

"How's the boss?"

"Curious about the realism of your new music video."

"So, nosey?" Dylan smirked.

Sighing at his good mood, I picked up a fork and thanked the gods for Dylan's choice in the restaurant. The gods made the desserts here, I swear.

"He's happy in love and hates that I'm not."

Eyebrows lifting, Dylan took a mouthful of his dessert. "He met someone? Was this before or after Ethan accused you of fucking him?"

Filling Dylan in on Sean and Holly, I summarized their relationship. "So, I guess the answer is before, but he was crying on my shoulder about losing her a second time when Ethan used it as an excuse to end us."

"He was an idiot to give you up, Jess."

"No more than you were."

"True, but I did it to save you, Jess. You wanted a family and a stable home. The band just got signed, and I had no intention of ever having a family. I can't have kids, you know that."

"Then why are you here now? What's changed?"

"You mean other than trying to be a good friend who is there for you when you need someone?"

"Dylan, I say this from the bottom of my heart, but as much as you suck as a boyfriend, I think we can all agree you are a worse friend. At least there is sex when you're a boyfriend."

Dylan's deep laugh filled the space around us. "Good point. Okay, so you want the truth?"

"Always."

"I realized that your expectations have changed. You always wanted kids when we were younger. But when you were with Ethan, you were willing to go without for him. Would you be willing to make that sacrifice for me? Say you will, and I'll be here, Jess. Between every band commitment, I'll come back to you."

Well, that was unexpected. It was also inaccurate. I never gave up on a family, Ethan and I just never discussed it again. "All these years and all I had to sacrifice was having kids?"

"It was more than that when we were younger. The band was constantly touring or in the recording studio. We have more time now. We have a dedicated fan base, and the label isn't pushing us to tour constantly. I can give you more time, Jess. I have the power to push back now." Dylan took a moment to consider me. "I'd like us to try again. As adults with a different outlook on life than we had thirteen years ago. If you aren't ready to jump into another commitment, that's fine with me too, but I'd at least like us to spend more time together to see if we have another chance at this."

Chewing the inside of my cheek, I watched Dylan. His words seemed sincere, but was I ready to attempt another relationship so soon? My chest still ached thinking of Ethan, and he'd been messaging since we ran into each other at the airport.

As if my thoughts summoned the ghosts of the future past, my phone buzzed.

<E:> Happy Valentine. I would have liked to take you out to dinner. If I knew where you were, I'd have turned up to do so. I miss you. I know I fucked up, but please, give me another chance?

Over the last month, there had been many variations of the same— each one I ignored. Just like I did tonight because it still hurt to think of Ethan and what he said to me that night. It took years for Dylan and me to be cordial to each other again, and that was after years of angry hate sex. Or at least, it'd been hate sex on my side of it, until it just became lust and the need to be fucked hard and without mercy.

"I can't risk my heart again so soon," I admitted. But I wasn't sure if I was answering Dylan or Ethan. Then the truth was, maybe I was saying it to both.

"I'll take whatever you can give me, Jess, even if it's just your friendship. It doesn't have to be physical."

When I cocked a brow, Dylan smirked.

"Okay, I want it to be physical, but I'll accept if it's too soon for you."

"I'm still hurting. Sex right now would be like it has always been for us. Angry hate sex."

"Huh, I always saw it as makeup sex. Yeah, it took a few years, but I'd hurt you pretty bad, so the penance was worth it."

Watching the grin spread across his face tempted me to pour my water over his head, but I didn't. Instead, I found myself smirking.

"You're an ass."

"You love me, though."

Taking a deep breath, I couldn't deny that I'd always loved him. The question wasn't if I still did, but if I wanted to chance my heart on someone who had already wrecked it once before.

Blowing out all the air in my lungs, I shook my head, Dylan's smile withering around the edges. "I can't commit to anything with you right now. But I'm not going to turn down a night of angry sex either. I haven't even been able to masturbate since Ethan left. Thinking about fucking you is the first spark of desire I've had in months."

Dylan's grin took over his face as he hailed the waiter.

"Best I get the cheque, and you home before it disappears again. I've been dreaming about you sitting on my face."

My chest flamed, all the way up my neck into my cheeks. Maybe Dylan was just what the doctor ordered to cure my heartache.

As Dylan paid the bill, I picked up my phone and messaged Ethan.

<Jess:> I want to be loved. You can't love me if you can't trust me. Let me go, E. We both just need to move on.

"Ready?" Dylan asked.

Putting my phone in my bag, I nodded. "Yes."

CHAPTER ELEVEN

MY BACK HIT THE WALL HARD, FORCING A GRUNT OF PAIN TO ESCAPE my throat and a wall hanging to fall to the floor with a smash further down the hall.

"Shit!" I tried to determine what we'd just broken.

"I'll deal with it," Dylan dismissed as he thrust deep. His naked body was a thing of beauty. Lean and sculpted, a great canvas for his ink addiction, courtesy of his best friend back home who ran a tattoo parlor.

Holding on for dear life, I wrapped my ankles behind his back, my hands gripping his shoulders as our panting mouths clashed and stole each other's air. One of Dylan's hands held my hip, the strong guitar-playing fingers of the other was massaging my breast as he fucked me into oblivion.

Over his shoulder, I caught glimpses of the mess we'd made of the house. Our clothes laid the path between the front door where he'd licked, sipped, and sucked me to orgasm as soon as we got inside, to the kitchen where Dylan swiped the island bench clear so he could lay me across it and fuck me to another orgasm.

The sofa was our next victim. I was bent over it while Dylan took me from behind to my third. Straddling him on the couch to a fourth, and then cushions on the floor and coffee table shoved aside where we'd tumbled for Dylan to come hard enough I'd have bruises from the floor on my back.

We stayed on the floor for recovery, then agreed on drinks before showering and going to bed. My near-empty glass slid off the far side of the island and smashed on the floor while Dylan took me hard bent over the bench. Then, after I came again, he turned me, wrapped my legs around him, and picked me up.

From what I could tell, we'd made it halfway down the hall before we'd hit the wall, literally. Then a few meters further, when I'd dropped to my knees and taken Dylan in my mouth, slurping his tart and salty cock covered in both our pleasure. After I'd moaned loudly, Dylan cursed, pulled me up, and shoved back into me again.

That got us here—a meter from the bedroom door where he was nailing me to the wall.

"Fuck, Jess! I've missed you so goddamn much!" Dylan groaned, then his mouth was latched onto my neck, sucking and biting as he pounded my body.

I needed this. Needed to be fucked hard into the next world. I needed Ethan fucked out of my system so I could move on. Get back to living.

"Fuck!" I screamed as Dylan's bite became too much, warring with the pleasure of his body obliterating Ethan's lingering hold on me.

The salt of tears coated my tongue, but Dylan kissed me hard, drinking my pain, absorbing my hate into his skin, bleeding my heartbreak for me, and that meant everything.

He could be my everything if I gave him the opportunity. I knew that. That he had come here to twist my heartache for his purpose, to take what he'd always wanted and denied himself, denied me. It didn't matter right now. Only the way my body was climbing to another climax was important.

Hissing, Dylan took his hand from my tenderized breast to slam his palm into the wall hard. "God, damn it, Jess!"

Pushing away from the wall, Dylan shouldered open my bedroom door, strode to the bed, and dumped me on it. "Turn around. On your knees. I'll have no fucking skin on my back left the way you're going."

"You love it."

Kneeling behind me, Dylan thrust into me, making me cry out with the stabbing pain deep inside.

"I love you." Then, grabbing my throat and stomach, Dylan pulled me upright against him. "Arms behind your back, grab your elbows."

Doing as he told me, I crossed my arms behind my back, squirming at the way this position pressed Dylan's big rock-god cock against all the best places inside me. Getting a vice grip on my arms with one of his large hands, Dylan held me close to his chest, his breath hot against my sweat-drenched neck.

"I'm going to fuck you hard until you come again for me, then, once my dick is dripping with your pleasure, I'm sliding it in your ass and claiming you as mine again. All mine. If you won't give me your heart, I'm going to own every other part of you until you learn to love me again."

Pulling his hips back, Dylan slid back into me gently, his body moving against me in total opposition to his words, but then he jerked his hips hard at the end of his slide, and I cried out. Hard didn't mean fast. Hard didn't mean violent skin slapping sex. For Dylan, hard could mean many things. In this instance, he was making hard love to me.

Rotating his hips, Dylan pulled back, slid in, then jerked hard to the end before easing the slight pain with another circle of his hips. My cervix was already bruised from our first fuck. I would struggle to walk tomorrow, but I didn't care. Dylan loved it. I was too caught up in the pleasure to consider anything but the way Dylan was driving me out of my mind with this slow, hard fuck.

My body coiled and tightened. Dropping his hand from my throat, Dylan gently rubbed my clit, his fingers drenched in seconds.

"So fucking wet, Jess. I've traveled the world, fucked all over it, and your pussy is still my favorite. I'll always come back to it. Always want it more than any other because you're more than sex to me, Jess. You're my girl, my heart, my muse, my fucking life."

His fingers dipped inside me, forcing me to make more room for him so his fingers and cock could both pleasure me. Then, removing his fingers, he used his hand on my forearms to lean me forward, then pressed those dripping music-makers against my starfish.

Forcing myself to relax, I moaned loud as the first one, and then a second of his fingers slid in. My body zapped with a pre-orgasm, an early warning of how good this next one would be, with a twinge of pain as he prepared me.

No one else got this. No one but Dylan had ever taken me this way. Dylan was the only one I'd allowed before. Ethan never asked for it, and I doubted it was his thing, and I'm not sure I would have said yes. Not before there was some commitment.

The first time Dylan took me this way, there was no discussion. Just his fingers, then his cock, and a mind-numbing orgasm that didn't make me regret it. Afterward, Dylan kissed the base of my spine and told me it was his. No one else's. I don't know why I complied all these years, but I'd just always felt that more kinky part of me—the part that liked rough, angry sex—belonged to him because I both loved and hated him.

"The moment you found me by that creek when I was sixteen, bleeding and broken, wishing for death. You were mine. My fucking angel. My light. I didn't live because my life was worth fighting for that day, Jess. I fought to live for you. You are what keeps me going when the darkness is suffocating. You, Jess. You're my everything."

Tears cascaded down my face, and then I was lost. My vision blacked out as I cried out my pleasure, my body contracting like a vice around him.

Cursing, Dylan held me tight, pulsing to keep me going. When I went lax, he let me go and pulled out. Then he was claiming me as he promised. My fingers gripped the sheets. Dylan grabbed my hips and fucked me as he came so hard I felt it despite floating away from everything. I was vaguely aware of us sprawling over the bed, Dylan still inside me, and then I melted into a puddle of nothingness.

———

Gray light filled the room when I woke. A heavy weight covered my back. Dylan was still holding me tight, and he was still in my ass, despite no longer being hard.

Groaning, I rolled back to get him off me, biting my lip on a moan when he slipped out of me, and his cum dribbled everywhere. Getting up, I went to the bathroom and cleaned up, showering despite the early hour. It was Friday, and I still had to work today, but I would miss my morning surf again because of Dylan.

Coming back into the room wrapped in my robe, I used a warm washer to clean Dylan's groin, so he didn't get stuck to himself. When cum dried, it could be like glue.

"Just cleaning you up," I murmured when he stirred.

Grumbling under his breath, all I caught was 'Angel' as he gently grasped my wrist, took the washer from my hand, lifted it to his mouth, and kissed my pulse point. "I'll shower and make you breakfast."

"You don't have to get up."

"I'm awake now," Dylan dismissed, walking into the bathroom, his back bloody and his shoulder blades covered in gouges, making me feel bad.

I shouldn't. Dylan loved a little pain with his sex. The first time I'd done it accidentally, he'd encouraged it, even asked for it from then on until I did it on instinct now.

Going to the bathroom door, I leaned against the door jamb, watching him wash and the way he winced as the hot water washed over his fresh cuts.

"You spoke about how we met last night."

Dylan's eyes flashed up to meet mine in a warning. Dylan's greatest secret. His biggest shame. He was a victim—a survivor.

When I was twelve, I'd gone bushwalking. It wasn't a big deal back then. We lived in a reasonably safe area, and kids were out and about on their own all the time. I'd gone to my favorite place, a little billabong fed by a creek when I heard someone crying—a teenage boy, badly beaten, bleeding and broken, wishing for death.

He never told me who did that to him. Whether he knew them, trusted them before they blackened his soul. All I knew was that it was a 'them' because Dylan told me to run in case 'they' were still there somewhere. Instead, I got him standing and all but carried him out of the bush to help.

"Have you ever spoken to anyone about that day? Other than the police?" Who he never told the worst of his injuries. The scratches and cracked ribs were nothing in comparison.

He'd never spoken of it again. The closest he came was when he slapped the non-disclosure agreement in front of me a year later and demanded I sign it.

We were strangers before that day. I met Teille at the hospital, and she asked my name and number so her parents could thank me. They'd appreciated what I did. Dylan didn't. Not then.

"I have a therapist," Dylan grumbled.

"Do they help?"

"Yes. You should try seeing someone."

Lifting my eyes into the top of my skull, I rolled them as I stood straight. "I'll get the coffee machine on."

"Jess," Dylan waited for me to look back at him. "Did I get too rough? You look sore."

"I'm fine. Tender, but not hurting," I assured. My back was bruised, and I'd need to conceal the teeth marks on my neck, but I wasn't bleeding like Dylan.

Leaving the room, I ignored the streaks of blood on my sheets, focusing instead on the smashed picture frame down the hall. Sighing, I started the coffee machine, grabbed the dustpan and brush, and cleaned up the broken glass and damage from last night.

CHAPTER TWELVE

Rockstar's Mistress

THERE IS NOTHING LIKE FINDING A MESSAGE ON YOUR PHONE FROM your ex after having wild sex with a former ex the night before to make you feel guilty.

<E:> I don't want to move on. I want you! I want you to unblock my number so I can call you. To unblock me on Skype so that I can see you. Talk to me, Jess. We can work through this.

"Everything okay?" Dylan asked as I shut off my screen and shoved my phone in my bag.

"Ethan keeps messaging me."

Shoving his hands in his jeans, Dylan didn't comment. We weren't there yet. "You want a lift to work. I can drop you off on my way out."

Considering the tender situation between my legs, not walking to work was probably a good idea.

"That'd be great. Thanks."

Following Dylan out to the car, we said nothing more. I wasn't sure where we stood or what was happening between us. My head was a mess, so work became my escapism to not think about things like always.

Dylan turned up with dinner that night, and we sat watching the sunset in quiet. Then, we cleaned up and went to bed, fucking like rabbits all night long. Then Saturday and Sunday, Dylan brought dinner over again. He didn't come Monday or Tuesday while Sean was there, but every night for the last two weeks, we'd eaten together, then slept together.

Dylan disappeared during the day, going to wherever he was staying. He didn't ask me to stay, and I didn't offer, but he held me while I slept, filled the space in my bed, and made the nights more bearable.

"Teille arrives tomorrow. Evan's flying in with her. Mathew and Jeremy will probably follow in the next couple of weeks," Dylan murmured against my head as we snuggled down, ready to sleep. "We've got a month until we start filming the next music video, and then we start doing promotional stuff ready for the tour in summer, so we need to start rehearsing as well."

"You're staying here?" I asked quietly, staring at the wall opposite the bed.

"I've found a place for us to stay and a rehearsal space, so yeah. We're going to be here for another four months at least. I'll be gone for two months after that for the European and American tour, then have three months off until the Australian tour," Dylan informed me. "But I'll come back in between."

"To me?" I asked quietly, tracing the outline of the bass guitar up his ribs. His favorite bass. The one he played on stage at every concert.

The four strings escaped the head at his left pec, twining from the pegs into a bramble of steel strings that tangled around the life-like sketch of a billabong. A textbook with a blood-covered razor blade resting on it sat on the bank. Beside them was a girl, her face hidden by her brown hair, her slim body naked and tucked up so you couldn't see anything. Her wrists were slit and bleeding. Her tears filled the pond, and the steel-string brambles shackled her wrists and ankles.

I wouldn't say I liked that tattoo. I hated knowing I was the girl. Not that I'd ever tried to take my own life. That was the pain he carried for his sister. So I went back to the detail on his bass guitar and the conversation we weren't having.

"If you want me, Jess. Every night I can, I'll come back to you."

Sighing, I stretched my arm across Dylan's torso, fingering where I knew an acoustic guitar adorned his right ribs. Dylan's fingers played with my hair, lulling me to sleep, where he'd tucked me into the nook of his shoulder.

"I like having you here. I sleep and eat when you're here."

I was still swimming when I got home each night, but sex was my outlet now instead of constant exercise. Not that sex with Dylan wasn't energetic. It wasn't always in the bed either. Dylan liked to fuck where the need took him, and nowhere in this house was unmarred by his lust.

Taking my hand from his ribs, Dylan kissed my pulse again, then held my hand to his chest. "Get some sleep. I'll be horny again soon."

It made me smirk. Dylan was a bit of a sex-fiend when he let it out. Teille told me he lived a celibate life when he wasn't on tour. Knowing what Dylan was like with me, I'd always found it hard to believe, but it made sense he made up for it when they were travelling, and women were throwing themselves at him.

"If you're staying, you should bring your stuff here. No point having to wear the same clothes every morning when you leave."

Dylan's chest stilled for a second, and then he took a deep breath. "Yeah?"

A tear escaped my eye, sliding onto Dylan's shoulder and betraying my heart. "Yeah. I'll give you a key in the morning."

Rolling me onto my back, Dylan leaned over me, wiping away the streak of tears that came from nowhere. Then, brushing his thumb over my bottom lip, Dylan shifted between my thighs.

"I lied. I'm horny now."

———

I was walking home from work a few weeks later when my phone rang. Frowning at the caller ID, I pressed the answer button, cutting off the music in my ear. "Greg? Is everything alright?"

"It's Ethan," the tired male voice that made my heart ache informed. "You blocked my number, and I needed to talk to you."

"Ethan," I mourned. My feet stopped. "Is Lou okay?"

"He's fine."

"Then why are you calling?"

There was a moment's pause, and the answer became apparent–the messages, the refusal to give up trying to get me to talk to him.

"I can't do this, Ethan. It still hurts just thinking about you. I can't do this. I'm sorry. I know you want another chance, but I'm not that sort of person. I don't give people a second chance to hurt me when nothing has changed. I can't put what you did aside and hold a civil conversation with you. Not this soon."

"It's been months, Jess. Five months. I've given you space. I've reached out. I've messaged and asked for a chance. I've asked your friends how I can find you so we can do this in person. You're not the only one still hurting. Five fucking months and I think of you all the time. I didn't even miss my wife this bad."

"Your wife cheated on you. You cheated on me!"

The line was quiet for a moment.

"We've talked about this. I didn't sleep with her."

"Then why were you in her room? Why were you naked and pulling your pants on? Why was she naked? Why didn't you go to Greg's room?"

"Because Greg wasn't answering his god-damn fucking phone! Because it ripped me fucking apart thinking you were cheating on me! When Greg messaged to ask me where I was, it was the first I'd been able to get hold of him. But it was too fucking late because you found me, and I realized I'd just fucked up my only chance of love because I expected you to hurt me just as everyone else I'd ever loved fucking left me, Jess. Everyone!"

Sinking my ass into the gutter, I curled in on myself, holding the phone tight as I sobbed at Ethan's rant. He'd destroyed us. Hurt us both because he was so used to being left. But it was too late. It was too late the moment he let me walk away from him in that hotel room and take that elevator down to the ground floor.

"Jess—" Ethan mourned as I cried my heart out.

My fist pressed to my heart, trying to hold the goddamned thing in my chest, but God, it hurt.

"Jess, tell me where you are. I'll come to you."

Shaking my head against my knees, I kept crying. I didn't want to. I didn't want to be this broken woman who couldn't keep her shit together—I never used to be. Ethan broke me.

Blowing out a breath, Ethan waited a few minutes.

"Greg showed me the new Burning Beds video. Nice to have my fuck-up immortalized for all the world to see. I understand now why being his muse pisses you off. I'm curious how much of it was true, though."

Squeezing my eyes tight, I tried to stop the flow of tears, but they kept coming like the dam was open, and the levy just broke.

"Jess, was Dylan sending you or me a message with that god damn song?"

A whimper escaped at the truth of those lyrics, of that video. Silence reigned a moment longer.

"Are you with him? I've signed that NDA. You can tell me, and I can't say a fucking thing to anyone. Just be honest with me, please?"

I knew Ethan didn't mean right now. If Dylan were here, he would have taken the phone by now and told Ethan never to call again. And while I knew there was no spoken commitment between Dylan and me, it was implied. So I gave Ethan the truth.

"Yes."

A long pause.

"How long?"

"A month."

Ethan must have done the maths in his head or known the song's release date. "Valentine's Day?"

"Yes."

"I guess he was waiting for you with a bunch of flowers like in the video too?" There was anger in his voice, along with grief.

"Yes."

This was torture. I hated this, but Ethan deserved to know. He ought to know he'd lost me because of his jealousy and fear. He needed to let it sink in that he was never getting me back.

"I guess he's the lucky bastard who knew where to find you. Even your father didn't know where you were, or did he lie to me?"

"Lou doesn't know."

"So, you're still in love with me, but with him? Is that fair to Dylan, Jess?"

With my breathing under control, I swiped at my tears, my pain dialing down. "Yes." Squeezing my eyes, I kept my forehead to my knees.

"Yes? That's it. That's all I get. Yes, you're still in love with me? Or yes, that's what Dylan deserves?"

Gulping down the raw honesty of those words, I cringed, my voice quiet with what I was about to reveal. "Both. I love and hate you both. You asked how much of that video was true. All of it, E. Everything. He broke me first, and now I'm living with him. Goodbye, E."

Pressing the hang-up button, I sat there for a long time, pulling myself back together. Once I'd recovered enough, I opened my messages and sent one to my dad.

<Jessie Girl:> I'm back living in Maui, and Dylan is with me.

Lou hated Dylan when we were friends. Not because he was mean or an ass, but simply because he knew how we came into each other's life. Dylan was irreparably damaged, and so Lou much preferred Ben. Maybe I let my dad influence my romantic choices, even with Ethan.

<Dad:> When you say with you…?

<Jessie Girl:> Living with me. Sleeping with me. I didn't want you hearing it from anyone else. I'll speak to you Sunday.

<Dad:> Thank you for telling me. I love you.

Tucking my phone away, I got to my feet and kept walking home. This time, I did divert to the bottle shop and bought that vodka. By the time Dylan arrived that evening, I was drunk, and when I told him Ethan had called, Dylan put the bottle away, stripped naked, and proceeded to fuck the anger and hurt out of me all over the house. I bruised, and he bled. Just like my fucking heart back in that gutter.

After that, Dylan and I fell into a routine. He was there every night, even when Sean came over, though he'd go out and give us space to work and be friends. Teille and I became close again, and she started joining me for horse rides and snorkeling on the weekends, followed by Saturday night drinks with her and my friends, or sometimes with Dylan and the band after rehearsals. The guys welcomed me back like a long-lost sister; and other than hearing all the gossip from their last decade of touring, it was like Dylan and I never stopped being what we'd always been to each other.

Except we weren't that either. Not anymore. I loved Dylan; I always had, but I wasn't that smitten young girl anymore. I was heartsore, and I didn't have it in me to free fall again. Not yet, anyway. I think Dylan knew, that he understood, and that's why this worked. Sex and friends. It was just what I needed.

Dylan was with me every night between filming for music videos for four months. They spent two days in Bora Bora to film Siren's Call and four days in Oahu for Ocean's Between—a song about friendship no matter the distance—and I went with him for both.

The media snapped photos of us together and suggested a romance, but those rumors went nowhere without PDA. Especially when they realized I was the same girl who stood beside him at his parent's funeral. Hell, one tabloid suggested I was a secret sister—the daughter of an illicit affair.

That was both funny and disturbing. More so when Dylan—who found it very amusing—spent an entire fuck session waxing poetic about how kinky it would be. Like we were royalty. I'd eventually gotten sick of it, got off his dick, and walked away, leaving him jonesing for me until he promised never to mention it again.

All wasn't right, but it was enough. My heart still hurt thinking of Ethan or even when I thought too hard about Dylan and me. But it was easier to ignore the deeper stuff. As Evan, Burning Beds' lead guitarist, told me, "Just live in the moment. Forget the past, and don't stress about the future. Just exist in the here and now. Love for today because yesterday is history, and tomorrow is still a fantasy."

Of course, Evan had been hitting on me at the time, trying to convince me to ditch Dylan for a night and give him a ride, or even convince Dylan about a threesome. Tempting as that second option was, Dylan just laughed it off, so no Burning Bed reverse harem scenario for me to reminisce about when they went on tour. Still, there was always the power of fantasy.

CHAPTER THIRTEEN

"So, Dylan. How long until the band's on tour now?" Sean asked from where he and Holly were perched out on the deck by the pool.

Grabbing a bottle of Rouge Lise and two beers, Dylan took them out to the table while I got the cheesecake out of the fridge and carried it out to join them. Dinners had become regular for the four of us over the last four months whenever Sean came out for the monthly report.

"Just a little less than two weeks," Dylan answered. "We'll be three weeks in Europe for some of the big summer festivals, and then five weeks touring Canada and the States."

"Are you sick of it yet?" Holly asked. "After all these years."

Lifting a shoulder and dropping it, Dylan took the dessert from me and put it on the table before taking his seat next to me.

"The traveling part got old quick. It's exhausting, and after I turned thirty, it seemed to be a little harder. But playing on stage in a sold-out stadium never gets old. Once I'm up there, making music and singing, I'm re-energized and in my happy place."

445

Sean glanced at me as if expecting me to be hurt by that comment because I wasn't Dylan's happy place. But I wasn't. I'd always known that performing, singing, and making music was the higher state of being for Dylan. His music was the reason he survived his adolescence. So I'd never try to take it away from him, and I certainly was never going to compete with it.

"Is the band ready?" I asked instead.

Finishing his cheesecake, Dylan relaxed back in his seat with his beer and gave me a smirk that could melt the panties of most women.

"Yeah. We've got the new songs down to a tee, and we've rejuvenated some of our earlier tracks. This week we have to finalize our setlists for the festivals and just do a bit of finessing."

Judging by the blush staining Holly's cheeks, she was still starstruck by Dylan's presence. She'd had to sign the non-disclosure agreement before she started joining Sean for visits, but she was happy to do so to get to meet one of her favorite bands. But, of course, protecting a celebrity's anonymity was nothing new for a hotel manager. You either knew how to keep your mouth shut, or you didn't keep your job long.

"How are the wedding plans coming?" I asked Holly. "Only four months out now."

Her family hadn't been happy about the wedding. Not her marrying Sean, that was fine. But when Holly decided to have a small beach wedding at Turtle Bay, with no media and none of her siblings in the bridal party, her family arced up. Holly chose to have Trisha as her one and only bridesmaid, and I was Sean's best man, though I'd be wearing a similar dress in the same color as Trisha.

"Good. I think I've got it all organized now. Just have the last dress fittings in two months, so no getting pregnant before then," Holly teased.

"Yeah, no chance of that!" I scoffed.

Dylan shifted, and I didn't miss the way his eyes flashed towards me. "I can't have kids, but you should heed your advice if that hickey on your neck is anything to go by," Dylan smirked, pointing to a dark bruise on Holly's neck.

Holly blushed, her hand going to the love bite, but Sean's brows bunched together, studying me.

"I'm sorry to hear that," Sean offered.

"I'm not," Dylan replied without pause. "I don't want kids. I won't even let teenagers come backstage at our concerts. From the time I aged up, I set the rule that backstage holders have to be twenty-one and over."

Sean's gaze narrowed on me with concern, but thankfully, he didn't push the topic.

"Will you be trying for a family straight away?" I asked, putting the focus back on the happy couple rather than whatever the hell Dylan and I were.

Not that we weren't happy—hard not to be with the number of orgasms we'd been having—but we weren't marriage material. I knew that. What we were now is all we'd ever be. I didn't know what made me so sure of that, but I was. That wasn't a bad thing either. We had great chemistry and were friends who cared too much for each other, but I would never encourage anyone to use us as the poster couple of relationship goals.

"Maybe in a few years," Holly answered. "I've got my new business to focus on for now, and I'm not even thirty yet."

My phone started ringing with my dad's ringtone inside. Frowning, I got up from the table and headed inside to grab the phone from the kitchen bench.

"Dad?"

"Jessie Girl, are you in Hawaii?" he asked, sounding breathless.

"Yes, why? What's wrong?"

"Come home, Jess. As quick as you can."

My world stopped spinning and froze. "Dad, what's happened?"

"It's your mother and sister. They were in a car accident. I just got the call and am on my way now."

Swallowing the lump in my throat, I stared at the photo of my parents I had on the side table. "How bad is it?"

"I don't know, Jessie, but it was bad enough that they are having to cut them both out of the car."

My mouth was dry. "I'll be there as fast as I can," I murmured.

"Thank you. And Jessie—I love you." Lou hung up before I could respond.

"Jess?" Dylan called to me from the kitchen. When I turned to face him, my expression must have said it all. He rushed towards me, taking my elbows in his hands. "What is it?"

"I have to get home. There's been an accident."

Flicking his eyes between mine, Dylan took a breath, checked his watch, and then he pulled his phone from his back pocket and pressed speed dial.

"Go pack your bags. I'll have Teille organize the plane for us, and we'll be there not long after sunrise tomorrow."

"Dylan…"

"Go pack, Jess. I've got this." His attention turned to the phone as he stepped away from me. "Teille, we need the jet as quickly as possible. It's Jess's parents. She needs to get home."

Swiping the tears already falling down my face, I rushed down to the bedroom, grabbed my cabin bag, and started throwing jeans, jumpers, underwear, and sleepwear inside. My eyes spied a black dress that was perfect for a funeral, and I paused, staring at it.

"What's wrong?" Dylan asked, coming into the wardrobe and packing a bag for himself.

"The black dress. Would packing it tempt the situation, or would it ward it off?"

Gaze moving from me to the black satin dress, Dylan grabbed it, rolled it gently, and shoved it into his bag along with a pair of sensible heels.

"I'll take it," he stated before heading to the bathroom. "It's a cold winter back home. Pack a jacket and boots."

By the time we were back out in the living area, Sean and Holly had cleaned up from dinner. Pulling me into a hug, Sean squeezed me tight.

"Don't you worry about a thing here! I'm going to stay and cover for you, no matter how long you need. Just go be with your family." Releasing me, Sean stepped back, and then Holly hugged me just as lights flashed out in the driveway.

"Our ride's here to take us to the airstrip," Dylan murmured gently.

Taking my bag, he led me out to the car and opened the back door for me, where we both climbed inside. Evan sat behind the wheel, Teille in the passenger seat because, legally, Teille couldn't drive. A result of the brain injury she'd suffered from Sharnie's vicious attack was that Teille had little spatial awareness and could not judge how fast other cars were traveling, or even the distance between her and another object. She always had bruises from running into things, but, in a car, it meant more prangs than a demolition derby.

"Let us know how bad it is when you get there. The rest of us can follow you over if we need to," Evan said.

"Why would you need to come over?" I asked, happy to focus on them rather than what could be waiting for me.

Evan's eyes met mine in the rearview mirror. "We still have a lot to get done before the tour. So if your trip home will be longer than a few days, it will be better for us to pack our stuff up and come home and finish rehearsals there. We can then leave direct from Sydney for the tour. Funerals usually take a week minimum to plan."

My lungs refused to expand or expel.

"Jesus, Ev! Some fucking tact, man," Dylan cursed, taking my hand. "Let's just get you back and see what's happened before we start stressing about what the next few days hold, okay?"

Nodding my head, I pulled out my phone. "Karla, it's Jess. I'm coming home."

"Passing through to work up north again?"

"No. Mum was in an accident. It's not good."

"Shit!" Karla mourned. "I'll call your dad, find out which hospital she's at, and meet him there. I'll keep you updated. Let me know if you need me to pick you up."

"I'm flying in with Dylan, so we'll meet you there. Just message me with updates. Flying private means I still get wi-fi in the air."

"Having a rockstar fuckboy has great benefits. Where do I get one?"

"His bandmates are all single," I smirked.

"Yeah, and probably disease-riddled as well."

"I'm clean and happy to be your fuckboy anytime, Karla," Evan called back from the front seat.

Chewing my lip, I glanced at a smirking Dylan. "Your volume is up pretty loud," he snickered.

Clearing my throat, I hit the keys on the side of the phone to turn it down and continued. "I'll message you our ETA once we have one."

"Okay. I'll let you know once I'm with Lou."

"Thanks. And Karla?"

"Yeah?"

"My dad's not a widow yet. So don't be a skank."

Karla laughed. "Babe, that's why you have nothing to worry about here. Margaret isn't stupid. She knows a line of women are ready and willing to help your dad mourn his loss in the best way. She's not going to step aside to let us have our wicked ways with him. I'll be in contact soon."

Hanging up, I gave the phone a small smile. "You better hope my mum pulls through this, Ev, or you are shit out of luck of ever scoring with Karla again."

"My sister told me she was engaged to that limp dick she's been with since high school?" Evan frowned.

He'd had a thing for Karla when I was hanging around as a teen, but other than the night of my seventeenth birthday, Karla never gave Evan a chance. She'd picked him as a manwhore from day one and wasn't willing to waste any energy on him.

"They broke up. For good this time."

Arriving at the small airport for domestic flights in Maui, Evan showed his ID to get through the gates to the area for private jets and then took us to where our ride was refueling.

Grabbing our bags, Dylan farewelled the others and headed up the stairs.

"Hey." Evan pulled me back into a hug. "I hope your mum's okay."

"Thanks, Ev." I went to pull back, but Evan held me in place.

"Jess, just remember he's got his demons. He wants to be there for you, but this sort of thing, watching you go through it, could trigger him."

When I gave Evan a quiet nod, he let me go. I hugged Teille and raced up the stairs onto the private jet. Taking my hand, Dylan pulled me into the chair, and then the door closed.

"The wind is behind us, Mr. Neptune. We should be landing in Newcastle eight hours from take-off," the pilot informed us over the speaker.

We'd just taken off and the wi-fi connected again when my phone pinged, and then there was a steady stream of updates for the next two hours while Dylan slept beside me.

<Karla>: I spoke to your dad. The ambulance is just leaving the scene of the accident now. Sharnie is en route with suspected head injuries, and Margaret is in critical condition. Lou said the car was a wreck, but that's all I know for now.

<Karla>: I'm at the hospital.

<Karla>: The ambulance just arrived. Margaret has suspected spinal and head injuries. They've got her in the trauma bay. Lou and I are outside. I'll message you as soon as I have news.

<Karla>: Sharnie is stable but needs to have her head scanned; nothing I couldn't have told them. They are doing tests to check on the baby first, and then they'll take her to radiology. They've just told your dad that your mum needs emergency surgery. I'll message you when we get an update.

"Hey, have you had any sleep?" Dylan murmured as he sat up from the oversized chair that he had fully reclined.

452

When I didn't answer, Dylan took the phone from my hand. "There is nothing you can do from up here. Get some sleep so you can be whatever your dad needs tomorrow."

Reclining my seat, I snuggled into Dylan, but I didn't sleep. Instead, I just drifted in the haze that borders between waking and sleeping. My gut told me all was not well. That it wasn't going to be okay. That tomorrow, my world would change, and not in a good way.

CHAPTER FOURTEEN

THE CAR DROPPED US AT THE HOSPITAL ENTRANCE.

"Find a park, and I'll call you once I know how long we'll be," Dylan told the driver.

God, if we were in any other situation, I might envy having people at your beck and call as he did. But, right then, I was just appreciative that he was there for me again when I needed to get on a plane without notice. Typing out a text to my dad, I let him know we were there as I rushed through the door into the lobby of the massive hospital. I didn't even have an idea of where to start looking.

<Dad>: Head to emergency. I'll come out and get you.

"They're still in emergency," I told Dylan.

Taking my hand, he walked me in the right direction. Since I'd lost Matilda, I hadn't been in this hospital, but it was significantly different and changed over the last decade. I barely recognized the place.

"How do you know where you are going? I wouldn't know my left from right here anymore."

"It's kind of a regular stop when we are home," Dylan answered cryptically.

"Should I ask?"

Lifting a shoulder, Dylan kept his eyes on where he was going. "When you grow up somewhere and become famous, everyone you used to know falls into two categories. The suck-ups–where even people who hated you are suddenly your old best friend–and those with 'tall poppy syndrome'. The latter sometimes result in an emergency visit." Dylan looked over his shoulder at me. "And the majority of the time, it's not me. Just so you know."

"You've never struck me as the violent type. The few times you've gotten in a fight, it was a valid reason," I replied.

Coming to a stop, Dylan cupped my face and stared into my eyes. "That right there, that's why I've always come back, Jess. You see the real me while everyone else sees the rockstar."

"Jessie!"

Turning towards my dad's voice, I found him holding open the door to a restricted area of the hospital. He looked like he'd aged twenty years overnight. Deep dark circles under his eyes, and his usually tan skin seemed pale in the hospital lights. Walking quickly, I was in his arms a moment later.

"Dad."

His body kept the door open as he hugged me tightly. "Thank you for coming so quickly."

"Thank Dylan. Without him, I'd still be sitting in the airport waiting to get on the plane home."

Lifting his head as I stepped back, Lou locked eyes with the shadow standing at my back.

"Dylan." Lou offered his hand.

"Mr. Butler."

"Thank you for getting Jessie home so quickly, and please don't think me rude, but I think you should go."

"Dad!" My mouth gaped open.

Not missing a beat and keeping his eyes on Dylan, Lou tilted his head toward the way he'd come. "Jessie's sister is in here. She's heavily pregnant and fragile right now."

Clenching his jaw, Dylan gave a shallow nod as his arm swept across my back, and he dropped a kiss on my temple. "I'll go get the hotel sorted. Call me if you need me. Otherwise, when you are ready to come and get some rest, I'll send the car to get you."

Turning without another word, Dylan started back the way we'd come, pulling out his phone as he walked.

"Dylan," Lou called. He waited until Dylan looked over his shoulder, his eyes dark with anger and old pain as he glared at my father. "Thank you."

Grinding his jaw, Dylan switched his gaze to me, the anger softening. "I'm here when you need me."

When. Not if. As if one look at my father told him how tonight would pan out already. Something shifted inside me. Like that look, those words started to prepare me for what was to come.

Walking down a corridor, we turned into a long room with a row of well-spaced beds down one side and a nurse's station sitting centrally on the other with toilets and trauma rooms on either side.

Stopping, Lou turned to look at me. "I need to warn you. Sharnie took a hard hit to the head in the accident. She's banged up, but the head is the concern, especially as she's had a change of personality as a result. They are monitoring her for a few more hours in case the concussion needs hospitalization."

"How bad?"

Taking my elbows in his hands, Lou looked me in the eye, and what almost seemed like hope shined out at me. "That's the thing, Jessie Girl. It's not bad."

I'd had that hope once. That Sharnie would be the sister and best friend I'd had before, but that died too long ago.

"Dad, the last time Sharnie's brain rewired itself, I became very familiar with the emergency room for years following."

"I know, Jessie. I just wanted you to prepare you."

He turned to walk on, but I grabbed his hand. "What about Margaret?"

Lou's throat visibly constricted. "She's still in surgery."

Frick! "How many hours is that?" I asked, pulling out my phone to check when Karla messaged.

"Only four hours. There was a wait for an operating room. The occupants in the other car got here a few hours before your mum, so they were already in surgery."

Other car? "Dad, what happened?"

Swallowing, Lou lowered his voice. "Sharnie's baby shower was yesterday. I'm not sure of the specifics, but your mother lost control of the car or failed to stop at a red light on her way home and impacted with a car of university students on their way out for the night."

I hadn't seen this look on my father's face since he stood by my hospital bed, watching me cry, holding the bundle that was Matilda in my arms.

"Two of the passengers in the other car didn't make it. The other three are in intensive care, still fighting for their lives. Sharnie is experiencing guilt for the first time since she was fourteen. I know it's going to be hard for you to believe this of her after everything she did to you, but the girl you are about to see is the sister you once loved. Give her a chance, please?"

Not sure what to say or feel, I gave a numb nod. While I was still trying to process everything that Lou had just laid on me, he led me to a curtained-off bed and stepped through.

On the bed, my beautiful, honey-blonde and heavily pregnant sister sat holding an ice pack to her bandaged head. Tears filled her already red-rimmed green eyes, making them more vivid.

"Jessie," she sobbed. "I'm so, so sorry for everything."

Standing there, I wasn't sure how to take her.

"I know it's not enough for everything I did. But it's true. I'm so very sorry."

"Okay, calm down," Lou cooed as Sharnie started bawling. "You heard the doctor. You need to keep calm for the baby."

I was frozen. This woman was not the Sharnie I'd known since her psychological break, but my sister before that had always been a fun, happy-go-lucky girl. So whoever this Sharnie was, I couldn't say she was my twin either.

"Where's Greg?" I tried for distraction.

"Still airborne," Lou answered, hugging his older daughter. "I left a message with Ethan to call me as soon as they land."

Putting my handbag down, I shoved my hands in my pockets. "When was the last update you got on Margaret?" Looking at his watch, Lou swept his hand over his face. "They wanted me to wait over near the operating theatre for updates, but I thought I should be here while Sharnie got assessed. Once Karla gets back, I'll go over and see if I can get an update. Maybe she's out of surgery, and they forgot I was here to update me."

"Where did Karla go?"

"My place to get me a change of clothes," Sharnie hiccupped as she calmed again.

Considering the top of her dress was covered in blood, I couldn't fault the need for fresh clothes. The thing is, I was more worried about Margaret. It'd been twelve hours since the accident already, and if she only went into surgery four hours ago, then it took them three hours after they realized she needed surgery to get her in a theatre. If I learned anything from watching medical dramas over the years, time was of the essence in emergencies.

"Why don't you go now, Dad? I can stay with Sharnie, and we'll come and find you if she gets released before you get back."

Looking at Sharnie, Lou didn't seem thrilled with that idea.

"Jessie's right, Dad," Sharnie assured. "Go find out that mum is okay. None of us will be able to relax until we know she's safe."

Interesting. That wasn't the Sharnie I knew. She would have made it about her, told dad he couldn't leave her until Greg arrived, or said it was fine, but then huffed and made a fuss about how much her head hurt.

Patting Sharnie's hand, Lou got up and hugged me. "Just text me if you need me."

"No, you ring me if you need me," I fired back. "Keep us informed."

Lou took off with a kiss to my temple, back out into the labyrinth of halls. Pulling out my phone with a sigh, I sent Karla a text begging for coffee, then another to Sean to let him know we arrived safely, but no update on my mum, and then put the phone away.

"I meant what I said, Jessie. I'm sorry about everything I've put you through." Her free hand moved over her swollen tummy. "About Matilda—"

"Don't!" I gritted my teeth, seething that she dared bring her up.

Sharnie's eyes filled with tears again as she shrank back on the bed. "Okay. I'm sorry."

The curtain pulled back, and a man our father's age in scrubs stepped in with a tablet device.

"Sharnie Dumont?"

"Yes," Sharnie almost whispered as she set the ice pack aside.

"I'm Doctor Shaw, the neurologist. How's the head feeling this morning?"

"Still hurting, but bearable."

"No blurry vision, blackouts…" the doctor continued to list off a list of symptoms and wait for Sharnie's response to each one, making notes on his device while she did. Then, taking out a penlight, he shined it into her eyes while he spoke and did a few other things.

"Okay, I've looked at the scans they did when you arrived at the hospital. You had some minor swelling in the brain that concerned me, but other than the headache, which is understandable, you're not showing any other signs that we should be worried about."

"What about the personality change? Isn't that a symptom?" I asked, causing the doctor to frown at me and check the tablet.

"Personality change?"

"For the last sixteen years, my sister's been an unfeeling psycho bitch, and now she's considerate of others and feeling guilty about stuff. Dad said he'd mentioned it."

When the doctor raised an eyebrow at me, then to Sharnie, my sister sank into her shoulders, tears leaking from her eyes again.

"She's right. I have a formal diagnosis of sociopath after suffering a drug-induced psychosis when I was fourteen. You normally couldn't leave Jessie and me alone together. I've put her in the hospital multiple times since the psychological break and have plotted to kill her numerous times. She miscarried her daughter because of me," Sharnie sobbed, wrapping her arms over her tummy. "And now, I know I did all those things and the insane reasons I justified hurting her, and I feel tormented by it. Everything I did…oh, God! Jessie, I'm so sorry. About Ben, about Matilda, about Ethan. I'm so, so sorry."

What now? "Ethan?"

She was nodding as her tears poured faster. "Greg confided in me that you two were together and that you were in love with each other. But he worried how Ethan's insecurity because of his ex cheating on him would impact your relationship's longevity. So, the next time Ethan was around, I mentioned you cheated on Ben with Dylan all those years while claiming Dylan was just a friend. I know you didn't, but I knew it would feed his doubts, that it would cause issues, and I laughed when I found out you broke up. Ethan doesn't even know I manipulated him to hurt you, Jessie. I'm so sorry. I can't believe I did that to you."

Really? Because this woman would be the only one who doubted that was all true. No one who knows the Sharnie I do would even question it.

"I can." Tears fell from my eyes as I stared at Sharnie. Then, getting up, I looked away because she looked remorseful for the first time ever. "I need the bathroom."

"Jessie—" Sharnie called as I pulled back the curtain.

"I just need the bathroom. I'll come back," I assured.

Because Sharnie the psycho bitch would never have copped to it unless she was gloating, and this woman was anything but. Still, it just ripped my shattered heart out of my chest.

"Can you hand me my phone, please? It's in my bag," Sharnie pleaded before I left.

Swallowing, I opened her bag, found her phone, and handed it to her before making my exit.

"I want to run a few more tests before we release you," the doctor excused himself behind me. "Give me a few minutes."

Just before I stepped into the bathroom, the doctor caught up to me.

"Miss..." he murmured, looking uncomfortable.

"Butler. Jessie Butler."

There was a moment of recognition on his face with the name, but I wasn't sure if it was because he knew my dad or he'd seen the tabloids guessing about my relationship with one of our country's hottest rockstars.

"I'm sorry, I just… your sister's situation—"

"If you tell me it's impossible she's suddenly sane and guilt-ridden, and that's she's faking it, I'll walk back in there and murder her. So please tell me she's a medical miracle to act human again suddenly," I answered sarcastically.

Doctor Shaw took a step back and cleared his throat with his eyebrows in his hairline. "Not a medical miracle, but also not faking it, I don't believe. Traumatic brain injury can change the way a person processes and understands information. Even a concussion can impact someone's psychological presentation long after the initial injury has healed. Common brain injury symptoms include anxiety, irritability, anger, depression, feelings of being overwhelmed, mood swings, or emotional lability."

"So, the concussion has reversed my sister's psychosis and given her a conscience again? I'm sorry. I can see it, hear it even. But I fail to believe that a concussion can shift someone's personality that dramatically."

"Her personality is still her own. People perceive it to be a shift of personality, but the true them is only buried by how they perceive and express themselves."

Feeling exhausted, I leaned against the wall. "What are you saying?"

"There is no cure for psychosis, but I believe your sister is trying to process her past behavior in a way her brain refused to all these years. Now, that might make her a nicer person again, or as her brain heals over time, the woman you've known since she was fourteen will slowly emerge again. But, unfortunately, there are no assurances other than the fact your sister has suffered a severe concussion and that it is going to impact the way her brain functions for a time."

Watching me take in this information, the doctor waited a moment then touched my upper arm kindly.

"I'm sorry it's not the optimistic answer you were probably hoping for, but it might help you cope with the way you're experiencing your sister today. I'm going to run some more tests, so it will be a few more hours before we can discharge her."

"Are you worried?"

"She had mild swelling in the brain, and she's heavily pregnant with high blood pressure. So it pays to be careful in these situations. Are you your sister's next of kin?"

"No. Sharnie's husband is a pilot and currently somewhere over the Pacific, so our dad is the temporary next of kin until he can get here."

"Is your father here at the hospital?"

"Yes, he's in the waiting room for the operating theatres hoping for an update on our mother. Unfortunately, she was in the accident with Sharnie."

Nodding as if he knew about Margaret, Doctor Shaw started tapping away on his tablet. "I'll order these tests, then go discuss my concerns for your sister with your father."

"I'll text him and let him know you're coming," I start to push the bathroom door open.

"Miss Butler. It may only be a temporary reprieve from the woman who has terrorized you, but I find these moments are usually given to us for a reason. Don't turn it away, if you can."

With that, he walked back to the nurse's station, giving directions to a nurse there. Closing my eyes, I pushed through the bathroom door, my feet kicking my figurative heart across the floor.

CHAPTER FIFTEEN

"How are you holding up?"

Lifting my head from where I was studying my toes, I took the coffee and then Karla's hug. "I feel like I've stepped into an alternate universe."

"The Sharnie thing?" When I nodded my head, Karla blew out a breath. "I'm finding it just as hard to believe, and she never even did anything to me, but just the way she talks is different. It doesn't have that razor's edge beneath the Splenda."

"Splenda?"

"Faux sugar. It's a term Lizzy and I started using for Sharnie and other women like her. The ones who fake sweetness to cover the bitch they are. We've dealt with enough of them at work."

It made my lips twitch with humor. Karla was a make-up artist who worked with many modeling agencies and movie sets, and Lizzy was in event management.

"Come on. Let's find my dad. They've just taken Sharnie for an MRI; she'll be a little while."

My phone started ringing with Greg's name flashing on my screen as we walked towards the surgical waiting area.

"Greg?"

"Jess, there's been an accident. I'm not sure if anyone's called you." Greg was breathing hard, probably rushing through the airport.

"They have. I'm here already."

"You're there already?"

"Yes. Look, Sharnie and the baby are okay. I've seen her already."

"Are you sure? Because she sent me this long and weird email about stuff I don't want to go into over the phone."

Frowning, I eyed Karla, who was navigating us through the hospital. "Well, she's got a severe concussion, and that's caused a personality change or something. She's feeling guilty about stuff, but health-wise, the doctor said she's okay. He's worried there was some brain swelling and her blood pressure is high, so he's sent her for an MRI, but other than that, just a nasty gash to the head."

"High blood pressure isn't good for the baby."

"They've got monitors on her. So if anything happens, they'll be on it like lightning."

"What about your mum?"

Closing my eyes, I swallowed hard. "She's still in surgery. I'm just going to find Lou and get an update. The neurologist treating Sharnie was going there to talk to him next because Dad's Sharnie's next of kin until you get here."

Pushing through a set of doors, we could see Lou across the waiting room talking to Doctor Shaw. I thought about putting Greg on loudspeaker and handing it to my dad, but it was better not to stress Greg on the drive.

"Okay, Jess. We just got to the car. Ethan's going to drive, so call me with any updates. We should be there in just over two hours."

"Drive safe."

Hanging up, we made our way over to Lou, me finishing my coffee and dropping it in the bin as we did. We didn't interrupt. We just waited nearby for them to finish talking. Doctor Shaw squeezed my father's upper arm and they stood up.

"I'll ask someone to come and give you an update about your wife."

After Doctor Shaw gave me a nod, he walked through the doors for the operating theatres.

"Dad?"

"They're worried Sharnie's blood pressure may be related to the headache," he sighed, falling back in his chair. "Doctor Shaw also performed the surgery to relieve the cranial pressure on your mother—whatever that means. They were closing her up when he left the theatre, so he's unsure why I haven't heard anything yet. He's gone back in to check."

Eyeing Karla and the coffee in her hand, Lou scrubbed his face. "Any chance I can have one of those, Karla, sweetheart?"

"I'll go get you one," Karla assured and took off in another direction.

Sinking into the seat beside my dad, I frowned when he took my hand and squeezed it.

"Did he say if Margaret was okay when he left the surgery?" I asked.

"He said she was in critical condition but stable, or he wouldn't have left. He should have got paged if something happened, so he thinks she's gone to post-op and they couldn't find me to update me."

When I was younger, I was an eternal optimist. I would have assured Lou that it would all be okay, that Margaret was strong enough to pull through this. That was before Matilda and before Ethan. Now, my head was full of doubts. 'They never forget to update the family on Grey's Anatomy. It doesn't bode well,' my mind kept telling me. My stomach turned, the air seemed thicker and warmer in this waiting room, and I'd started to feel cold.

"I've been here for nearly two hours already," I muttered. "Nothing good takes this long to fix anymore. They can replace your heart with someone else's in less time than she's been in there, Dad." My voice was a little pitchy and hitched as I fought down my rising anxiety.

Saying nothing, Lou squeezed my hand again. We sat there in complete silence until Karla returned with a coffee for Lou twenty minutes later. Then we returned to silence again for another twenty until a woman in scrubs came through the door, pulling a scrub cap from her head to show sweat-soaked white hair pulled back in a chignon. She eyed us as she stopped at the desk, spoke to one of the staff, and then came over to us.

"Mr. Butler, I'm Doctor Emilia Cazaz. I'm sorry we've taken so long to update you on your wife."

"Lou is fine. These are my girls, Jessie and Karla. How is she?" Since we were in kindergarten together, Karla had been part of our family, and Lou often considered Karla and Lizzy just as much blood as Sharnie and me. Considering I'd been in-absentia for the last decade and Sharnie was a psycho, he probably preferred them too.

Eyes coming to me, the doctor smiled, but as she took in Karla, her eyes double-blinked before considering Lou and me again. I couldn't blame her. While I didn't look anything like my twin, we were all Caucasian. Karla looked like her Mongolian mother and had her Russian father's height and blue eyes.

Forcing a smile, the doctor gestured we should use the consultation room, then walked ahead of us to swipe her staff card to unlock the door and held it for us to file past. Once we were all inside and seated, the doctor took a deep breath and started explaining the surgery my mum needed.

"Margaret arrived here with a severe head injury, multiple crush fractures to her limbs and chest. Some of her rib bones were quite brittle in places, and when they fractured, they did so like glass. The shards of bone splintering in every direction."

The surgeon kept her hands in her lap, hidden by the table, but the way her forearm muscles were shifting beneath her skin, she either had itchy legs or was wringing the crap out of her scrub cap.

Tears fell free as I read the sympathy in her eyes. Snatching up Lou's hand, I squeezed it tight.

"Unfortunately, despite our best efforts, the injuries Margaret sustained were too much for her body, and she was pronounced dead a short time ago."

Karla swore and burst into tears, but mine were already falling. Lou's jaw worked a few times, his eyes turning glassy as his body shook. "She was a donor."

Swallowing, the surgeon kept her face stoic. "Unfortunately, the trauma that Margaret suffered has made most of her major organs not viable for donation, but there are other options available. I've organized for our grief counselor to come and talk to you, and the donor team will also be down soon. I understand you had a daughter in the accident also?"

Nodding his head, Lou cleared his throat. "Jessie's twin, Sharnie."

The surgeon glanced my way, then took a deep breath. "Doctor Shaw feels, considering your sister's blood pressure, head injury, and pregnancy, that it would be best not to tell Sharnie about her mother just yet. Instead, he'd like to get the MRI results and consult with Sharnie's obstetrician before they give her any difficult news."

Lou's jaw dropped open. "You want me to lie to my daughter?"

"Just for a few more hours." Rising out of her chair, the surgeon gave us a sympathetic look. "I'm sorry for your loss. You can use the room as long as you need." Getting up, the surgeon left the room.

Karla broke down crying.

"Oh, honey," Lou pulled her into a side hug, rubbing her back and soothing her.

Getting up, I walked around the room, my fist pressed to my mouth as I tried to hold my emotions inside a little longer. I couldn't let loose yet; someone would need to keep it together to tell Sharnie, and she'd likely attack whoever broke the news. I'd rather it be me than Dad.

Tears fell down my father's face as he consoled Karla, but he didn't break down. He'd do that later in private. Our watery gazes met, and the pain in the depths of his nearly broke me, but like my father, I would wait.

My phone vibrated in my pocket. Taking it out, I looked at the screen.

"It's Sharnie. She's back from the MRI and wants an update on mum."

"I'll go sit with her," Lou started to say, but I shook my head.

"No, Dad. If you go, she'll know something is wrong, and then you'll have to lie to her," I argued. "I'll go. She already hates me anyway. If she finds out that I lied to her later, it's not going to make things any worse between us."

"Jessie Girl…" Lou sighed, but he didn't debate my words.

"You should eat. Karla will stay with you for the administrators to come and talk to you, then you both need to get some lunch. I'll text you any updates on Sharnie."

Leaning down, I wrapped my arms around my dad, squeezing him tight, the tears falling faster for a moment, then I pulled away and headed for the door.

Stopping off at a bathroom, I cleaned my face up. Then, pulling out my phone, I called Dylan.

"How's Margaret?" he asked on answering.

My voice hitched and tears fell as I managed to keep my voice somewhat normal. "Dead." My chest ached as a sob broke free.

"I'll be there in twenty minutes."

"No," I squeaked. "Sharnie isn't out of the woods yet. We can't tell her about Margaret, so I have to pretend it's all okay and go sit with her."

"What the fuck, Jess? Why you? Your Dad is there, and her husband should be there."

"If Dad goes in there, she'll ask why he's not with mum, and Greg just landed a short time ago, so he's probably halfway down the freeway right now."

"Jess, you owe that bitch nothing. Let her suffer on her own, and I'll come and get you."

Shaking my head, I stared into my eyes in the mirror, red-rimmed and full of grief. I needed to pull myself together, or Sharnie would know as soon as she saw me.

"It's not about Sharnie, Dylan. There is an innocent child at risk."

"Fuck Sharnie and her brat. She murdered your baby without an ounce of remorse, just like she killed my sister. Twice!"

Closing my eyes, I didn't let Dylan's venom penetrate. His hatred for Sharnie was more than well deserved. Not just what she did to Teille, but he was there through most of the abuse I suffered as well.

"I get your anger and distaste, and I assure you that if it were just Sharnie, I'd be nowhere near her right now, but it's not. I lost my baby. I wouldn't put my worst enemy through that, so I'm going to stay until Greg gets here. Then, I'll stay until Lou doesn't need me. He's a strong man, but he loved Margaret with all his heart. I'm worried how this will affect him."

"As Evan said, it'll take a while to organize the funeral. I'll call Teille and get her to organize the house and for the band to come out, then call our manager to change our flights for the concert to be from here. Call me when you need me." Dylan hung up before I could respond.

Sighing, I looked at my blank screen, opened my call history, and pressed Greg's name.

"Hey, we're about thirty minutes away. How is everyone?" he answered.

"Sharnie is back from her MRI, and I'm just on my way to her now. They're concerned about her high blood pressure and have told us she needs to stay calm and relaxed. You'll probably be here before we get any further updates. Text me when you are in emergency, and I'll come and get you."

"Thanks, Jess. How's Margaret?"

My breath rushed out of me, more tears falling free as I struggled to find the words. Not because I couldn't say them. I could, even though it hurt. But I knew I was on speaker, and I didn't want to distract them from the road.

It didn't matter. My silence was answer enough because Ethan cursed, and his hand pounding the steering wheel a few times came through loud and clear.

"Jess, I'm sorry," Ethan muttered.

Sniffling, I focused on what I needed to do.

"We can't tell Sharnie yet. The doctors won't let us, so Lou is staying away, and I'm about to lie to her, give her false hope so that her baby will be okay. When she finds out, no matter her personality change, she's going to hate me, and that's okay. She's hated me for so long I wouldn't know how to deal with her any other way."

That hurt, despite it being the absolute truth. Sharnie was my twin, and growing up, we'd been best friends, but I couldn't deny how her being nice to me all of a sudden was creeping me out.

"Jess, she doesn't hate you," Greg mourned. "She'll understand."

No, she wouldn't. I wouldn't if the roles reversed, and Sharnie was way more dramatic and irrational than me.

"I'll see you soon," I answered, then hung up the phone before it got weirder.

Rewashing my face, I patted it dry and got my shit together to face my sister.

By the time I got back to Sharnie, she was sitting up with some cap on her head.

"It's an ice cap," Sharnie pointed to it. "It's designed for people with intense migraines. It's like an ice pack for the head but also doubles as a pair of skins or something. The doctor told the nurses to put it on me after the MRI. How's mum? Did you get an update?"

Taking the seat beside her, I gave a shallow nod. "The surgeon came out while I was there. The surgery is taking so long because of something to do with her bones. She suffered quite a few fractures, and one of her bones splintered or something. Doctor Shaw was the neurosurgeon for her before he came to see you. He told dad that she was in critical condition, but he wouldn't have left the theatre if he didn't feel it was safe to."

Sharnie blew out a breath and relaxed. "Poor Mum. She's going to be in so much pain. She'll probably be stuck in hospital for a while too." Then, reaching out, Sharnie took my hand and squeezed it. "Hey, you should stay with Greg and me while you are here since you don't have a room at Mum and Dad's anymore."

I'm sure I resembled a rabbit in headlights. "Did you hit your head or something?"

Smirking, Sharnie tugged at the bandage peeking out from under the ice cap. "Well, duh!"

It made me chuckle despite remembering waking in the middle of the night with Sharnie standing over me, a knife in her hand poised to stab me in the heart. A shiver raced down my spine at the memory.

"I'm good. I'll stay with Dylan."

Sharnie released my hand so quickly I got whiplash. "I didn't realize you were still friends?"

Noticing the hate in Sharnie's eyes, I sat back, recognizing the Sharnie I knew too well. Interesting that Dylan was the trigger for her to emerge.

"Yes. I'm still in regular contact with both Dylan and Teille." When Sharnie's teeth gnashed together on Teille's name, I lifted a brow. "You never told me what made you lose your shit with her that night."

"I was high."

"Pretty sure it wasn't the first time. You were high fucking Ben the first time, and that had already happened by the time you flipped out."

Sharnie's steel gaze came to me. "Ben told you?"

"I only found out last year."

"When you were home for the wedding?"

Glancing at the monitor, I noticed Sharnie's blood pressure. Taking a breath, I exhaled. "It doesn't matter. It's in the past. Let's talk about the baby. Do you know the sex? Have you decided on a name?"

Still glaring at me, Sharnie ground her jaw. "It's a boy. We're calling him Scout."

"Scout Dumont. I like it." I forced a smile.

"Are you and Dylan together?"

Her question surprised me. Even when Dylan and I were close as teenagers, she never asked about him. Sharnie never acknowledged he was part of my life.

"As a romantic couple? No. I wouldn't have gotten involved with Ethan if we were. So have you got the nurse—"

"Are you fucking him?"

"Jesus!" I sat back in my chair, shaking my head. "Why is this a thing for you? I told you we are friends."

Sharnie's eyes narrowed. "You are, aren't you?"

Getting up, I shook my head. There was not a chance in hell I was confessing anything to Sharnie. She'd sell it to the highest bidder just to get two minutes of fame. A nurse came over, checking the machines.

"What's going on?"

Shaking my head at her, I swallowed and looked back to Sharnie.

"You need to relax. Your blood pressure is too high. My being here is agitating you, so I'll go check in with Dad and get something to eat. Do you want me to bring you something?"

Grabbing my wrist, Sharnie dug her nails in. The machine beside her started beeping erratically, getting the attention of the rest of the nurse's station.

"You weren't even pretty, and Dylan only ever had eyes for you. He never even acknowledged I existed, but he couldn't stop looking at you even when you took up with Ben. You're Plain Jane, but every guy I wanted, wanted you! Daddy's perfect fucking Jessie Girl."

"Sharnie, you need to calm down," the nurse was saying, then she was telling one of the nurses to draw up some drug to administer.

Sharnie flinched and pressed her free hand to her head, but those evil eyes stayed glued on me, her nails drawing blood from my wrist. "Teille was going to tell you about Ben and me. She knew I'd fucked him first, and she was going to tell you. But I wanted you and Ben together because then maybe her gorgeous older brother would finally look at me! He was so talented that it was obvious he would make it big, and it was me who should have been on his arm. The beautiful twin. The photogenic twin. Not the boring nerd-next-door twin who would never fit into his world. Not you!"

My mouth was hanging open, absolutely stunned. The nurses working on the other side had pretty much the same reaction.

"You nearly killed his sister. He was never going to look at you with anything but hate," I replied calmly and sadly, lowering my voice as not to escalate things, but it didn't matter.

"I loved him! I deserved him. Not—" Sharnie's grip loosened as the pupil in her right eye got bigger all of a sudden until the iris was nearly non-existent. Shit!

"Sharnie," I whispered.

The nurse noticed too, and then I was being pushed out, and the screen pulled across as Sharnie started fitting on the bed, and a code went up that brought doctors and nurses running.

My phone went off as the cacophony of alarm reached its peak. I started running to the doors and shoved them open, looking for the face I knew was waiting. Greg came bounding over. He took one look at me, and his skin drained of color.

"Jess?"

"Down the hall to the right. Just follow the sounds of chaos."

As he raced through the doors, I stepped out into the waiting room only to find my body pressed against a solid chest, a familiar scent permeating my nose as hands that knew my body almost as well as my own rubbed my back.

"Jess. What happened?" Ethan murmured in my ear as he held me to him.

"I think I just killed my sister."

CHAPTER SIXTEEN

THE MOUTH OF THE HUNTER RIVER SPARKLED OUTSIDE, RIPPLES moving through caused by one of the big ships leaving the Newcastle Port. Early birds were taking advantage of the sunny winters day already jogging, strolling, or riding along the Honeysuckle foreshore. A week ago, when Dylan brought me back to the hotel, I'd spent several hours out there just sitting on the edge of the harbor, watching the ships come and go.

"Jess?" Greg's voice pulled me back from the view and to the phone on speaker in my hand.

"Yes, sorry. I'm here."

"I know I'm probably asking a lot of you, but Lou and I want to be here with Sharnie."

"Of course. It's fine." Cringing on the lie, I turned away from the view outside to see Dylan standing with his arms crossed in the doorway of the bathroom, a towel slung low around his waist, water still dripping down his naked chest from his shower.

"Thanks, Jess. Ethan has keys to my place and offered to drive you over in my car—"

A hiss escapes my lips at a different pain, and I sink my ass on the window seat.

"But if you would be uncomfortable at our place, Ethan can pick up some things before he comes to get you, and you can stay in your hotel room," Greg hurriedly added.

My eyes drifted to Dylan again. His eyes were not happy as he watched me. The request itself or the companion offered as a chauffeur might have caused that look alone.

"Can I let you know when I get there? I need to discuss it with Dylan first."

Greg took a deep breath. "Dylan's here with you?"

That made me wince. "Yes. Sorry, I thought Lou would have told you."

"I can't say he has, but surely he wouldn't have an issue for one night?"

Taking in the way that Dylan suddenly stood straight, glared at the phone, and stormed back into the bathroom to finish getting ready to go practice with the band, I think Greg underestimated just how deep the waters of hatred towards his wife ran in this hotel room.

"I think your place is the better option." Something loud cracked down on the countertop in the ensuite.

"You could both come and stay with me until after the funerals. We've got a nice guest room downstairs, and I can't say that I wouldn't mind the help for the next few weeks."

Now he was pushing my generosity. "I need to talk to Dylan. I'll be at the hospital in an hour. Dylan will drop me off on the way to rehearsal."

"The whole band's here?"

"They followed Dylan over. They leave for the next tour next week, and Dylan wanted to be here for me."

"He seems like a nice guy. Does he treat you right?"

"We're not having this discussion, Greg."

Greg was quiet for a beat, probably building up the guts for his next ask. "Will you come and see her?"

"She hurt me, Greg. A lot more than I ever realized." It started because of the man in the bathroom if Sharnie's last words to me were to be believed. And Dylan was just as angry as I was about this nightmare.

"I know the part she played in you and Ethan. She confessed it in the message she sent me. I'm so sorry, Jess. I only told her about you and Ethan so she'd get over her paranoia about you and me. I just wanted to be able to come home and not have things thrown at my head again."

Dylan dropped onto the bed and started pulling on his boots.

"I'll see you soon." Hanging up before Greg could continue down that avenue, I put my phone in my purse and watched Dylan. "He's invited us to stay with him until after the funerals."

"No." Shoving his foot into the second boot, Dylan wouldn't look at me.

Nodding, I expected that answer. "I'll stay there tonight to help out. But, I'll be back here tomorrow."

Dropping his foot on the floor, Dylan stood up. "Why? This isn't your problem. You owe that bitch nothing."

Lifting my eyes to Dylan's, I accepted his rage and kept my voice even. "It's not about owing anyone anything. It's about being a decent human being."

Dylan scoffed, "She deserves nothing decent. She deserved what happened to your mother to happen to her. She deserved what happened to you to happen to her. She deserved to have her head caved in with a textbook—like she did my sister!" Dylan's voice rose with each new sentence. "Do you know what it does to me that she did that because she wanted me? That it was her jealousy of you and me before there even was you and me that cost my sister everything? Teille went through years of hell and multiple surgeries. She tried to kill herself. She can't ever drive. She couldn't finish school. She can't even fathom having a fucking relationship, which means she'll never get married and have kids. But the bitch who did that to her got to do all of it. And you expect me to be fine with you going there and spending the night to fucking help her?"

Fuck, I shouldn't have told him. But we'd always wondered what set Sharnie off that night, and I couldn't not tell him after all this time. But it was wrong. Now he blamed himself. And I'm pretty sure he blamed me. Bowing my head, I swiped at the tears leaking from my eyes.

"You should be grieving your mother. The mother that bitch killed, along with three university kids. Just in case you forgot that Margaret should not have needed to drive that night, but Sharnie manipulated her to get behind the wheel. This is the least of what she deserves."

"And what about Greg?" I shot out of my seat, so Dylan wasn't standing over me. "Does Greg deserve to suffer just because he was married to that bitch?"

Clenching his jaw, Dylan stepped back, but he didn't continue his rant.

"I'm not doing anything for Sharnie. I am helping Greg and his child and my father, who is grieving the loss of his soulmate. Greg's parents live in Melbourne. They are flying in tomorrow and will be here to help Greg with everything after that."

Turning around, Dylan grabbed his jacket from the bed and started pulling it into place. "And what about Ethan?"

Surprised by the question, I frowned. "What about Ethan?"

Pocketing his wallet, phone, and hotel key, Dylan half-turned to face me. "He's meeting you at the hospital and driving you back to

Greg's. Is he also staying the night to help?" When I stood there blinking at him, unsure what to say because it hadn't even occurred to me, Dylan huffed and shook his head. "You are so selfless that you didn't even consider how he could use this situation to force you to listen to him finally."

Mouth falling open, I shook my head. "Ethan loved Margaret, and Greg is like his brother. We are just doing what needs doing."

"A-ha." Dylan chuckled angrily. "And he needed to have his arms all over you while you grieved your mother."

My mouth snapped shut. I'd still been in Ethan's arms when Dylan showed up at the hospital to bring me back to the hotel last week. I hadn't called him. He'd just shown up, and it just happened to be ten minutes after Sharnie suffered a ruptured aneurysm.

"You still want a lift?" Yanking the door open, Dylan walked through the lounge area of the penthouse suite we were in, heading for the main entrance. "I'll see you downstairs."

Evan and Teille, who were staying in the other rooms, rose from their seats on the sofa. Dropping my sorrowful ass on the end of the massive bed, I hugged myself and let the pain and grief of the last week out.

Someone sat on the bed beside me and put an arm around my shoulders. Cursing, I swiped at the tears.

"Don't take it to heart, Jess. I warned you about his demons. Add the bitch-witch to the equation and sprinkle it with a little jealousy about your ex on the scene, and it's a clusterfuck waiting to happen," Evan soothed.

"I can't win. If I don't help out, I let my family down. If I do, I hurt Dylan and Teille. Either way, I'm going to hurt someone."

Sighing, Evan squeezed me to his side. "Are you married or engaged to Dylan?"

"No."

"Are you in a committed, loving relationship that you think will lead to marriage?"

Swallowing the ugly truth, I closed my eyes as more tears escaped.

"No."

Evan softened his tone. "Do you love your family?"

"Yes."

"Then you've already made the right choice. Teille would do the same if the roles reversed. Don't let Dylan's anger and issues cause you more heartache by neglecting those who need you. Go do what you need to do." Dropping a kiss on my head, Evan stood up and left.

Glad that Evan took the time to comfort me and not hit on me for once, I got my shit together, shoved a change of clothes and pajamas into an oversized handbag, and headed downstairs.

The ride to the hospital was quiet, since no one was willing to talk in case it set Dylan off again. He'd been tense since he picked me up from the hospital, but when I told him what Sharnie confessed two days later to explain why I allowed Ethan to comfort me, Dylan turned cold as ice. Oh, he was still fucking me, but it was the violent, hate-filled sex that we'd had before he moved in with me. Except this time, it was him hating on me instead of me hating him. It felt like I was seventeen years old, and Dylan had just dumped me all over again.

When the car pulled up to the curb of the drop-off/pick-up area of the hospital, I opened my door, not even bothering to say anything, but Dylan grabbed my wrist as I was halfway out and waited for me to turn to face him. Then, blowing out a breath, he swiveled his hold until his fingers threaded mine, and he held my hand, lifting it to his mouth for a kiss to my first knuckle.

"I understand where you are coming from, Jess. However, it doesn't mean I agree or have to fucking like it," he murmured.

Closing my eyes, I turned away, my hand slipping from his as I stepped out of the SUV he'd hired and shut the door. Without looking back, I made my way into the hospital and to the high dependency ward, stopping by the coffee shop on the way for breakfast.

"Jessie Girl," my father sighed with relief when he came out of the HDU to meet me—wrapping me in his arms and squeezing me tight. He'd done this each time he'd seen me since Margaret died. Not that I complained. I hugged him back with the same heartache thrumming in my chest. The last seven days had been hell for all of us.

"Any change?" I asked.

Lou's hold stopped my diaphragm from expanding as he tensed. When he pulled back to meet my eyes, I already knew the answer.

"When?"

"Sometime this afternoon." When my eyes drifted over Lou's shoulder in the direction I knew Sharnie was, he cupped my cheek. "I know you grieved the loss of your sister a long time ago, but if you wanted to—"

"That woman in there isn't my sister, dad. She's my tormentor."

Taking my hand, Lou nodded. "I know Jessie. I'm not asking you to, just offering the opportunity just in case you needed it."

Chewing my cheek, I considered the chance to punch her one more time might be therapeutic, but I couldn't see Greg, Lou, or the hospital staff being okay with that.

"Has Greg got the paperwork ready?" I was here for a specific reason. To help Greg out so he could stay by his wife's bed.

"I'll go and get it." I didn't move to follow him. Since Sharnie had come out of surgery, I hadn't gone past the doors for the HDU.

"Miss Butler," a familiar voice greeted, albeit with a sorrowful tone.

"Doctor Shaw."

"Are you here to say goodbye?"

"No," I answered firmly. "I said goodbye a long time ago."

Bobbing his head as if he understood, Doctor Shaw gave me a sad smile and went to move on.

"Wait," I took a step to catch his attention again. "How long does it take?"

Smoothing his brow, Shaw kept his voice low and respectful. "It can be minutes; it could be hours or days. There's no way to predict it. Unfortunately, with the state of your sister's health, I suspect it will be sooner than later."

"I'd like to do something, as a present for Greg and the baby. If you'd allow it? I might even need help."

"A present?" Shaw furrowed his brow at me again. It probably wasn't the right word to use considering the situation, but I wanted Greg to have this one thing, for Scout to have this one thing.

"When I was twenty-one, I miscarried. She was born stillborn. I at least got to hold her once. Sharnie should have that, even though she won't be conscious for it. Scout should have that one moment in his mother's arms before—" Choking up a little, I swallowed as my eyes filled with my emotions. "I want to give that to them."

Watching me for a moment, Shaw glanced toward where Sharnie lay and then back to me, his own eyes a little misty. "You'll need to be here at two. I'll help."

"Thank you."

With a twitch of his lips that resembled a sad smile, Shaw gave me a singular nod and went to the nurse's desk. Lou returned with the papers I needed, and I headed off to do my part in today's 'administrating the loss of a loved one' hell.

I was waiting for rounds to end to get another doctor to sign-off when Ethan found me. He didn't say anything. Instead, he just sat beside me, exhaled hard, and bowed his head.

"How's Greg?" I asked, the silence between us uncomfortable in a way it never was before.

"Heartbroken. Freaking out. Exhausted. How are you?"

"Just tired."

"Just tired? Your mum died, Jess. I know you weren't talking, but—"

"We made up. Sort of. The week I ran into you at the airport. After finishing the work trip, I went home and then met up with Sean and Holly for the flight home. We made our peace."

Watching me with grief in his eyes, Ethan reached out and took my hand, squeezing it. Returning the gesture, I took my hand away.

"And I'm more tired than anything because Lou has moved all his focus to Sharnie and Scout and supporting Greg, so I've been dealing with all the paperwork and organizing Margaret's funeral." And trying to get it to happen before Dylan flew out for his tour because he agreed to be there with me if it was before he had to leave. Then again, that was before I told him of Sharnie's confession, and he started hating me, so it was probably the last thing he wanted to do with me right now.

"Did you go to see her?" Ethan asked.

"I went with Dad to the morgue."

Before Ethan could ask any more questions, a woman in scrubs approached with a sad smile.

"Morning, Jess. Do you have the paperwork?"

"Morning, Adriana." Handing her the papers in my hands, she checked through them, then applied her signature and gave me back one set.

"Okay. Let's go get him." Rubbing her hands together to create a little excitement, she scanned her staff badge at the door to the outer door to the NICU and held it for Ethan and me as he pushed the pram through. We all disinfected our hands, and then we waited as Adriana went to Scout's crib, giving him a big smile before she picked him up.

"Okay, little man. Your favorite aunt is here to take you home today. You've proven to be strong and resilient, and I've signed off on letting you go out into the world and give it your all."

Adriana gave me that sad smile again after passing the little bundle of a white blanket to me. I'd been here daily to sit by Scout's side since he was born via emergency c-section when Sharnie's brain bleed occurred. Greg came by when he needed to stretch his legs, Lou too, but they'd mainly stayed with Sharnie, so I ensured I was here for Scout each day while Dylan was at practice.

Saying farewell to the pediatrician, we made our way to another cafe to relax and grab some lunch while we waited for the time I needed to go back to the HDU.

"You're a natural." Ethan watched me give Scout a bottle of formula Adriana mixed up for us before we left. "You should stay and help Greg raise him."

Lifting my head, I glared at Ethan. "Excuse me? Did you really just suggest I give up my career, the home I love, my friends, and come back here and play mummy to my abuser's kid?"

"Shit, Jess, I—"

"Shit, Jess, is about right! I'm doing this to help Greg until his family arrives. Then I'm staying long enough to bury my mother and ensure my father is okay. I'll be going back to my life and job as soon as I can, Ethan. Newcastle isn't my home anymore, and I have no responsibility to this child or its father. I especially owe Sharnie nothing, and she's not going to be the reason I turn my world on its head a third time."

Running a hand down his face, Ethan sat back in his chair, looking scolded. "You're right. I'm sorry. It just came out."

Yeah, sure, it just came out. "Do yourself a favor and don't even suggest that shit to Greg. You'd just leave him disappointed when I get on the plane to leave again."

Pursing his lips, Ethan nodded, but something in his eyes seemed overly guilty. Like when someone promises they won't do something after they've already gone and done it. Trainees gave me that rabbit in the headlights too-late promise all the time.

Fuck! Had Lou and Greg already been thinking about this? I hoped not, because I wasn't staying.

Just before two, we were in the HDU. Greg was surprised but happy to see his son.

"He should get the chance to be in her arms at least once," I said.

Nodding, but with his throat too choked up to say anything, Greg handed Scout back to me and went back to hold Sharnie's hand. I stepped out of the way while the medical team came in to explain everything that was about to happen—and then they disconnected the lines, took the tube out of her throat, and turned off the machine.

Looking up at me, Doctor Shaw gave me a nod and tilted the backrest of the bed up a little. I came forward as he set Sharnie's arms in a cradle, and I placed Scout in her hold, resting his little head right above her still-beating heart.

Stepping back, I found the right angle to make it appear Sharnie was smiling down at her little man, did a few close-ups of him on her chest, and then we had Greg come in beside her and add his arms to support Sharnie's for a few more, including one where the tears fell from his eyes as he kissed his wife's head.

It took all of two minutes, but mine was the only dry eyes by the time it finished. Taking his son in his arms, Greg held him and sobbed as he kissed his little head.

"That was a beautiful thing you did," Shaw murmured as he came to stand where I was, as far from the bed as I could get. "My wife died giving me my third child. Those photos will be everything to that kid one day."

"I know."

Watching the monitor, Shaw nodded. "It won't be long now. She's already slipping to the next world."

"She's reigned over hell for a long time now; it won't be too hard an adjustment."

Barely resisting a smirk, Shaw checked his watch and noted something in the file on the tablet in his hand.

Coming over, Greg put Scout back in my arms and pressed a kiss to my cheek.

"Thank you, Jess."

Smiling down at the little boy in my arms, I softened my voice. "I did it for him. We'll see you soon." Turning, I headed out with Ethan by my side, pushing the pram. Ethan pulled out his phone and read a message as we exited the hospital.

"She's gone."

Nodding once, I kept my focus on Scout.

"Come on, Scout. Time to go check out your new home."

CHAPTER SEVENTEEN

"You hate me, don't you?"

Tires revolving over wet tarmac was my only response. Tapping my phone, I placed it on my thigh to watch Dylan. His hands tightened on the wheel as he navigated us from the graveyard to my parent's house.

"If you take this on yourself, if you blame you or me for Sharnie's actions, she wins. Even dead, she wins."

Dylan's knuckles turned white at the mention of Sharnie's name, his jaw clenched, but he didn't say anything. This had been our entire morning. He played the part and held my hand at my mother's funeral, but from the time we woke this morning, he'd not said a single word to me.

Sighing, I woke my screen and looked at the picture Dylan was tagged in last night when he and the band went out for drinks. The one with his tongue down a woman's throat while he pressed her against the wall. Swallowing, I closed the app and slid my phone back into my purse.

Dylan knew I'd seen it. His phone chirped with an alert the same time mine did. We saw the pictures at the same time, and I knew when he got to the one that had stolen the air from my lungs because he lifted his head, appraised me, then dropped his phone back on the bed and went back to getting dressed.

He gave me no excuses, no apologies, and no denial that it was anything more but a passionate kiss of a drunk rockstar and one of his adoring fans. He just kept getting dressed in his suit, and after a few deep breaths, I did too.

Pulling into my dad's driveway behind my father's car, Dylan cut the engine, then turned to look at me for the first time since we left the hotel room.

"I've reserved the penthouse for another week for you. Use it. You'll suffocate if you stay with anyone. You need your time alone at the end of each day to slowly let your grief release," Dylan spoke quietly into the cabin around us. "You've got the car another week too. Just drop it off when you finish with it. Teille will organize to collect my stuff from your place and my key left on the kitchen counter for you."

"Jesus!" I whispered, wiping a tear from my cheek. "You have a knack for timing when it comes to disappearing from my life, Dylan. Take my virginity and throw me out. Attend my mum's funeral and dump me between the grave and the wake."

A car double-parked behind us, and I glanced over my shoulder to see Evan. He wasn't at the funeral. Dylan was attending the wake for at least an hour before Evan picked him up for them to head out for the tour, but I guess plans changed after that picture showed up. Or maybe they changed before that.

"I hope the tour goes well. Goodbye, Dylan." I went to open the door and get out, but Dylan caught my hand, wrapping the car keys in my palm.

"This isn't goodbye, Jess. At least not permanently. I need time to deal with what you told me. I need to process my feelings about everything and then see where that leaves us."

"That photo from last night seems to leave us in the same place you left me thirteen years ago." Scrunching the skirt of my black vintage velvet dress in my fists, I staved off the tears. "Why do guys keep cheating on me? It's not for lack of sex. I know I'm good for that—but one fight, one misstep in our relationship, and you all run out and dive into the nearest cunt you can find that's not mine. Why?"

Blowing out a breath, Dylan reached up and cuffed the back of my head, forcing me to meet his eyes.

"For starters, I didn't fuck her. And from what you told me, Ethan didn't fuck his flight attendant either, and Sharnie blackmailed Ben. So that's not a thing. Secondly, you are the best fucking sex I've ever had, Jess, because I care about you, which makes it more than fucking. If this were just about us, if I weren't used to a particular lifestyle, I would never leave your bed. I wouldn't let you out of it either.

"Thirdly, this is nothing like the last time. I was a fucking mess, and you were so fucking innocent. It's not that I couldn't bring you with me, but I wouldn't. You deserved your pretty life with a picket fence and babies. You still fucking do, and I'm never going to give that to you.

"Lastly, I don't hate you, resent you, or blame you in any way, shape, or form for your sister's insanity and jealousy. I also can't bear to come home in two months, after you see more of those kinds of photos from the tour, and have you look at me like you did this morning. I have loved you most of my life, Jess, but I'm always going to end up hurting you. I know it, and so do you. It's why you kept me at arm's length for the last decade. It's why you never let this build into something more. The last few months have been the best I've had off stage, but they were only available to me because you loved someone else, and he wrenched your heart out."

Watching the tears pour from my eyes, Dylan bowed his forehead to mine as he exhaled. He was right. I didn't let myself get attached again. I couldn't. Not because I didn't love him, but because I'd still been in love and hurting from Ethan, and I didn't trust Dylan not to smash the shards of my heart that remained.

"You are the other half of my soul, Jess, but in this life, we are never going to be each other's happily ever after. My demons ripped my soul to shreds, and we can't meld together how we should. Maybe in the next life, we can try again." Kissing my forehead, Dylan pulled back, lifted my face, and kissed me as if he was trying to find the bits of us that fit and get them to fuse.

Dylan was right. Our connection was in tatters, and it was never going to work. Pulling back breathless, we stayed as close as we could, our tears merging and falling together.

"Don't hate me, Jess. You're still the only one who makes my heart keep beating away from the music. Even if I can't have you, I need the illusion."

With my eye pressed to his cheek, I breathed through the sorrow.

"I've never hated you, Dylan. I just hated watching you tear yourself apart, and the way you made my heart your collateral damage."

Dylan's next kiss was slow but just as passionate, and I knew it would be the last. Pulling back, Dylan got out of the car, walked to where Evan was waiting, got in, and they rolled away, leaving me crying in a rented luxury sports car in my father's driveway.

I don't know how long I sat there crying or how many people arrived, saw me falling apart in the car, and chose to respect my privacy and go inside without making a thing of it, but eventually, the car door opened. Strong arms scooped me out of the car just enough for that body to slide in beneath me, and then the car door shut again, and those arms cradled me against a familiar chest swathed in a black suit and black button-down.

"God, Jess." Ethan held my face to his chest and let me cry all over him in the passenger seat of the enclosed car.

I cried for my mum, Scout, who would never know his mum, Matilda, Teille, Dylan, me, and Ethan–because he lost his mum when he was too young.

By the time I calmed down, the wake was well and truly in progress, but Ethan and I stayed in that confined space even longer. He held me while I just sat there breathing. The pain of it still occasionally wracking my chest. Eventually, I grabbed up my purse, pulled out a pack of tissues, and started wiping my snot and tears off Ethan's nice suit before I cleaned up my face.

"Lou saw me like that?" I finally asked. Ethan went with Lou in the limousine provided by the funeral home. Dad asked me to go with him, but I'd elected to ride with Dylan, considering how things were between Lou and Dylan. I'm glad I did. At least he said goodbye this time.

"I told him I'd take care of you; he needed to be in there."

Still cradled in Ethan's arms, neither of us moved to get out of the car.

"I should go in. Sean and Holly came all this way just to be here for me," I murmur eventually.

Squeezing me once more, Ethan relaxed his arms but didn't make a move to let me go.

"I don't think I can get out of the car with how we are sitting," I added quietly when we both failed to move.

Without a word, Ethan opened the car door, twisted in the seat, then heaved up, taking me with him, waiting until he was standing before releasing my legs. Once I had my feet under me, I glanced around. The drizzle of rain was keeping everyone inside.

Placing his hand in the small of my back, Ethan escorted me inside and helped me out of my jacket.

"Thank you," I murmured, tears still filling my voice.

Meeting my eyes with his red-rimmed ones, Ethan licked his lips and caressed my cheek before withdrawing his hand as if the touch of my skin burned him.

"I meant what I said when we met, Jess. Your family is important to me. If you need me, as a friend, I'm here. Especially today. Nothing makes you feel alone more than going stag to a wedding or a funeral. I know you're with Dylan, but if you need a shoulder, mine is free."

The longing in Ethan's eyes was more than any friend, but I appreciated that he would put that aside. The fact it echoed around the hollowness of my aching heart was a problem I had to deal with alone.

"Thank you. I should use the bathroom."

Giving me a nod as I backed out of the foyer, heading for the powder room, Ethan blew out a breath as I turned from him. "I need a drink," he muttered.

Closing my eyes on the pain in his voice, I closed the bathroom door and cleaned myself up. When I made my way out to where the wake was taking place, the first arms to greet me were Sean's.

"Where's Dylan?"

"He had to leave for the tour to start."

Stepping back, Sean stared into my eyes. "He couldn't hold over until tomorrow?"

Chewing my lip, I averted my gaze from the intensity of those ocean blues. Using his finger to make me meet his eyes gently, Sean cocked that brow at me. "What happened?"

"Sharnie. Isn't it always Sharnie?"

Grumbling under his breath, Sean pulled me in for another hug.

"I'm sorry, Jess."

Nodding against Sean's chest, I pulled back and swiped a tear away before I lost my composure again.

After talking to them a bit, Karla and Lizzy found me and joined the conversation, excited to meet Sean after all these years of hearing about him. Karla waited until Lizzy had Sean and Holly's attention to ask me quietly about Dylan's absence. Unlike Sean, Karla accepted Dylan leaving for the tour without question.

As the guests left, I was sitting by my father's side nursing Scout and giving him a bottle when Sean came over to offer his condolences to Lou. His ocean eyes took me in, holding the baby, but said nothing as he stepped closer and smiled as he appraised Scout.

"He looks just like you, Greg," Sean offered.

"Let's hope he has his father's personality too," I added.

Sean smirked, and while Greg gave us a quiet smile, his eyes filled with tears. "I'm not sure how I'm going to raise him by myself, to be honest. I can't quit my job, but to keep it might mean having to move back to Melbourne to be near my family so they can help out."

I watched Lou rub his lips together and lower his head. He'd lost his wife and daughter, and now he was going to lose his only grandchild. Deep blue eyes observed me from the other side of my father. Ethan, waiting for my reaction. His suggestion I stay coming to mind.

Gazing down at my nephew, I gave him a sad smile; my heart ached for his father and mine. Releasing a sigh, I took the bottle away and put the cloth nappy I used as a towel over my hand, and rolled Scout to his left side as I sat him up. He released a beautiful burp.

"It's a pity you don't live in Hawaii. I could take care of Scout while you are flying."

"True. All of my resorts have a creche for staff and guests," Sean added. His eyes were sad but with a sparkle in them.

"You could always hire a nanny," I suggested.

"And I'll be here," Lou reminded Greg.

"Dad, I thought it might be nice if you fly back with me and spend some time in Hawaii."

"I still work, Jess," Lou replied, his heart not really in it.

"Yes, but you have a few weeks left of bereavement leave." Reaching out, I took his hand. "Just a couple of weeks. Some time away, plenty of golf to be found, and time with me?"

Ethan's brows drew together as he watched the interaction.

"I'm going to be around. I'd be happy to take you around some of the best golf courses Hawaii offers," Sean added. "Holly has a few jobs, but we would only be gone a few days at a time."

When Lou stayed quiet, I slipped my hand into his. "Nothing needs to be decided right now. I'm here for another week no matter what."

Getting up, I handed Scout off to Greg, then turned and kissed Lou on the cheek. "I told Sean I'd give him and Holly a lift back to the hotel. I'll see you tomorrow."

"Thank you for organizing all this today. It was beautiful," Lou murmured, pulling me into a hug. "I'm glad that on your last visit you made an effort to clear things with your mother, Jessie Girl. It's good that you were able to forgive each other before this happened."

Holding back tears, I gave him a silent nod, then turned and started walking out with Sean, his arm going around my shoulder in comfort as we left.

CHAPTER EIGHTEEN

"WE'LL STAY IN SYDNEY FOR THE REST OF THE WEEK. HOLLY WANTS to spend some time with Trisha and discuss wedding things," Sean mentioned over breakfast the following day.

Sean and Holly stayed at the same hotel as me to be close if needed.

"I'll meet you at the airport before our flight."

Once again, Sean booked my flight with them. This time I think it was to make sure I didn't end up at the airport alone with Ethan. There was no reason to mention the two times I'd already spent alone in a car with Ethan, since Ethan hadn't even brought up what happened between us.

Reaching across the table, Sean covered my hand with his. "If you need more time here with your family, I can cover for you."

"Honestly, I'm keen to return to my own space and job."

Pursing his lips, Sean side-eyed his fiancé but stayed quiet. Not that Holly missed it. Instead, she looked at her watch and shot out of her seat. "I haven't finished packing. I'll meet you upstairs, honey."

Coming around the table, Holly kissed me on the cheek, then dashed away, allowing Sean to say what he wouldn't in front of her.

"Jess, your mum died. Your dad has no one else. If you want to stay, I'm happy to give you a good reference—"

"Woah! Stop right there." Blinking wide eyes at Sean, I shook my head slowly. "I am not moving back here. Greg and Ethan are like sons to Lou. They will be his family if he decides to stay. I've offered for Lou to visit me, but he needs to grieve first, and Dad won't do that with me around, Sean. He'll want to be strong and not show his pain to me. That's what parents do."

Sighing, Sean nodded agreement but then tilted his head to assess me. "And you?"

"You saw my breakdown. I think everyone did."

"No. Ethan, Holly, and I stood on the upper path blocking everyone's view for a while, then once the majority of guests arrived, Ethan went down to the car to be there for you."

Confused, I looked up. "I'm surprised you let him?"

Sean's face dropped. "Jess, I didn't get a chance to say anything. When it was obvious that you weren't recovering, he marched down there without a word and took you in his arms. If you had tried to stop him, I would have stepped in, but you didn't." Dropping his head, Sean peered at me and cocked a brow, but when I frowned, not understanding what he was trying to suggest, he blew out a breath and shook his head.

"When you get back, I want to talk to you about Maui."

That just made me even more self-conscious. "What's wrong with Maui?"

"Do you want to be there? I know you, Jess, you run from your heartache, and I worry when you get back, and Dylan is all through that house, it's going to trigger you to run again. So, I want to get ahead of that."

Sitting back, I watched Sean. "How?"

"Turtle Bay. I'm officially taking on the general manager's role, and I want the best of my managers taking care of my baby."

My mouth gaped a little. I loved Turtle Bay and would normally have jumped at it, but I'd always stayed with Sean when I was there.

"No offense, but I don't want to room with you and Holly. I heard enough at the Hideaway."

Smirking, Sean shook his head. "Well, that's fair, but you could buy one of the new villas on the outskirt of the resort. Make it your home. You are renting out your place at Ewa Beach to Mayla, so you have the capital for a loan, or I'm happy to do a rent-to-buy agreement with you, whatever you prefer."

The new Turtle Bay estate was Sean's latest project. An exclusive row of houses that skirted the resort on the far side of the golf course. An idea he got from my place in Ewa Beach, except only the houses were available to purchase. The ground they sat on still belonged to Cassidy Resort, and the strata included the cost of renting the land, but it gave you year-round access to the golf course and the resort facilities. I'd have loved to live there and steal Sean's horse to go riding all the time.

"Can I think about it?"

"Of course."

"Can I have one of the villas near the beach end?"

Lifting that god damned brow, Sean smirked. "You could have the one next door to mine."

A smile bloomed across my face. There were three waterfront villas at the beach end of the estate, and at the opposite end, looking over the bay, were two more nestled next to Sean's current bungalow. One of those, Sean designed for him and Holly. She didn't know it yet. Sean was making it a wedding present, and then his old bungalow would get renovated for guests.

"Do I want to know what a waterfront villa will cost me?"

"About the same as my place in Maui was going to cost you, but it has three bedrooms and direct access to the beach. And to be honest, the bay is cheaper, quieter, and protected during storms, so it's the better end to live."

That would make the villa a much better investment in the long run, even if I didn't take the job transfer.

"I'm not saying yes to the job yet, but I will take the villa. If I don't move across, I can rent it out as a holiday house."

Sitting back in his seat, Sean assessed me. "Can you afford to buy two places?"

"I'm happy to keep renting Maui for now. The inheritance I got from Margaret will be a sizeable down payment for the Turtle Beach place."

Smirking, Sean took out his phone and sent a message. "Consider the villa next door to me yours."

"I better get going. Karla is coming to help me clean out Margaret's stuff today. I'll see you at the airport in a week."

Standing up, Sean hugged me tightly. "I'm a phone call away if you need me for anything, Jess."

"Thank you. For being such a great friend and boss. I may not be lucky with love, but I've never wanted for the best friends I could have."

Sean wiped away an errant tear from my cheek, smiling down at me. "I think you are very wrong, Jess. I think you have two men who love you so much it scares them, and they've made mistakes due to that fear."

"Love isn't meant to hurt you."

"Come on, Jess. If it doesn't hurt, you're not doing it right. And speaking from experience, losing someone is the best way to recognize just how much they mean to you. As I'm sure your guys can well attest." Lifting his eyes above my head, Sean barely resisted a smirk as he focused on someone.

Looking over my shoulder to see what Sean was grinning at, I spied Ethan out in the hotel lobby with Scout's pram. Frowning, I looked back at Sean. "Did you call him?"

"No. I wouldn't do that to you." Walking with me towards the door, Sean lowered his voice. "Did you want me to hang around?"

"No, you've got a train to catch. I'll see you next week."

"Okay." Squeezing my shoulder, Sean gave Ethan a nod then headed upstairs to help Holly with their bags.

"Morning," Ethan greeted when I stopped by him. "Is everything okay?"

"Yeah, Sean's just trying to lure me back to work for him in Oahu. What are you doing here?"

Ethan's Adam's apple bobbed as he swallowed. "I, ah, didn't mean to interrupt. Greg has errands to run this morning and asked me to watch Scout. He wasn't settling, so I took him for a walk along the foreshore then it started raining. We were closer to here than home, and I thought we could take shelter here if you didn't mind? Just until the rain lets up."

I finally noticed how hard the rain was coming down; an hour ago, the skies were blue, and the sun shone. Thankfully, Ethan had the rain cover over the pram.

"Are you okay, Sir? Are you visiting Miss Butler?" The manager offered Ethan a towel. It was an easy thing to assume, and since I was staying in the penthouse which a rockstar had rented out for me, the staff were extra courteous where I was concerned.

"Yes. The baby is my nephew." I advised the manager while Ethan used the towel to pat himself dry as best as possible. Let the manager assume Ethan was my brother-in-law. "We might grab a coffee, and then I'll give you a lift home on the way to Lou's," I suggested, indicating the dining room.

"If you wanted to go up to your room, we can send your guest's clothes to be dried for him and have the coffees brought up to you," the manager urged, and I understood he didn't want Ethan dripping water all through his dining room.

When I chewed my lip thinking about going somewhere private with Ethan, he handed the towel back to the manager. "It's fine, Jess. But I wouldn't turn down the lift home if that's available?"

Since I was planning on leaving straight after breakfast, I didn't need to go back upstairs. So I nodded, thanked the manager, and went to the valet desk to get the car brought up for me and borrow a car seat for the baby.

"I thought Greg's parents were helping him with Scout?" I asked as we made our way along the foreshore before the road would swing around to the beaches.

"That was my understanding, too," Ethan grumbled. "But then they decided they had to go with Greg to the funeral parlor to help organize Sharnie's funeral, and he should leave the baby with your father or you for the day. Greg knew you were busy today and didn't want to ask for more help than you have already given, so he called me."

"Have they taken care of Scout even once yet?"

"No. They're not interested in their grandchild whatsoever. They don't even call him by name, just 'the baby'. Last night, his father was subtly suggesting that Greg would be better off giving Scout up for adoption and finding a new wife to have a family with."

"What the hell?" I gawked at Ethan, who was grinding his teeth.

"I know. Once Sharnie's funeral is over, he's pissing them off, and we'll sit down and work out the best way forward. Your idea about the nanny may be the way to go."

Pulling up in front of Ethan's apartment building, I parked the car. "I'm here for another week. I'm happy to help out and take care of Scout a few hours each day to give him a break. He's got a lot on his plate. I'm happy to keep Scout with me through Sharnie's funeral if he doesn't want to take him as well."

"You're not going?" When I just stared back at Ethan, his brows drew together over his deep blue eyes, and then he turned away with a sigh. "I'll let him know. Thanks for the lift."

Getting out of the car, I grabbed the pram from the boot and wheeled it over under the awning of the front door for Ethan, so he didn't have to juggle the baby and pram. Then before he could say anything more, I raced back to the car to get out of the rain, gave them a wave, and drove away.

I parked the car behind Margaret's at Dad's place and went inside.

"Dad, I'm here."

"Kitchen," Lou called back.

Coming around the corner, I found Lou standing at the bench in his pajamas, staring at a half-eaten omelet on the counter.

"Dad?"

"I haven't had to make breakfast in thirty-five years. It tasted too good. It wasn't burnt or rubbery, and I hated it and couldn't keep eating."

Stepping forward, I put my hand on Lou's shoulder as he sagged and shook, and then I held my father as he broke. I was wrong. I thought he wouldn't cry in front of me, but I think he was waiting for me to be ready to catch him.

An hour later, Lou was showered and sitting eating the breakfast I had made him.

"Your mother was a terrible cook, but I ate everything she made me and loved her for trying. It wasn't fair on her that your grandmother was a gourmet chef, so I decided that I wouldn't hold her to that level when we married. I got used to it after a while."

Smiling, I sat down with a fresh coffee for us both. "I remember Nanna coming around with ready-made meals while you were at work, so all Margaret had to do was put them in the oven and heat them for you."

Lou frowned. "She did?"

"Six days a week until I was old enough to take over the cooking. After that, Nanna told me she trusted me not to poison you."

Lou looked amazed. "I never knew."

"That's because Margaret still managed to burn everything or not cook it long enough. Do you remember when I was six, you told Margaret dinner was lovely, and she'd finally mastered that lasagne? That was when I started helping her with dinner and setting the timer according to Nanna's instructions."

Staring at me a moment, Lou started chuckling, and then it evolved into full-on laughter. "Margaret never told me. After you moved out, we just started going out for dinner or ordering in regularly. She said it was because she didn't see the point in slaving away in the kitchen for just the two of us."

"Do you remember when she tried to cook jacket potatoes in the microwave and managed to burn them to the point they caught on fire and melted Nanna's microwave-safe container?" I offered with a smile.

"Your grandmother never forgave her for that."

"Melting the container or setting fire to potatoes?"

Chuckling, Lou tipped his head. "Both, probably. Poor Greg. Sharnie had about as much culinary ability as Margaret. You were the one to take after your grandmother. You should have become a chef."

Smiling on the happy memories of learning to cook beside Nanna, I bowed my head. "I've rarely cooked since I left home. It's just not as satisfying when you cook for yourself." When Lou frowned at me, I grinned. "Except breakfast. I still make a full breakfast. Rolled oats, french toast with bacon, juice, and coffee. Just like Nanna made them."

"When I come to visit, you better be cooking for me each morning."

That perked me up. "You're going to come and stay with me?"

"Not straight away, but you're right. I didn't come to visit all these years because of Margaret's fear of flying. That excuse is gone now. I want to see where you live and your life, Jessie. I want to know my daughter and be part of her life."

Should I be hurt that I was only worth the effort now that I was all he had left? No. I knew he'd wanted to visit many times before, and Margaret and her fear prevented it. This year, they'd been planning a trip after Margaret had attended therapy for five years to overcome her fear.

Lou's phone pinged. "Greg's booked Sharnie's funeral. It's the day before you fly out."

"I offered to watch Scout while you are at the funeral."

Blinking at me, Lou took a moment to put his phone down and rub his lips together. "You're not going to attend?"

"Dad, I understand that there was something wrong with her brain, but the amount of hurt Sharnie caused me… I can't forgive it, and I'm not going to go to her funeral and pretend to be sad that she's dead because I'm not sad. Not in the least. What I already knew would have been enough to stop me from feeling sorry for her, but the things I found out during her moment of guilty conscience…."

Taking a deep breath, I calmed myself down before I ended up yelling at someone who didn't deserve it.

"She's the reason Ethan hurt me, Dad. And her last act of hate before she died just killed any chance Dylan and I had of making a go of things. So, no, Dad. I'm not going because the desire to pour petrol all over her coffin, light it up and sing 'Ding Dong the Witch is Dead' is too fucking tempting after everything she did."

Observing me, Lou swallowed hard before inhaling deeply. "Tell me everything, Jessie Girl. Everything she did that you never wanted me to know. You've protected her long enough. Let your hate for her die here with her. Let me shoulder the burden I should have always carried as your father that you refused to let me."

My eyes filled with tears as I met Lou's eyes. He was right. I'd never told them half the things Sharnie did to me. Only what I couldn't hide because it left physical scars.

"You don't want this, Dad. You'll hate your daughter, and Karla should be here soon."

"You protected your sister. Even when you hated her, Jessie, you knew she was sick and didn't want to turn us against her, and you suffered your mother's hate because of it. You gave up your family so the sister you once loved would still have someone. I love you, and you are all I have left. She can't lose us now, and I am sick of losing you because of your subconscious need to protect her. Tell me the truth. I've waited long enough to learn it."

As tears spilled over my lashes, I took a deep breath and spilled my sister's sins. I emptied the pit of hate and hurt that had grown inside of me until Lou got up from his seat, came around and took me in his arms, and told me how sorry he was. How strong, beautiful, and loving I was to have endured all of it and never told my parents the worst.

A superstitious part of my brain wanted to pour salt over the dining room table as if the evil that I spoke needed containing or it would infect this house and all within it. But it already had a long time ago, and while I'd run away, it tainted me and always would. That's how trauma works. Even when you heal it, it stains you, leaving a shadow on your soul that will never know the light again.

As a result of my trauma, I didn't believe that there was the possibility of heaven or hell when I died. This life was hell enough for some. It was Dylan's hell, and it was mine. Dylan only escaped his torment through music, but it lingered in the tainted parts of his soul.

I'd just escaped hell by surviving Sharnie. My sister's death was the end of my torment. And didn't I feel like shit for thinking it, let alone believing it to be the absolute truth?

"It's okay, Jessie Girl. It's okay. She can't hurt you anymore." Pulling back, tears in his eyes, Lou took my hand and led me across the room to the wall where he took a photo of Sharnie before walking me out to the backyard and the barbecue.

Smashing the frame, Lou put the picture on the grill. "My mother did this with me when my grandfather died. You never knew him, but he was a horrible man who tormented and beat his children. I often wondered if Sharnie got his genes." Lou handed me the fire starter. "Your grandmother told me this helped her burn him out of her life. Fire cleanses, in a way." Lou kissed my head and put his mouth to my ear, keeping his arm around my shoulders to comfort or support me. "Do it."

Swallowing the sorrow in my throat, I admit there was pure satisfaction when I clicked the lighter and set it against the photo paper.

As the picture curled up and charred, the ink blistering, Karla arrived, stepped up beside me, and put her arm around me as we watched Sharnie become ashes.

Then Karla threw her arms in the air and yelled, "Ding dong, the witch is dead!" at the top of her lungs. I loved her so much for saying it for me.

CHAPTER NINETEEN

"HERE YOU GO," GREG HANDED ME A GLASS OF WINE.

Closing the book I was reading, I accepted the drink and sat up straighter. "How'd everything go?"

"Good. The service was lovely, and the wake was both eye-opening and painful." Taking the seat next to me, Greg lifted his beer to his lips, taking a long pull. Sipping my wine, I didn't interrupt his thoughts.

"I never really spent much time with Sharnie's friends. Ethan was the only one who ever came over and hung out here. Having just spent several hours meeting and listening to the people your sister hung out with, I'm left wondering if she truly had any friends."

"I can't speak to the last decade, but up until she went batshit crazy, she did."

Chuckling, Greg considered me, then took my hand. "Lou said you grieved your sister years ago, but you still had a private farewell for Sharnie. Would you tell me the worst thing she did to you? Not everything, just the worst."

"She was your wife, and everything I've seen tells me you cared for her, so out of respect, I think what you already know is enough." Then, glancing around, I realized Greg was alone. "Where are your parents?"

"Flying back to Melbourne."

"Already? I thought they were going to help you with Scout?"

Slouching in his seat, Greg fidgeted with his beer bottle. "I told them to go. They never wanted kids and were shit parents, always too busy with their work and lives to bother with their accidental heir. I wrongfully thought that now they've retired, they may want to try being grandparents. They made it clear that would interrupt their lifestyle, so I told them to go."

"Are you going to manage?"

"Lou has offered to help out, and I've already called a nanny agency to interview live-in nannies. It's not an expense I can afford. Pilots don't earn as much as everyone seems to think, but Lou pointed out Scout's inheritance could be used. I'm hoping to have it all sorted out before going back to work in two weeks."

Taking a minute, Greg then sat up to lean on his knees, staring at the floor a moment longer before he turned his head to meet my eyes. "Jess, I know about Ethan."

Frowning, I cocked my head. "Know what about him?"

"I know Sharnie is the reason he broke your heart."

"Does Ethan know?"

"Yes, I told him when Sharnie confessed it to me."

Gaping at Greg a moment, I lifted the wine glass and swallowed the rest.

"I should go." I had dropped the car back that afternoon, so I could just get on the train in the morning, but Greg's place was only a thirty-minute walk from the hotel.

Greg stopped me from getting up with a restraining hand on my wrist. "Before Sharnie died, she sent me a message. I didn't know what was happening. I got off the plane, and there was this long admission from her. I thought she must have been drunk, but then I got Lou's voicemail about the accident and Sharnie's emotional state, and it made more sense. Jess, the majority of the message was about you. How guilty she felt. She confessed everything. I think you should read it."

Wait. What? Sharnie's last message to Greg was about me?

"I'm not sure I want to," I admitted. "It was enough to get the in-person confession."

"So, she did tell you?"

Exhaling, I slumped against the couch. "Yes. More than I needed to know. Sharnie told me she deliberately fed Ethan's paranoia with lies. Then right before she died, she told me why she tried to kill Dylan's sister. I made the mistake of telling Dylan because we've never known what set her off that night, and now Dylan can't even look at me." Huffing, I shook my head, put the empty wine glass down, and snatched Greg's beer from his hand. "Sharnie has destroyed every relationship I've ever had. She killed any chance of Dylan and I making a go of it from her death bed. It only took her eighteen years, but at least she didn't get the satisfaction of knowing she finally succeeded." Putting the bottle's rim to my lips, I took a drink.

Taking out his phone, Greg opened his messages.

"I'm a horrible person—the worst. I pretended to be somebody so you would want me because you made the mistake of mentioning your father is a movie producer the night we first met, and I talked about my dream of being an actress. Marrying you was just a step to getting what I wanted. Scout was an accident. I never wanted kids, and now I'm stuck with one. I somehow have the life my sister wanted, and I can't help feeling it's some trick of Karma. Like

Karma knew I hated this idea and forced it upon me to punish me for stealing Jessie's ideal future."

Tears streaked down my face as Greg read out the message. Sharnie's admission of only marrying him to get to his father seemed to have no impact on him, and I didn't know how he could have received those words from his wife and stood at her funeral as if she'd loved him.

"I wish I could say that stealing Jessie's dream was the worst act I committed, that the affair I had was one of mutual passion and that I loved Ben, or that I was sorry that I caused my niece's death. But, at the time, they were all collateral damage in my hatred towards my sister. I convinced myself she deserved everything she suffered because she got between me and what I wanted. She stole the future I wanted in my head, and so I took joy in taking her dream from her."

Stealing a glance my way, Greg took his beer back and swallowed a mouthful before handing it back again.

"When you told me the change of your roster to include Hawaii as your main run was because Ethan was in love with Jessie, I saw an opportunity to hurt Jessie again, and I took it. Please tell Ethan I lied. Jessie never cheated on Ben. Dylan and Jess were only friends back then. They were in love, everyone knew that, but they never acted on it as far as I know. Make sure he knows I lied. I can't undo all the harm I caused Jessie in my obsession with tormenting her, but destroying her relationship with Ethan might be reversible if they both know I caused it."

When Greg considered me, I lifted the beer and took two consecutive mouthfuls.

"There is something else. I don't want this baby. I won't be a good mother, and you know that. I hoped having you as the father would void the bad mother I might be, but we can't leave Scout to our parents if anything happens to us. Yours are selfish, and mine don't need that responsibility. Jessie would be a great mother. I stole that opportunity from her, but she was so happy about becoming a mum. So if anything happens to me, you should give Scout to Jessie to raise. She'll let you be part of his life, but we know you can't be a single parent. Jessie would be able to do it. I know because she's always done everything she put her mind and heart into doing.

"You never know, if Ethan and Jessie can forgive each other for the lies I told, maybe she won't have to do it alone. Either way, if something happens to me, our son will need Jessie. She'll come home for him. She's selfless like that. She gave up her home and family so that she wouldn't have to hurt our parents by telling them how evil I am, so I know she'd do this for her nephew.

"Forgive me for the lies and manipulations. If you choose to leave me, I won't blame you. You deserve someone who loves you. I won't fight you for custody either because Scout deserves a better mother. Hell, if Ethan and Jessie can't make it work, maybe you could marry her. That's just the kind of thing I deserve to happen to me. If I don't get to see you again, take care, Greg. You were the only guy I could stand long enough to come close to loving."

Closing his phone, Greg put it on the table.

"How did you even stand at her funeral today and not spit on her grave?" I asked, astounded by how calmly he read that message.

"Being able to cope well under pressure is part of my job requirements, but despite how she felt about me, I did love her when I married her, Jess. I wouldn't have otherwise."

Handing Greg back his beer, I sighed.

After taking a few mouthfuls, he turned to face me and handed me back the bottle.

"I can't give up my job, Jess. It's all I know and the only way I can provide for Scout. I would love you to share custody with me. To be there for him when I can't be, but I won't ask that of you. You have your life, and I'm not going to be like everyone else and demand you sacrifice what you've built for me."

Swallowing the last of the beer, I set the bottle on the coffee table. "Good, because I won't. I've lost enough for that bitch. I'm not letting her take my career and life from me too. I'm sorry if that sounds selfish to you or leaves you in a bad place, but Sharnie was wrong. I'm not selfless anymore. She taught me not to be."

Turning to face Greg, I smiled and took his hand. "I have enjoyed helping out with Scout this last week. I would love to be part of his life if you want, but I'm not moving back here to do it." Leaning in, I kissed Greg's cheek. "I'm sorry she didn't love you, Greg. She's right, and you deserve to find a woman who will."

Getting up, I grabbed my bag. "Let's catch up when you have another layover. I want to stay a part of your life if it doesn't hurt you to be my friend."

Rising out of his seat, Greg gave me a sad smile. "As I said last year when we met. It was a shame you and Sharnie hated each other. I would have liked you as a sister. I guess she's not here to prevent that anymore."

Pulling me into a hug, Greg held me tight. "I'm not the only one who deserves to be loved, Jess. For what it's worth, Ethan still loves you."

Groaning, I pulled back. "I think I've had enough drama this last twelve months. My poor heart needs time to heal before I consider jumping back in the surf for another try of catching the perfect wave."

Smirking, Greg started walking me to the door. "I'll text you when I'm back at work and organize lunch or something. Dinner seems too much like a date." Taking out a slip of paper, I handed it to Greg and continued to the door as he read it. "Who's Lizzy?"

"She's one of my best friends. She was at Margaret's funeral. Her husband left her at the beginning of the year because he couldn't have kids. She only works locally and has experience looking after her brother's young kids, so she offered to help out with Scout until you can find a nanny."

"Thanks, Jess."

Walking to the hire car on the curb, I gave Greg a wave, then dropped into the driver's seat. After buckling the belt, I dropped my head against the headrest and breathed. There was no reason to feel guilty for choosing my happiness above family responsibilities. Was there?

"Friggin' Sharnie!" I snapped.

That message she sent Greg felt like another one of her manipulations. And if it was, it nearly worked. It took more effort than I cared to acknowledge not to cave and consider staying. I'd avoided the guilt for the last two weeks by not considering it an option because it shouldn't have been. My life wasn't here anymore, and I didn't want to give up what I had in Hawaii.

Blowing out a long breath, I muttered "I owe her nothing" to myself. Then, sitting straight, I started the car and drove back to the hotel. I needed another drink or three, so I wouldn't stay up all night overthinking things.

It only took one drink in the cocktail lounge before my mind turned to Sharnie's confession. Picking up my phone, I hesitated only a minute before pressing call.

"Jess?" Ethan's voice came down the line. "It's late. Is everything alright?"

"I'm leaving tomorrow morning. Have a drink with me and tell me why you broke my heart. I'm ready to listen."

CHAPTER TWENTY

THE SOUND OF A TOILET FLUSHING DISTURBED THE DREAM OF ETHAN fucking me as a man possessed all over the hotel room. Opening my eyes to see sunlight streaming in through the window, I checked the clock and was relieved to see it was still early. That's when the night of drinking slapped me up the back, front, and sides of the head, and I dropped my head back to the pillow with a groan.

What was it about turning thirty that prevented your body from coping with a night of excess like it did at twenty-nine?

A knock at the door reminded me I'd ordered room service before bed.

"I'll get it," Ethan announced.

"Thank you."

Forcing myself to sit up and face the morning, I assessed how I felt. My body ached, but it was a pleasurable pain, unlike my head. Frowning, I lifted the sheet to cover my naked chest and then peered through narrow slits at the room. It was a mess, just like the bed.

Pillows and clothes were strewn all over the floor, picture frames hung askew on the walls, and the bed itself looked like it had endured a week's worth of frantic fucking.

"Okay, breakfast for the hungover one." Ethan carried a tray into the room and placed it at my feet. Lifting the lid off one plate stacked high with toast, Ethan jammed a slice between his teeth and then moved around the room to collect clothing items.

Ethan took bites of his toast as he moved, then dropped the towel around his waist with no shame of his nudity—not that he had anything to be ashamed about—and started yanking on his jeans.

"I have to go home and get my uniform and layover bag. I'll pick you up in two hours," Ethan explained.

"Pick me up?" I asked, chewing my bite of buttered toast slowly.

My question made Ethan smirk. "Check your phone." Then, pulling his shirt over his head, Ethan watched me collect my phone from the side table and wake the screen to find a text message, a voicemail, and a newly saved video.

"Did we sleep together?"

Laughing, Ethan dropped on the mattress and started yanking on his shoes.

"There wasn't much sleeping, Jess. Which was irresponsible of me considering the flight today, so I'll need to sleep in the car on the way to the airport."

"We had sex?"

Ethan froze and looked at me. "Shit, you don't remember?"

What I thought was a dream echoed through my mind, and I bit my lip as heat rushed through my body.

"I think I do; I just thought it was a dream," I countered, putting my hand to my forehead and cringing at my voice. "To be fair, my head is a bit wishy-washy this morning."

Turning back around, Ethan finished getting dressed. "Do you remember what we talked about at least?"

Nodding my head only slightly, I summarized what I told Ethan last night.

"Knowing Sharnie's part changed nothing. You still allowed her to get in your head, and you were the one person who should never have believed a thing that woman said about me," I answered quietly.

Huffing, Ethan stood and came back to my side of the bed. Grabbing another slice of toast, he held it out to me, then collected another for himself.

"The wrap-up is that we talked and decided to be friends, then you asked me to come upstairs to keep talking when they closed the bar. Talking about Margaret started you crying, which led to lots of fucking. I've got to go. I'll meet you downstairs in two hours, and don't forget to check your phone." Shoving his wallet in his pocket and grabbing his keys, Ethan left.

Chewing the piece of toast, I opened the message to see it was from Ethan telling me I'd agreed to catch a ride with him to the airport today and to be ready by nine. It was sent before the bar downstairs shut. The voicemail was also from Ethan.

"Jess, this is for you in the morning because you are pretty tipsy, and I don't want you to hate me. We've just had sex, and I've come to the bathroom to call you because it was fucking incredible. I've missed you so god-damn much, but I know you're not ready to let me back into your life as more than a friend.

"You told me Dylan ended things with you before he left, and I hope to God that you got that right because I was wrong that night I ended things with you, Jess. You would hate yourself for cheating on someone, especially when you love them as you do him. Please don't deny it; it was there in your eyes when you told me everything Sharnie said to you at the hospital and the fallout from it.

"When I leave this bathroom, I will crawl back between your legs and spend the rest of the night helping you forget all the hurt: mine, Sharnie's, and Dylan's. You deserve everything good, Jess, and one day, I hope you let me be part of your life in a more permanent way again. I promise I'll never hurt you like that again if you give me another chance, but I also acknowledge now is not the time for that.

"So, before you freak out about letting me comfort you, I want you to know that's all tonight was for both of us. What we did was born of shared grief and heartache. The loss of your mother and each other. You trusted me to take care of you, and fuck, it makes me feel even worse that I didn't trust you more when you handed me your heart. But I know what I lost that day, Jess, and I will never risk losing it again if you give me another chance."

There was a knock on the door in the background and my voice telling Ethan I needed the bathroom.

"Just a sec," Ethan answered, then sighed. "I guess what I'm trying to say is, I love you, Jess. But I know tonight isn't forgiveness, so don't freak out in the morning, okay? We were just two people grieving together in the most intimate of ways. Oh, and in answer to the question you asked me. I meant what I said, Jess. It's a yes. I'm on board whenever you're ready, even if you don't want me as part of the package. I'll see you in the morning."

The call disconnected, and I swiped away the tears streaming silently down my face. Then, swallowing all the emotions swelling up inside, I choke them back down and clear my throat a few times to get myself under control.

Sniffling, I opened the saved video and pressed play.

"What the hell…?"

The video shows the top of Ethan's head between my naked thighs, and the sound effects coming through the phone leave no doubt about what he is doing down there. The sounds made me bite my lip so hard it's not funny.

"God, I love your mouth on me," I moan in the video.

Ethan looks up at me with a lazy smile and glazed eyes. Then, he stares right at the camera and darts his tongue to flick my clit, making me buck beneath him.

"What are you doing, Jess?"

"Sorry, I couldn't resist."

The camera swings to the side as I remember I was going to turn it off, but Ethan grabbed my wrist and brought it back to focus on him.

"I don't mind as long as it's just for you, okay?"

"I'll password protect it."

Grinning with mischief, Ethan winked at the camera and then dived back in to feast.

Shutting off the video before it went any further and gripping it to my chest as my body heated, I panted a little at the effect it had on me.

"Damn," I whispered. I'd forgotten how naughty Ethan could be when it came to sex.

Clearing my throat for a different reason now, I put the phone aside and gobbled down my breakfast. I was downstairs, checked out, and waiting by the door when a car pulled up, and Ethan opened the back door for me to see him in the back seat.

"Jess."

The driver got out and put my bag in the boot, and then I slid in beside Ethan.

"How'd you score the driver?"

"I'm paying for it. Greg normally drives, and I pay for petrol, but I'll just get a driver while he's on leave. Allows me to sleep for the drive. Better than the train."

"Can't argue with that. What time is your flight?" I asked, settling into the seat.

"An hour before yours."

Shoving a small travel pillow between the headrest and frame, Ethan slouched down, spread his legs wide, and got comfy.

"Ethan?"

"Yeah, Jess?" He sighed, eyes closed and already settling into sleep.

"Thanks for the message and the video."

Smirking with his eyes still closed, Ethan patted his lap. "Feel free to sleep on me again."

Smiling, I ducked from under the shoulder belt and curled up on the back seat, using Ethan's thigh for a pillow. His hand ran up my covered arm to rest on my shoulder, and as I started to drift off to sleep, I thought about the other part of my dream this morning.

"I want a little girl with your hair and eyes."

Ethan's fingers squeezed my shoulder, but the soothing classical music the driver was playing stole me away to sleep quickly after.

Three hours later, the driver roused us to let us know we were approaching the airport. Sitting, I spent a few minutes fixing up my appearance, so did Ethan, just in time for the driver to pull into the set down zone.

Getting out of the car, I stretched while the driver got our bags out for us, then it was just Ethan and me walking into the terminal.

"Thank you again for the lift," I yawned as we walked through the sliding doors.

"It made sense, Jess," Ethan smiled then looked at the board. "Which flight are you?"

Taking out my ticket, I looked at my flight code then looked at the board. "I'm over there." I gestured towards the counter where the airline checked luggage and issued boarding passes. "I guess I'll see you in a few weeks?"

Ethan's eyebrow went up as we headed for the line, especially when I stepped into the priority boarding, but he didn't mention that I was flying business class.

"A few weeks?"

"Greg and I are going to catch up on his next layover. I assume you'll tag along?"

Ethan's face softened. "You'd be okay with that?"

"We're friends, aren't we?"

Lips twitching in a restrained smile, Ethan leaned down and kissed my cheek. "Always. Are you going to the lounge to wait for your flight?"

"Yes, I'll meet Sean and Holly there."

"Well, maybe I'll see you there. If not, take care, Jess."

The way Ethan's eyes glimmered made long forgotten butterflies alight in my stomach.

No. No. Stop that shit. Love hiatus is in effect, remember?

"You too, Ethan."

As I stepped forward to the counter, Ethan walked away. He got fast-tracked through customs, so there was no point in him waiting to walk through with me. Plus, I promised to pick Mayla up some stuff duty-free.

"Superstitious?" the lady at the counter asked when I handed over my passport and ticket.

Confused by the question, I frowned. "Sorry?"

She gestured at Ethan's retreating form. "Some couples are superstitious about taking the same flight as their husbands in case something happens, then one of them is still there for the kids."

"Oh, no, this is just the flight my boss booked me on," I dismissed that notion, then glanced across in time to see Ethan take a final look back before he disappeared. Our eyes stayed connected for a moment, and I kept looking long after the door slid shut behind him.

"How long have you been married?" the lady at the counter asked.

"We're not. We broke up just under a year ago. We are just friends now."

The lady's eyebrows hit her hairline. "Oh!" But her smile seemed to get bigger instead of diminishing. Her eyes glittered at me, suggesting she thought I was playing things down or in serious denial. I didn't try to justify things further. She could think whatever she liked. The only people who needed to know the truth were Ethan and me.

Forty-five minutes later, I'd passed through customs and done my duty-free shopping, making my way to the lounge with my regulatory sausage roll and caramel milkshake in hand when my phone buzzed.

<Sean>: Just got to the airport. I will meet you in the lounge.

<Jessie Girl>: I'm already here.

<Sean>: Okay. We'll see you soon. Holly asked if you needed a pie and sausage roll?

<Jessie Girl>: I already got mine.

<Sean>: Of course you have. Honestly, Holly must think she's dealing with an amateur. See you soon.

After checking into the lounge, I searched for a seat but instead found Ethan. Smiling, I went to the table he occupied and waited until he lifted his eyes from his tablet device.

"Can I join you? Sean and Holly are probably thirty minutes behind me."

"Of course. What have you got there?" Ethan asked as he sat up straight and put his tablet aside.

"International travel tradition. I always get a sausage roll, pie, and caramel milkshake before leaving the country. I never know when I'll get one again."

"I guess it is irregular for you to come home as much as you have been," Ethan considered.

"Until last year, I hadn't been back to Australia in ten years. Three times in one year seems a little excessive after so long."

"I noticed you still travel on an Australian passport. Do you have a work visa for the US?"

"I did. I won the green card lottery in my third year in Hawaii. So now I use my Australian passport to arrive and leave Oz and my American passport to arrive and leave Hawaii. Saves the long queue in customs that way."

"Pity you don't have a European passport for the same reason," Ethan joked.

"I do."

His face dropped. "What?"

"Lou was born in England, remember? I've had dual citizenship since I was born."

Still frowning, Ethan considered. "So, your kids would be entitled to three different passports at birth?"

Waggling my hand back and forth, I scrunched my face. "Australian, instant yes. American, yes, especially if I have them there. But, of course, British is two generations removed, so they'd have to apply for it."

"Huh, and you barely travel?"

"I travel for conferences, and I've gone on the occasional holiday. I just rarely came here."

Ethan considered me. "Maybe you won't have such an aversion to coming home anymore."

Giving him a sad smile, I set the rest of my food aside, no longer hungry. "Maybe. Do you want the rest of this?"

Ethan eyed the pie and sausage roll. "Remember what I told you about pilots needing to stay healthy?"

"Yeah."

"That's not healthy."

"Neither is that coffee you are drinking."

"It's healthy for my passengers after I stayed up all night worshipping a goddess," Ethan chuckled.

My cheeks heated, but we fell into casual talk until Sean and Holly arrived, and then Ethan asked them all about their wedding before going to get ready for his flight.

Neither Holly nor Sean said anything about Ethan being there, for which I was grateful. Our focus turned to what happened when we got off the plane, which for me was a night at my old place with Mayla before flying back to Maui.

Twenty-four hours after landing in Hawaii, I was standing in the kitchen of my place in Maui, tears caressing my cheeks. Dylan was everywhere, both in memory and physically. No one had come to pack up his stuff and leave the key like promised.

"This was why we always used hotel rooms before," I growled.

Pulling out my phone, I dialed Sean.

"Jess, ready to accept my offer?" His voice was gentle despite the upbeat tone.

"I hate that you know me this well."

There was the sound of a car door closing and Sean walking across gravel before a knock sounded at my door.

Frowning, I turned and opened it. Sympathetic ocean blue eyes met mine as Sean tucked his phone away, a couple of packing boxes by his leg.

"No, you don't."

Engulfing me in his arms, Sean held me to his chest, my tears making his shirt wet.

"What are you doing here?" I murmured against his shoulder.

"We sailed over this morning to help you pack. Kilikina isn't hacking the manager's position. She wants to go back to dealing with events, so I need you back at Turtle Bay pronto."

"What about Maui?"

"Nalani is doing a great job. It seems you train your assistant managers well, Jess. Either way, I need you on Oahu, and I think you need to be there too. So we're going to pack you up today. Your team is having a farewell dinner for you tonight, then we'll come back and watch a movie, and tomorrow, we'll sail you home."

Stepping back, Sean gazed down at me like a big brother.

"No more running away."

CHAPTER TWENTY-ONE

"WHAT ARE YOUR PLANS TODAY?" I ASKED, PUTTING A CUP OF COFFEE in front of Lou as he finished his breakfast. Then I took my seat at the outdoor breakfast table I had set up to look over the beach. Not that I didn't eat nearly every meal out here this summer. While I loved my places at Maui and Ewa Beach, my new home at Turtle Bay was heaven.

The outside had a Hamptons-style facade, with a similar floorplan to my place in Ewa Beach but a bit more spacious. The main bedroom was twice as big as my old place and looked over the beach, which only encouraged my habit of sleeping with the balcony doors open.

Even though Sean's new place was a wedding present for Holly, they moved in once it was ready so Sean could rent the bungalow out and make money from it during peak season.

Summer was also the reason for my long work hours right now, but Sean agreed to cover for my day off tomorrow.

That was part of our agreement of me taking over the Cassidy permanently. Whenever I wanted to take a vacation, Sean would cover me. He felt it would work out better that way and give him peace of mind, especially with how much leave he owed me.

So my best friend was now my neighbor; and since Holly and I got along like sisters, it had led to many dinners and movie nights together, though I made sure to limit the movie nights so that I wasn't intruding on their couple time.

A month after I moved in, Lou came to visit. We were nineteen days into his three-week stay and my last day of work for the week. I took tomorrow off to spend the entire day with Lou before he flew out the following day.

"Ethan and Greg flew in last night. They are driving up this morning, and then we're playing golf with Sean for the day."

It made me smile. "I think Sean has liked having you here. He's had an excuse to play golf at all his favorite courses."

"It's been good getting to know him. Sean's a good man. Holly is a fortunate woman."

"Yes, she is. Though, she's lovely as well. They suit each other very well."

"Yes, they do. Sean invited me back for the wedding in three months."

Sean had already told me he would extend an invitation to Lou. "Well, my guest room is yours anytime you want to visit, Dad. It's been great having you here."

Smiling at me, Lou took a sip of his coffee. After a moment, I looked back over at him.

"You know, if you wanted to live here, I'd love that too. I know your life is back home, but I have loved having you here."

"You don't think you'd get sick of your old man crowding your space?"

It made me chuckle. "Please, you've seen the hours I keep. By the time I get home, you're only a few hours from going to sleep, and I'm out surfing before you get up in the morning. But we do get to have breakfast and dinner together regularly, and you'd have the house to yourself all day long, of which you'd spend half of it swinging a club out on the green."

My place wasn't near the golf course, but it was only a short buggy ride to the tee-off for Lou.

Smiling out at the water, Lou sighed. "It would be a lovely place to retire, but Jessie Girl, there is a matter of visas and what-have-you."

"I'm sure we could work it out."

"I'll think about it." Then, finishing his coffee, Lou observed me. "Are you feeling better? You looked a bit pale over breakfast."

"I'm fine. It's probably just the heat and being dehydrated or something."

"You're not pregnant, are you?" Lou asked. "I know Dylan didn't want kids, but accidents happen."

My laughter filled the space around us. "God, Dad. Dylan had a vasectomy before he turned twenty-one. So there is no chance he got me pregnant."

Lou's eyes rounded. "Oh. I didn't know. Still, I hope you took precautions considering his lifestyle."

Still smiling, I shook my head. "He has regular testing, so I know he's clean. But, yes, we always practiced safe sex. God, I was even using condoms with Ben. Ethan's the only one I've ever thrown caution to the wind with, and that was only that one…" my words fell away with my smile as the jagged memories of the night of Sharnie's funeral flashed in my head.

Not realizing where my mind went, Lou reached across the table and took my hand.

"I'm sorry, Jessie Girl. I didn't mean to dredge up painful memories."

Shaking my head, I recovered my smile and put my other hand over my father's.

"It's okay. I'm okay, Dad." Rising out of my seat, I kissed Lou's cheek. "I have to get up to work. Enjoy the day with the guys."

"Would you join us for dinner tonight?" Lou asked, following me into the kitchen. "Sean and Holly will be there too."

Rinsing my cup, I put it in the dishwasher. "That sounds lovely. Just message me where and the time. I'll make sure to finish on time tonight."

Satisfied with the smile on Lou's face, I grabbed my work bag and headed out for the path which went behind Sean and Holly's new place, past Sean's old bungalow and up to the resort, updating my fitness app and tracker with the morning yoga and surf as I walked. My eyes darted over the menstrual health section of the app for reassurance. Then, exhaling a long breath, I put my phone away and got my head into work mode, leaving everything else behind.

Later that evening, I sat between Holly and Lou in the hotel restaurant, eating our dinner. We had waited until the main dinner rush was over, which allowed me to work a little longer and meant the night was a bit cooler, which was good because the humidity was killing me this week.

"Are you sure you don't want a drink, Jess?" Greg asked as they ordered another round.

"I'm sure. I've let myself get a bit dehydrated this week, so I'll grab another coconut water and cranberry juice, please."

"Ooh, me too." Holly put her hand up.

The waiter cleared the table and left, and the talk returned to the cost of living in Hawaii, which was significantly higher than in Australia when it came to food. It was nothing new to me, so Holly and I started having a separate conversation about the wedding and Trisha's plans for her hens' party.

"If we get through the night without male strippers turning up, I will consider it tame by Trisha's standards," Holly laughed as someone leaned over my shoulder on the other side, placed my drink on the table.

I turned my head and waited as our server dropped his mouth to my ear.

"Kilikina is having a freakout in the kitchen, and Chef asked if you'd come to mediate, please?"

"Is it about the Hanson wedding tomorrow?" When the waiter nodded, I sighed and gave him a nod in return. He moved on to set down everyone else's drinks. "I have to go deal with an issue. Excuse me for a moment."

Making my way to the kitchen, I found Hanley standing with her arms across her chest while Kilikina pointed at her tablet aggressively.

"What's going on?"

"The bride's mother changed the menu for tomorrow, and the bride only just found out, and Kina here thinks I can magic ingredients out of my ass to fix it," Hanley answered, then turned her back and went back to handling her domain, having palmed the problem off to me.

Sighing, I went to Kilikina. "Okay, give me the de—"

Before I could finish what I was saying, one of the kitchen hands took a pot from the burner and poured the liquid over a steak. The steam hit me, and my dinner tried to make a reappearance.

"Jess? Are you okay?" Hanley frowned, coming towards me as I covered my mouth and hurried to the sink, but nothing came up.

Turning on the tap, I scooped up some water then splashed my face before putting my now-cold hand to the back of my neck.

"Yeah, I just..." Grabbing a glass from the tray for the kitchen staff, I filled it with water from the cooler and skulled it. Then, feeling much better, I put the dirty glass in the wash rack and turned back to my two managers staring at me wide-eyed. "I'm fine. I'm a little dehydrated from all the exercise I've been doing and the humidity this week. Kina, let's take this outside, and we can come back to Hanley with a solution."

Stepping out, Kilikina and I went over the menu changes. Then, we determined what we could fix by overnighting stuff and what would need to remain because there was no overnighting stuff from the mainland without passing that expense onto the bride to argue it out with her mother.

By the time I got back to the table, Sean and Holly were gone, and just Greg, Ethan, and Lou remained.

"Sorry about that. Weddings cause no end of drama."

"By the sounds of it, Sean's will be no different," Greg chuckled.

"Yes. Holly's parents have certain expectations and are not happy that Holly has told them to show up or not, but keep their opinions to themselves," I smirked. "Considering they just wanted a quiet beach wedding, they've convinced me of the benefits of ducking down the courthouse and saving the money for a better honeymoon."

As I took a drink, I got caught up in how Ethan was watching me. I felt like the delicious candy on the other side of the shop window that he wasn't allowed to consume.

Taking out my phone, I kept it out of sight and typed out a message.

<Jess>: Take a walk with me tonight? We need to talk.

Putting my phone away, I tuned back into the conversation, catching Ethan checking his phone and his eyes coming to me before giving me a slight nod and sliding the phone away.

"Before we turned in for the night, Mayla suggested we could stay with her until I found a place. Since we've been staying with Mayla on layovers, I've gotten to know the area. I like the location and proximity to the airport, and it's not that far from you and Jess. Sean said Scout can go to the daycare at either his Ko Olina resort or here, depending on who he's staying with, and he'd give me the staff discount as family."

I knew that Mayla and Greg kept in contact after Ethan broke up with me, but I didn't know that Greg and Ethan stayed there whenever they were in town.

"When did that start?" I asked, frowning across the table.

Greg hesitated. "Mayla didn't tell you?"

"I knew you were still going out dancing and drinking, but I didn't know you were staying in my place."

The guys gave each other an uneasy look, then Greg licked his lips. "About three months after you and E broke up. E kept going back there, trying to convince Mayla to tell him where you were. When that didn't work, he asked me to try and get your location. Mayla wouldn't betray you, but we had fun together, and she offered for us to stay there instead of a hotel after a few nights out. I didn't like her getting a taxi home alone, so it worked out better for her safety," Greg answered, careful about his words.

Frowning, I sat forward. "Have you been having an affair with her?"

Greg's eyes widened, darting them to my father and back to me.

"They're not fucking," Ethan answered. "They're just friends, but—" Ethan eyed Greg, causing Greg to bow his head and look guilty. "Probably only because being more wasn't possible until now."

Lou cleared his throat, avoiding looking at Greg, probably struggling with how to feel about his son-in-law developing feelings for another woman while still married to his pregnant daughter. Still, Greg didn't do anything wrong.

"Jessie Girl, I think you missed the important part of what Greg was just saying." Lou sat back, and suddenly all six eyes were on me.

"I'm moving to Oahu, Jess," Greg clarified. "I want you and your dad to be part of Scout's life, you're the only family we have, and I don't want him growing up without it, so I asked work to make Oahu my home base, and they've agreed to the transfer from the start of next month. Would you still be willing to help with Scout, Jess? To take him occasionally while I'm working?"

Shit! Fuck! As if I didn't have enough to get my head around tonight.

Blinking at Greg, I glanced at Ethan and Lou, then Greg again.

"But what about Dad? If you are here, he will rarely get to see Scout."

Greg's eyes went to Lou, making my eyes go to him. He was grinning.

"I guess that makes it my turn to tell you my news," Lou started, and I think my breathing stopped, panic filling me that maybe Lou's medical appointment in Sydney over Christmas last year wasn't as innocent as he made out.

"I've enjoyed my time here over the last three weeks, Jessie Girl. I've enjoyed having you in my life again, and I don't want to go home to an empty home full of memories that will make me miss you all. I have a pretty sizeable nest egg that would allow me to retire and live my life comfortably.

"Sean's connected me with an engineering firm here, and they've offered to sponsor me for a visa and have me do consultancy work for them since my expertise is building on sand and around water."

My mouth fell open. "You're moving in with me?"

Inhaling deeply, Lou took my hand. "I love you, Jessie Girl, and I know what you were saying this morning about your hours, but you are a grown woman and have lived on your own for quite some time. I've moved around you as a guest, but living there would probably cause ripples for both of us after a while. So, this morning, before Ethan and Greg arrived, Sean showed me the designs and locations for stage two of the estate here. I picked a place along the fairway and paid the deposit. It will be three more months before I can move into my house, but it will take a few weeks to get things tied up at home and move here, so if you are still happy for me to stay with you until my place is ready, then that would be great. In the end, I'll be close enough to be part of your life, but not too close to be annoying or underfoot.

"And I'll be helping to take care of Scout because you shouldn't be taking that on full-time. You like to get out and have adventures on the weekend, so I'll take Scout every weekend Greg is working and alternate weekends when he is home because Greg deserves time out too."

Forcing my mouth closed, I smiled between my father and Greg and jerked towards Lou to hug him.

"This is the best news. It will be so good to have you both here and be part of Scout's life." Sitting straight, I wiped the tear from Lou's eye before it could spill, then wiped my own.

As I looked back to Greg, my gaze caught on Ethan, who was sitting there watching, nursing his beer, focusing entirely on me again.

"But, that leaves Ethan with no one. You're both his family back home, and Greg, you are best mates, and you always fly together. That's not fair to separate you two."

Ethan's mouth twitched as Greg laughed and punched his mate on the arm.

"Do you want to tell her, or should I?" Before Ethan could draw breath, Greg turned a beaming smile on me. "E's coming too, Jess. We're all moving here for you because you're our family, and you've been alone long enough."

Now I wasn't sure how to react. "Will you be finding your own place too?"

Shaking his head, Ethan put his beer back on the table.

"Right now, I'm leaving my options open. I'll be staying with Greg and Mayla initially, and then Lou's offered for me to stay with him once he's in his place until I find where I want to be. Considering I usually play golf with your father on my days off, that seems the better choice for the short term. But I don't want to make a choice yet." Ethan's gaze seemed to heat me from the very core of my being. "I'd like to see what doors get blown open by this wind of change."

Swallowing hard over my physical reaction to Ethan's words and look, I licked my lips and nodded.

"That sounds like a good approach. Of course, you don't want to make any hasty decisions."

"Nothing hasty about it, Jess. We've been throwing this idea around since you left. We're all committed to being a family. If you'll have us?"

Jesus, help me! I swear my tongue was swollen in my mouth from the passion in Ethan's eyes as he spoke those words, holding me prisoner as he picked up his beer and took another mouthful.

Forcing myself to swallow and clearing my throat, I grinned at Greg and Lou.

"Are you all sure about this? It's a big move."

"We're sure," Greg answered. "Nothing is holding us home anymore, Jess. Just promise not to run off to another island or country again because chasing you around the globe will get expensive."

Blushing, I cringed as my smile melted away. "I can't promise, but I think Sean will find a way to prevent me from disappearing on you. He seems to be able to predict my reactions now and plan ahead."

A hand slipped over mine, and when I looked up, Lou watched me with a look that felt like my heartbreak was echoing through him. Then he turned his attention to the men he looked at like sons.

"Well, we're going to have a drink and sort out some of the details for the move. Did you want to join us, or do you want to go home and relax after a long week of work?"

"Actually, Jess and I need to talk before we finalize this move, so why don't I walk her home, and I'll meet you guys at the bar," Ethan suggested.

He wasn't trying to hide that we needed to discuss how this move would affect us. They probably wanted him to make sure I was okay having him around first anyway because as much as we'd agreed to be friends and called a truce for the funerals, we based that friendship on him living there and me living here. Oahu as an island was about the size of Sydney in Australia. It's big, but it's not big enough when you have friends and family in common.

"Jessie?" Lou checked quietly. When I nodded, he got up and kissed my forehead. "I love you."

After Greg and Lou had headed for the bar, Ethan finished his beer and stood up, and I followed. We walked in silence while leaving the resort, and it wasn't until we were on the path towards the bungalows that Ethan started speaking.

"Are you okay with this, Jess? Don't lie to save my feelings. If having me around will hurt you, I'll find a place near Greg and try to stay out of your way. I don't want to take Sharnie's place as your tormentor."

As we reached the crossroads that headed to the rocks, the bungalows, or the bay beach, I indicated we follow the path to the latter.

"It's a nice night for a walk on the beach."

Not giving Ethan the chance to say no, I walked ahead on that path, and then once I hit the sand, I took my work shoes off and waited for Ethan to be ready to keep walking.

"I need to know how you feel about this, Jess. I need you to be straight with me," Ethan tried again.

Looking ahead, I licked my lips. "Well, in theory, I have no issue with you moving here or being around my dad, Ethan. You've been part of his family for a long time now, and I know he looks to you and Greg like his own sons. I think you both love him like a father too. I wouldn't take any more children from Lou. He's buried one already."

Ethan shoved his hand in his pockets. "But?"

"Are you capable of just being friends with me, Ethan, or are you hoping to use this to embed yourself in my life in the hopes it can rekindle the flames you doused?"

"If friendship is all you are comfortable with, that's all I'll ask. But I'm not going to stand here and lie that I'm over you. I still love you, Jess, and if being here somehow could open your heart to me again, I would be here for that too. I promise not to hurt you again if that ends up happening because I know the pain of losing you now, and that is not something I would ever inflict on myself twice, and I certainly never want to see you breaking like I did that night ever again. What I did to you, to us..." Ethan shook his head and let the words fall away.

"If you were willing to give me a second chance—and I know you are not ready for that yet—but if at some stage you are, I think we need to take it slow again. So, yes, I'm capable of just being your friend, Jess, but I'm not going to deny I'm hopeful that one day our friendship might shift and bloom into love again."

Accepting that response, I kept my eyes forward. Greg and Lou needed Ethan. He was their family more than I was. Yes, my father loved me, but he knew I could survive without them. I'd done it for a long time already.

Yet, I craved having a close family again, having my dad here, and being a part of my nephew's life. Hell, I liked Greg and felt the same brotherly connection with him that I did Sean, and I loved Ethan. Denying that would be pointless, but I wasn't ready to trust him again. I needed time to mend my heart and piece it all back together.

My eyes filled with tears as I considered how to word my next question.

"What we talked about before I left Newcastle. The message you left on the phone. Are you sure you could do that? Are you sure we could just be friends, that you wouldn't use those circumstances to barge into my life, that you could not hate me if all I wanted were to be friends?"

We walked several meters in silence, and I knew Ethan was thinking his answer over before he gave it. Then, finally, his steps slowed, and Ethan stopped walking and turned to face me.

"I'm not going to say it wouldn't be hard. That I will ever get over you, but if that's what you want, it's still more than I could ask for, Jess. I'm the one who destroyed us. You gave me your heart, and I obliterated it, and I'm sure as shit not over-dramatizing that because I saw it happen.

"I watched the woman I loved break, witnessed the light in your eyes dying like you were bleeding to death in front of me, and the way you looked walking away from me, it's haunted me since. Even you offering me friendship is more than I deserve, so if I can do something to see the light come back to your eyes, I'll do it, Jess."

"You told me…"

"That was before you, Jess. Those opinions, they were before I realized you were my everything. Before I walked into that hospital, and you fell into my arms and cried in them. Before I watched Scout put into your arms and wondered what it would have been like if that was our child you were holding. Before Dylan stood beside you at your mother's funeral and all I could think was he was standing in my spot. The place I gave up and regretted ever since. Every limitation I placed on us, on our relationship, crumpled to dust when I ruined us."

Taking a breath, Ethan collected my hand from my side and held it in his.

"You changed my mind about everything, Jess. When you are ready, if you gift me a second chance, I will give you everything you deserve and desire. I would marry you tomorrow, and if you want a brood of kids, I will happily exhaust myself getting you pregnant time and time again. And I will be a good dad, Jess. I didn't have one, but my grandfather raised me well, and I also have your dad as a role model. But, most importantly, I will be your friend, no matter how much or how little you allow me to be in your life, because I love you, Jess, and that hasn't diminished one bit since I lost you. So, if loving you as a friend is all I'm allowed, even at arm's length, it's what I'll do."

Tears streaming down my face, I closed my eyes and focused on breathing. Ten breaths, and I opened them again, staring into the deep blue windows to Ethan's soul. I didn't doubt he meant every word he spoke. The passion of his words reflected in the expression of his face and the depth of his gaze. Blowing out a breath, I nodded my head.

"Good, because I'm pregnant, and it's yours."

CHAPTER TWENTY-TWO

PUTTING THE BAG DOWN BY THE DOOR, I RANG THE DOORBELL.

"Are you looking forward to seeing your Dada?" I asked. The gorgeous boy in my arms answered with a big smile and blowing bubbles. "Of course you are."

The door swung open, and Ethan stood looking out at me, a smile hesitating on his face, taking me back to when I'd broken the news to him.

———

"Fuck, Jess!"

Ethan took my face in his hands, the space between his brows scrunching.

"Are you sure?"

"That I'm pregnant, pretty certain. That it's yours? Well, it was that or immaculate conception, and since we didn't take precautions and I haven't had a period since Margaret's funeral, I feel pretty confident in both statements."

Stepping back, Ethan scrubbed his hand through his hair.

"Shit! Are you okay? I know we talked about me being your baby daddy if you decided to go it alone, but neither of us intended it to happen that night."

His concern made me chuckle. "Didn't we? I mean, you knew I wasn't taking contraception, and you didn't wrap it up any of the four—"

"Six," Ethan corrected.

"—times that we did it that night."

Interlacing his fingers behind his head, Ethan lifted his face to the sky.

"I'm pretty sure I was more focused on making you come so hard and loud that you forgot all the reasons you had to cry."

Choking on a laugh, I bit my lip. "Well, you certainly did that. I forgot all reasoning. Obviously, you did too."

Dropping his arms to his sides, Ethan gazed back at me, swallowed hard, and averted his eyes to the ocean.

"This conversation. You were telling me that you're going it alone. You don't want me."

Stepping forward with a sigh, I touched Ethan's cheek to bring his eyes back to me.

"I love you, but I'm not able to take the risk and jump straight back into this. Let's start with friendship and see where it leads for us."

"And the baby? We never got around to discussing my role in my child's life. Or if I'm going to have a role other than the sperm donor?" Ethan's fingers tickled across my lower belly gently.

"God, Ethan! How big a bitch do you think I am? We can co-parent, you can walk away, or we can find something else in between. We can sit down and nut out details once you know what you want; just don't hope it will lead to anything between us other than what you have now."

———

Ethan takes me in with a sweep of his eyes the same way he did that night. "Hey, we weren't expecting you for another hour."

"I know, but Mayla asked me to come a bit earlier so we could go snorkeling together before she goes shopping with Greg."

"Oh." Ethan's barely-there smile vanished. "I was hoping to catch a lift home with you. I'm playing golf with Lou this weekend."

Sick of standing still, Scout started fussing in my arms.

"Ah, do you think I could come in?" I asked Ethan.

Blinking his eyes wide open, Ethan automatically reached for Scout, taking him from me as he stepped back. "Shit, yes, Jess. Sorry. Do you need to sit down? Put your feet up? A cup of tea?"

"I'm not even three months along. Chill out!" I whispered harshly, following Ethan inside. Whispering, because Ethan was the only person I'd told about the baby, and I'd made him promise to keep it under wraps until I reached the second trimester in two weeks.

A month after telling Ethan, I was still trying to work out how I would tell Lou or Sean that I got knocked up on a one-night stand with my ex. Lou only flew back to live with me four days ago and brought Scout with him, so I'd just had my first few days of parenting a baby and going to work.

Luckily, the morning sickness had settled by the time Lou came back, and I only had random bouts now after hot showers or around certain foods. I'd started avoiding the kitchen at work to avoid any more triggers.

Gritting his teeth, Ethan looked around, then focused on Scout.

"Greg is showering. He shouldn't be too long. Mayla just finished her morning yoga when we got home from surfing," Ethan explained, but in a voice meant to make Scout think he was talking to him. "I can't wait until you can come out surfing with us, little buddy."

Rolling my eyes at Ethan because that baby was years away from getting on a board, I set Scout's bags on the floor next to the lounge.

"In answer to your request for a lift, if you can wait a couple of hours, I'm happy for you to catch a ride. I'll pick you up on the way back through, around ten?"

Ethan's eyes came back to me. "Thank you. I'll call Lou and tell him."

"OMG, is that Scout?!" Mayla gasped as she came down the stairs, rushing to Ethan to gush over the three-month-old baby. Mayla came from a big family, and as one was of the eldest, she'd grown up with babies. So she probably knew how to take care of Scout better than everyone currently in his life. "Can I have a hold?"

Smirking, Ethan handed Scout over, and Mayla automatically started bouncing as she walked around the lounge and spoke to him.

"While Mayla has Scout, do you want to grab all his stuff out of my car?" Dad brought his playpen, pram, and bassinet over with him so that we'd have furniture for him when he got here.

"I thought Mayla and Greg were buying Scout's furniture today?" Ethan asked as we got to my car. When I moved back to Oahu, I'd taken my car back, but Mayla had a new little run about already.

"Just the big stuff. We only had this temporarily, but I'll go shopping tomorrow to fix up the nursery for my place." Placing a hand over my still-flat lower abdomen, I smiled. "If things go well, Scout will be moving into his next stage by the time this one comes along, and the oopsie can use the same furniture."

Glancing around to make sure no one was watching, Ethan came closer, his fingers gently caressing my hand covering our child.

"Oopsie? Way to give it an unwanted complex straight out of the gate."

"What do you want me to call it? Daddy forgot to wrap it up?" I lifted a brow in challenge.

Smirking, Ethan's free hand came up to my face and fluttered along my jaw, betraying an intimacy that he was forbidden. And damn if I didn't want him to kiss me and remind me how he got me knocked up in the first place.

Ethan stared into my eyes for a moment, his smirk growing, then he dropped his eyes to my hand, still cupping my womb.

"How about Joy?"

"You think it's a girl?"

"I would like you to get your dream. But I chose joy because what happened between us was an outpouring of grief, and I'd like to think the outcome of our emotional vent will give you much joy. The way you talked about Scout that night and how it rekindled the desire to be a mother—it's the same for me, Jess. Holding Scout, helping Greg care for him, I remembered that kids were on my list before Natalie betrayed me, and I want that. I was surprised but ecstatic when you hit me up to be your baby daddy that night just on the chance of being a dad. But I don't think I'd want this with anyone else, Jess. Clucky or no, had any other woman offered for me to fertilize her eggs—"

"That is not how I said it."

Ethan chuckled. "I'm paraphrasing. But had any other woman asked, it would have been a hard no because I couldn't imagine having kids with anyone but you, Jess. You are not just a lover. You took the time to get to know me and be my friend, and I know we can make this work even if we are not in a relationship."

Returning his eyes to mine, Ethan lowered his face towards mine, hovering an inch above me as his thumb wiped away a tear I hadn't even felt escape.

"I know you can't trust me with your heart, but I promise you, I will love our little bundle of joy unconditionally, and I will keep loving

544

you in whatever capacity I'm allowed. But as your friend and the father of that precious cargo, I will fuss and care for you, no matter how much that annoys you."

Ethan drifted closer, and just as his lips came close to mine, the door opened, and he swept to the side of me before pulling back and taking a step away, collecting the bassinet and frame.

"Sorry, I got caught up in how you were looking at me," Ethan apologized before walking back inside.

"Hey, morning," Greg greeted, pulling me into a hug. "Thanks for doing this, Jess." Pulling back, he took me in, and the space between his eyebrows creased, then he peered after Ethan. "What did E do this time?"

"What?" I widened my eyes, only to feel a few more tears shake loose. "Oh, no, it wasn't—" Taking a breath, I smiled and shook my head. "We talked about Scout and how he reminded us we wanted to be parents ourselves once. That we'd sort of forgotten it after getting our hearts broken."

Greg frowned harder. "You and Ethan discussed having kids when you were together?"

Yeah, he knew his friend well, judging by the disbelief on Greg's face.

"No! Noooo!" I quickly corrected him. "When I was younger and when Ethan was married to Natalie."

Clearing his face, Greg made a silent 'oh' as he collected the portable playpen from the trunk and swung the bag over his shoulder before removing the pram.

"Did he never mention kids before?" I asked, closing the car back up.

"Back then, yes, but we were both young, and it was a futuristic thing. Not something we were rushing out to do. But E hasn't mentioned kids since. Hell, he told me I was crazy getting married and having a baby now because we'd never been so in-demand with women. Men in their thirties are a hot commodity, you know. Old enough to be experienced and considerate of a woman in bed, but still young enough to get hard, have a good recovery, and financially more secure."

"While I'd love to take your ego down a notch, I can't argue with any of those points," I sighed.

"You're missing E's D, aren't you?" Greg snickered.

"And on that note. Mayla!" I called out her name, laughing when Greg's shoulder bumped me on his way back in, chuckling his heart out as he did.

"What'd I miss?" Mayla asked, coming out ready to go.

"Your new boyfriend giving me shit."

"He's not… we're not," Mayla stuttered.

"Save it. I know you two are mooning for each other." Then, sinking into the driver's seat, I started the engine.

"It's too soon, isn't it?" Mayla asked, hurrying to join me in the car. "His wife only died three months ago."

"There is no minimum or maximum for grieving, Mayla. Everyone processes their grief differently and along with varying timelines. Some people are ready to date again weeks after their spouse dies, others may never date again, and it doesn't mean those who moved on quickly loved less either. The need for human connection is a personal thing. Some crave it more than others."

Mayla rubbed her lips together, fidgeting with her shorts.

"I think the more sensible reason to take things slow is that he's a newly single dad," I offered quietly. "It's not just about the two of you."

Looking over at me, Mayla smiled quietly. "You're talking to the chick with six younger siblings to three different dads. That, I get."

Mayla glanced down at my chest and then cleared her throat while waiting for a heartbeat. "So, your rockstar knocked you up?" When I bit my lip, she laughed. "Seen my mum through six pregnancies, remember? It's either you got implants, or you're pregnant. Since you already had a nice rack, I'm thinking the cause of your boobs swelling above your bikini top like that is pregnancy hormones."

Licking my lip and biting it again, I glanced at Mayla.

"I'm pregnant, but it's not Dylan's. We broke up before he went on tour."

"Explains some of the photos I've seen of him up to his usual antics," Mayla shrugged off, then narrowed her eyes at me. "So, it was Ethan?"

My eyes opened wide as I swung to look at her, having to concentrate not to oversteer and kill us both. "Why him?"

"Because you've never been a fast mover. So for you to do the horizontal mambo so quickly, it would need to be a familiar dance partner, and the only one of those you had access to was the pilot who made you get all gooey-eyed while he was holding a baby just a few minutes ago. Probably because you pictured him holding the one he inseminated you with recently."

Swallowing hard, I focused on the road.

"So, it was Ethan?"

"Yes."

"One for old time's sake that led to a mistake? Because I've been there, done that, on…" Mayla pretended to count on her fingers, and after using them all and both thumbs, she shrugged. "Numerous occasions."

"I asked him for a baby. Told him I wasn't going to wait for love anymore. I've been in love, and that hasn't worked out, but I want to be a mother, and I'd like the father to be someone I cared for, even if all we could be was friends."

"And being the good friend he is, he dropped his pants and said, 'No need for a turkey baster. This one comes with orgasms galore'," Mayla imitated Ethan poorly, but it had me laughing until tears fell from my eyes.

"Fuck, Mayla. I'm trying to drive."

"Yeah, but I'm right."

Grinning her way, I met her eyes for a moment. "Yeah, you are. I lost count."

The admission had Mayla laughing like a hyena, but she didn't admonish me or stress me about being a single mum. Instead, she looked my way and beamed at me once she calmed down.

"You're going to be a great mom, Jess. And if I were the betting kind, I'd put good money on you and Ethan finding out how to love each other again."

"The loving each other isn't the problem. It's the trust."

"Are you going to let him help raise his kid?"

Frowning, I pulled into Kahe Point Beach Park. "Yes, of course."

"Then you'll trust him again. Take it from me, trusting a man with your kids is harder than giving them your heart."

"Good dads can be bad husbands, just like good husbands can be bad fathers."

"I know. My dad was an asshole to my mum, cheating on her and shit, but he's great to me. I don't think I would have got this far without him." Mayla's lips pulled up on the side and cracked her door. "Come on, let's get in the water and stop being mushy. Jeez, pregnant women are always so emotional!"

Laughing at Mayla's shit-stirring, I got out and grabbed my snorkeling bag, and locked the car before following her towards Kahe Point.

———

"Have you watched the video you made in Newcastle since getting home?"

Struggling to restrain a grin, I let only the side of my mouth lift as I drove the Veterans Memorial Freeway north. "Yes."

"How many times?" Ethan smirked in the passenger seat.

Nearly every time I'd gotten myself off over the last two-and-a-bit months. Ethan performing the lip, sip, suck was erotic as hell, even on video. "Once or twice."

Licking his bottom lip, Ethan side-eyed me. "Any chance you'll send it to me?"

"You want to watch yourself growl me out?"

Stifling a laugh, Ethan turned his head to look at me. "I want to listen to the noises you make while I choke one out."

"Oh." Biting my lip, I thought about it. I mean, it was his face in the video. Unless someone knew what I sounded like coming, the video wasn't a threat to me. "I'll send it to you if you send me a video of your dick while you rub one out with the sound on."

Lifting his eyebrow at me in the Sean Cassidy style, Ethan considered me for a long moment.

"What? I like to watch!" I told him defensively.

His lips twitched. "I'll go you one better. You can film me masturbating. Tonight. But you have to strip down to your underwear and sit with your legs spread while I do and let me come all over you."

"Ethan!" I groaned. That would be so hot. "This is not within the boundary of just being friends."

"I don't know many friends who ask for videos of each other getting off or for their friend to knock them up."

Pulling up at the lights that would put us on the Kamehameha Highway, I chewed my lip continuously. At the same time, I considered the cost versus watching Ethan stroke his dick and having a lifelong memorial that could certainly soothe the lonely nights.

As the lights turned green, I accelerated with the traffic and made a counteroffer.

"I'll agree to the underwear, but I want to lick your cum off your body afterward."

"Jesus, Jess!" Ethan gripped the growing bulge in his pants, pushed his feet into the floor, and adjusted the way he was sitting. "You have a fucking deal, but we might need to do it as soon as we get back. I'll tell your dad we're running late."

Laughing, I checked the oncoming traffic and indicated before swerving off the road and into the car park for the Dole Plantation.

"What the fuck, Jess?" Ethan stared at me with wide eyes, holding onto the car door.

"You'll have to wait for tonight, but I need my pineapple soft serve to hold out until then."

Ethan started roaring with laughter as I climbed out of the car and headed for the building. He knew Dole Whip was my sexual frustration food. Of course, it was also my PMS food, but there was no doubt why I needed it right now.

Catching up to me on the stairs, Ethan shoved his hands in his pockets, a broad grin across his face as we walked across the veranda. Neither of us spoke another word about what we had just agreed to for the rest of the drive.

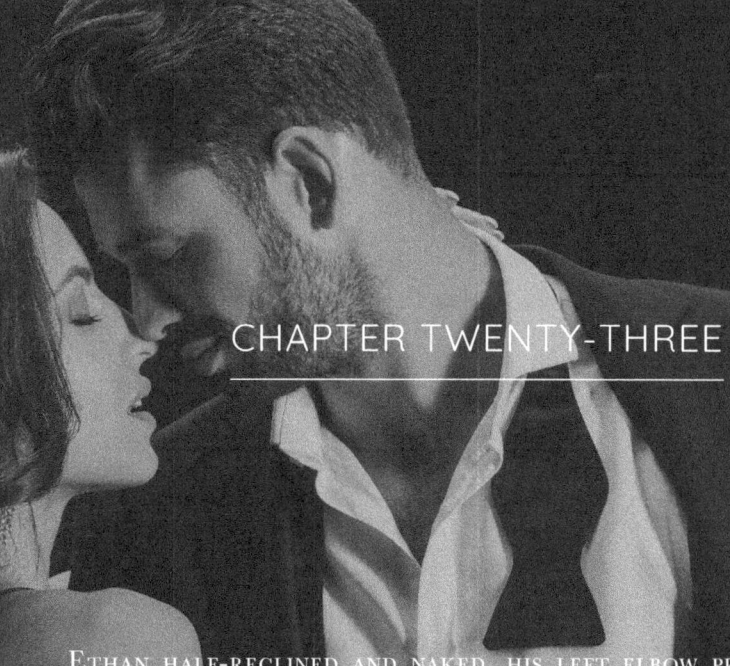

CHAPTER TWENTY-THREE

ETHAN HALF-RECLINED AND NAKED, HIS LEFT ELBOW PROPPING HIM, crunching his defined abs while his right stroked his long, thick cock will be embedded in my memory forever. Not only because I have it on video, but because it's the hottest thing I've ever seen in my life.

The male fantasy porn that saturates the market with aggressive deep throating, anal, and asphyxiation portrayed as normal instead of the kinks they are, didn't do anything for me. But Ethan masturbating was hot as fuck.

The camera view didn't include his neck or face. I was keeping it anonymous for safety's sake, but everything below was there for me to drool over. Off-camera, Ethan's eyes were focused on me sitting on the sofa opposite the bed, in the sexiest lingerie I owned, my bottom lip caught between my teeth and panties drenched.

Not that the delicate mesh lingerie covered anything. It was entirely see-through, and the look on Ethan's face when I undressed in his hotel room for him, subtly giving him a show to help get his motor revved, was priceless. If we'd still been a couple, Ethan would probably have had his throbbing cock buried in me already while he fucked me hard and fast to punish me for teasing him like that.

"God, damn, Je—" Ethan groaned and dropped his head back, cutting himself off before breaking the agreement. No faces, no names. It was okay to be naughty as long as safe practices were in play.

The neediness of my sex was too much. Sliding my hand up my thigh, I kept the phone pointed at Ethan's rhythmic movements while I started rubbing over my clit in circles. When Ethan lifted his head again, his eyes zeroed in on my hand, and his breath rushed out.

"That's it, baby. Rub that pussy for me. I can see how wet you are; you want my cock, don't you? You want me inside you, stretching you open, and fucking you until you come all over me."

Ethan's hand was pumping hard and fast now, my fingers matching his rhythm. Keeping my eyes locked with his, I had to bite my lip to keep my moans within, causing a metallic taste to coat my tongue as my body tightened, ready to launch over the precipice to nirvana.

"That's it. Come for me, baby. I want to feel your pussy squeeze my cock and milk it dry. I want to fill you with cum, then lick your pussy clean until you come over my tongue."

Throwing my head back, I opened my mouth but held my voice as my body arched at the sudden pleasure taking me over. Wave after wave of ecstasy hit me, and in the background, Ethan cursed and grunted.

Looking up just in time, I licked my bloody lip as Ethan squeezed his shaft and spurted his cum all over his abdomen. Ethan dropped back to lie on the bed, his legs hanging over the end. Ethan cursed softly, covering his face with his left hand, his chest and abdomen heaving with the exertion.

Turning off the video, I set the phone aside, made my way to the bed, and followed through on the last part of our bargain. Once Ethan's stomach was clean, I licked the tip of his softening cock before I remembered he wasn't mine anymore.

"Shit, sorry." I pulled back as it twitched, and Ethan growled.

His left hand grabbed the back of my head to stop me from escaping, his eyes the deepest blue I'd seen them in a long time.

"Don't stop and don't apologize. If I didn't want your mouth on me, I would have stopped you before now. But, if it involves you and my dick, I want you to assume I'm on board because I can't even imagine a scenario where I won't be."

Grinning, I licked along the length once.

"You say that now, but just you wait another four months when I resemble a whale with swollen ankles and feet."

Fisting my hair, Ethan urged me to look up and meet his eyes.

"Jess, do you think I love you because of how you look? That's not how love works. The first night we met, my attraction was for your beauty, but it had shifted to something more intense because of the chemistry between us even by the end of that first night. I've been in love with you for a long time now, and I know your beauty goes beyond the superficial."

Staring up at Ethan's eyes, I struggled to hold back tears, both of regret for what we lost between us and the yearning deep within me to forgive him for everything and demand he be mine again. But I couldn't do that. Not yet.

Dropping a kiss on Ethan's hip to thank him for those beautiful words, I pulled away, crossed the room, and dressed.

"So, I was thinking, could we have dinner tomorrow night before I head south? You, me, Sean, and Holly?"

Pulling my summer dress over my head, I turned to face Ethan. He'd pulled his boxers on, but nothing else.

"You want to double date with Sean?"

"I never said it was a date." Ethan smirked. "I liked Sean, but my accusations also damaged any chance of us being friends, and things are awkward when he joins Lou and me for a round of golf. He's always civil, but he gets defensive if you come up in conversation. Not that I blame him. Lou explained he's like an older brother and protective of you, so I understand why he doesn't want the guy who broke your heart hearing that you work long hours and barely eat enough to be conscious."

"My father does not say that?" I gaped at him.

"He worries, Jess. You know that."

Sighing, I roll my eyes. "So, you think having dinner together will show Sean we're friends again, and he doesn't have to give you the evil eye anymore?"

"I'd like to try and smooth things over with him since I'm going to be around a lot more now."

Standing there blinking at Ethan for a moment, I looked away and swallowed my tongue as I slipped my ballet flats into place.

"I'll ask when I get home."

"Thank you."

Grabbing up my phone and keys, I started for the door but stopped, fidgeting with the keyring rather than looking at Ethan.

"Are you home on Saturday two weeks from now?"

"I think so. Why?"

Licking my lips, I caught the edge of my lip between my teeth but then winced and let it go before I caused it to bleed again.

"I'm having my first prenatal scan. So we'll be able to see our baby if you want to come with me?"

"I'd love to," Ethan answered without hesitation, taking a step forward and capturing my hand. "Thank you."

Lifting my gaze to meet his eyes, I smiled a little, nervous about how this would work between us but happy that he wanted to be part of his child's life.

"I'll message you Sean's answer."

Opening the door, I slipped out into the hall and made my way downstairs using the staff-only access areas, hoping to avoid some of the front-of-house staff who were more prone to gossip.

I was nearing the path to the bungalows when I heard my name called. Turning, I spotted Sean sitting at the outdoor bar, waving me over. Smiling, I headed his way.

"Hey, what are you doing up here on your lonesome?" I asked, taking a seat.

"Holly's on a work call." Lifting a brow at Sean, I waited. I loved using his weapon back on him. "It's Benjamin Henderson."

"So? She chose you."

Fidgeting with his empty glass of beer, Sean scrunched his nose. "True, but he's an ass, and the way he talks to Holly as if they are still something just rubs me the wrong way. For our relationship and her work, it's just easier to come and have a beer. Plus, Holly usually feels guilty about me having to leave my home while she talks to the jackass and likes to make it up to me when I come back." Smirking, Sean gave me a wink, then looked me over. "Where are you coming from?"

"Ethan's here."

"I know. Didn't know you two were hanging out again?"

"No, we're not. Just—"

"Drinks or are you eating like old times?" one of the bar staff offered as they collected Sean's empty glass.

Sean smirked and lifted a brow at me.

"I could go for a burger."

"Two burgers and beers it is," Sean decided.

"No beer for me. Just a virgin mojito, please."

Sean lifted his brow and sat back, crossing his arms all casual-like.

"You were saying?"

Taking a breath, I wished having a beer right now was an option.

"Trying to make the friend thing work. He's here. Quite often, when I do the handover, he's there; and of course, he'll be moving in with Lou once his place is ready, so we need to be able to be around each other and interact."

"Can you?"

Nodding my head, I gave Sean a quiet smile. "He's a decent guy. Besides what went down between us, I like talking to him. We get each other. Ethan suggested we might all have dinner tomorrow. You, me, Holly, and him. He will be around a lot more and doesn't want things to be awkward between you when you are both hanging out with Lou."

Tilting his head, Sean considered me. "Okay."

"Okay?"

"I think it's a great idea. Maybe if I can see that you are comfortable around him, I can stop worrying about how his presence is impacting you. I'll book us a table for six tomorrow night."

Frowning, I considered Sean. "That seemed way too easy."

Sean just lifted his brown and continued to smile at me.

"What?"

"You're just friends? That's it? There's not something more happening between you?"

"What do you mean?"

Leaning forward, Sean put his elbows on the table and gave me the sort of eye contact reserved for an inquisition. "I mean, the way he comforted you at your mother's wake was pretty big, Jess. Grief, along with another romantic disappointment, can stir up many emotions, and sometimes people act on those feelings. But then they feel guilty about it, which leads to all sorts of tripping over themselves."

Swallowing, I glanced to the bar and wished they'd hurry up with the drink order.

Reaching over the table, Sean took my hand to stop me from fidgeting with my bracelet.

"I've known you a long time, Jess. You have never turned down a drink off duty, but I've not seen you touch a drop of alcohol in the last month. So, I'm guessing you got plastered sometime after Margaret's funeral and woke up in Ethan's bed, and now you're avoiding alcohol because you blame it for giving into your feelings. And now you are trying to convince yourself that you and Ethan can just be friends because you feel guilty."

"You might be on the right track," I choked, grateful that our drinks arrived at that moment, and I could suck in a big mouthful and pretend it was alcoholic.

"Oh, thank God, because Holly guessed that you were pregnant."

Freezing like a deer in headlights, I stared at Sean with wide eyes. Sean started laughing.

"I know. But it was the only other reason for your sudden aversion to alcohol." Sean chuckled, but his smile fell away as I averted my eyes and sat back, chewing my lip. "Jess?"

Staring off towards the beach, I closed my eyes, took a deep breath, and turned back to meet Sean's intense look—surprised that he didn't seem worried or panicked, so he was doing better than me.

"The night before we came home, I told Ethan I'm not ready to forgive or trust him again. But, I also told him I'm sick of waiting for the right guy, so I want a baby, and I asked him to be the father, and Ethan surprised me by agreeing to knock me up whenever I was ready." Lifting a shoulder, I tried to play the next part off as no big deal. "It just so happened that we gave it a good try before I came home, and now I'm pregnant."

The side of Sean's mouth lifted and dropped back down as Sean tried hard to keep his expression under control.

"And where does that leave you and Ethan?"

"Currently, as friends. I've got a lot happening in my life. Lou moving here, taking on a partial parenting role for Scout, and I'm still a broken wreck inside. Dylan helped me heal a little, but it was more like covering up the mess with a sheet and pretending not to see the Ethan-shaped lump underneath.

"The talk we had that night, and the subsequent message he left me explaining his feelings, helped a lot more, but I think I only have the energy to deal with what is already in front of me, and that sheet is just going to have to hang there until I'm ready to pull it off."

"Or the wind blows it off and forces you to confront the fact you two are still messily in love with each other," Sean offered, smirking over the lip of his beer at me. "Are you raising this kid together?"

Rubbing my hand against my flat tummy, I gave Sean a quiet smile. "We've agreed to co-parent. Ethan's helping with Scout as well, so it's been like training for us."

That made Sean laugh. "Fuck, you both got clucky over the psycho's baby and decided to make your own."

Reaching forward, I shoved Sean's shoulder. "Shh! Only you, Mayla, and Ethan know right now."

Shaking his head, Sean kept laughing. "Plus, Holly and your father."

"Lou knows?"

"He made a sly comment today after asking me if Holly and I would try for a family straight away. He said it's good when cousins are the same age and grow up together. Holly has been hinting you are up the duff for a few weeks, but Lou's comment today affirmed her suspicions." Sean shook his head. "When Holly first said 'up the duff', I had to look it up. That's an Aussie term if ever I heard one."

"So, are you?" I asked with a smile of my own.

"Am I what?"

"Planning to get in the family way straight away?"

Laughing loudly, Sean shook his head. "Like I told Holly, I'm going to keep practicing as often as I can, and it's entirely up to her when she opens the door on her end."

It made me grin and shake my head as our meals appeared. Sean ordered another to go for Holly, then picked up his burger.

"So, I guess we better discuss maternity leave."

CHAPTER TWENTY-FOUR

"Please welcome Mr. and Mrs. Cassidy!"

Party poppers exploded as Trisha and I walked into the reception ahead of Sean and Holly, hand in hand. Applause for the happy couple deafening us.

We stopped behind our seats and waited for Holly and Sean to get themselves situated to get to the bridal table. While the wedding ceremony took place on the beach, the reception was in an open-air event tent set up in the corner of the resort pool area. The pool bar was servicing the reception, with the restaurant catering.

Everyone took their seats, and immediately the first course was served.

"So far, so good," Trisha murmured to the rest of us at the bridal table. "I'm so glad Sammy and Roger made it, but oh my God! I preferred her pregnant and unable to drink. She can put away more alcohol than a seasoned alcoholic for someone so tiny. How is she even upright today, let alone smiling and laughing?"

"First time in months I've been glad to have an excuse not to drink." I chuckled, handing Sean a couple of paracetamol.

Accepting my offering, Sean gave me a wink before filling his bride's water glass and slipping the pills into her hand under the table.

"I have to say. Holly spent so much time warning me about you, Trisha, that I was unprepared for Sammy last night. I'm glad we got attending staff backfilled, because I don't think Mayla and Nalani would have survived work today. They thought they were hardcore and could keep up with Sammy."

"Hell, I thought I was hardcore until last night with Sammy," Trisha mourned. "Now I'm suffering imposter syndrome."

Chuckling, I glanced across the tent, deep blue eyes capturing mine for a moment before turning back to the other members of their table. Ethan sat on one side of my father, Greg on the other, with Scout in the pram beside him.

Greg and Scout were staying in the nursery tonight. It was all decked out now as Scout's bedroom, but I'd kept all the colors neutral so that it would suit Joy no matter if it were a boy or girl.

After I told Sean about Joy, I had to tell Lou. It was close enough to three months, and it wasn't fair to keep it from him. Lou didn't ask who the father was, but I think he knew straight away.

Since then, Ethan had confirmed to Greg and Lou the baby was his, so that cat was out of the bag. Lou wasn't upset, and over the last few weeks, I'd caught him watching me and smiling while I cooked breakfast for us, or we danced around the kitchen cooking dinner together at night.

"Practicing?" Sammy asked as she took a seat beside me. I was feeding Scout while Greg and Mayla danced. With the meal, speeches, and main entertainment finished, all that was left was the dancing.

"My nephew," I answered with a smile. "He lives with me when his dad is flying."

"And which one is the dad? The tall, dark, broody one who can't take his eyes off you?" Sammy indicated to the area where Sean, Lou, Ethan, and Senator Cassidy stood talking.

"That's the dad's best friend, Ethan. Greg was married to my sister."

"Holly told me about the accident. My condolences."

Giving Sammy a sad smile, I didn't say anything. Losing Margaret was a complex emotion that was still fresh.

"So, Holly tells me you are quite the trainer. Have you thought about focusing your skills and outsourcing them?"

I started laughing. "Sean warned me you'd try and poach me for this new venture you have happening with Holly."

"He should have told Holly not to brag about how good you are if he wanted to keep you."

Shaking my head, I sat Scout up to burp him. "Sean's not just my boss. He's my best friend, and I'm loyal to him. So if you want me to consult for you, you need to get him on board, not me."

Giving me a big smile, Sammy took a sip of her drink. How she could stomach more alcohol was beyond me.

"Noted. Now, back to the tall, dark, and broody. Is that your man?"

Glancing toward Ethan, I smiled when I caught him watching me again. The look of adoration on his face as he watched me with Scout was now familiar since he'd seen the image of our child at the ultrasound two weeks ago. Ethan gave me a wink before he leaned sideways and murmured something to Sean, bringing his ocean blue gaze to Sammy and narrowing with suspicion.

"Ethan's the father of my child," I answered, suddenly unwilling to deny there was anything between us.

Sammy's grin widened. "Thought so."

A shadow fell over us as Ethan came to my side. "Sorry, ladies. Sean told me I have to rescue Jess before Sammy convinces you to go work for her husband."

Sammy and I both started laughing, Scout joining in on my lap.

"Can I have this dance, Jess?"

"Here, I'll take the baby," Sammy offered, helping me hand Scout over. "If I have him in my arms while I talk Sean into sharing you, he's less likely to murder me."

Taking Ethan's hand, I let him lead me onto the open-air dance floor just outside the tent and pull me into his arms.

"You are the sexiest best man I've ever seen." Ethan chuckled as he held me close, his hand slipping precariously close to my derriere as we moved. "You're all boob in that dress."

"To be fair, they have swelled since my last fitting."

The beautiful coral satin with peach overlay dresses Holly chose for Trisha and me were perfect beach wedding attire, but were a little too tight around the bust. Mine because of the sudden increase in my boobs, and Trisha's because there was only so far the seamstress could let the dress out to fit her natural assets.

Firming his hold on me, Ethan smiled down at me. "I wasn't complaining. The view is excellent from where I'm standing."

Slapping his upper arm, I chuckled. "Stop it." When Ethan just smirked at me, but his focus came back to my eyes, I sighed. "Has Lou said anything about Joy and us?"

"Just that we are grown-ass adults and capable of deciding for ourselves what will work best for his grandchild and us. As long as we are happy, he doesn't need to know anything else."

"Huh, he said the same thing to me."

Ethan smirked. "Your father loves you, Jess. He'll stand by you no matter what."

"I know." I smiled up at Ethan, then shifted to rest my head against his chest as we moved.

"Are you happy, Jess?"

Thinking about it, I smiled. "I would say I'm content with my current circumstances."

The air rushed out of Ethan's lungs. "That's good."

Pulling back, I met his gaze. "That doesn't mean things won't change. It's just where I need to be right now."

Giving me a nod, Ethan kept us moving, the side of his mouth twitching, but he kept his thoughts to himself.

"What?"

"Just the way Lou, Sean, and Greg are watching us." The sparkle in Ethan's eyes told me he was being cheeky.

When I casually turned my gaze toward my family, they stood there watching us dancing, all of them with big smiles. While that wasn't new for Greg, Sean was a surprise, but it shouldn't have been after how well dinner went a few weeks back. None of them were saying anything, but it was all there in how they smiled whenever Ethan and I interacted.

A more upbeat song came on, and Ethan stepped back, swung me under his arm, and our quiet moment was over—but we still had lots of fun dancing and laughing the rest of the night. Greg even took me for a few rounds on the dance floor, showing off his ballroom skills and putting Ethan to shame between dancing with Holly and the girls.

It was a great day, and by the time I fell into bed exhausted but happy, I wished I'd let Ethan come and stay, even if it was just to cuddle up for the night.

———

"Are you sure about this?" Lou asked, watching me finish feeding Scout his bottle a few weeks after the wedding.

"A hundred percent. Teille said the courier would be here before ten to get Dylan's stuff, and then Greg and Ethan should be here by twelve. So, you go have a morning game with Sean, and then while the guys help move you into your new place, I'm going horse riding with Holly and Mayla."

"I don't understand why it's taken them so long to organize someone to collect his stuff. It's been four months already."

"The two-month tour got extended with extra performances, so they are just winding down before the next leg in two months."

"Still, I'd prefer someone be here with you. You're only fifteen weeks along. What if——?"

"Dad, I'll be fine. The courier will come and get Dylan's boxes and leave again. It's no stress. I promise I won't even help move the boxes." Not that there was much in them—some clothing and notebooks for his songwriting.

"You can't blame me for being worried, Jessie Girl. Not after——" he cut himself off, but I wasn't letting it slide.

"Matilda? You can say her name, dad. And I understand your concern, but this is Dylan."

"Yes, Dylan. The boy you saved. The boy you loved, and when he broke your heart as a teenager, you cried for a week straight. The man who broke up with you after your mother's funeral. That guy."

"Dad," I said his name calmly as I rubbed Scout's back to keep him calm while his grandfather got angry. Lou had never liked Dylan, so I was sure he was happy to see the back of him each time he walked out of my life. "I'll be fine. The night I lost Matilda was entirely a different scenario. Now you're upsetting Scout and missing out on green time. We'll see you later."

Grumbling under his breath, Lou picked up his golf clubs, gave Scout and me a kiss on the head, and left.

"Don't you worry about your grandpa; he's not cranky at anyone, just worried. Your Aunty Jess has a habit of giving her heart to men who are clumsy with it."

Scout gave me a big smile right before a big burp.

"My thoughts exactly, little man." Putting his bottle aside, I shifted Scout into his rocker and put some Baby Einstein on for him. Scout immediately started kicking his little legs. "Let your food settle, and then you can have tummy time."

Grabbing the bottle, I cleaned it up, and by the time I was heading back over to put Scout on his playmat, there was knocking at the front door. With Scout safely strapped into the rocker, I went to answer the door expecting a courier, only to find Dylan on the other side.

Frowning, I glanced at him. "Teille said a courier was coming to pick up your stuff."

Inhaling deeply, Dylan hung his head. "That's your way of saying you don't want to see me."

"It's me saying I didn't expect to see you," I replied, crossing my arms and lifting a brow. "It normally takes you a few years to get the guts to talk to me again after you pull an asshole move like dumping me at my mother's funeral."

Dylan's tongue flicked the side of his mouth as his hand scrubbed through his hair.

"I'd like to say I'm older and wiser now, but I think we both know that's not the case. Can I come in?"

"Did you at least bring the key to Sean's place in Maui?"

Slipping his hand in his pocket, Dylan withdrew the key and offered it to me. Taking it, I stepped back to let him in before shutting the door.

Dylan scanned my place as he removed his cap and sunglasses and placed them on the hall stand. "Nice place. Are you renting this from Sean as well?"

"It's mine. Well, it will be once I pay it off," I answered as I headed back into the living area and checked on a cooing Scout. "Tummy time, little man."

Setting Scout down on his play mat, I turned back to Dylan to see him staring at Scout like he was his arch-nemesis. "Is that the psycho's child?"

"Greg's son. Yes."

"And he what? Gave him to you?"

"No. I take Scout on the weekdays that Greg is away for work. Normally Lou would have Scout this morning, but since I had to hang around for your stuff to be collected, I told him to go have a round of golf."

Dylan looked confused as I moved toward the kitchen and poured us a glass of water.

"Lou moved here a month ago. He's currently living here with me. Greg also transferred his home base to be here in Oahu so that I could be part of my nephew's life."

"For free childcare," Dylan snarked.

Shrugging a shoulder, I drank my water and went to sit on the floor by Scout to keep an eye on him.

"It's good practice for when I have my baby."

Gritting his jaw, Dylan averted his eyes. "I guess that answers my question about where we stand."

"You answered that yourself when you ended things with me between my mother's funeral and her wake, Dylan. What the hell were you expecting? You and I both know that nothing has changed. You might have processed your shit with Sharnie and your sister, but you will do the same thing again in two months when it's time to go on tour again."

I moved to where Dylan was standing and put my hand on his forearm.

"You were right. As much as we love each other, we can't work. Our broken bits don't fit, and I keep cutting myself on your jagged edges, trying to make us work."

"Jess." Dylan's voice was full of so much yearning it hurt.

I cupped the slight bump in my abdomen with my hands, taking a step back.

"I'm pregnant, Dylan. I will have my own child to take care of in six months, and I know how you feel about kids, so I know this is goodbye."

Dylan's eyes filled with fear as he took in my hands and the tiny baby bump they outlined. "That's not mine! It can't be."

"It's not," I assured.

Lifting his eyes to mine, Dylan looked lost, and it broke my heart to see that pain surface after so long.

"You know what happened to me. You know I can't be around kids."

"I do, but you walked out again. And I realized that women had raised children by themselves throughout history. I am thirty-one, financially secure, have a good career, and have a good family around me. I'm sick of sacrificing my dreams for someone else, Dylan. If someone truly loves me and values me, they'll bend to meet me. Look at Lou, Greg, and Ethan. I wouldn't stay in Australia and give up my career to help raise Scout, so they all packed up and moved here."

"Ethan?" Dylan's head snapped up. "Is he the father?"

Swallowing, I maintained eye contact. "I asked him for a baby. He gave it to me with no restrictions. We're not in a relationship; he's just the baby daddy."

Grinding his teeth, Dylan shook his head. "I moved here for you first, Jess. Doesn't that count for something?"

"Yes. It's why we had those four months together, Dylan. But you gave me up, and I want to be a mum. So when the opportunity presented itself and Ethan was willing to give me that without demanding I come back to him, I took it because I'm sick of Sharnie destroying all the happiness in my life."

I cupped Dylan's face, tears falling from my eyes as I met his gaze, watching him soften under mine.

"I know you have your demons. That what they did to you haunts you, and you worry you will turn into the same sort of monster. But feeding your fear only gives it power."

"That's easy for you to say. The person you fear is dead."

"You're wrong." Taking my hand back, I wrapped my arms around myself protectively. "Like you, I am who I fear. Sharnie was my twin, and she went crazy. She was a sociopath. Sharnie was the monster I could see and predict. Getting away from her was easy. The fear that I shared the same DNA and that I could snap at any moment and become someone's monster made me run.

"Dylan, the night I rang you and begged you to get me out of there, to take me anywhere, just do it quick. I didn't plead to escape because I feared Sharnie or couldn't deal with losing Matilda. I did it because, for the first time, I wanted to hurt them. I yearned to cut them open and make them bleed as they did me. I could taste their blood and hear their screams, Dylan. That's how bad I wanted it. And I realized this was the moment. It was where I let my sister turn me into a monster worse than she was, or I got the hell out of dodge and removed the temptation. So, I ran."

"Jesus, Jess, you are nothing like your sister," Dylan scolded, then pulled me into his arms. "Everyone has felt like that. Everyone has hurt so bad that they want to hurt someone else, to make them feel the pain they are suffering. That doesn't make you crazy or insane. It makes you human–unless you act on it. Then yes, you are a nutcase in need of being locked up like your sister should have been. But you could never be that person, Jess. I know you. You couldn't hurt a fly."

"I'll have you know—I'm a fly serial killer. Fly swatters, Mortein fly spray, whatever gets them away from me."

Huffing, Dylan tightened his hold a moment, then slowly pulled back, taking a step away and observing me.

"I'm sorry, Jess. I handled things back there badly and for leaving you like that. But you're right, I keep hurting you when all you've ever done is love me. You deserve better. I hope this baby and Ethan give you all the happiness in the world."

"Ethan and I aren't back together," I clarified.

Dylan smirked and looked up at me through his eyebrows as he rubbed the back of his neck.

"Not back together yet. Yet, being the important word, Jess. Come on, you love the guy, he loves you, and you are about to have his baby. Ethan fits where I haven't all these years."

Dropping his hand, Dylan sighed. "I'm kind of envious of him, you know. The way you looked at him that night we flew to Bora Bora, I knew he would be the guy to take you from me for good. I thought it was a sign when he fucked up and broke your heart. That it was a chance for me to steal you back again, but I think it was Karma giving us closure. I needed to be with you when you got that call and when you stood by that bitch's side when she finally told you why she destroyed our lives; you, me, and Teille. It was so the three of us could finally sever these bloody ties between us. I realize that now."

He might have been right, but maybe it was his chance to prove I meant more than he'd ever let me believe, and he blew it. "Dylan?"

"Yeah?"

A small smile teased the side of my mouth. "You're morbid as fuck."

A grin spread across Dylan's face as he let out a small chuckle. "I know." His eyes went to Scout, lying on his back, smiling up at the mobile above him on the playmat. "I know we are done-done, but we can still be friends, right?"

"Sure. Just don't write any more songs about me."

Smirking, Dylan brought his gaze back to me and took my hand in his, caressing my knuckles before placing a kiss on them.

"No deal. You're my Muse, Jess. Without you, there are no songs, and without music, there is no oxygen. You're my tree. Your roots keep me grounded, and you take my toxic shit and make it air I can breathe."

Smiling sadly, I squeezed Dylan's hand, then stepped away. "Let me grab Scout, and we'll show you to your boxes."

CHAPTER TWENTY-FIVE

"Jess!"

Looking up from where I was finishing a cheese board, I smiled at the handsome gentleman calling my name in greeting.

"Senator Cassidy," I returned his greeting and set down the knife to accept his welcoming embrace. "I didn't know you were coming today."

Pulling back, still holding a good bottle of top-shelf scotch, the senator gave me his trademark grin.

"Your dad and I got talking at the wedding a month back, and I promised that I'd come out for a round of golf again once he got settled. He's a brilliant man, that dad of yours, and he makes for good company."

"That he is," I agreed. At Sean and Holly's wedding, Lou and Sean's dad forged an immediate bond as widowers and after they discovered their love of golf, became fast friends. I got the impression Senator Cassidy liked being there for Greg, too, as someone who lost his wife while he still had two young boys.

When his eyes dropped to my belly and there was nothing to see, the senator's smile dropped a little, then he quickly refocused. Holding up the scotch, Senator Cassidy looked around the kitchen. "Where should I put this? It's my housewarming gift."

"There's a bar in the outdoor kitchen on the patio." Gesturing to the doors that folded open to connect the indoor and outdoor living space, I smiled up at Mr. Cassidy and smoothed my hands down my top to cup my rounded belly. "And don't let the top fool you. There's more than a bump there now. It's still fairly small, but I've only just gone eighteen weeks."

His natural smile returning, the senator put out his hand, then stopped away from the tummy.

"May I?"

"It doesn't kick or anything yet." I shrugged and permitted him.

Rubbing his hand over the roundness, the senator laughed. "Doesn't matter. It's for good luck. Just like rubbing a Buddha's belly."

Scoffing, I playfully slapped at the senator's shoulder and stepped back around the kitchen bench to finish preparing the cheeseboard.

Holly greeted Sean's dad on her way inside to help me. Things were still awkward with them, but he was slowly winning her over.

"What can I help with?" Holly asked, eyeing the platters I put together for Lou's housewarming guests to enjoy. There were new friends he'd already made on the course here, and a couple of old friends from home had come to visit along with Sean and Holly, Greg and Mayla with Scout, and Ethan who lived here with Lou now.

Indicating the cured meats intended for the charcuterie board, I added some strawberries between the cheeses.

"So, are you loving having your house to yourself again?" Holly asked as she started rolling and positioning the meats.

"Yes, and no. I loved having dad there, but I have missed not worrying about disturbing someone when I can't sleep or just being able to do my own thing."

"You'll have to enjoy that while it lasts. You'll be sharing your place permanently in only a handful of months," Holly said, with a pointed eyebrow lift and eyeing my tummy. "You won't be able to surf in the morning any more soon, and then once Joy is born, you'll constantly have two babies to take care of regularly."

Looking outside to Mayla playing with Scout, where Greg held him in his arms, I smiled.

"I think by the time Joy comes along, Scout will only be coming north for his weekends with Pop or family get-togethers."

Following my gaze, Holly smirked. "I'm glad I'm not the only person seeing that. So you think those two will work?"

"The only reason they aren't together already is that they are both trying to be respectful."

"To your sister?"

"To my dad. Sharnie didn't warrant that sort of respect, and though Greg loved her when they married, she treated him appallingly. So, I think them taking things slow is out of respect for the man who lost his daughter, but also to navigate how they work with Scout in the picture."

"By all accounts, Mayla loves Scout, and he loves her. So I don't think there is an issue there." Holly chuckled.

"Well, I noticed Greg hasn't exactly filled his weekends looking for his own place either."

"He should just buy your place for him and Mayla to live, now that Ethan is living here."

"That'd be nice. Then I can pay off my place."

"Which brings me to my next question. Why is Ethan living here instead of with you? You get along, and you plan to co-parent. Wouldn't it be easier if he moved into your spare room?"

My focus flicked over to Ethan, laughing at something he and Sean were discussing while gesturing out at the fairway. For two weeks, Ethan had lived five minutes down the road from me. He'd joined us for surfing each morning he was home, and we'd taken some long walks together just to talk and hang out now that I wasn't allowed to ride horses anymore.

Chewing the corner of my lip, I turned my gaze to Holly.

"Wait until you are pregnant, with all these hormones, and tell me you could keep a bedroom door between you and Sean each night. I mean, Ethan didn't knock me up holding hands. There's a reason I fell all over him the night we made Joy. The guy fucks like a sex god. Mix what he can do with the way I still feel, and all these feel-good hormones, my lovesick heart and Ethan-obsessed vagina will convince me to marry him by tomorrow."

Pursing her lips, Holly turned bright red, then burst out laughing. Grinning, I put the finishing touches on the finger foods and picked one platter up. "Reason enough?"

"Oh, yes. I'm not even pregnant, but my heart and vag ganged up on me to forgive Sean, so I understand."

"I thought it was the sun chair through the roof that convinced you?"

Holly waved that near-death experience away.

"No. That was just fate forcing us together again. But, honestly, I'm still not convinced Sammy didn't cause that storm and throw that sunbed my way. That woman is a force to be reckoned with when she wants her way."

"How is Sean going with avoiding signing me up for training?" I chuckled as we carried the platers outside.

"He's dodging her phone calls, and if Sean sees Sammy's name on my screen, he runs for it. So I think you should prepare for Sammy to rope you into creating a training program sooner than later."

Lifting a shoulder in indifference, I set the platter down.

"I already have one written, but it's fun seeing Sean trying to give that little bulldog the runaround."

"I'm telling Sammy you called her a bulldog." Holly laughed.

"That's fine. Sammy doesn't scare me."

"Really?" Holly looked amazed. "I mean, your association with a bulldog wasn't far off the mark."

"I had a sociopathic twin sister whose entire life goal was to hurt me. Sammy is child's play."

Swallowing her laughter, Holly looked horrified. "Oh, God, Jess. I'm so sorry. I shouldn't have insinuated-"

Chuckling, I waved her concern away. "I wasn't offended, Holly. It is what it is. The bonus of having dealt with that is that I have a backbone of concrete, and I don't scare easily. Sammy's determined, but she's got a heart of gold. I kind of like her."

A smile bloomed on Holly's face. "Wait until you get to know her. She's wonderful."

"Ladies," Ethan greeted as he came and helped himself to some of the food. "This looks great, Jess."

"I'm going to go get a drink." Holly smirked and gave me a wink as she headed for the bar.

"Subtle. Real subtle, Hol." I laughed.

Smirking, Ethan watched Holly walk off, then came closer.

"So, surfing tomorrow morning?"

Rubbing my belly, I nodded. "Don't know how many more I'll get before it gets too uncomfortable to lie on the board, so yes."

"Did you have plans tomorrow afternoon? I was thinking of taking a plane out and flying a loop of the islands if there's one available."

"I'd love to, but honestly, just driving in a car without airflow triggers my morning sickness. I'd hate to think how being up in a plane would affect me right now."

When Ethan's face fell, I felt terrible because I knew flying was his first love, and I was the only woman he'd ever shared that with before. But there was something else he loved just as much.

"I wouldn't say no to riding on the back of your bike, though." Ethan had shipped his bike over. Other than clothes and a few mementos of his grandparents, that's all he'd moved to Hawaii. I sidled closer, letting my arm brush his. "We could take a ride down to the Dole Plantation and get me some pineapple juice." I couldn't have Dole Whip anymore. I literally cried when the doctor told me soft-serve ice cream put me at risk of miscarriage.

A grin split Ethan's face as he assessed me. "You think your father will let you on the back of my bike while you are pregnant? Jess, he threatened to shoot me for taking you on the bike when there wasn't delicate cargo."

"Don't tell him." Then, smiling, I grabbed a carrot stick, stuck it between my teeth, gave Ethan and saucy wink, and went to join the party.

"God, give me strength!" Ethan exhaled hard behind me.

———

Pressing my hands and knees into the board, I forced it down into a duck dive beneath the wave about to break.

Coming back to the surface, I continued paddling out behind the break to the lineup where other surfers were sitting assessing the incoming waves.

"That was a nice cutback." Ethan complimented my last ride. "You've really improved over the last year."

Coming up beside him, I sat up and straddled my board. "Thanks. Sean's been giving me pointers."

"Where is the happy couple this morning?" Ethan scanned the lineup.

"Probably practicing making their own joy." I chuckled at their absence, and Ethan joined my joke.

Since returning from their honeymoon a few weeks back, they would occasionally miss the morning surf in favor of making their own waves. Not that they told me this. I'd just been unfortunate to hear them. That was the problem with your newlywed friends as neighbors and both of you leaving your bedroom doors open for the ocean breeze in summer.

"This set has my name on it," Ethan decided as he turned his board and started paddling.

Watching Ethan's powerful arms and shoulders drive into the water as he paddled to catch the wave, I chewed my lip and tried not to remember all the times those arms lifted me and carried me while he kissed the hell out of me. Or the way his shoulders felt beneath my fingers as he powered into me.

"Down, girl!" I cursed myself.

Shaking my head, I turned my focus back to the waves, watching them come and go while I tried to sort out my feelings from the lustful need. It was more challenging than you think.

One of the reasons I desired Ethan so much was because the chemistry between us was always off the charts. Even the night we conceived Joy, it was still as mind-blowing as that first week after meeting the night before Greg and Sharnie's wedding.

The sex had always been earth-shattering. When we first met, being with Ethan felt as natural as breathing. We just orbited around each other and worked flawlessly. But we lost that rhythm between us when he started coming to visit last year, and we always felt like we were out of step with each other.

Maybe we fell apart last time because we were both on guard for it. I'd struggled those months with communicating with Ethan, and I think that was because I knew he meant something more than what we'd agreed to, which put a different kind of strain on our relationship. So maybe, we both weren't ready last year.

"Penny for your thoughts?"

Turning my head, I realized Ethan was back beside me. He smiled and tilted his head as he swept his wet hair back off his face.

"You were studying the horizon pretty hard, Jess. You only go that far away when you are problem-solving. So, share the problem; let me see if I can help you talk it out."

The fact Ethan recognized this about me meant something, didn't it? For months now, we'd hung out as friends, enjoyed each other's company, and not once did Ethan try and make it more, or push me to reconsider our situation; even though, at times, I caught him watching me with sheer longing and a pinch of heartbreak on his face.

"I was thinking about our last weekend together. The plane ride, the picnic up the lookout, and how you told me you were in love with me. You broke my heart, Ethan."

"I know, Jess. I was an idiot. I've been thinking about it a lot, and the best I can come up with is that I was happy with my life, and then you came out of nowhere, and suddenly I craved more. But just as quickly as you blew into my life, you were gone again, leaving me shaken up and unable to settle back down. I think it was the same for you, and it's why we couldn't let go. Yet, after you left, it felt different, like you walked on eggshells around me. And I think that, coupled with my uncertainty, set us up for failure," Ethan confirmed my thoughts with sorrow all over his face.

It was always there, our grief over what we'd lost. Nonetheless, there were moments over the last few months where we smiled and laughed and just enjoyed each other's company. There was an ease between us now, like that first week in Newcastle. It was as if we'd come full circle. Maybe, we never could have worked as something casual with an open ending. We tried to force what we felt for each into that box to prevent getting hurt. Had I never left Newcastle that first time, I think we would have ended up happy without trying, just as we were now. Well, mostly.

Meeting Ethan's deep blue gaze, regret swimming over the surface, I asked the truth of my heart. "If I let you back in, how can I be sure I won't be making the same mistake again?"

Taking my hand, Ethan caressed my face, his eyes full of certainty as they saw deep inside me. Both of us raw in our honesty. "Because I never make the same mistake twice, Jess."

As Ethan pulled me closer to him in the water, our eyes locked on each other, our mouths getting closer, I opened my heart one more time.

"I like us like this. We just gravitate around each other, and being with you makes me happy, as it did when we first met. It's easy. I don't want us to become hard work again."

"Me neither, but I know we can do this, Jess. If we just roll with the waves, we'll be okay."

Smiling, glad we were finally on the same page again, I let those butterflies loose through my tummy again. "Okay."

"I love you, Jess."

"I love you too."

Ethan lowered his face that last bit, and just as our lips touched, the ocean rolled beneath us and knocked us off our boards. Coming back above water to cheers and claps from the lineup, I grabbed onto my board and realized a bigger swell had come at us without us seeing, giving the other surfers some entertainment.

Across from me, Ethan was laughing, sweeping his black hair back off his face.

"Maybe we should head back to shore? Did you want to have breakfast with me?" I asked, ignoring our audience.

Ethan's eyes locked on me, desire and longing making them sparkle in the morning light.

"Definitely."

CHAPTER TWENTY-SIX

I'D PULLED MY WET SUIT DOWN TO MY WAIST LIKE USUAL FOR THE walk back to my place, Ethan sharing a funny incident about their last flight as we walked.

Pushing open the gate to my side yard, I smiled back at Ethan. "Oats and French toast for breakfast?"

The side of his mouth kicked up. "Sounds good."

Setting my board in its stand, I pushed my wetsuit down my legs and threw it over the clothesline to dry while Ethan propped his board in the second board holder.

"I can't drink coffee anymore, but I can make you some. Frankly, I still love the smell of it. I can't believe everything I have to give up for this baby. No coffee, no Dole Whip, no horse riding, soon I won't be able to surf. I didn't realize how my life now consisted of what the doctor considers risky activities until I thought back to the last time I was pregnant, and the only thing I had to stop was coffee," I complained to Ethan as I opened the laundry door.

"I can think of a few things you enjoy doing that you won't have to give up for the baby," Ethan chuckled, following me inside.

"Like what?" I turned to face him.

Hot lips breathed warm air across my mouth as Ethan's hands captured my face and angled my head just right as we backed into my laundry.

"Kissing me."

Ethan's kiss was everything. Slow but firm, his tongue curling into my mouth to taste, tease, and arouse me. It was coming home after a year abroad and wondering how you ever left him in the first place. Wrapping my arms around his neck, I vowed never to leave home again.

"Me touching you," Ethan breathed into me.

Pressing me to the back of the laundry door, Ethan unclipped my bikini top, then pulled the straps from my shoulders to free my swollen breasts. The cool ocean breeze blowing through the still open door hardened the peaks, sending lightning sparks to my core when Ethan brushed them with his thumbs.

"Riding me."

Smiling against my mouth as I moaned, Ethan caressed down my body to find my hips. His mouth dropped to my throat as his fingers gripped the top of my bikini bottoms, peeling them down my legs, his mouth drifting south as he squatted to help me step out of them, placing a tender kiss on my rounded belly.

"I apologize in advance for all the noise your mama is about to make, but you'll love her all blissed out and happy," Ethan murmured with an evil smirk across his face.

As Ethan rose, I laughed and wrapped him in my arms. "The noise is the least of what you should be apologizing for doing. You're about to jostle the poor thing around in there."

Grinning, Ethan pressed my body to the internal door, pressing his thigh between my legs until I gasped as he rubbed against my sex.

"We'll start gently; get her used to it."

We stood there heavy petting in the laundry, Ethan encouraging me to grind against his thigh for a good five minutes before he pulled back, pulled the cord on his board shorts, and ripped open the velcro to shove the material to the ground, leaving him just as naked as me.

Grabbing my ass, Ethan lifted me to his waist, shoved the external door shut, yanked open the internal door, and carried me upstairs to my bedroom.

Dropping me to his bed, Ethan walked to my open balcony doors and closed them. "Don't want to disturb Sean and Holly's morning by outdoing them." Ethan gave me a cheeky wink as he pulled the California blinds into place to prevent early morning beachgoers from seeing inside.

My eyes stayed glued to Ethan's tanned athletic form the entire time, chewing my lip at how his cock stood rigid against his hard abdomen. The hardcore surfer's body was still a mouth-watering sight.

As Ethan walked toward me, he stroked his cock once, then ran his hand up to his abdomen to his chest. My eyes followed the action and the light, nearly non-existent trail of hair up the center of his core to where it disappeared at his rib cage, leaving the solid pecs and shoulders hairless. The urge to kiss every part of that muscled physique rose like it did whenever he stood naked before me. That is, until I reached his eyes.

Those deep blue penetrating eyes that stripped me bare the first moment I met them and every time since watched me, waiting, taking in every inch of my sun-kissed pale flesh.

I'd forgotten how vulnerable and exposed I always felt under that gaze as if his eyes did more than see the curves of my body, but he could see to the very soul of me. It was always as if he could see all my hopes, fears, hurts, and joys.

The first time he looked at me like this, the night of Sharnie's wedding, I knew I would fall in love with him. That night, I'd sat up covering myself with my dress, unsure if I was willing to let that happen. Today, there was no hesitation. I loved this man already. There was no holding back anymore because I was all in.

Ethan's lips twitched in a smile as he knelt on the bed. Leaning over me, Ethan took my face in his hands tenderly as he smiled with pure happiness. He pulled my mouth to his, leaving only millimeters between our lips as I looked up to meet his adoring eyes.

"I love you, Jess," he murmured as his lips brushed mine, his nose rubbing mine. "I'm never giving you up again." Another brush of lips as he set his weight forward, lying me back beneath him. "For keeps this time."

Ethan's thumb and finger closed over a nipple, his thigh pressing against the moist heat between mine, making me gasp and arch. Then, dropping his mouth to my neck, Ethan pinched the pulse of my neck, trailing down to my shoulder.

Covering my body with his, Ethan kissed me slow and deep, groaning into my mouth when my hand found the tip of his seeping cock and spread his pre-cum around the smooth head with my thumb.

Adjusting his body over mine, Ethan smoothed a hand over the flat of my tummy, caressing the bump in my womb before slipping over my wet heat, swirling through my slick need, and pressing two of his fingers into me.

When I first slept with Ethan, I determined he was patient, meticulous, and an overachiever just by his approach to sex. So it didn't surprise me when I found out he was a pilot who regularly held the lives of hundreds of people in the palm of his hand. He had that pilot calm in his demeanor. It took a lot to rattle him, and it was something I adored about him, especially in the bedroom.

Kissing me slow and deep, Ethan matched the rhythm of his fingers as they fucked me, his thumb rubbing gently around my clit until my body tightened and exploded as I whimpered into his mouth.

Empty orgasms were still a little painful. My nerve endings caught fire as my body clenched and released, trying to milk Ethan's fingers for more.

"I love the sounds you make for me, Jess," Ethan whispered as he pulled back, shifting his position.

Swiping his index finger over my lips, Ethan grinned before kissing me again, licking the tart taste from my lips in the process. He still moaned a deep guttural sound when he tasted me like he was eating the best dessert. God, that rumbling in his throat had my pussy flooding and clenching with longing every time because we knew what came next.

Getting to all fours, Ethan kissed his way south, kneeling on the floor and using my hips to pull me closer. Eyes locked with mine, Ethan dropped his face and licked straight up between my folds, swirled around my clit, then backtracked and delved into me with a feral rumble that vibrated his tongue against my good spot, causing my eyes to roll back in my head.

"Fuck, I've missed how you taste, Jess. So fucking sweet."

Gripping my hips, Ethan ate my pussy with the same enthusiasm as Pooh Bear with a jar of honey, making me grab the sheets and cry out to the bedhead as another orgasm swelled and broke over me minutes later.

Chuckling, Ethan pulled back, dropping delicate kisses to the insides of my thighs as I panted and moaned, slowly riding the waves to shore again.

"That's why I shut the doors," Ethan snickered, pressing a kiss to my pubic bone before dropping his chin to scrape my clit with his stubble, making me shiver and cry out again.

"You're evil!" I moaned as Ethan dotted my baby bump with kisses.

"You love it." He laughed.

Yes. Yes, I did!

"How are you coping in there?" Ethan asked my belly, then lifted his gaze to mine. "You think she's okay?"

Smiling, I sat up, caressing his jaw, loving the way his scruff scratched the palm of my hand. Of course, he'd shave when he showered and be back to my clean-faced Ethan, but I did love it when he went a day without shaving.

"You heard the doctor. Sex during pregnancy is perfectly safe for the first two trimesters." We didn't correct my doctor when she assumed Ethan and I were in a sexual relationship. He was the father; obviously, we had sex. It was easier not to confuse her with the complications of our relationship at the time.

"Your father—"

"Whoa! New rule. No bringing parents into the bedroom during sex. But just to be clear, what Lou is worried about is not a factor here, Ethan. I'm not about to walk in on you banging my psycho twin sister the day before our wedding, am I?"

"Even if she were still alive, there would be zero chance of that ever happening, Jess."

"Then there is nothing to worry about, is there? I've passed the risky first trimester, and the scans were all good. If the next scan shows an issue, we deal with it then, but otherwise, we just be happy and assume everything is healthy."

Caressing my jaw, Ethan smiled. "You're beautiful, Jess. Everything about you. You have this amazingly positive outlook on life despite everything you've been through. The beauty of your soul lights up your eyes, mesmerizing me. The warmth of your heart infatuates me. How fucking hot and sexy you are totally annihilates me."

"God, Ethan, when you say shit like that," I breathed against his lips.

Grinning, Ethan crushed his mouth to mine. Then, with a low groan, Ethan yanked my hips forward to meet his, where he knelt between my legs and wrapped me around him. Holding me tight, he rose, then climbed up onto the bed, crawling into the center with me wrapped around him, our mouths feeding at each other passionately.

As Ethan pinned me to the mattress beneath him, his cock nudging my entrance, my body was burning up with need. Ethan shifted his hips until his tip was right where we wanted it, and then he pushed inside.

"Oh, God!" I gasped, pulling away, burying my head in his neck, breathing his intoxicating warm amber scent mixed with the salt of the beach as Ethan stretched me around his girth.

"Fuck, Jess, you're squeezing me so tight you're going to break me. Relax, baby. I've fucked you eight ways from Sunday plenty of times. You know you can take it."

I'd typically accuse a guy of an overinflated ego, but Ethan earned his when it came to his cock and how he could make me sing with it. But, hell if I didn't feel like a virgin all over again right now.

Growling when I didn't relax, Ethan pulled out and rolled us to put me on top. "Let's try this," he soothed. Kissing my neck, my shoulder, Ethan caressed his hand down the arch of my back, over the rise of my ass to reach my thighs, then dragged me along his body. Finally, he hauled me over his generous cock until the slick head pressed against my opening.

"You're in control, Jess. Take me as deep as you want me," Ethan assured as he peppered my jaw with kisses and nibbled my ear.

Moaning, I pressed my hips back and down, Ethan meeting my movement with a gentle thrust, his hands on my hips assisting until he was seated deep inside me.

My eyes rolled back in my head as I uttered prayers of worship to his glorious cock, making Ethan laugh and pulse against my cervix.

"Oh, God, Ethan. Do that again, and I will come already."

"Then get that ass moving already, or I'm going to bend my knees and fuck that pussy into tomorrow, Jess. You feel too damn good just to sit here."

Smirking, I pushed up to sit, lifted my hips, and then slid down his length again, causing groans of pleasure from both our mouths. Then, taking a moment, I rolled my hips.

"Just let me..." I began rocking and rolling to take Ethan even deeper, slowly getting my body used to him again.

Caressing his hands up my waist, Ethan palmed my breasts, rolling and tweaking my nipples as I eased him even further until it was as deep as possible. Then Ethan spread his legs, bent them up, and pushed up from below to be balls deep.

Praying to a higher god, I raked my nails down his chest, leaving red marks as I fell forward and bit his neck.

"We good?" Ethan checked, his hand soothing along my spine, the other sweeping my hair back so he could drop a kiss on my shoulder.

"Yes."

"You sure?"

"Fuck me, Ethan." Then I clenched tight around him.

Growling deep in his chest, Ethan gripped my hips, lifting me the length of him, slowly, before driving me back down hard as he thrust up with his hips. With each of my descents, he slammed into me from below, fucking me slow and hard, making me cry out with every thrust until I either came or slowed things down.

Pushing up to sitting, I forced Ethan's legs down and took a moment to catch my breath.

"You okay?" Ethan asked as he came up onto his elbows.

"Yes, I just don't want to come yet," I assured, leaning forward to kiss his gorgeous smirking mouth slowly, licking his lips before pressing it into a deep kiss, our tongues wrestling while my hips wiggled to take him deeply again.

Shifting his weight to one arm, Ethan curled the other around my waist, flattening his palm in the small of my back as we kissed to keep my pelvis angled, so every move rubbed my clit against him. The guy knew my body too well.

Sliding up slowly, I started riding him. Loving the way he hit all the right spots, firing off pulse after pulse of pre-emptive pleasure.

Kissing down my throat, Ethan used his palm to force my back into an arch until my breasts were at his mouth. His tongue lashed my nipples, sending rippling pulses of lightning to my womb, causing me to struggle to keep control as my body contracted around him.

Glancing down, I watched as Ethan held me in place with his strong arms, his tongue slowly circumnavigating my nipple before flicking the tip, then sucking it with a bit of nip of teeth that had me cursing and riding him faster and harder.

Ethan glanced up, capturing me with his focus as our bodies rutted like the world's end was coming, his deep blue gaze holding my ice blue eyes in a trance. His tongue circled and flicked, and I lost my rhythm.

Grinning, Ethan closed his mouth over the stiff nib, teeth scraping, sending a cascading trigger to my pussy. Throwing my head back, I repeatedly cried out his name as I came so hard that I swear I blacked out, and my body was left paralyzed by the intensity.

"Oh, fuck, Jess!" Ethan yelled, then he gripped my hips and bucked beneath me as my sex clutched him tight, milking him as he throbbed and came inside me.

As my body relaxed, I opened my eyes to meet Ethan's smiling eyes. Caressing his stubble, I admired how gorgeous he was.

"For keeps this time, Jess," Ethan breathed, turning his face to kiss my palm before bringing those soul-deep eyes back to mine. "I love you."

I fell into him as our mouths connected, pinched, and delved in passionate surrender to our feelings for each other.

We stayed like that, me cuddled against his chest until my tummy rumbled with hunger, causing us both to laugh and the jostle making Ethan's satisfied cock to pulse with life again.

"Mmm, I think I need to feed you before I make love to you again," Ethan murmured to the top of my head.

"We could fuck in the shower then go down for breakfast," I proposed, eager for more of Ethan but very aware that my morning sickness would kick in if I didn't eat soon.

Ethan's cock hardened against me. "You're a nymph." He chuckled and gave my ass a little slap. "Come on then. Get up before I just roll you over and sink into you again."

When I groaned at the suggestion, Ethan growled and threw me onto my back, thrusting inside me and making me gasp as he started a hard and fast pound.

"Not fast enough, Jess. Let's see how quickly I can make you praise my name again."

Two minutes. That was the answer. The egomaniac timed it. Then he carried me to the shower and tried to beat that record again. By the time we made it downstairs and were sitting eating breakfast, the smiles on our faces were as big as they come.

"If you keep looking at me like that, you're not going to be able to sit on my bike later without feeling me," Ethan threatened.

Trying to suppress the dirty thoughts running through my head, I looked out at the beach. "You're not playing golf today?"

Lifting a brow, Ethan checked his watch and sighed. "I've missed tee-off already. Anyway, I'd prefer to spend the day with you, if you're okay with that?"

Blushing, I glanced back at Ethan and sipped on my chai latte. "That might be nice."

"Did you have plans?"

"I was going to go shopping for some maternity clothes. There's no squeezing these boobs into my bras anymore, and getting my jeans to button up is becoming hard. If the belly pops in the next few days, I'm screwed."

"Pretty sure I already took care of that this morning," Ethan answered cheekily. "But shopping sounds like fun. We could get a few more things for the nursery, and there are a few new clothes I should get."

Intrigued, I tilted my head. "Like what? I thought you brought all your clothes with you?"

"Well, your father suggested pajama pants."

I nearly spat my chai across the table. "Should I ask?"

"I've been sleeping in the downstairs bedroom at his place, which also looks over the fairway."

"Oh!"

"There was a gathering of lady golfers a week back." Ethan shrugged. "Lou also mentioned that young children have a habit of climbing into bed with mummy and daddy, and it is a good idea to have things tucked away when that happens."

Biting my lip, I laughed as I imagined that scenario, but then I realized I was imagining being in bed with Ethan when it happened, and that didn't worry me. My smile grew, and I settled back, finishing my breakfast.

"So, shopping, and then a ride this afternoon?"

"Only a small one. I'm not taking you on the highway. Lou will kill me."

Rolling my eyes, I agreed to the terms.

"I'll head back to Lou's and get dressed. Should I bring some clothes for tomorrow back with me?"

Trying to restrain my smile, I went up on my toes and kissed Ethan's cheek. "Couldn't hurt. Maybe a toothbrush and stuff too," I murmured as my fingers stroked his stubble. "But leave this for today? I want to feel it between my legs later."

Growling, Ethan pulled me into his arms and kissed me hard. "I'll be half an hour."

Dressed in his board shorts, Ethan didn't even take his board with him as he jogged back to Lou's place to change. Thirty minutes later, he pulled up on his motorbike by the garage and came inside with a duffle bag that he set down just inside the door.

"Ready?"

Ethan didn't go back to Lou's any night before flying out again. Over the week, more of his stuff appeared at my place, and I made room for him in the wardrobe without comment. Not from Ethan, not from me, nor from Lou about the fact Ethan wasn't coming home to sleep.

When Ethan returned home from work, he came straight to me; but he had to make do with a passionate kiss by the door until bedtime due to Scout being there.

Ethan never stayed at Lou's again. No one said anything about Ethan moving in with me. Our friends and family all took it in as if he'd always been there, and I loved them all for not making a thing about it.

It wasn't all a smooth transition.

At five months, the belly popped, and surfing wasn't possible anymore. For a few days that irritated me, since Ethan was still hitting the surf with Sean, but then Holly announced she was expecting and asked if I'd like to do yoga on their beach deck of a morning with her.

Around the same time, Mayla suggested she take some responsibility for Scout while Greg was away so they could form a bond. Honestly, that bond was already there, but Ethan didn't complain about getting to come home and not worrying about the baby in the house on arrival.

"There will be another baby here soon cockblocking me twenty-four-seven. So I need to take advantage of the baby-free house while I can," Ethan justified as he bent me over the kitchen bench.

"Dinner will burn," I complained.

Looking over his shoulder, Ethan reached out and turned the flame down.

"It's on simmer. Now, grab the bench, baby. It was a long flight home, and I want to try and beat that two-minute record."

He didn't. But two minutes thirty from start to me crying out his name wasn't a bad effort.

Our little Joy had her father's appetite for trying to beat records because four months later, two weeks before I was due to take maternity leave, and three weeks before she was due, Livanda Maggie Dylan Knight was born after only an hour-long labor.

And before you jump to conclusions, Dylan was Ethan's grandmother's name. Trust me, it caused Ethan no end of heartache deciding whether to add it or not, but in the end, the love for the woman that raised him won out.

The day I held my daughter with her mop of black hair and her big blue eyes in my arms was the happiest day of my life. I cried, holding her, her little arms waving everywhere until the nurse helped me wrap her up and put her on the breast.

When Ethan took his little princess in his arms and I saw the pure love on his face as he looked from her to me, well, there weren't any words to convey that level of happiness.

EPILOGUE

"Did you hear the new songs?"

Yawning, I swung my legs out from under the covers and pulled on my robe, switching the phone to the other hand to get my arm in the second sleeve and heading out to the kitchen in the two-bedroom apartment I woke up in to make coffee.

"I did. Morbid AF is pretty funny."

"And Roots Entwined?"

"Brought a tear to the eye, but I like them, and they deserved to go platinum. Congrats on that, by the way, and on writing songs that no one directly involved with me relates to me."

"Even though they do, and you know it."

Stirring my coffee, I tapped the spoon on the side of the cup.

"Did you call me at seven in the morning to see if I liked the songs you released a month ago?"

"No, it's just been a while since we spoke, and I thought that was a good conversation starter."

Taking my coffee to the lounge room sliding door, I slid it open and stepped out onto the balcony overlooking the grounds of Sean's Ko Olina resort and the private lagoon.

"Yes, but seven in the morning when you know I was up late doing bridal party stuff and now have a wedding to prepare for today?"

Sighing, Dylan cursed under his breath. "You sure you are okay with me coming today? If it's going to make you uncomfortable—"

"Dylan. We covered this already. If I weren't okay with it, you wouldn't be here. We're all friends now. Things were fine at Livvy's christening last month, weren't they?"

"You mean other than Ethan telling me he'd drown me in the baptismal font if I so much as looked at your boobs again?"

Smirking at the memory, I sipped my coffee. "You were staring."

"They weren't hiding in that dress."

"I think it was when I was breastfeeding that was the trigger."

"Well, I never thought watching a baby suck on your boobs would be erotic. Fuck, there's a song in that. Hold on while I find my notepad."

"Don't you dare! And we won't have to worry about that today. I stopped breastfeeding after the christening."

"Why?"

"Argh, six months of being a cow was long enough, thanks. There are teeth, and she's eating solids now. The formula is fine. It also means I can drink wonderful things like coffee and alcohol again."

Dylan snickered on the other end of the phone.

"What?"

"Just how much our conversations have changed."

"Motherhood does that."

"You're happy?"

"I'd be happier if I was still in bed asleep."

"You know what I mean."

Smiling as I heard the toilet back inside the apartment flush, I took a deep breath, inhaling the coffee I was holding. "Yeah, Dylan. I'm happy. Are you?"

"It's a constant work in progress, Jess. I'll see you at the wedding."

"I'll be one of the ones in the pretty dresses up the front. You can't miss me."

With a laugh, Dylan hung up, and I finally took a sip of my coffee as an arm wrapped around me, and Ethan nuzzled my neck.

"Dylan having an anxiety attack about seeing you today?" Taking my coffee, Ethan took a sip.

"Yeah." I wrapped my arms around Ethan's neck, loving how he naturally pulled me tight against him. "Are you okay with him?"

"I can't say I enjoy seeing how he looks at you, but considering that I was much the same a year ago, I can't fault him either. Hell, I think he handles it much better than I ever did. Most of the time, I could believe you were just friends all this time."

"Years of practice," I answered, stealing my coffee back and taking a mouthful. Then, rubbing my hand up Ethan's chest, I stared into his eyes. "Now, should we discuss you turning up drunk at the bridal suite at three this morning, throwing me over your shoulder like a caveman, and bringing me back here just to spoon me?"

"I wasn't drunk. Just happy. Greg was drunk."

"Noted. But Greg didn't haul Mayla around like a Neanderthal."

Leaning closer to my mouth, Ethan smiled. "Well, as it got time to go to bed, I realized that having you in the same hotel and sleeping apart was just wrong. I hate going to bed without you beside me, Jess. I do it enough when I'm away for work. So I'm not going to sleep apart from you when we are both here. Plus, how often do I get to wake up with you and one of us not having to get up and take care of Livvy? Speaking of which." Ethan smirked and tugged me back inside. "You've got an hour until anyone will miss you."

Laughing, I put my coffee down on the table we passed back to the bedroom, taking full advantage of a childless morning.

Three hours later, I was back in the bridal suite, showered and in my underwear and robe, my make-up done and hair in rollers while the nail artist did my nails.

"How do you not have bags under your eyes? I could kill Greg for waking us up with his carry-on last night."

"I always sleep sounder in Ethan's arms than without."

"You know that whole scene this morning was so Ethan could kidnap you."

"No, it was because your drunk fiancé wanted nookie. Ethan was just opportunistic."

"Honestly, how did we end up with the thirty-five-year-old guys who act like horny teenagers whenever they are outside a cockpit?"

"What makes you think they are any better in the cockpit?" I laughed.

"I would hope they are focusing on not crashing the plane."

"Enjoy it while it lasts," the nail artist interrupted. "Give it another five to ten years, and they'll prefer to sit in front of the television with a beer than do anything romantic. The sex will be boring and take him all of five minutes before he rolls off you and goes to sleep snoring so loud you can't get yourself off or sleep."

Mayla and I just stared at her with our mouths hanging open. Even the hairstylist stopped working on Mayla's hair to gawk at the salty nail artist.

"You're done," the nail artist declared and started getting things ready for the next person in line.

"Thanks." Getting up from the seat, I moved to Mayla's other side and lifted a brow.

'I know,' Mayla mouthed. 'But she's a good artist.' Then, flashing her beautiful nails at me, Mayla winked.

It made me smirk. The woman could perform nail art, that's for sure.

"So, you work here and are getting married here?" The hairdresser asked.

"Why not? It's a beautiful location, and I get a staff discount," Mayla answered.

After Mayla and Greg bought my place from me, they couldn't afford a lavish venue. So they decided to put the majority of the money towards a honeymoon. Scout would be staying with Ethan and me or Lou while they were away. Mayla had never really left Hawaii, so Greg was taking her on a whirlwind mini-tour of Japan, Singapore, and Australia.

Looking my way, Mayla lifted a brow. "Have you thought about where you and Ethan will get married?"

"We haven't talked about marriage. Ethan told me he'd never get married again when we first got together, so I'm content just living in sin with him."

"Yeah, but you've thought about it, haven't you?"

Lifting a shoulder, I realized I hadn't really had time to daydream about weddings. Maybe I didn't want to get my hopes up. I was content having Ethan come home to me after each flight and having Livvy. She had Ethan's black hair but my pale blue eyes, and she had Ethan besotted with his little princess.

"Come on, Jess. Where? At Turtle Beach or back in Maui?"

Screwing up my nose, I considered the options. "Sean and Holly already did the beach wedding at the Cassidy, and while Maui is beautiful, it doesn't resonate as the place I want to marry Ethan. I don't know. I'd want something small and intimate with just Lou and our best friends there. It'd be nice to have it somewhere away from the mainstream. Somewhere quiet and peaceful where we could stay on for the honeymoon afterward, but separate from most of our guests."

As I described what I wanted, the perfect location came to mind, and I felt heat rush to my cheeks as I envisioned the exact spot I would like to stand and say my vows to Ethan.

"You know where you want to get married, don't you?" Mayla asked, watching me.

"Yeah. I know. But as I said. We've not even discussed it."

"Okay, honey, you're all done," the hairdresser told Mayla, holding up a mirror so she could see the way her long black hair fell in waves down her back. "Your sisters can help you into your dress, and I'll finish off Jess's hair."

"Thank you." Mayla smiled, admiring the flower behind her ear before vacating the chair for me.

While Mayla's sisters were here to get ready, they weren't in the bridal party. It was just me standing up for her, with Ethan as Greg's best man. Mayla decided that since I introduced them, I should be in the bridal party, but if she had one sister, she had to have them all, which meant Greg had to come up with six more groomsmen, and the cost would have blown out.

Instead, Mayla let her sisters organize the traditional pre-and-post-wedding events. That included the hen's party two nights ago, the welcome lunch yesterday to welcome all the guests who came for the wedding, and the luau and entertainment last night in place of a rehearsal dinner.

After the wedding today, there would be the traditional reception, and then tomorrow would be a farewell brunch before the bride and groom went off for their honeymoon. It was an entire weekend of activities, and while I loved the aloha vibe and the whole celebration with family... It was all a bit much for me.

But an hour later, as a ukulele player sang a Hawaiian song and I walked down the aisle, my eyes locked on Ethan; I couldn't help thinking about what it would be like to marry Ethan for the first time. What our perfect day would look like.

Ethan smiled at me the entire way down the aisle, even when Greg gave him an elbow and said something which only made Ethan's smile grow. Livvy was in the front row on one of Lou's knees, Scout on the other, both dressed up for the day.

As Mayla reached Greg and he took her hand in his, the officiant blew the pū–a conch shell horn–to start the ceremony. The celebrant followed this with the "Oli Aloha," a traditional Hawaiian chant to prepare the space for blessings and to welcome the happy couple and their guests.

After the ring blessing and exchange, Mayla and Greg exchanged Leis. Greg's a Ti leaf lei, and since Mayla was from Maui, she chose the pink Lakelani rose for her lei to represent her island of birth. Mayla even went full traditional and performed the Hula for Greg at their reception. Then he took her hand, led her out onto the floor, and danced her around for their first dance, showing off his ballroom background and wowing all the guests when he picked Mayla up and spun her around like Patrick Swayze in Dirty Dancing.

"I think you should perform the Hula for me later, in the privacy of our hotel room," Ethan murmured as he took my hand for us to join Greg and Mayla on the dance floor.

"If you think my feet aren't already killing me, you are wrong. I'm missing Holly's decision to go with thongs for shoes for her wedding. As soon as this dance is over, I'm losing these shoes."

"I think as soon as this dance is over, we should get lost somewhere private, and you let me under that skirt."

"I feel like you have a one-track mind tonight." I chuckled at his response.

"Do you know how long it's been since I could bang you all night without a baby waking up halfway through and cockblocking me at every opportunity? If Livvy keeps that shit up, she's never getting a sibling."

Laughing, I just shook my head at Ethan. As much as he complained, he was adept at finding quality time, even if it was a quickie in the shower. Hell, other than the six weeks of 'hell no' time after Livvy was born, I don't think we'd gone a day without sex when Ethan was home. I loved the intimacy and the orgasms too much to say no, and Ethan loved getting us both off as many times as he could in the time allotted.

"Okay, but seriously, I miss the way you used to greet me home after work. Nothing says 'I missed you' like you greeting me at the door naked and letting me fuck you against the entry wall."

"Well, why don't I speak to dad and see if, on occasion, when you will get home from work late in the evening, he can take Livvy for the night so you can get a good night's sleep and be ready to give her all your attention come morning? That way, I can give you a warm welcome home."

Ethan's eyes lit up. "You think he would?"

"Considering how much he loves his weekend with Scout, I think he would love to babysit for us whenever we need it."

When Mayla started keeping Scout with her while Greg was flying, his visits with Lou were the only time I saw him, away from us all getting together. So while Lou took Scout during the day, Ethan and I took him at night so that Dad could get some rest.

It also meant that when Livvy was born, Scout was around, and he adored Livvy like a little sister. And now that she was crawling, she wanted to be there with him if Scout was there. Thankfully, Scout hadn't started walking yet, but he wasn't far from it. And once he did, Livvy would be determined to walk just to follow him.

"You know him staying with us for three weeks straight will make her very upset when he has to go back home, right?" Ethan mused. "We should give her another sibling quickly."

"You know there are only ten months between her and Scout which probably accounts for their closeness. She may not like her sibling as much. And let's remember that I'm a twin and that there have been twins in the maternal line of my family for the last five generations. So you risk the chance of getting two for the price of one if you knock me up again."

Ethan's steps faltered as he blinked wide eyes at me, then slowly closed his mouth and considered. "Okay, let's not rush into anything. Livvy has Scout, and Sean and Holly just had Ava, so she's already effectively got a brother and sister. That's more than enough."

Barely restraining my laughter, I nodded in agreement and didn't add anything. I knew Ethan wanted a little boy. But in all honesty, I felt like I had my miracle in our little girl, and I didn't feel the need to rush into a second pregnancy; especially since she did have Scout and Ava to grow up around.

Truth be told, I was slightly terrified of having twins. It was not because of the work it takes, but it would kill me if one of them ended up like Sharnie, not only with the mental illness but also hating her twin and taking delight in hurting them.

"Hey, Jess. We've got plenty of time. I'm happy with how things are for us right now. We can wait another year to talk about it and decide if we want to add more joy to our lives or if one bundle was more than enough," Ethan assured. "She's already one more than I thought I would have."

Ethan placed a gentle kiss on my lips, then rested his forehead on mine. "It'll be alright. Whatever scary scenario you're imagining right now, don't. We've had enough misery in our lives. Only happiness is allowed."

Smiling up at Ethan, I was ready to kiss him again when a throat cleared next to us. Pulling back, we found Lou with a teary Livvy in his arms.

"She wants her Dada, so I thought I'd take my daughter for a turn on the floor."

"Does my princess want to dance with her Dada?" Ethan asked, taking Livvy into his arms. She smiled immediately, her tears forgotten as Ethan rubbed her back, then dropped a kiss on my cheek. "I might go stand with Greg and Sean for a bit. Save me a dance later?"

"Absolutely."

Watching Ethan walk off with Livvy, I smiled, then stepped into my father's hold and danced around the floor with him.

Later that evening, I held a sleeping Livvy, Mayla had Scout nearly down in her arms, and Holly was feeding Ava while we all sat talking.

"It's good that Ethan and Dylan can be civil to each other." Mayla watched where the group of men had gathered.

"Is there a reason they shouldn't be?" Holly asked. "I mean, I know they both want Jess, but it's not like she cheated on one with the other or anything."

"I guess not." Mayla shrugged. "I've never really seen exes get along, especially when they still love the same woman."

"I guess, but wouldn't it be more awkward for Jess as the woman in the middle between them?" Holly asked.

"Sitting right here," I reminded them.

"But Ethan knows Dylan is still in love with his girlfriend, and he was insecure once about her friendship with Sean, so I can't imagine him being okay with her and Dylan staying friends."

"Hey!" I clicked my fingers at Mayla. "Sitting right here, and don't go saying that shit. I just got over that last lot of shit and trusted Ethan with my heart again. If you start putting those worries in my head or his, it could undo everything."

"Shit! Sorry, Jess."

"So you should be. And just so you know, Ethan and I already talked this shit out before Livvy's christening. We agreed I'll always tell him when Dylan calls, and if he wants to see me, it has to be when Ethan is home."

"Ethan has to supervise?" Holly checked.

"No, but he wants to be home, so if I'm upset after seeing Dylan, he's here for me. And if Dylan tries anything, he can kill him; and if Dylan tempts me, I can come home and fuck him until I remember who I belong to now and why I chose him."

Holly and Mayla were quiet for a moment. Eventually, it was Holly who blinked and looked at Mayla.

"I can't decide if that is the most romantic alpha-male thing I've ever heard or if we should be counseling Jess on healthy relationships."

"Oh, before you follow that second chain of thought, can I remind you about Benjamin Henderson and your deal with your wonderful husband when it comes to him?"

Holly's mouth dropped open, closed, and she nodded. "Point taken. Romantic alpha-male it is."

We all laughed at Holly's reference to the books she started reading after her breakup with Sean, which she'd gotten Mayla and I addicted to over the last year. Which, of course, led to a conversation about the latest books we were reading.

Not long after, Lou turned up with the twin pram and helped settle Livvy and Scout in before giving me a kiss goodnight. "I'll keep them until brunch tomorrow morning."

"You think Livvy will last another night?" I checked, unsure how it would go since she'd already had two nights without her mum or dad. Before this, she would only stay with Lou one night and be crying for me in the morning.

"As long as Scout is there, she's fine," Lou assured. "She barely even notices you aren't there while he's around."

"Sounds like a future-friends-to-lovers book in the making." Mayla chuckled.

"Dude, they are related. Remember?" I scolded when Lou looked horrified.

"Oh, sorry. I tend to think of Scout as Greg's son and forget you were related to Scout's biological mother." When Lou glared at Mayla, she held up her hands. "I'm sorry. To be fair, I never met her, and no one but Greg talks about her, and he doesn't like to discuss her too much. I'm not sure if he's worried it'll upset me or because it still hurts him."

"Probably both," Holly offered.

Pursing his lips, Lou nodded. "I'll see you all in the morning."

After Lou walked off with the pram, Holly and I gaped at Mayla. She held up her hands in surrender. "I know. It just slipped out. I forget he is the psycho's father sometimes. I mean, he's so nice, and I can totally see that he's your dad, Jess, so I just can't connect him with the woman I heard all those horror stories about."

"Does Greg not talk about her to you?" I asked.

"He used to. He was miserable towards the end, and he used to talk to me about how he felt he had made a mistake. I think it makes him feel guilty now, though, not just feeling like that about her, but that he told me some of the stuff she did. Then she died, and he couldn't take those words back, but he didn't want to say bad stuff about her anymore. I think he wants to remember only the good things, so if Scout asks about her one day, Greg can tell him what he liked about her, why he fell in love with her."

"Greg's a great guy. I don't know how she ever caught him," I admitted.

"Me neither, but I'm glad she did," Mayla smiled. "If she didn't, you wouldn't have met Ethan, and that wouldn't have brought him here chasing you, which wouldn't have resulted in me meeting Greg and falling for the fool. So, it took a little heartbreak to meet my soul mate. But he and Scout are totally worth it."

Grinning at Mayla's love-struck happiness, I couldn't help but look across the room, seeking out my own. Meeting my eyes, Ethan smiled, then excused himself from the others, coming over to offer me his hand.

"I promised you at least one more dance before the night was over."

Taking Ethan's hand, I let him pull me up. "Fair warning, I'm doing this barefoot. Do not step on my toes."

Laughing, Ethan pulled me close. "I'll try to avoid them."

As a soft, slow song started playing, Ethan pulled me into him and swayed with me in his arms on the dance floor.

"Is this the sort of thing you had planned when you were marrying Ben?"

"Dancing barefoot, exhausted, and dying for my bed?" I checked.

Chuckling, Ethan shook his head, then gestured to our surroundings. "This sort of big event?"

"Well, I didn't do a lot of the planning back then. Margaret and Ben's mother sort of controlled all of it, and I just got to pick colors, bridesmaids, our dresses, and even that they wanted the final say over. So, they planned it to be like this, but it's not what I would want for myself. My tastes were always different from Margaret's."

"If you could have your perfect wedding, what would it entail?"

I laughed, giving Ethan a weird smile, causing his forehead to crease in confusion.

"What?"

"No, it's just Mayla asked me the same question just this morning, and up until then, I hadn't thought about it, so it's weird that you're asking today."

"You really hadn't thought about it?"

"Really. You were very certain about marriage not being on the cards back when we first dated, and since we got back together, I've not considered it."

"Fair enough." Ethan shrugged. "But when Mayla asked this morning, what did you think about?"

"You, me, Lou, the kids, Greg, Mayla, Sean, and Holly at the Hideaway in Queensland."

"The Hideaway. That's Sean's adults-only resort?"

"My idea would be that all the others stay at The Retreat on the other side of the island, which is family-friendly, and we stay at The Hideaway. That way, Lou has Livvy close by, but not so close we can't enjoy our honeymoon."

"And that's where you'd want the wedding to happen?"

"Yeah. When I thought about it, I saw us at the lookout where you told me you loved me for the first time, but that made me think of the lookout over the cliffs at The Hideaway, and I decided that would be the place. We could do it all there, surrounded by our family, but far enough away to have plenty of privacy. Nothing fancy. A nice simple dress, a celebrant, and rings, and I'm good to go."

We kept swaying for a moment.

"That sounds kind of perfect. What time of year were you thinking?"

"I don't know, either early September or late March."

"March is still six months away. Plenty of time to organize a wedding, don't you think?"

Frowning, I pulled back. "What do you mean?"

Grinning, Ethan tipped the bottom of my chin. "I mean..." Stepping back, he got down on one knee and took a velvet box out of his pocket. The music cut out, and when I looked around, all our friends were right there, standing in a semi-circle around us, watching, big smiles on all their faces. Even Dylan was smiling, but the lost boy look was all over his face.

"Jessie Butler." Ethan pulled my attention back to him and the beautiful vintage engagement ring he held. "You are the love I never dared to dream I would find. Will you do me the honor of marrying me?"

Tears streamed down my face, this moment seemingly impossible only moments ago suddenly happening, and I was so glad it was Ethan. He was the only guy with whom I could genuinely imagine having a forever. I'd always known Ben and I wouldn't last, and after Dylan broke my heart the first time, I knew that marrying him would never happen. But Ethan? Ethan, I'd felt that forever with the moment we met; I just hadn't dared imagine it or get my hopes up, just like he hadn't with me.

"For keeps?" I checked; my voice was breathy and barely audible.

Smiling large, Ethan stood up, cupping my face and wiping away my tears with his thumbs. "For keeps."

"Yes, please."

Smile turning into a winner's grin, Ethan swept me up in his arms and kissed me until I was desperate for oxygen. Cheers broke out, clapping surrounding us as Ethan kissed me again and again.

Stepping back, Ethan took my hand and slid the ring onto it. It was a little big for my finger, but we could fix that.

"It's beautiful. You picked this out?" It was precisely the ring that I would have picked for myself.

"Sean and Dylan helped me."

My eyes widened. "Dylan?"

"Yeah. I figured they were the two people who knew you best other than me. Is that weird?"

"No, just unexpected."

Stroking my cheek, Ethan pulled me tight against him. "You two were friends for years before anything blossomed between you. He's part of your life, Jess. I'm not stupid. Whatever happened between you two as kids formed a bond that can't break. I think you both have tried, but it's just twisted it all out of shape. Loving someone means accepting they have a past and might have loved someone before you, but that past will only threaten your future if you make it an issue in the present."

"Those words sound way too wise and open-minded for you."

Smirking, Ethan hovered over my lips. "They're your dad's. We talked a lot about how I messed up. What I know is that I trust you, Jess, not just because I love you but because I know you. I know how loyal you are to your friends, so I don't doubt you will be just as loyal to the man you give your heart to–I'm just glad that lucky bastard is me."

Blinking away more tears, I wrapped my arms around Ethan's neck tugging him closer. "I love you, Ethan. You'll always have me if you love me and treat our family and me well."

"For keeps?"

Smiling up at Ethan's adoring eyes, I kissed his lips. "For keeps."

The End

JOIN THE BEAUTIFUL AND DEADLY

Join Ebony's Mischief List

Sign up to Ebony's mailing list for the following perks:

- latest news on new releases
- heads up on upcoming promotions
- exclusive freebies like coupons to read Ebony's stories on Radish for free
- first chance at Giveaways
- get a free book

Go to https://ebonyolson.com for more information

IN MY TOWN, THERE ARE TWO
KINDS OF PEOPLE; THOSE FROM
THE SOPHISTICATED ELERI,
AND THOSE FROM THE
GANG-RUN RIVERSIDE.

THE NATURAL DIVIDE IS THE
ELERI RIVER.

THE HUMAN DIVIDE IS MONEY.

A STANDALONE ROMANCE
SUSPENSE WITH A TOUCH
OF THRILLER.

CALYPSO

An Eleri Royals Novel

EBONY OLSON

CALYPSO

I was wet!

Actually, wet might have been an understatement. I'd walked five kilometers in torrential rain. Two kilometers of that in heels, which seemed like a feat in itself. I'd taken my heels off when my second blister busted, and the pain became unbearable.

Not that I was unhappy. I was damn near elated. The date my mother had set me up on was horrible. The asshole son of one of her colleagues was a self-entitled and arrogant son of a bitch. When he tossed me out of his car forty minutes ago because I wouldn't put out, I'd smiled and waved goodbye.

Why? Because doing my mother the favor of dating her colleague's son had bought me a two-week holiday in Hawaii. That's why I didn't care how sore my feet were, or how wet I was skipping towards the late-night Pitstop Cafe. The fact I resembled a drowned rat couldn't steal my happiness either.

The Pitstop is a heritage-listed building in the middle of nowhere but on the main road to everywhere. Close to ten years ago, it opened as a cafe with a seven-eleven service station attached.

Bouncing to the doors with a smile on my face, I was daydreaming about the bikini I should buy for my vacation in Hawaii. That was the only reason I went on this date from hell. Once I was under cover of the awning, I attempted to wring myself of excess water. The glass doors slid open, and the buzzer sounded to let the employee know he had a customer.

Joshua, a high school senior and night shift employee, stepped around the corner from the cafe. His blue eyes going wide as I stepped inside the doors, Joshua's pouty mouth moved, but no sound came out.

Under normal circumstances, I would have no idea who Joshua was, since he was two years behind me at school. But I tutored him for my two senior years. Even a quarter of the way into my second year at university, I continued to mentor Joshua. So, we knew each other well.

"Band-aids?" Smiling at Joshua, I pulled my dripping, sable-colored hair back off my face. That was my one regret tonight, wearing my hair down. Catching my reflection in the glass windows, I looked like the psychotic dead girl from 'The Ring.' Instead of crawling out of the television, I was walking through the door.

"The second row from the back," Joshua answered, then dashed around the corner back into the cafe.

Okay, I guess I've looked better, but I wasn't used to that reaction. Looking behind me as I squatted to get a packet of band-aids, I realized I'd left puddles in my wake. As if on cue, Joshua appeared, setting up a wet floor sign before moving towards me as he mopped the floor.

"Sorry. I did try and squeeze all the water out before I came in."

"It's okay. I've been mopping all night." Joshua smiled, holding out a dry towel. "Give me your coat. I'll hang it in front of the fire in the cafe."

Lowering my handbag and heels to the floor, I unbuttoned my ivory duffel coat and swapped him for the towel. "Thanks, Josh." Gracing me with his natural smile, Joshua went back to the cafe. He'd changed a lot in the last four years. No longer the cute kid, Josh had filled out a little and was previewing the handsome man he'd become. At eighteen, Joshua wasn't there yet. There was still a boyishness about him that made me think of him as a kid.

After using the towel to dry my face, hair, and legs, I grabbed the band-aids with my stuff and walked over to the counter. Retrieving my comb out of my bag, I slicked my hair back into a ponytail. Joshua still hadn't come back, so I took out a make-up wipe and my compact and cleaned all the make-up off my face. The mascara smudged black around my eyes, but I cleaned it until it looked like eyeliner.

"Now you look like yourself," Joshua teased, coming to serve me on the other side of the counter. Picking up the band-aids, he scanned them. "Need anything else?"

"A hot chocolate and something hot to eat."

"Kitchen in the cafe is already closed, but there are a few hot dogs left if you want that?" Joshua offered, pointing to the hot dog machine.

I eyed him. "Two hot dogs would be awesome, as long as there is cafe quality hot chocolate to go with it?"

Grinning, Joshua rang up the hot dogs for me. "Grab your food and come next door to get warm." He handed me my change, his eyes dropping to my cleavage before he moved around to the cafe.

Glancing down, I found my nipples high beaming through the sapphire silk of my dress. As far as dresses go, it was conservative. It showed more leg than anything else. But when you've walked barefoot through torrential rain in Autumn, your body tends to showcase that you are cold.

Wrapping the towel around my shoulders like a shawl, I grabbed my hot dogs. With my handbag over my shoulder, heels in one hand, hot dogs in the other, I moved round to the cafe. If I'd been paying attention, I would have noticed the voices coming from the cafe before I walked around. I didn't.

At first, all I noticed was a table with seven men sitting around it playing cards. An assortment of hoodies, leather jackets, and sport team jackets hung from the back of the chairs. It didn't faze me. The Pitstop was a favorite hangout for a lot of the local youth during the week. Usually, they'd all be at a party by now on a Friday night.

It wasn't until one of them lifted his head to watch me, and the others followed suit, that I became unsettled. Most appeared to be decent, but at least half of them could pass for members of a drug syndicate in a Hollywood movie.

At the far end of the table, were the last set of eyes I expected to see hanging in a service station cafe on a Friday night. Crystal blue, those eyes were almost a perfect match for my dress. Thick long lashes surrounded those eyes as they dropped to scan my appearance. My gaze lowered to his perfect cupid's pout, enclosed in a couple of days' worth of scruff.

Pulling my focus back, I took in the olive skin and the mop of unruly black hair. He wore a long-sleeve heavy metal shirt with a hood. While generous in size, the clothing couldn't hide his broad shoulders and physique. Biting my lip, I turned my focus forward, ignoring Aaron Wish, the catalyst of my raging hormones. Now, the only part of me that had managed to stay dry all night was as drenched as the rest of me.

Like Joshua, Aaron had been a scholarship student - the poor kid at a costly college. Rumors claimed him to be a local drug lord, womanizer and voted most likely to become an assassin. Despite this, I'd crushed on Aaron Wish something fierce from age fourteen. A year ahead of me at school, I want to say that when he left for university, my crush went with him, but it didn't.

As an Excelsior student - an advanced learning student - I chose to leap ahead with my university studies. This meant taking two first-year units each semester for my two senior years of high school.

So, instead of Aaron vanishing from my life, we'd ended up having two university units together. Last year we had all the same subjects and one class together each semester this year.

The saving grace I had, was that Aaron Wish didn't even know I existed. Sure, he remembered me from school, but I hid up the back of my classes at university, so no one even knew I was there.

Joshua slid a mug of hot chocolate across the counter to me as I reached it. "There you go, Caly. Go sit by the fire and thaw yourself out."

Putting my money on the counter to pay for the drink, I gave Josh a warm smile. "Thanks, Josh." Taking a sip while I waited for the change, I then dropped it all in the tips jar.

"You're too generous, Caly," Joshua sighed. When our math teacher suggested Joshua get tutoring, he'd had to admit that he couldn't afford it. His scholarship only covered the school fees and uniforms. So, I'd volunteered to tutor Joshua for free. In exchange, Mr. Downs wrote me a glowing recommendation for early entry to Eleri University. Despite no longer being bound by that deal, I'd grown to like Joshua and wanted to see him get into medicine as he hoped.

The table by the fire was far enough away from Aaron Wish and friends that they'd hopefully forget I was there. Putting my back to the group, I took a large mouthful of my hot chocolate. Retrieving my mobile from what I was grateful was a waterproof handbag, I pressed call.

"How'd the date go?" Penny, my best friend and roommate, answered on the second ring.

"It was a total bust. The bastard ditched me halfway between Charlie's and the Pitstop Cafe because I wouldn't blow him." Taking a big bite of my hot dog, I moaned at getting some decent food.

"That asshat! It's pouring rain, and he left you in the middle of nowhere at night?"

"Yep," I answered around my food. Unladylike, I know, but I was cold and starving. Charlie's was a five-star restaurant that barely served enough to satisfy a gold fish's appetite.

"Shit! Where are you now."

"Pitstop. I've busted my favorite pair of heels, I've got blisters the size of Mount Olympus, and I'm drenched to the bone. But I have a holiday to Hawaii secured in the bag."

"No wonder your mum had to bribe you to go out with such a prick."

"Agreed. Can you pick me up?"

Penny groaned, "God, Caly. If you'd phoned an hour ago, I'd be in the car in a heartbeat. But I went over to see Simon. There is a party on at his place, and I'm about three drinks over the limit already."

My head dropped in disappointment. "Well, shit!"

"I'm sorry, hon. Can you afford a cab?"

Not really. "Yeah. I'm guessing you're staying with Simon tonight, so I'll see you in the morning."

"Okay, hon. Let me know when you're home safe." Penny was the motherly one out of the two of us. Wild but caring.

Hanging up, I took another bite of the hot dog as I contemplated how I was going to get back to campus tonight. It was over a thirty-minute drive from the Pitstop. Slumping down in my chair, I pulled out my iPad and searched the bus timetable using the cafe's free Wi-Fi. The only bus that came by here towards the campus for the rest of the night was still another hour away.

With some free time up my sleeve, I logged onto my blog site and wrote a new post while I devoured my food. Hitting the publish button, I finished my hot chocolate and called my mother.

"Caly, I didn't expect to hear from you until tomorrow," my mother's voice came over the line rushed.

"I expected to get your voicemail. Aren't you at a conference in Singapore?" My mind raced over the schedule I'd memorized for my mum's whereabouts this week and the calculation of time difference between countries.

"I'm just walking into dinner. How did the date go?"

"He wined me, dined me, then dumped me by the side of the road when I wouldn't let him sixty-nine me. I've already blogged it, so you can read it when you get a minute."

My mother's heels stopped clacking across the marble floor. "Are you safe?" She asked with genuine concern. My mother was a high-powered businesswoman in the world of biochemical engineering. She'd given birth to me between replying to work emails and directing her team via phone calls. She worked from home for two weeks, and then I went to work with her.

"I am. I broke those Jimmy Choo's you got me for my birthday last year, but I'm safe. The blisters are worth a holiday to Hawaii."

Releasing a small laugh, the echo of her high heels striking marble started up again. "A deal is a deal. Tell me the dates in summer you want the flights booked and where you want to stay, and I'll get it organized."

"Summer is too far away. How about during winter break?"

"I'm heading into dinner. We'll catch up next week and discuss it then. Love you."

"Love you too, mum," I replied as the call disconnected. With a sigh, I looked at the time and then checked my cash flow.

Despite my family being well-off, my mother insisted on me earning my way. This meant I was very strict with my budget with what I made from work. Don't get me wrong; I wasn't doing it tough. My mother paid for my student fees and dorm costs. But all day to day expenses were mine. For that reason, I budgeted enough each week for coffee's and transport to work, or to go to the bar with my friends.

There was enough cash for the bus ticket home and a least one more hot chocolate. Getting up, I made my way back to the counter, which, unfortunately, took me close to the table of men.

Keeping my eyes on my destination, I didn't let the shenanigans at the other table catch my attention. Glancing up from the book he was reading at the counter, Joshua smiled when I stopped in front of him. "Hot chocolate or something stronger?"

"Unless you sell Bourbon, it's hot chocolate." Putting my money on the counter, I picked up his book. "Mary Shelly's Frankenstein?"

"Set reading," Joshua informed me.

With a nod, I placed it back down so he wouldn't lose his page. A masculine laugh burst out behind me. The way it heated my body better than the fire had made me cringe.

"What's so funny, Ayah?" One of the guys asked.

"There's a blog called Blue Balls that I started following in high school. It's by a girl who calls herself Nymph," Aaron chuckled. "It started off as a blog about all the ways her boyfriend used to try and get her to have sex with him. They broke up a few years back, and now it's about her dating life."

It was like instant freeze, holding my breath, realizing he was reading my blog. My mum and Penny knew it was my blog, but I'd never told anyone else. The desire to get my stuff and wait at the bus stop was overwhelming, but at the same time, it impressed me that he liked it.

"Is it dirty?" One of the guys asked.

"Sometimes, but it's not graphic sex or anything," Aaron answered. "It's still all about what guys say or do to get girls to have sex with them. Like tonight."

Now, I wanted to melt in a puddle of embarrassment as he started reading.

"I went on a blind date. Normally, I would never do a blind date. Let's just say someone coerced me into it, and no matter how bad it went, I was still going to be the winner. So, I went on this blind date with a guy in his mid-twenties. He's the son of a successful businessman. He's good-looking, well-educated, and wealthy. I couldn't understand why this guy needed to be set up on a blind date. Accepting he may be too busy to meet women; I went along thinking I would at least enjoy a nice evening."

Chuckling again, Aaron took a sip of his hot beverage as he scrolled the screen on his phone. "He arrived on time, was dressed well, and even opened the car door for me. So far, so good. He took me to a posh restaurant. Not my scene, but, obviously, he was trying to impress. He insisted on ordering for me; instant turnoff, and then proceeded to talk about himself and how good he is at everything. I was bored before the entree arrived."

Joshua pushed my mug of hot chocolate across the counter, along with my change. He was also listening to Aaron and captivated. "After two hours of listening to this guy talk himself up, and replays of American Psycho happening behind my eyes, the waiter arrived with the dessert menu. Finally, the night was looking up. The desserts at this restaurant were orgasmic. So, considering it was the only orgasm I was getting tonight, I was all for dessert. You know what Ego did? He told the waiter we wouldn't need dessert. He followed this up by leering at me over the table and saying, 'You're hot. You don't want to ruin it by eating desserts.'" Aaron burst out laughing.

His friends made combined hissing and sounds of imminent danger. "Ouch!" One guy laughed. "I'm surprised he's still walking."

Aaron started again. "So, we leave the restaurant. I plan to say goodnight; I understand why no one will date you, good riddance when he pulls the car off onto a side road. Ego then proceeds to remove his seatbelt, unplug mine, and push his seat back as far as it will go. Unzipping his pants, Ego pulls out his Johnston, and tells me to climb aboard."

"This guy is an idiot!" someone exclaims. The others murmured agreement, and I nodded. Chuckling at me, Joshua leaned over the counter to hear better.

"Needless to say, I refused his offer. Both for moral reasons, and the fact that he was either flying at half-mast or, in my experience, was not god's gift to women. If you get my meaning. Ego then informs me that if he shells out, I need to put out. When that didn't work, he tried to negotiate for a blowjob. On my refusal, Ego acknowledged he'd settle for a happy ending."

"Jesus! This guy should stick to paying for it," Aaron's friend laughed.

"When I failed to meet his demands for me to 'take care of his needs,' Ego, ever so politely, climbed out of the car. Coming around to my door, he took my upper arm and forcibly removed me from his car."

The crowd grew quiet. "I don't like where this is heading, Ayah." One of the more dangerous looking guys warned.

Aaron put up a placating hand. "Don't worry; I've already read it through. She's safe, or she wouldn't be blogging about it already." The big guy sits back, crossing his arms in suspicious patience.

"Where was I? From his car. He grips me rather tightly and tells me to get on my knees or walk home. Now, I must tell you, Ego hadn't bothered putting his little fellow away. It was still poking out like a hitchhiker's thumb. Yes, it's cold, and we were getting rained on, so I'll give him some shrinkage allowance. But it had been warm inside the car, so not that much."

By now, all the guys are holding up their thumbs and snickering. "Give the girl my number. Shrinkage need not apply," the big guy leans in with a grin. His eyes lift to me, and he winks. With a chuckle, I pick up my hot chocolate and take a drink while the big guy lets his eyes check me out.

"So," Aaron shakes his head with a laugh, "on my knees or walk. All ladylike, I lift my knee rather forcefully. As he falls to the ground cursing, I politely decline. The queen of England would nod approval at the grace in which I handled the matter. Collecting my bag, I enjoyed the walk home. Of course, who do I trip over on the way? Lancelot. The one place I wasn't wet from the rain, I am now." Putting his phone away, Aaron chuckled.

"Is Lancelot her fuck buddy or something?" Joshua asks.

Spitting up my mouthful of hot chocolate, I quickly covered it as all eyes turned in our direction.

Frowning in consideration, Aaron leaned back in his chair and shook his head. "No. He's the one guy she's never talked about more than a mention here and there."

"So why call him Lancelot?" Joshua considered. "Lancelot was Guinevere's affair. I would think they must be sleeping together, especially with her saying she tripped over him."

Aaron smiled, shaking his head. "He's been on the scene since she was with her ex-boyfriend. She called him Lancelot for being her temptation, not because they hooked up. He's always mentioned in passing," Aaron clarified.

The big guy was watching me again. "Speaking of ladies out walking by themselves at night... what's a pretty thing like you wandering around in this weather for?"

All eyes turned to me. "My roommate had a few too many drinks at her boyfriend's party tonight and decided to crash there the night. I'm going to wait for the bus and get back to campus so I can sleep in in the morning," I bent the truth.

"Except you work the weekends," Joshua corrected me. If there weren't a counter between us, I would have kicked him in the shins.

"Yeah, but I'm closer to work if I stay on campus, so I get to sleep a bit later. Plus, I get my bed to myself instead of sharing with some jock who thinks he's entitled."

"Hey, I am entitled," one of the guys at the table pouted in humor.

"Not to me, you're not," I winked. All the guys laughed.

"What about me?" The big guy asked.

"What about you?"

"Am I entitled?"

Opening my mouth to answer, Joshua beat me to it. "Dude, no. Caly is spoken for." Blinking at Joshua, I didn't refute it. Picking up my mug, I started walking back to my seat.

"Of course, she is. She's too fit not to be," the big guy complimented. "I can still give you a ride home."

Chuckling, I saluted him with my mug as I walked. "Thanks, but the bus doesn't require me to get on my knees and worship, so I'll take that option, thanks."

All the guys chuckled and returned to their card game. Taking my seat, I opened an eBook to read while I waited for the bus. About ten minutes later, chairs scraping across the floor caught my attention. Aaron and his friends were leaving. They all made their way outside except for Aaron and the big guy. Instead, the big guy came to stand beside me. "My offer for a lift is still there. No expectations. I don't like women being out and susceptible at night. Bad things happen, even on busses."

"Thank you, but my mother taught me never to hop in a car with a stranger." He was being nice, not sleazy, so I gave him a friendly smile.

He returned my smile. "You're friends with Josh?"

Tilting my head, wondering where this question was leading, I nodded.

"And you live on campus?" His smile grew when I nodded again. He looked over to where Aaron was straightening up the tables. "Ayah?"

"Yeah, man?" Aaron stood up, looking our way.

"Give Caly a lift back to campus. I'll sleep better knowing she made it safely."

"No, really-" I tried to object.

The big guy put his hand on my shoulder. "Josh will be in the car for most of the ride, and Ayah lives on campus, so he's going there anyway. Aren't you Ayah?"

Aaron folded his arms across his chest, face stern. "Yeah. I'll get her home safe."

The big guy smiled. "Thanks, dude." He patted my shoulder. "Names Dwayne, by the way. Josh can give you my number if you ever stop being spoken for." With a wink, Dwayne walked out.

Aaron's soul-eating eyes were still focused on me. "Pack up. Josh is closing up. We'll wait in the car." The lights in the shop area went out a second later. Biting my lip, I shoved my iPad back in my handbag, along with the Band-Aids I was going to need for work tomorrow morning. Grabbing my coat off the chair, I pulled it on. Collecting his leather jacket, Aaron yanked it on, his eyes still on me.

Swallowing the massive glob of saliva filling my mouth, I picked up my empty mug and took it to the counter.

"Leave it. The morning shift will deal with it," Aaron told me.

When I turned around, Aaron was holding my bag and shoes in his hand, analyzing the broken heel.

"You are very dressed up for a house party. Don't know many girls who would kill a pair of fancy heels and walk in the rain to the bus stop, rather than take the couch."

Taking my bag and Jimmy Choo's from him, I shrugged off his interest. "I'm not the average girl."

Aaron squared himself to face me. "Caly Zilla, popular, but always reserved at school. You dated one of the most popular boys in my year and were top of your class. You're rich but rarely showed it, right down to you even working as a tutor to give yourself spending money. And, you were an Excelsior student," Aaron listed off. "You were a year behind me at school, and yet, you've been at uni since I started."

"There a year before, actually," I corrected.

"I'm in my third year, and you are in half of my classes."

"I know." My face and neck became hot. I wasn't sure if I was blushing because Aaron noticed me, or because I'd acknowledged seeing him.

Aaron's eyes lit up. "Let's go wait in the car."

"Does this lift carry the expectation of a blowjob?"

"No expectation, but I wouldn't turn one down if you feel the need to say thank you," Aaron teased.

Rolling my eyes, I followed him out to the car park. Opening the door to a two-door sports car, Aaron pressed the lever for the front seat to slide forward. "Josh needs to get out first, so you'll have to take the back seat."

"There is an irony in that comment, I'm sure," I scoffed, stepping forward.

With a smile, Aaron slid the seat into place, locking me in the back of his car. Closing the door, he walked around, dropping into the front seat. "You look good in the back seat," he winked.

"You probably say that to all the girls you get in your back seat."

Aaron grinned. "Do I look like I fit in that back seat?"

No, no, you don't. At well over six feet, Aaron Wish stood a head taller than me, and his shoulders were twice my breadth. I wasn't short, but Aaron made me feel it in his presence. Taking a deep breath, I decided to divert the conversation. "So, did you become an assassin like your classmates predicted?"

Smiling, Aaron pressed the button for the engine to start. "Can't fit many weapons or bodies in the trunk of this car."

"How does a guy on scholarship afford a car like this?"

Aaron's smile faded. "It was a payout from the job I did through school."

"God, I wish I could afford a car."

"The rich girl complaining about money to the scholarship kid is ironic," Aaron huffed.

"I'm pretty sure the scholarship kid owning a car worth more than my annual income, is questionable."

Aaron met my eyes in the rearview mirror. "Life giveth and life taketh away."

My smile faded too. My hand went to the necklace at my throat. I couldn't remember a time I hadn't worn the locket. Even at school, where jewelry was banned, my mother got special permission for me to wear it. It was a gift from my father to my mother. I'd never met him, had no idea who he was. As far as I knew, he was gone from her life before I was born. The locket was all I had of him.

The passenger door opened, and Joshua slid in. Doing up his seat belt, Joshua smiled at me. "Catching a lift to campus?" When I nodded, Joshua's eyes flicked to Aaron. "She's the reason my grades are good enough to get into medicine next year; keep her safe."

Meeting Joshua's eyes, Aaron huffed. "I know. I will."

There in the dark, illuminated only by the dashboard light, I saw a resemblance in their facial structures that I'd never noticed in daylight. Aaron was all dark and brooding compared to Joshua, who was light and upbeat. Joshua was more auburn in his hair, and his skin a little paler, but their silhouettes and eyes were a perfect match.

"Are you two related?" I asked as the meaning of that clicked in my head.

Aaron smiled. "Josh is my baby brother." Putting his arm across the back of the passenger seat, Aaron looked at me as he started reversing. "He's been telling me all about you for years."

Keep Reading Calypso

ROMANCE SUSPENSE BY EBONY OLSON

Hotel Series

HOLLY CLAIRE TRILOGY

Holly's Trilogy: Books 1-3 Hotel Series

(Compilation of Henderson, Cassidy, & Holmes)

JESS BUTLER TRILOGY

Best Sunset: Books 4-6 Hotel Series

(Compilation of Best Man, Best Layover, & Best Knight)

Standalone Books

Black Mark: The Complete Saga

Calypso

Rain: A Dark Past Romance

Protective Instinct

DARK FANTASY / PARANORMAL ROMANCE / FANTASY BY EBONY OLSON

Standalone Books

Of Shadow and Light

Boundary

Silver Rogue

Halos

Hierarch Series

Succumb

Numinous

Masked

Exodus

Burning Immortality (Coming 2022)

Raven's Wing Trilogy
(Radish Fiction Exclusive)

Phased

Mer Tales
(Radish Fiction Exclusive)

Indigo Shores

Anthologies

Booktober: A Halloween PNR Anthology

ABOUT THE AUTHOR

Ebony lives in Sydney, Australia, with her husband, daughter, and six rescue cats. She loves to read fantasy, thrillers, and paranormal romance, spending most of her free time with her nose in a book or writing.

Having always possessed an over-active imagination Ebony spent her younger years regaling friends with fantastic stories, holding her audience captive with the passion and suspense of her characters plights. In adulthood, she shows no signs of stopping her imagination from spreading across as many pages as it can find.

Website: http://ebonyolson.com/
Ebony's Mischief & Mayhem Peeps

facebook.com/EbonyOlson.Author

twitter.com/Ebony_Olson

instagram.com/ebony_olson

amazon.com/author/ebonyolson

bookbub.com/authors/Ebony_Olson

goodreads.com/Ebony_Olson

www.ingramcontent.com/pod-product-compliance
Lightning Source LLC
Chambersburg PA
CBHW070240140726
47909CB00017B/18